RETREAT

RETREAT

J. F. Gonzalez

Midnight Library

A limited edition hardcover was previously published by Thunderstorm Books.

Cover art by Kealan Patrick Burke

INTRODUCTION

Brian Keene and Cathy Gonzalez

Jesus "J. F." Gonzalez passed away on November 10, 2014 after a heroic but brief battle with cancer. *Retreat* is the last novel he completed before his death (the working title had originally been *Executive Retreat*). However, he left a number of other novels half-finished (including a sequel to Retreat, two prequels to Survivor, and several more novels, as well as a dozen or so short stories). He also left behind copious amounts of notes on which authors he wanted to complete these various projects, how he wanted them to end, and where they should be published.

Jesus considered all of his fictional works as part of a larger fictional mythos. In diary entries, and in conversation with peers and publishers, he referred to this mythos as the "Dark Worlds Saga".

In a diary entry from May 3, 2008, he writes:

"Over the past several days, I've had additional ideas on this, as well as an idea to link this novel with several other books, eventually tying everything in to a common mythos and thread. I also have an idea to utilize one of the minor characters in this to a series of novels in which she is a central character.

My first thought was to link books through the Hanbi demon in

Primitive. *There could be several cycles of my books that are linked together.*

The Clickers cycle is composed of Clickers *and* Clickers II, *and is in turn linked to Brian Keene's Labyrinth cycle. An unwritten third Clickers novel can explore the Dark Ones more, possibly linking them to Hanbi.*

The Survivor cycle is Fetish, Survivor, and Bully. *All have the common threads of William Grecko, the Eastside Butcher, and the snuff film ring from* Survivor.

The Corporation, Primitive, *and* Back from the Dead *make up the Hanbi cycle.*

Shapeshifter, Conversion, *and* The Beloved *are stand-alones for now, but future books can be tied very loosely to them.*

Executive Retreat *can be tied to the Survivor cycle. The Clickers and Hanbi novels can be linked.* Shapeshifter *can be linked to* Executive Retreat *by way of characters knowing Bernard Roberts. That gives us, in reality, two large cycles. How to tie them together?"*

The glimpses into Jesus's diary give you a good idea of how his mind worked. Like some people have to sleep with the window open, he lived with his mind open to new ideas and experiences. He wasn't in a hurry to categorize everything, but rather he'd roll input around on his brain to explore the possibilities. Cathy and he both agreed that it's easier to see connections when your ideas are fluid instead of pigeonholed into tidy, defined spaces. He listened to all kinds of music, read all kinds of writing, talked—and listened—to all kinds of people. That's not to say he loved it all (you didn't want to get him started on certain pop stars or conservative news outlets), but he was always open to the experience.

Long-time readers know that Jesus did, in fact, link his Hanbi cycle with the Clickers cycle, via *Clickers III* and—in more detail—in *Libra Nigrum Scientia Secreta*. And *Retreat* begins the job of tying these different cycles together. His partially finished sequel to *Retreat*, for which he left behind extensive plot notes and a synopsis, further tie the individual cycles together, forming a complete and cohesive Dark Worlds Saga. Jesus's diary entries also detail plans he had for books beyond the *Retreat* sequel, with a recurring character who would have delved further into all of his fictional creations.

Unfortunately, Jesus did not get to see what he considered to be his crowning literary achievement to completion, but it is with great honor and respect that we are determined to see it fulfilled, and to share it with you, his readers and fans.

Brian Keene and Cathy Gonzalez
December 2015

RETREAT

PROLOGUE

Twenty-Four Months Ago

She was nervous, and she tried not to let it show as Bill Richards looked over her resume from across his cluttered desk.

She would have felt better about this second interview if Bill's office was in an actual office building, the kind of structure that housed insurance companies, law firms, and other businesses of white-collar dealings. Instead, his cramped office was in a small industrial park, the kind of place that housed commercial printers, graphics shops, small-time distribution centers, and machine shops. When she'd undergone the initial phone screening two weeks ago, she'd learned that the job she was applying for was with a company called Apex, Limited; they were involved in mutual funds and provided financial services to the investment community. It had sounded very impressive over the phone and she'd pictured, at the very least, a quarter space on the second or third floor of the aforementioned office building, with most of the space taken up by cubicles.

Her first interview had been conducted at a classy restaurant downtown, the Marquee, with an HR representative named Cindy Leiber. It was obvious Cindy had a slew of appointments that day for the same position. Cindy assured Carla that once called back for a second interview, it would be with the Senior Vice President of the Western Division, in his office—

Apex was a small firm and Cindy handled the Western Division's HR business remotely out of her home office. Now Carla was finally at this second interview, sitting in a drab office with very little personal effects; no potted plants or paintings hanging on the wall, no framed family photos on the desk. Aside from the desk was a filing cabinet, a credenza, and a few chairs. That was it.

The lobby had been even less inviting, and Carla had the feeling this was a two or three person firm. The position she was interviewing for was that of a secretary. Fifteen dollars an hour. Crap wages, but she needed it. Anything was better than her present situation.

Bill saw something in her résumé. "It says here that you used to be a Business Analyst at..." His brows furrowed as he read the resume. "Braun and Meyers?" He looked at her questioningly. "Is that correct?"

Carla nodded. "Yes, sir."

"What does Braun and Meyers do?"

"They're a Financial Services firm."

"Oh!" Bill seemed surprised by this. He brushed aside the *faux paux* quickly, running his pen down the résumé. She would have thought Bill would have known this, being that Apex, Limited was involved in the financial services industry. "Your employment with them ended in April of last year and you worked at Walmart, then Corporate Financial, then as a waitress at Ruby Tuesdays."

Carla had rehearsed this part a thousand times. "I got laid off at Braun and Meyers," she said. "I didn't get a severance package, and the unemployment benefits weren't enough to cover my expenses. The Walmart job was just a stop-gap. I'd hoped to make something of the Corporate Financial position, but it wasn't right for me and—"

"Why not?"

His question didn't trip her up the way it might have somebody else. "My degree is in finance and a week after I got my position at Corporate Financial, which was a consulting gig through a head hunter agency, my department was eliminated due to downsizing. I was transferred to customer service. Not really my thing. I stayed on long enough to get another job through the agency that I thought would lead into a long-term thing, but that didn't pan out either. The company they placed me with had budget cuts. I was one of over a dozen consultants that were let go."

"That would be your stint with Paragon Consulting?" Bill asked, looking at the résumé.

"Yes."

"I see." Bill was nodding. He flipped to the next page of the résumé. "There's not much here," he said. "Another series of jobs at retail outlets and fast food chains..."

"I needed to make some kind of money to pay my bills," she said.

"How long has it been since you've had a position in your chosen field?" Bill asked.

"Over a year."

Bill nodded. "I admire that. Your résumé demonstrates determination and resourcefulness."

"Thank you," Carla said. She folded her hands in her lap, trying to keep them from shaking. She really needed this position. The last eight months of underemployment had left her destitute; she'd lost her car, her apartment, and was living out of a Motel 6 while she waited tables at Ruby Tuesdays during the evening. The pay was for shit, but it kept her from being completely homeless.

As Bill read the résumé, Carla reflected on her situation. She'd always been a take-charge kind of girl. Her father might have paid for her education, but she'd paid the rent on her apartment through a series of part-time and summer jobs while slogging her way toward the sheepskin. She didn't want a hand-out; she wanted to *work* for her money. She wanted to earn it fairly. And while her father told her he'd admired that, he'd wanted to support her financially through college as well, which she'd refused. Chalk that up to her fierce streak of independence. It had contributed to the strained relationship she'd had with her parents since she'd turned thirteen. And while she could have gone to Dad for financial help when she was laid off, a mixture of pride and the residue from their strained relationship prevented her from doing so. Thinking about it, even now, brought the old hurt back to a simmering boil.

To say that she was estranged from her father was an understatement. She never wanted to see him ever again. It was that simple.

Carla pushed those feelings to the back of her mind. She closed her eyes briefly, took a breath, opened them. Bill was nodding to himself, a satisfied look on his face. He looked up at her, a smile cracking his face. "I'm impressed by what I see, Ms. Taylor. Your credentials speak volumes, as do your accomplishments and background."

"Thank you," Carla said.

"How long have you lived in Casper?"

"Almost two years."

Bill looked at her job application, which she'd filled out and mailed in two weeks ago after receiving a phone call in response to her résumé. One of the conditions of pre-screening job applicants was to submit to a background check due to the sensitive financial nature of the position, which Carla was only too happy to undergo. Carla had filled out the necessary information on the background check at her first interview, which had taken place a few days after the initial phone screening. Once she'd passed the background check, she'd had to undergo a drug screening—again, she had no issue with that. She'd never done illegal drugs, and she was only a casual drinker, usually a glass of wine or two with dinner on the rare occasions she went out with friends. Now that she was on this second interview, it was clear she was a serious contender for the position. "You were born and raised in Pasadena, California, but you moved to Wyoming. Why?"

Carla was prepared for this question, too. "I wanted to advance my career. Braun & Meyers had an opening in their Wyoming office and I applied for it. I wanted the position, and I didn't care where the geographical location of the job was. I'm not tied down by location, Mr. Richards. My opinion is that one should follow their dreams wherever they may take them. Braun & Meyers had the perfect position to match my skills, talent, and interest, and that position just happened to be in Casper, Wyoming." She smiled. "And here I am."

Bill Richards laughed. "Very good." He looked back down at her job application, eyes moving back and forth from it to her résumé, checking for consistency. "You were with Braun & Meyers for nine months and were laid off. Why not move back to Pasadena? I would imagine the Los Angeles area would provide you with better networking opportunities."

Carla shrugged, side-stepping the personal issues. "I like the area. I thought I could make a go by staying here and finding another position in my chosen field."

"Did you cast your net wider in your job search?"

"Oh yes."

"And no serious interest?"

Carla shrugged again. "It's this post-recession economy. It's really done a number on the financial services sector."

"Yes, it has." Bill's features turned grim for a moment. "I take it your family is from California?"

Carla nodded. "Yes."

"I come from a fairly large family myself. Six kids."

"Really? Wow! My family isn't very large, really. It's just my brother and myself."

"Large families are remarkable in this day and age, huh?"

"I guess so," Carla said.

"What kind of hobbies do you have?"

"Hobbies?" This was an out-of-left-field question.

"Yes, hobbies. Do you like movies? Do you like jogging, swimming, that sort of thing?"

Carla considered this, wondering if it was a trick question.

Employers did that sometimes, and they had all kinds of agendas behind them. Was the question intended to weed out the candidates who valued their personal time, or was it the kind of question to weed out the kind of employee who might spend way too much time at the office? Carla decided to play it safe. "I have a few interests. I used to belong to the local gym, and I like jogging."

"So you have an interest in physical fitness, then?"

"I suppose you could say that."

"That's good. I like living a healthy lifestyle myself. Eat good, exercise, that sort of thing."

"I always eat healthy."

"Wonderful!" Bill smiled, jotted something down on a notepad next to her application.

Carla chuckled. "Sometimes I like going out dancing. You know, with my girlfriends."

"Where to?"

Carla named a few places in town, nightclubs she'd gone to with some of the girls from the office at Braun & Meyer's when she'd still been employed there. "I haven't kept in touch with them lately, though," she said wistfully. "I've been so busy."

"I can imagine," Bill said, running his pen down the application again, scanning it for more tidbits of personal information. "Having fun is imperative to a good life. Good food, good drink, good times."

"Well, I've never been much of a party girl," Carla admitted.

"Good for you!"

"I like to stay healthy."

"I can see that," Bill said, looking at her job application. "You don't smoke, which is good. Helps with our insurance underwriter. And by the way, you passed your drug screening. I know we do things differently here, and I appreciate you agreeing to undertake the medical test prior to our second interview."

"That was no problem," Carla said. "I don't do drugs anyway, so I had nothing to hide."

"Good!" Bill folded his hands in front of him. "It must be hard now without the health insurance."

Carla sighed. "Very hard. Knock on wood, I haven't had to see a doctor since my layoff, but I chalk that up to trying to live a healthy lifestyle."

"So you haven't had any serious illnesses?"

"None whatsoever."

"That's good to hear."

Carla was anxious to talk more about the position and how she could use her education and skills to help with Apex, Limited's goals. "You mentioned to me on the phone that the position was for an Analyst."

"Yes," Bill Richards said, picking up his pen again. "Everything I described to you on the phone is pretty much what the job entails. You'd be analyzing business documents for our clients, creating reports, that kind of thing. Your background is ideal for the position, and I like the fact that when you're faced with adversity you don't back down. You keep on fighting, keep working the angles to reach your goals. You're calm and focused, all admirable traits we're looking for."

Carla smiled, a warm feeling spreading through her. "Thank you, Mr. Richards."

"The only concern I have is your place of residence," he said, looking at her job application again. "The address you gave us is for a local Motel 6."

"Yes." Carla nodded. She hoped this would not present a problem.

"Not that it's any of my business, but I imagine that once you start with Apex, you'll be able to afford a better place to live."

Carla sighed, the nervous feeling dissipating faster.

"What I'm getting at is this." Bill regarded her frankly, his smile open and friendly. No sense of judgment here. "Our policy on personal time off is limited to four hours a month after your thirty day probationary period. You will accumulate two weeks of paid vacation time at the end of your one-year anniversary of employment. I imagine at some point, you will need some personal time off to deal with moving into a new apartment, yes?"

Carla nodded, relief flooding through her system. "Yes, of course."

"You will probably want to visit family at some point too."

"No, I don't," Carla said. "I just want to put my nose to the grindstone and get to work."

"So you won't want to take any trips to California to visit your parents?"

Carla smiled. "No. At least...not so soon." No need to reveal to Mr. Richards any of her family problems. Besides, she had no intention of contacting her father. Her mother, maybe (her mother hated speaking to her father now, anyway), and *definitely* not her brother, Robert, who was a chip off their father's block. Robert would call Dad the minute Carla got off the phone with him, telling Dad in no doubt excited terms that he'd just talked to Carla. And after three months of relative peace and quiet, thanks to Carla's constant moving from motel to motel during her spate of homelessness, she knew the minute Dad had an idea of what section of Casper she was in, he'd be on her trail again. He'd been tracking her down relentlessly since the estrangement. The only good thing homelessness had done was it had allowed her to slip through the cracks. With no permanent address or credit card, it was harder for him to find her. She wanted to keep it that way.

She wished Dad would leave her alone. She could never forgive him for what he did.

Bill smiled, breaking her thoughts. "Well, I'm sure if you need a day or so to deal with moving, or to deal with visiting a family member, we can arrange something."

"I might need a day or a few hours here and there for moving," Carla said. "But I'm not that close to my family, so I really doubt I'll need the time off to deal with family issues."

"Very good. So, would you like to accept the position?"

Yes! Relief flooded through her. Carla couldn't help but smile wide. "Of course. I'd love to."

"Wonderful!" Bill reached for the phone on his desk and pressed a button. "Mr. White?"

A voice spoke through the intercom. "Yes, Mr. Richards?"

"I'm very pleased to inform you that we've found a suitable candidate. Can you and Mr. Brown step into my office please?"

"Right away, sir."

"Thank you." Bill Richards released the intercom button and rose to his feet. He held out his hand to be shaken. "Allow me to be the first to congratulate you, Ms. Taylor."

Carla stood up and was shaking hands with Bill Richards, feeling good about today, feeling ecstatic that she'd been offered the position, when the door to Bill's office opened and Mr. White and Mr. Brown entered.

Carla turned to acknowledge them and didn't know what hit her. The last thing she saw before one of the men punched her in the face was a third man standing behind them in the hallway. This man was of medium height, slightly overweight, with graying hair, dressed in dark slacks and a gray sweater. He made eye contact with Carla and smiled at her as one of the other men delivered a crushing blow to her face. She felt an explosion of pain across her nose and forehead, a scattering of stars across her vision, and then blackness.

CHAPTER 1

Rick Nicholson was day-dreaming at his desk when there was a tentative knock on the door to his office.

He started, tearing his gaze away from the window which he'd been looking out of. He quickly gathered the papers he was working on and swept them into his tan briefcase, closed and latched the lid and quickly stowed it under his desk. On days like this, he couldn't help but be captivated by the landscape outside. Nestled near the Ashley National Forest in Sweetwater County, Wyoming, the Bent Creek Country Club & Resort was certainly the most visually attractive job location he'd worked at. Rick had been the operations manager of the resort for almost two years since leaving his law career behind in Denver, Colorado. The income he now earned was considerably less, but he was *definitely* happier.

The knock on his office door came again, more firm this time.

"Come on in," Rick said.

The door opened and Carmen Hernandez poked her head in. "Excuse me, Mr. Nicholson, but can I speak with you, please?"

"Sure," Rick said. He beckoned for Carmen to enter and she did, closing the door behind her. She settled down in one of the two chairs positioned in front of his desk, looking nervous. Rick wondered if she was having trouble with the Daniels couple. One of the waitresses had lodged a complaint against them last night. Claimed they were sexually harassing her. Rick had found himself in an uncomfortable position; how to balance the needs of the employee in accordance to state and federal employment law against sexual harassment in the workplace, and how to avoid ruffling the feathers of Bent Creek's extremely wealthy clients. Bent Creek Country Club was more than an exclusive country club that catered to the very rich; its members were rich, powerful people who paid for the privilege of being able to do whatever they wanted to do within the club's gates. Last year another client, Drew Samples, had paid one of the groundsmen to grovel like a dog in front of him and lick his shoes in return for a crisp ten thousand dollar bill. The bastard had laughed about it with his snobby friends for days afterward.

"What's up, Carmen?" Rick asked.

"Brian isn't here," Carmen stated.

"Brian? You mean Charlie's partner?" There were two Brian's on the payroll. One worked in maintenance with Charlie Thompson, a big burly man who resembled a football lineman; the other Brian worked in the resort's laundromat.

Carmen nodded. "Yes. He's not here."

"What do you mean, he's not here?"

Carmen shrugged. Rick watched her from across his desk. Carmen was ten years his senior and originally from Guatemala. One of a team of twelve maids who serviced the Bent Creek suites, Carmen sometimes worked twelve-hour shifts turning beds, cleaning and dusting rooms and lavish suites, and performing other cleaning duties on the grounds. She was a good worker. Rick heard nothing but good things from her team leader.

"He's not here. He was supposed to be servicing the generator outside the pool house this morning and Charlie can't find him. I went to his room and he's gone."

"You sure he isn't elsewhere on the grounds?" The Bent

Creek Country Club sat on forty square miles of rolling forests, creeks, and picturesque prairies. Many of its members hunted quail and deer during hunting season, and hiked the rugged canyons in the summer.

Carmen shook her head. "No. Charlie called him, but he isn't answering."

Rick shrugged. "I don't know what to tell you, Carmen. You sure Brian didn't just skip out?"

"Skip out?"

"Yeah. We had that happen last season. One of the pool boys slipped out toward the end of the season. Packed his bags, skipped out on a week's pay. It happens." *Especially when the Board makes me hire guys on work release*, he thought to himself.

"No, Brian wouldn't do that," Carmen insisted. The look in her eyes, her body posture, told Rick all he needed to know. Carmen's concern was deeper than worrying about a co-worker. Rick flashed on the previous month of the season; hadn't he seen a lot of Carmen and Brian during their off-time together? Hanging out at the employee's-only bar-and-grill, away from the rest of the establishment? Sitting by themselves in the corner booth, away from their other co-workers? Rick believed he *had* seen that. Experience told him they were seeing each other. Another thing to look out for in this day and age of the workplace from an employer standpoint—a jilted lover can always file a sexual harassment claim against an employer for turning a blind eye to the relationship. They could claim the company allowed a fellow employee to sexually harass them.

Rick frowned slightly. What was he thinking? He'd had a one-night stand with one of the waitresses who worked the lounge, which was run by five-star Chef Jim Munchel, just a few nights ago. Despite the fact that it had been mutual, that it was she who had come on to him, Rick realized he shouldn't have allowed it. He also shouldn't have tried to follow up with her, hoping for a repeat performance. The waitress, Anna King, had treated that night as if it hadn't happened, and she'd surely never responded to his overtures to pick up where they'd left off. Thinking about it now, and his thoughts on Brian Gaiman and Carmen Hernandez, only emphasized that he had to get through the next few days and then this season was officially over. That meant getting to the bottom of this Brian Gaiman thing.

"Are you sure?" Rick asked her gently.

"*Sí*! I'm sure!"

Rick knew he had to tread lightly here. He was sure Carmen knew that Brian was on work-release. Hell, the guy had been pretty frank about that to Charlie, his maintenance partner, on the first day. He'd also been honest about it to the few Bent Creek clients who'd privately praised the young man's resourcefulness and work ethic to Rick. Brian wouldn't be the first bad boy to sweep a woman off her feet and then skip town on her.

"You *do* know that Brian is on work-release, right, Carmen?"

"*Sí*!" Carmen cast her eyes downward, as if ashamed she'd gotten herself involved with Brian. She forced her gaze back up to Rick's. "But what does that have to do with the fact that he's missing?"

Rick told her about the pool guy from last season. As he related the story, Carmen grew silent. "And that guy wasn't the first, either," Rick said. "Paul Westcott told me we get at least one guy a year who skips out sometime during the late summer season. These guys are recently released from prison, they're restless, they want to see their families, and they see this area as a place to make a clean escape. It happens."

Carmen shook her head, confusion on her features. "No, not with Brian. He wouldn't do that. He wanted to...how do you say? He wanted to stay on the right track."

"I'm sure he did, Carmen, but—"

"He would not have run off without telling me!"

Rick regarded Carmen from across his desk. If there was any doubt to his suspicions that Carmen and Brian were having a fling, those doubts were gone now. It was all spelled out for him: ex-con with a seemingly heart of gold woos pretty older woman and promises her the world, then ditches her abruptly. He'd seen this movie many times.

Rick shifted gears quickly. "Tell you what," he said. "I will call Charlie to my office and have a talk with him. I'll also call Paul and have him send somebody down to Brian's quarters to check things out. How does that sound?"

"*Si*!" Carmen said, nodding vigorously, looking relieved that Rick was taking her complaint seriously. "*Gracias*!"

"No problem." Rick stood up and ushered Carmen to the door. "I'll let you know if I hear anything. In the meantime, if *you* hear anything, or if Brian contacts you or even drops by, let me know. Okay?"

"*Si*, Mr. Nicholson. *Gracias*!" Carmen headed down the hall, small and compact in her light blue maid uniform. Rick watched her go, noting her trim figure for the first time. *She looks like she's lived a hard life, but she has a nice figure*, he thought. *I can see Brian helping himself to some of that.*

Rick stepped back into his office and closed the door behind him. He went to the window overlooking the north side of the property. The sky outside was a deep blue, with only a faint hint of clouds. To the right, far off in the distance, was a mountain range. To the left, vast plains and rolling hills. The Bent Creek Country Club & Resort was smack dab in the middle of the most beautiful stretch of land in the United States. Aside from taking up forty square miles of rolling wilderness, the facility boasted three hundred luxury rooms and suites, as well as a five star restaurant run by one of the top chefs in the world, Chef Jim Munchel. The facility also boasted a salon, a massage and steam room, two indoor pools, a large Olympic-style swimming pool, two gyms filled with state-of-the-art exercise equipment, basketball, racquetball and tennis courts. There was a gift shop, a newsstand that sold magazines, newspapers, and the latest best-sellers. There was also a small medical clinic on the grounds staffed with a physician's assistant and a registered nurse. Knock on wood, so far the few medical emergencies that had sprung up had not required the services of a physician. For contingencies sake, there was an ambulance on the grounds, the nearest hospital only five miles away down Route 5.

There was a stable with over a dozen pure-bred horses for various riding activities. There was a thirty-hole golf course, as well as a squash court. A firing range was nestled at the rear of the grounds near an accessway that merged into the vast wilderness of the national park, for hunting (during season).

In short, it was everything anybody could ask for in a vacation resort.

Rick Nicholson reflected on what had brought him to his current position as manager of operations of Bent Creek Country Club and Resorts as he looked out his office window. Even if he had not left his position as a partner in White, LaChance, and Weinstein, the law firm he'd been working at since graduating from law school, he never would have been able to afford the one hundred thousand dollar entry fee and the fifty thousand dollar yearly dues to be a member of Bent Creek.

He'd been on the fast track to a partnership with the firm. Before he left, the senior partner, Mick LaChance, had pulled him aside and asked Rick to seriously reconsider his resignation. "Think about your future," he'd implored. "Think about all the good you can do with us, all the good that will follow in your personal life if you stay on. At the rate you're climbing, Rick, I can guarantee there will be a spot for you as a senior partner before you're forty."

The problem was, Rick had never wanted to be a lawyer. That had been his father's idea.

And now Dad was dead. Exposure to Agent Orange in 'Nam had led to cancer a decade ago. Rick had been in his final year of law school then and had finished, mostly to please his mother, who was devastated over his father's passing. Rick himself had been in a numbed haze the next few years; finishing school, applying for and getting the job at White, LaChance and Weinstein, and then the years of long hours and no social life being a young lawyer often entailed. By the time he woke up and poked his head out, a good part of the first decade of the twenty-first century had passed and he was approaching thirty-six. He'd never married, rarely had time for a serious relationship, much less a romantic fling, and he still lived in the same apartment he'd moved into when he'd passed the bar exam. And he realized, with some degree of regret, that the life he'd been leading was not his; it was the life his father had wanted him to live.

After taking stock of his finances and realizing he could afford to quit his position at the firm, he did. His decision surprised everybody, including all three senior partners, who still refused to accept his resignation. "We're calling this an extended sabbatical," Keith White told him at his going-away party, which had been held at a swanky downtown bar. Keith was the only partner he could trust to confide in completely, and Rick had told him everything; his self-doubt, how he'd felt pressured into becoming a lawyer by his father, how he needed time to get away and simply discover himself. "Take as much time as you need. We'll hold a place for you," Keith had said.

Rick had appreciated the gesture and still kept in touch with Keith, who kept asking when he'd be back at the firm. The honest answer was Rick didn't know.

No sooner had Rick left the firm when his mother was stricken with cancer. Rick moved to Boulder, Colorado, to be closer to her. After four months, she insisted he resume his work. He hadn't told her he'd quit the firm, so he'd headed back to Denver and tried to start over.

Only he wasn't entirely sure how to do that.

Rick sighed. He sometimes wondered if he'd hit a mid-life crisis a bit early. He'd always wanted to be something other than being a lawyer. When he was in high school he'd wanted to be a commercial artist, but his parents had squashed that particular idea (*how the hell do commercial artists make money, anyway?* his dad had asked one evening in that tone of voice Rick always hated; disapproval. *Go to college, be a lawyer. Don't waste your life chasing a pipe dream.*). Later, he'd wanted to be an airline pilot. By then he was studying pre-law and the switch to aeronautical engineering would have added another two years to his undergraduate degree. Besides, Dad would have been furious for flushing that money down the toilet. Nope, Rick was going to be a lawyer, whether he liked it or not.

Rick never liked being a lawyer. He was very good at it, but he didn't like it.

And now with Dad gone, he had a chance to reclaim his life and do something for *himself.*

Only he wasn't sure how to go about and do that.

Because Rick had not changed his lifestyle since leaving his position at the firm, he quickly found that his finances were dwindling. Not wanting to alert his mother to his unemployment status, he'd shifted gears quickly and cast a line out for gainful employment.

He found it as an Operations Manager for the Bent Creek Country Club and Resorts, in Wyoming, which he got courtesy of a lead from a former colleague of a competing law firm he still hung out with on a social basis. "Why not just ask for your old job back?" the colleague, Jim Smothers, said one night over beers at a bar and grill they frequented.

"Because I hate being a lawyer," Rick had responded.

"Yeah, I hate it too," Jim said. "But the money's sure good."

Thanks to his education and excellent referrals, securing the position with Bent Creek was easy. This was Rick's second season here, and he was fairly certain that at the end of this season he would be offered a position at the holding company that ran the facility. Rick was hoping this was the case; he'd come to like the work he was doing as Operations Manager. He was liking it so much that he was discovering what was becoming very clear to him: his hidden passion—running a business.

Over the past few months, as this realization had grown

stronger, Rick realized that landing this position had been a godsend. He found that he really liked running a company. He liked the ins and outs of it, the mechanics of making sure the day-to-day operations ran smoothly. Sure, there were hiccups along the way, but Rick had a flair for navigating around nasty turns and surprises. His quick thinking and logical way of doing things, holdovers from his years in the legal profession, lent considerable assets to his new role, and he thrived in it. Maybe getting this job, which was originally intended to provide cushion income while he did some serious soul searching, was what he needed to find his true passion in life.

With this realization in mind, during the six months he was unemployed after last season ended, Rick had reached out to one of the lawyers with his old firm about an old business proposition he'd floated some time back. Mike had only been too eager to get on the horn and contact the other players. By the time this season at Bent Creek was underway, the preliminary groundwork of their plan was in place. Rick had been doing his best to run things for it on his end up here, but that required stealth at times; he knew upper management generally frowned on employees working on their own businesses, even on their off time. Employees were generally expected to devote one hundred percent of their efforts and energies to their employers, as well as their loyalty. If what Rick and Mike were planning worked out though, Rick might not need to work at Bent Creek for much longer. In fact, this might be his last season. He'd been hoping the Board would offer him a permanent position, but he couldn't count on that. In fact—

The phone on his desk rang, snapping him out of his thoughts. So much for reflection.

Rick picked up the phone. "Rick here."

"Hello, Rick." It was Paul Westcott, Chief of Security. "Got a second?"

"Sure thing."

"Are you going to the meeting tonight?"

"Wouldn't miss it."

"Great! I wanted to touch base with you on the north end of the property and what proposals the state Games and Commissions are planning for next year's season."

And with that, Rick was back in his new world; plotting and planning the best way to run the most efficient business he could ever lay his hands on.

CHAPTER 2

Eighteen Months Ago

When the private detective was finished looking at the photographs, he looked across the desk at Joe. "How long has she been missing?"

"Six months now," Joe said. Even now, admitting this aloud still made his hands shake, his stomach flutter with fear over what could have happened to his daughter.

"And you say the last time you spoke to her was two years ago?"

Joe nodded. "Yes."

"You were estranged from her?"

"Yes."

"Why?"

He sighed, wondering how to explain this. The grandfather clock in the entry hall tolled, chiming five o'clock. Right on cue, the jingle of keys and the sound of footsteps through the kitchen—his maid, Juanita, leaving for the day. Once the private detective left, he'd have the house to himself again.

"Carla has always been fiercely independent," he told the detective. "Something I've always admired, by the way. She gets that from me, so we butted heads occasionally when she was a teenager. Nothing too serious, just the usual teenage rebellion crap. But then...around the time she graduated from college, we had a disagreement over a position that had been offered to her. A big oil company, *Al Azif*, Ltd, had offered her a very generous position, but it was at their world headquarters in Saudi Arabia. Carla wanted to take it, and I tried to talk her out of it."

"Why?"

"The honest answer is two-fold. I didn't want her to move out of the country because I couldn't stand the thought of her being half a world away. Any parent would understand." He looked at the private detective. "Are you a father?"

The private detective nodded. "My son is four, my daughter seven. I know what you mean."

"I knew that if she went to Saudi Arabia, I'd be worried for her constantly. You know how they treat women over there, right?"

The private detective nodded.

"*Al Azif* is a private company, and despite the fact that they have many Americans on their payroll, including American women, it is required that all women, regardless of their nationality or religion, live by Sharia law in Saudi Arabia. I pointed this out to Carla and we had a big fight about it. The biggest one we've ever had. I think she rebelled against me for the simple fact to rebel. She was taking this job and she didn't care if she was going to have to clothe herself in a burqua while out in public."

"I see," the private detective said. He'd introduced himself to Joe as Dean Campbell over the phone when they had their first conversation a few days ago. Joe pegged his age as mid-thirties, average build, average looks. He was perfectly suited for his profession.

"She accepted the position and our argument grew more heated," Joe continued. "To be honest, I was afraid for her safety at this point. Kidnappings in Arab countries are routine, and ransoms are rarely honored. Caucasian women command high prices on the Arab slave trade. I have more than enough to pay a ransom, but that wasn't the point. I did not want Carla to be in any danger, period. I did not want her living under Sharia Law, and even if she stayed on the straight and narrow in accordance to their customs, she would always have the risk of running afoul of the *mutaween*, or the Morality Police, for whatever imagined infraction they considered offensive: being seen in public with a man who was not her husband or relative, accidentally showing a hint of ankle, being a woman."

"Those rules even apply to foreign workers?" Dean asked.

"Oh yes," Joe answered. "It applies to everybody living within the kingdom. No exception is made for tourists or foreign workers who are in the country on work visas. That's a large part of the reason why the U.S. Embassy discourages American citizens from travelling there for any reason."

Dean made a note of this.

Joe continued. "Call me politically-incorrect, but I didn't want her to be living under such barbaric conditions. Carla's acceptance of the position was contingent upon her arrival in Saudi Arabia within three days. Because our argument over this incident spilled over into the next day and involved her mother, which drew out the conflict even longer, that window of opportunity closed and the employment offer was rescinded."

The private detective raised his eyebrows in surprise. "That's odd."

"It isn't if the talent pool is promising," Joe answered. "I later found out that the offer was made to another burgeoning executive. A young man, by the way. He's still over there."

"Safe, I presume?"

"I don't know, because two days after their offer to Carla was rescinded, she accepted another job offer, this one in Casper, Wyoming."

"With Braun & Meyers?"

"Right."

"She was laid off from that position nine months later and drifted through various jobs," Dean said, reading over notes he'd obviously taken a few days ago when they'd had their first phone consultation. "She lost her apartment, lost her credit, her car, and you had a hard time keeping up with her."

Joe sighed. Even now, thinking about it, created a deep pang of sorrow and regret that had not eased with the passing of time. "When she moved to Wyoming, she left no forwarding address. I had to pester my son to get information on her. She wouldn't talk to me on the phone, wouldn't meet with me. I even flew out there and tried to make amends with her."

"She filed a police report against you?" Dean said. The private detective looked across at him, eyebrows raised.

"Yes." He nodded. "I had to hire a Casper-based private detective agency to keep tabs on her. She somehow found out I was having her followed and did everything she could to shake off my tail. Being homeless didn't help. She didn't *have* to be homeless. I could have helped her find a new position, especially with my contacts, but she didn't *want* my help. Even without my help, she should have had no problem finding a position. But with the economy the way it is." He shook his head in despair. "The last place she was traced to was a Motel 6, just outside the city."

"You've reported her missing?"

"Yes."

"What do the Casper police say?"

Joe sighed, the first signs of frustration becoming evident in his voice. "They wouldn't take me seriously at first. Said there was no evidence of foul play. The police gained access to her motel room and the place was clean. She left no suitcase, no personal belongings. The only thing she was guilty of was skipping out on her bill."

The private detective pursed his lips. "I can see why the police wouldn't want to get involved. Did you tell them what you just told me? About your estrangement from her?"

Joe nodded, feeling the last nail being driven into that particular coffin.

"Did they at least *try* to do a search for her?"

"No."

"What about you? Did you put up missing flyers or anything?"

"Yes. And nothing has helped."

The private detective was silent for a moment. He opened the folder he'd brought with him: notes on the case. He read them over, his features reflective. Contemplating.

Finally, the private detective looked across the large mahogany desk at him. "I have to be honest, Mr. Taylor...this isn't going to be easy. I've had some success in cases like this before, but it could take a while."

He was prepared for this. "I don't care how long it takes. I just want you to find her. I just need to know...if she's okay."

The private detective nodded, his face solemn. "Of course."

CHAPTER 3

Anna King felt a brief moment of irritation as she approached the next table in her station.

Her waitress shift at Bent Creek Resort's massive dining room had only started an hour ago, and dinner service was already proving to be unbearable. The presence of the Daniels couple was the first thing that had set off her unease; upon seeing them, she'd felt a twinge of anxiety roll through her.

The second thing that had set it off was the scumbag at table seventeen, who was vacationing with his parents. The scumbag had skinned both his knees during some outdoor excursion earlier in the day. As Anna approached their table to take their order, he'd been in the midst of changing the bandages Ellen Wood, the resort's nurse, had affixed earlier that day. Anna had barely gotten a cursory "Good evening, I'm Anna King and I'll be taking care of you tonight. Can I start you off with a cocktail?" No, she hadn't even been given the courtesy of finishing this introductory script. Instead, Mr. Daddy Warbucks had thrust a pair of bloody and pus-filled bandages at her and said, "Here, take care of these."

The moment the bloody, pus-filled bandages touched her hands, Anna had dropped them in disgust and made a sound. She didn't remember now what it was. Probably *ugh*! She couldn't help it. It was instinctual.

That *faux pas* had resulted in a verbal dressing down in Alex's office. "I don't care if those bandages had the bubonic plague on them," Alex had said. "Your job is to serve our guests, no matter how outlandish their requests may seem to you. Do you understand?"

Anna understood perfectly. "Yes, Mr. Lillywhite," Anna had been forced to say.

"Good. Don't let it happen again."

It hadn't mattered that immediately after she'd dropped the bandages, she'd quickly summoned a bus boy to dispose of the mess. Mr. Lillywhite, who was the manager of the restaurant, made it clear on her first day that her job as a waitress was not only to take customers' orders and deliver quick service, she was to indulge in whatever whim the customer had, no questions asked.

The Daniels couple were the worst. Shane Daniels was an arrogant twit. Slim with short graying hair, he reminded Anna of a weasel. He had a southern accent that told Anna all she needed to know: rich southern boy who thought everybody who held a service job was just another nigger to mistreat. Niggers were niggers, regardless of what race and nationality they were. His wife, Jackie was no better. Jackie wasn't much to look at, with shoulder-length wavy blonde hair, big tits, and a face that brought new meaning to the term 'horsey'. She seemed to exist for the sole purpose of providing a life support system for her twat, which Shane indulged in every evening, or so he told everybody around him. "Jackie and I were getting it on last night, did we keep y'all awake?" he'd brayed loudly to their equally snobby friends at their table that first night. Over the past four nights he'd made an effort to let everybody around them know how much he and Jackie fucked. Jackie, to her credit, grinned stupidly during Shane's drunken boasts. Anna recognized the glazed look in her eyes every evening; the way she'd laugh five seconds after everybody else started laughing, as if from a delayed response. The woman was zonked out of her mind. Probably on Oxy or some other opiate. Anna didn't blame her. If Anna had the misfortune of being chained to Shane Daniels, she'd probably be full-on junkie, too.

Anna approached her next table, doing her best to put what was turning out to be an incredibly shitty night behind her. The customers at this new table were a youthful looking couple; blonde, tanned, and physically fit and attractive. The guy looked boyishly handsome, the woman his perfect trophy wife. Anna smiled warmly at them. "Good evening! I'm Anna and I'll be taking care of you tonight. Can I start you off with a drink?"

The man smiled at her. "You're the Epsilon who's taking care of us?"

Anna kept her smile. "Actually, I'm an Alpha in disguise, sir. But I'll be glad to take your order."

The man started, the surprise evident in his features. His wife seemed to not know how to respond. Anna was surprised by how quickly she'd lobbed that lame attempt of an insult his way. It was obvious this customer was well-educated, his reference to Aldous Huxley's novel *Brave New World* clearly demonstrated this.

"Well, then," the man said, smiling back. He glanced at his wife, then turned back to Anna. "It's refreshing that the help is educated, wouldn't you say so, dear?"

"I suppose," the woman said, her smile fake, plastic.

"With that in mind, it would be great to get to know you a little better at some point during our stay," the man continued. "It's rare that we come across one that is well-read."

"I'm sure it is, sir," Anna said, playing her role well. "I would welcome that very much."

The man turned to his wife. "Perhaps this can be arranged then?"

The wife nodded, her smile seeming to be one of amusement. Anna watched carefully, getting the impression wifey was simply putting up with her husband's flirtations with her. She turned to Anna. "I apologize for my husband's blunt treatment of you. You have to realize, most of the help we deal with here are rather shallow people."

"Of course, ma'am," Anna said, nodding. "I understand."

The man was regarding her with a look Anna recognized—desire. "You *are* a rather attractive woman, if I may say so."

"Thank you, sir. I appreciate it."

"About that wine..."

"Yes?"

The man turned to his wife. "How about a bottle of the Cabernet?" The woman nodded, and he turned back to Anna. "A bottle of the Cabernet, please."

"Wonderful! I'll bring that to you right away." And with that, Anna headed to the bar, ignoring the Daniels couple, who appeared to be the center of attention again at their table.

She was almost out of her station when a lone customer seated at one of the booths signaled to her. Anna smiled at him and approached. "Yes, sir?"

The man smiled back. Anna had liked him from the moment she'd taken his drink order fifteen minutes ago. He was tall, with dark hair that was boyishly long but not enough to be considered rebellious, and almost movie star handsome features. In a way, this did not make him stand out in this crowd. Most of the men at the Bent Creek Country Club and Resorts were very handsome men. Anna had found herself fantasizing about some of them, and it had gone no further than that. It was nice to have erotic fantasies, but it was their personalities that had extinguished the flame of attraction for her. Every hottie at Bent Creek either had the IQ of a toaster or they were arrogant, pompous pricks. This customer was neither. "I've decided," he said.

"Great! What can I get for you?"

The man read off the menu. "I'll have the Tiger prawn ravioli with the creamy fennel puree, and the light lobster bisque."

"Very good," Anna said. "I will put that order in. Would you like another glass of *Pinot Noir*?"

"No thank you," the man said. He smiled at her.

"Very good." Anna nodded and made her way to the kitchen.

Anna reached the queue and jotted the guest's order down and handed it to the chef who manned the pass, who took it and turned to the crew in the kitchen. "Tiger prawn ravioli with the creamy fennel puree and light lobster bisque."

Anna went to the kitchen and traded a glance with Martin Coslaw, the aging bartender who maintained duty behind the bar. Stooped with age, Martin had served the privileged at Bent Creek for over twenty years. He was her favorite co-worker by far. He had a million stories about Bent Creek, and had given her some unsolicited advice on her first night: *keep your head down, don't let your emotions get the best of you, and remember—at the end of the day, these people mean* nothing *to you.* It was valuable advice.

Martin approached the bar. "What's needed, dear?"

"Fresh bottle of Cabernet," she said.

Martin nodded and called the order back to one of his assistants, who ducked out the back to the wine cellar. Martin reached behind him for glasses and a bottle of Cutty Sark. "Night's gonna be hell," he said, not missing a beat. "A lot of the guests did a big hike through Pike's Canyon."

"Great." Anna knew very well what this meant. The pampered and privileged who'd made this hike would be raring for not only relaxation, but partying at the expense of those who had to work here. Last weekend a bunch of them had hiked Pike's Canyon and the party that had followed resulted in a waiter being fired by Alex when the man wouldn't clap his hands and hoot like a seal on command. "But your *friend* is doing it!" the man had said, pointing to one of the groundsmen, who, according to Martin, had been too embarrassed and scared to not comply.

"I don't give a shit," the waiter had said. "*I'm* not doing it and *you*, can *fuck off*!"

"Yep," Martin said, finishing off the drinks and placing them on a ticket at the waitress station for pickup. "Most of 'em are here now."

"The Daniels party wouldn't be one of them, would it?"

"I'm afraid so."

"Great. Just what I need."

Martin's assistant emerged with the bottle of Cabernet and a bottle opener. He set them on a tray. Martin set a pair of wine glasses down on the tray and gently pushed it toward her. She smiled at Martin, who nodded and winked, and with tray in hand she headed back to her station.

She tried to tune out the noise from the Daniels table as she approached the customers who'd ordered the wine. She set the empty glasses down, then opened the bottle carefully. The couple smiled in anticipation, trading glances with each other. Anna wondered if they were on a weekend romantic getaway or something—she hadn't seen them here until today, and the season ended in two days. Anna poured them each a glass and waited while they took a sip. The man nodded in approval. "Very good. Thank you."

"Can I get you anything else?" Anna asked.

"At this moment, no," the man said. "But thank you."

"Very good. Do you need a minute to look at the menu?"

"Yes, please," the woman said.

"I'll be back shortly, then." Anna nodded and turned away from the table, prepared to head to another table when Shane's voice called out to her.

"Waitress! Waitress, please!"

Groaning inwardly, Anna turned around and put on her best smile. She approached the table, thinking *use your best skills at method acting, kid. You're going to need it with this group.* "What can I get for you?" she asked.

"We have a new person in our party," Shane said, smiling drunkenly. Jackie sat beside him, laughing at something. Shane cocked a thumb at a balding man wearing a white golf shirt. "He'd like to place an order."

Anna directed her attention to the newcomer. "What can I get for you sir?"

The man took a quick glance down at his menu. "I'll have the Peking Duck in Mango Salsa."

"Very good, sir." Anna turned her attention to the others at the table. "Can I get anything for anybody else?"

"My room, tonight," Shane said, a leer on his face. "You got nice titties. Between you and Jackie, I can have a tittie sandwich!" With that, he laughed drunkenly.

Anna felt herself go flush with embarrassment as laughter erupted around the table.

"I'll go put the Peking Duck order in," Anna said. She made to step away when Shane grabbed her by the wrist.

"Hold on a minute," Shane said. His grip was strong.

Anna gasped, her heart lodged in her throat. She steeled herself for more abuse. "I didn't say you could go," Shane said.

"Sir, I have to put your friend's order in."

"You asked me if I wanted anything else." The man's breath was heavy with 151 Rum. His snooty friends were hiding their amused laughter behind cupped hands. "I could have a talk with your manager if you do that to me again."

"I'm sure you could, sir," Anna said, struggling hard to keep her emotions at bay. "Now, if you'll let go of my wrist, I will put in your friend's order and check on your food."

Shane seemed to consider this, then released her. Jackie laughed again, looking at Anna and not really seeing her. Anna rubbed her wrist, which was numb from Shane's grip. "Go check on our food, bitch. And be quick about it!"

Without a word, Anna headed toward the kitchen, her rage threatening to overwhelm her.

When she reached the pass, she called out the Peking Duck order. Then she asked for a status check on Table 13, which was the Daniels table. A moment later the pass chef called back. "Five minutes, Anna."

"Thank you," Anna said. She glanced back at her station. The half dozen tables she serviced were all taken care of with no service expected until Table 13's was up. She retreated to the bar and glanced at her watch. One hour left till her measly fifteen minute break. Damn.

"The Daniels couple at you again?" Martin asked. He'd sauntered over during a break in the action from filling waitress orders.

"I would so like to bash that motherfucker's face in," Anna muttered.

"I saw him grab your wrist," Martin said. "Not that anything will happen, but you might want to mention the incident to Rick."

"Rick? Why?"

Martin shrugged. "He's new. Young. Very personable. He's the best thing the staff has had in an operations manager for some time. Alex won't do shit for you. He's so far up Wayne's ass, he's breathing the man's bad breath." Wayne Salle was the CEO of the Bent Creek Country Club. "But Rick? He may be management, but he's been very good to us so far. He tries to smooth things out between customers and staff. We had a waitress last year who went through the same thing with the Daniels couple. Rick told Alex that he was to have her moved to another station every time the Daniels couple happened to be seated where she was supposed to service tables. Made Alex abide by it, too. I'm sure Rick would do the same for you if you explained the situation to him."

"Alex has already chewed me out once tonight," Anna said, not looking in the direction of her station. No sense in telling Martin that Rick probably wouldn't help her, not after the other night.

"It still wouldn't hurt," Martin stated. "Seriously, Anna. Don't let the Daniels couple do this to you. They've had three waitresses fired in the past two years, and they made one of my best bartenders quit. I know Wayne insists on going above and beyond the call of duty in making these people happy, but let's be serious. The Daniels couple have been abusing Wayne's rules for too long. I bet if you told Rick what happened, he'll have a word with him about it."

"You think?"

Martin shrugged. "I don't see why not. Something like this might take his mind off a bigger problem he has. It might drive him to actually do something about the Daniels couple for once."

"What kind of big problem does Wayne have all of a sudden?"

"You haven't heard about the missing money?"

"What missing money?"

Martin leaned forward, his voice lowered so they wouldn't be overheard. "Here's the Cliff Notes version. One of the guests, guy who's CEO of some investment bank in New York, had money stolen from his room sometime early this morning. Paul and his staff are freaking out over it."

"Really?" Anna felt a small burst of excitement at the news. A theft at Bent Creek Country Club and Resorts? It seemed unheard of. "How much?"

"A quarter of a million dollars."

"*What—*" Anna stopped, realized her voice had taken on a higher note of excitement. She lowered her voice. "Two hundred and fifty thousand dollars? In cash? Who'd be stupid enough to leave that much cash lying around in their room?"

"Somebody who thinks of two hundred and fifty k in cash the way you or I would think of five bucks," Martin answered.

Martin had a point. Still, it boggled the mind. "Somebody broke in to his room? How'd this all happen?"

"I don't know all the details," Martin said. He grabbed a dishtowel and began wiping down the end of the bar Anna was standing at, trying to appear busy. "But what I heard was that the guy in question had the cash stashed in a briefcase he kept in his room. Made no bones about having it, either, at least to his friends. The money was supposed to be for some private gambling he and his friends were going to partake in. Highly discouraged, of course." Anna nodded. Bent Creek didn't have many rules, but one of them was that management frowned on gambling. "Anyway, I guess he checked his briefcase this morning and the money was gone. He flipped out, called security, and Paul and his guys have been tearing their hair out ever since."

"He didn't put that cash in the room safe," Anna observed. All the rooms and suites had stainless steel safes, each one equipped with its own combination lock.

"Obviously not," Martin answered. "Depending on what denominations the guy had, that much cash might not have fit. He surely didn't claim the money when he checked in."

"You think somebody in housekeeping could have done it?" Anna asked.

"That's the obvious choice, but it looks like they already might have a suspect. Do you remember Brian Gaiman? Groundskeeper?"

Anna shrugged. She'd only been on the job long enough to know everybody in the dining room and the kitchen on a first name basis, but not the names of housekeeping and the maintenance people, much less anybody else. "Sorry, the name doesn't ring a bell."

"Brian's one of the groundskeepers," Martin continued. "They should have more on staff, if you ask me. Anyway, Brian skipped out late last night or early this morning. Nobody can find him. Groundskeepers have keycard access to all the rooms and suites."

"That doesn't mean he stole the money," Anna said.

"Brian's an ex-con. Served just under two years for aggravated robbery, burglary and other things. He was on work release."

"Oh." That changed everything. Anna had no idea Bent Creek management would allow a guy on work release on the premises.

She voiced this to Martin, who began making drinks for

a new order that Carol, one of the other waitresses, had just delivered. "I heard management has a work release program," he said. "It has something to do with their corporate structure or something. Some kind of charity thing they're involved in. Bringing guys like Brian back into the mainstream, helping them out, that kind of thing. Guess it gives them the warm and fuzzies in their otherwise cold and calculating capitalistic hearts."

"Is that the only proof they have?" Anna asked.

"Brian's work area the previous day was in the East Wing of the resort," Martin answered. He finished the drinks—a Manhattan and a Screwdriver—and placed them at the edge of the bar for pickup. "The guest who reported the theft is in the East Wing. In fact, Brian was seen in the area a few hours before the guy turned in that night. Paul and Rick put two and two together. I mean, who else *could* it be?"

"You got me," Anna said. She glanced toward the kitchen, saw the first of her orders had just been placed at the pass. She turned to Martin. "Duty calls."

"Okay," Martin said. "And Anna?"

"Yeah?"

"Talk to Rick. You may have to work here like the rest of us, but you don't have to take Shane Daniels's shit. Tell Rick what happened. You owe it to yourself to get him involved now, while he's still new and green to the job. You shouldn't have to put up with the Daniel's shit for the next two days we're here."

"I will." Anna smiled at Martin. She liked Martin a lot, and had come to think of him as the older brother she'd never had. Or maybe uncle was a better word. "And thanks."

"Don't mention it." Martin turned back to his job and Anna headed to the kitchen to retrieve her first of many orders for the night.

CHAPTER 4

Seventeen Months Ago

Joe Taylor was on the phone in his home office, talking to Danielle Winters, a childhood friend of Carla's. Tracking Danielle down had not taken much effort, but arranging a conversation with her had proved challenging. Danielle was a third year medical student at Harvard.

"Anything you can tell me will be a big help," he told Danielle.

"I wish I could remember something," Danielle told him. She sounded tired and worried over the phone. "I just can't. I told that detective everything I could remember."

"I know, and I appreciate it," Joe said. "That's why I thought I would call. If there's anything you're nervous about telling the detective, you can tell me."

"I'm not nervous about anything," Danielle said.

"Okay." Last week, Dean Campbell had uncovered forensic evidence from Joe's personal home computer that was dated from before the estrangement. The evidence indicated Carla had used this computer to access her email account on Gmail. Messages had been sent to Danielle from Carla's account in which she confided quite a lot, much of it involving her considering a stint as a high-class call girl to help pay for college. According to the email documentation, and what Danielle had told the private detective, Carla had not gone through with it.

"I wish I knew more, but I don't," Danielle continued. "We only spoke once every few months anyway. School has been crazy, and with her situation it's just...it's been *crazy*."

"I understand," he said. In the four weeks Dean Campbell had been on the case, he had not been able to turn up any new evidence. Carla's trail ended in Casper, Wyoming and went dead cold. Much like the Casper Police Department, who'd done a cursory investigation, Dean had been able to go no further than verify she'd lived in a few motels in the area after her job layoff and eviction from her apartment. There were no arrest records, no hospital records, no record from the airports, train or bus stations that she'd left the city or the state. The last job she'd held was through a temporary agency, who reported sending her out for a short stint as a receptionist at a manufacturing firm four weeks before she disappeared.

"You *did* talk to her when she lived in Casper, though, right?" he asked Danielle.

"Yes, I did."

"And you talked to her after her layoff from Braun & Meyers?"

"Uh huh."

"Did you send her money?"

Danielle sighed. He knew her parents were well-to-do, that Danielle was attending Harvard on their dime. "I offered to send her money but she wouldn't let me. In fact, she refused. Said if I sent her anything that it would be testing our friendship."

He sighed, closed his eyes. That would be just like Carla to decline help when it was offered, even if she desperately needed it. "You still maintained the friendship, though."

"Of course! Carla's my best friend."

He and Danielle had already danced around the subject of his and Carla's estrangement. It had been the first thing they'd talked about when they spoke six weeks ago. Back then, Danielle had been hesitant to speak to him, was distant, but he'd bridged the gap with her quickly when he learned that Carla hadn't been entirely revealing to her childhood friend on the specifics regarding what led to the fractured relationship with her father. Carla had told Danielle that her Dad was too controlling, was using his influence to steer her toward a job for one of the companies he had a controlling interest in, and that he'd sabotaged a lucrative job offer for an oil company. What she *hadn't* told Danielle was that her father had been largely hands-off on her job search, that he'd simply made the offer that he could help her get a foot in the door with one of his companies. Carla also hadn't told Danielle that the oil company who'd made the job offer was *Al Azif*, that the job location was at their international headquarters in Saudi Arabia, and that she was required to live there. He'd explained to Danielle his concerns for Carla living in a Muslim country that operated under Sharia Law, that American women were held to those same standards. When Danielle learned that, she'd said, "Carla didn't tell me *that*." In the weeks that followed after learning this, Danielle had been a fount of information. Unfortunately, that information hadn't been very helpful.

"You told the detective that the last time you talked to Carla, she'd just been let go from the receptionist job and was living in a motel. Do you remember which one?"

"No. They all blur together now."

"There was a Roadside Inn, a No-Tell motel, a Motel 6..."

"Yeah, there was a Budget Inn, too."

"Okay." He jotted this information down. "But you don't remember which one she was staying at the last time you spoke to her?"

Danielle sighed. "Sorry. I don't."

"But she was still in Casper?"

"Yeah, she was. We'd talked a few weeks before."

"What did you talk about?"

"Carla wanted to get another job that would get her enough money to leave Casper," Danielle said. "I told her if she left at the end of the semester, I was taking a job in Connecticut and she could live with me."

"What'd she say to that?"

"She declined."

He sighed. That was Carla, all right. Tenacious as hell. She was not going to run back home with her tail tucked between her legs. He wished she had, though.

"Anything else?"

Danielle paused. "The last time I talked to her she said she was going to look into one more job."

"What kind of job was it?"

"It sounded kinda good. A financial thing. She wasn't really making a big deal about it. In fact, she mentioned it to me in passing. I completely forgot about it until just now."

He decided to take advantage of this reawakening of Danielle's memory. "When did you last talk to her?"

"August 7th," Danielle said, pausing again briefly. She'd told Dean Campbell the same thing. "Yeah, it was August 7th. I'm pretty sure of it. That was a Sunday. Carla said she was going to look into this job on Monday. I distinctly remember that."

"Did she tell you how she found out about the job?"

"The employment section of the Sunday paper."

"Was that the only job she was applying for?"

"There were other ones, too. She bitched that there wasn't much out there to apply for. Bullshit secretary jobs, mostly, and then this one, which kinda leaped out at her. She didn't have much hope for it, but she was going to apply anyway."

"And it was a financial job?"

Danielle paused again, as if she were thinking. "Actually, I think it was a business analyst position. I don't remember the name of the company."

"What paper was the ad in?"

"I have no idea."

"Okay." He wrote down *Sunday newspaper, August 7th, employment section, business analyst*, and circled it. "This helps me quite a bit, Danielle. I can't thank you enough."

"I hope I was able to help." Danielle's voice took on a nervous tone. "I'm really worried about her. This just isn't like her."

"I know." Carla may have severed ties with her father, but she was a loyal friend and had kept in touch with Danielle throughout her troubled times.

"Please keep me in the loop," Danielle asked. "If there's anything I can do—"

"I will call you."

"And if I can think of anything else, I'll call *you*."

"Please do. And thank you."

"Thank you, Mr. Taylor."

They hung up.

Joe looked at his notes, deep in thought. He flipped through the desk calendar he had for last year, found August 7th and traced his finger to August 24, the day the Casper detective and his own private detective claimed Carla had skipped out on her motel room bill, leaving a week's back rent. Seventeen days, from the last time Danielle, or anybody else for that matter, had seen or spoken to Carla. August 24th, the last day on record that she was in Casper.

Seventeen days in between.

A lot could happen in seventeen days.

He sighed, feeling a pit of dread in his belly.

What the hell had happened to his daughter, Carla?

CHAPTER 5

Rick Nicholson glanced at his watch, hoping this evening's meeting with the board members and the executive staff would go quickly. As the last of the board members filed in to the conference room, briefcases and slim leather folders in hand, Paul Westcott passed by and clapped him on the shoulder. "How're you doing, Rick?"

"Okay," Rick extracted a sheaf of papers from his briefcase and laid them out in front of him, ready to get to business. He offered Paul a warm smile. "Busy day, huh?"

"Tell me about it." Paul sat down next to him. He was about to lean forward and say something else to Rick when Wayne Sanders quickly brought the meeting to order.

Standing at the podium at the head of the long conference room table, Wayne addressed the group with his sonorous and commanding voice. He was a small man, slim and balding, his face finely chiseled as if it had been cut out of granite. He wore perfectly tailored suits, favored colorful ties, and was usually soft spoken. Rick had only seen him angry once. When Wayne got angry his entire head turned a deep red; a vein would pulse in the center of his forehead, and his voice would change to a low growl that...well, it was rather scary, actually. Thankfully, that had only happened once, which was enough.

Wayne nodded at the assembled throng. "Good evening, ladies and gentlemen. Why don't we get started?"

As the meeting got underway, Rick did his best to pay attention to what was going on. Cathy Becker presented the financial report to the group, which was met favorably. Gary Zimmerman reported that he had struck a deal with Dimension Films and Universal Studios to offer sneak previews of both big budget A-list talent films, and Cannes and Sundance quality art house films for next season. This, too, was met with approval. Mark Robinson gave a brief report on the IT side of the business; once again, he recommended the company seriously invest in virtual remote backups, and once again, Wayne said the board would consider it. Rick suppressed his grin. One of the many things the IT Director had spoken to him about privately was the firm's inability to invest serious money on the best systems to efficiently and securely run their operation. "My budget's so small, I feel like I have to string everything together with baling wire and little balls that run down paths that hit something that triggers a spring that bounces up and hits another spring that strikes a match that provides heat to a burner that...well, you get the analogy." Rick did. He was under similar budget constraints.

"Once the season ends, I've established an adequate VPN system on the network that will enable a more secure connection," Mark continued. "I'll be able to shut down the system remotely after the private event—Casey Security will take over with monitoring the outside security system and the physical grounds."

This, too, was met with approval. Rick was fairly computer savvy, but there were things in place at Bent Creek that were beyond him. He knew that Mark had established various security methods up the wazoo, and the wireless network and hotspots for the guests were top notch. One thing Mark insisted on maintaining—and the Board agreed vehemently with him on this—was maintaining strong network and internet security for the resort's guests. It was important for the guests to have remote access to sensitive financial data and, if possible, to make financial transactions while on resort grounds.

Working with some of the best internet security specialists and consultants in the field, Mark maintained an extremely tight and impenetrable network.

Kyle Smart was next. He gave a quick rundown on the sporting and gymnastic equipment, reported that they were in need of a new stair master in the gym, and reported that one of the horses, an Appaloosa mare named Goldy, was beginning to show her age. "Jackie Daniels loves that horse," he went on. "Unfortunately, I'm afraid Jackie will want to take Goldy out tomorrow. Dr. Cauble has already advised me that Goldy needs to be retired. I need some guidance on how to handle this."

Wayne nodded. This was a sensitive issue. Jackie and Shane Daniels were Bent Creek's best clients. The couple dropped over a million dollars a year at Bent Creek, and to turn down her request to ride her favorite mare, Goldy, would not go over well. At the same time, to adhere to her wishes would not be in the mare's best interest and would not make Dr. Cauble happy. Chris Cauble was a good vet, but he was not on staff. Rick was pretty certain that Cauble was the kind of man who would report Bent Creek to the SPCA for Animal Abuse at the first sign.

"Call Dr. Cauble," Wayne said. "Ask him to evaluate Goldy. If he is of the strong opinion that she be retired, ask him for a recommendation for a new stable she can be sent to. If he can get her off the grounds tomorrow, that would be ideal. In the meantime, make arrangements with Randy Temple that we're interested in obtaining a new mare for the club. A young one." Randy Temple was an Appaloosa breeder in the area who owned a fifty-acre horse ranch on the north end of the county.

Kyle nodded, made a notation in his spiral-bound notebook. Case closed. If they were lucky, Jackie Daniels would sleep in until early afternoon and would not be ready to go riding until very late, around five or six. Goldy would be off the grounds by then; at least that's what Rick was hoping. Besides, tomorrow was the last day of the season, too.

Wayne turned to Rick, addressing him. "Mr. Nicholson?"

Perfect timing. Rick had his notes out and ready to go. "Operation wise, we've run a smooth ship. We're all set for our last day." He continued by reporting on a minor annoyance—the destruction of one of the suites by the adult children of one of their clients who'd trashed it in a drunken party—as well as detailing the dining room and bar inventory levels, office administration supplies, and maintenance equipment. "Chef Munchel reports that he is down to the appropriate levels of stock and food in the kitchen for the private party and banquet after we close for the season," he concluded. "Likewise, housekeeping is almost finished with laundering the sheets and towels, and I have a graveyard shift in place for Wednesday night to finish. That shift will be the last of the staff to leave the premises on Thursday until next season.

Wayne nodded in approval. After the season closed tomorrow, September 24, and the last of the guests left, Bent Creek would be left with a skeleton crew of only eighteen to handle the private party that had rented the facilities for the five days following its formal closure. Rick had stayed on last year for a similar private party to supervise this skeleton crew; he'd be doing the same this season.

"Very good," Wayne nodded. "Chef Munchel reports the possible addition of a late arrival for the private event. Aside from that, everybody else is already present, including the staff."

Rick nodded. Last year, the skeleton crew had been cherry-picked personally by Wayne at the last minute. It was a condition of employment for Bent Creek; if you did exceptionally well and were noticed, Wayne tapped you for the extra duty upon closing of the season. The ten employees (actually, eight—two of them had abruptly quit within the first two nights and left the premises) who'd been chosen last year had walked away with a nice little bonus at the end. "My report on employee performances will be on your desk by tomorrow morning," he said.

"Good. As discussed earlier, and in accordance to past work

structures, we'll only need a handful of staff. One housekeeper, one groundsman and maintenance worker apiece, one member of the athletic department, one or two staff members to run the theater, and three of Paul's staff to assist with security. With the exception of one member of the wait staff, Chef Munchel will be flying solo. After all, this is his show." Wayne smiled slightly. The only thing Rick Nicholson knew about the private party was that they had hired Chef Munchel, who was a world renowned chef, to prepare dishes exclusively for them from his personal recipes. Rick knew that the price for such a party usually ran in the tens of thousands of dollars; one of the partners at the law firm had hired a well-known chef for a similar affair, at his Aspen home. Chef Jim Munchel was even more well-known and in high demand, so the fee for his services would have to run in the hundreds of thousands. Chicken feed to the dozen or so guests who'd booked Bent Creek for the season's conclusion.

"I assume you'll retain Charlie Thompson for maintenance duties?" Rick asked.

Wayne nodded, his features contemplative. "Yes. It was rather unfortunate that Brian Gaiman left so suddenly." He looked at Paul Westcott. "Do you have an update on Gaiman's whereabouts and the latest news on the theft?"

At the mention of the theft, all eight board members and members of the executive staff seemed to take notice. Some shifted uncomfortably in their seats, others sat up straighter, their attention more focused. If news of such a brazen theft got beyond the gates of Bent Creek, it could bring unwanted attention.

"Well, this is the first time a theft has happened at Bent Creek," Paul said. "The victim, Parker Goode, is still very angry about it. Frankly, I don't blame him."

There were several nods of understanding around the room. Wayne was pacing the small area at the head of the big conference room table where he was holding court. "Yes, I don't blame him, either," he said. "Mr. Goode is also part of the private party that has booked the premises for the five days after our formal closing. Have your men examined his room for evidence?"

"Absolutely," Paul said. "There's no sign of forced entry to the front or back doors to the suite, and the lock wasn't forced open on the briefcase. Parker said the briefcase wasn't locked. Of course, he didn't think anybody would break into his suite in the first place, and now he's mad at himself for not locking the briefcase."

"No reason to be angry at himself," Wayne said. "Until now, we've run a very secure resort."

"Of course," Paul continued. "Which is why we were on this the moment it was reported."

"You found no fingerprints? No forensic evidence?"

"None whatsoever. My team went over the entire room. The first report I received was this afternoon. Initial forensic reports indicate that the only trace of DNA from hair fibers we've recovered from the room is Parker's."

"He hasn't had any other guests in his room, then?"

"No."

"And what about fingerprint evidence?"

"We compared his prints with those recovered. They're a match. We also matched prints with two of the housekeepers that have turned his room. We've searched their quarters and haven't found anything."

"Are the housekeepers cooperating?"

"Very much so."

"What is your assessment of them?"

"They didn't do it," Paul stated. Rick could tell Paul was adamant about this. "They're both exceptional workers, and when I questioned them they didn't give me any overt signs that they were lying." Paul would be able to spot evasion; in a past life, he was a homicide detective for the LAPD.

"What about our missing maintenance worker?"

Paul sighed. Rick caught his eye and nodded. They'd talked about Carmen's report earlier, and Paul told Rick that he'd let Wayne know about it. "Carmen was one of the housekeepers who turned Parker's room. She reported Brian missing this morning to Rick."

Rick cut in. "She seemed rather upset about it, too."

"We turned Brian's quarters and found nothing," Paul continued. "We also turned Charlie's room, and questioned him extensively. He was rather angry at the fact. Claimed Brian gave him no cause for alarm despite his background."

One of the board members, a tall, handsome man named Robert Barker, spoke up. "If I can cut in here real quick with a comment?"

Wayne acknowledged Robert with a nod. Robert nodded back, cleared his throat. "Myself and a few other members of the board have brought up the validity of revisiting the charter in our bylaws regarding the work-release program. In light of this recent event, I wonder if it's a subject that merits discussion for a future meeting."

A smartly-dressed woman whom Rick didn't know by name, murmured agreement. Other board members nodded silently. The only other board member Rick knew by name, Emily Wharton, said nothing. She was jotting down notes on a laptop.

Robert continued. "While it's hardly evident that our missing maintenance worker is the culprit in the theft of our guest's money, I think his disappearance will bear further investigation. The missing money is obviously no longer on the grounds." Robert directed his gaze to Paul. "What are you doing to locate Brian?"

Paul shrugged. "The state police have been informed of the theft. They also have Brian's photo and vital stats."

Rick cut in. "Paul and his team are cooperating fully with the state authorities and are doing admirably well under the circumstances."

Paul continued. "We're making an effort to locate Brian's family and known contacts, both outside the prison system and his old cronies."

"That's all very good, but what about the future?" Robert was obviously concerned, and several of the other board members bore similar expressions. For the first time, Rick felt a sense of unease coming from the board members. It was something he couldn't put his finger on, but they seemed to be uncomfortable with the theft and Brian's disappearance. "Until the other members of the board and myself can discuss our work-release program and whether or not to revise or eliminate it altogether, I believe there must be some discussion on how to better screen future candidates from this program."

"Agreed, and I share your concern," Paul stated.

"We can discuss that part of our by-laws at the winter meeting," Wayne stated, nodding at Robert, his gaze sweeping across to the other members of the board. "Until then, we should address the matter at hand." He turned to Paul. "As an ex-con on work release, Gaiman's parole will be revoked when he's picked up by the police. My suggestion is to cooperate with law enforcement if they need your help. I assume they have Brian's photo and vital statistics. Have they talked to Carmen?"

"I'm not sure."

"Carmen will be rather busy over the next twenty-four hours with the last day of service. If the police need to talk to her, they can do so at the conclusion of the season. Unless, of course, Brian is found before then." Wayne smiled. "And I suppose if that *is* the case, it won't matter then, will it?"

"I guess not," Paul said. He was jotting down notes in a spiral notepad.

Wayne turned back to Rick. "Anything else, Mr. Nicholson?"

Ignoring the tinge of unease he'd felt, Rick looked at his list and quickly brought the board up to speed on the rest of his agenda items. When he was finished, Wayne thanked him and moved on to Pete Pellegrino, Bent Creek's Business Administrator. Pete was in his early sixties, balding, and always wore spotless long-sleeved white dress shirts with dark slacks and either dark red or blue ties. As Pete started his report, Rick tuned the meeting out. It was almost done. In less than a week he'd be heading back to Denver with enough money to live on for the next year, maybe more if he stretched it out. He could spend more time with his mother—he'd been meaning to get out for a quick visit this season and had been unable to due to his workload at Bent Creek. Maybe now he could see her. She could use more than the visit; she could use the extra money he was planning on giving her. Mom hadn't been doing so well financially since the cancer had taken his father and had now come to lay claim to her body. Why have health insurance when it didn't pay for even half of her visits or medications?

As Pete Pellegrino ran down his list of items in his presentation, Rick glanced casually at his watch. Hopefully this would wrap fairly quickly, then he could get back to his quarters and give Mom a call, see how she was doing. Then he could relax a little bit, take advantage of one last meal in the dining room. Unlike the other staff members of Bent Creek, Rick and the other members of management were allowed to eat in the dining room and drink in the lounge. That would change when the season closed, however. For the five days that followed, Rick would have to eat at the little bar-and-grill in the employee lounge, which would be the only thing running aside from his skeleton crew. Meals for the skeleton crew were to be provided at specific windows—breakfast between 7:30 and 8:00, lunch between 11:30 and noon, dinner between 5:00 and 5:30. Anything beyond that, like snacks, would have to be procured prior to the bar-and-grill closing and reheated in the room microwave. Chef Munchel would do double-duty between his own kitchen and that of the bar-and-grill during the private event, hence the small window of time. He would be spending most of his time preparing his extravagantly exotic and, most likely, expensive meals for the wealthy clients who had hired him for this private soiree.

Rick leaned back in his seat, feigning interest in the meeting and thought about how much he was looking forward to not only the close of the season, but that of the private party and his fall and winter sojourn in Denver.

CHAPTER 6

He'd been tied up for three days now. Tied up, gagged, left in the dark in God only knew where, and he'd long given up on anybody coming to rescue him. It just wasn't going to happen.

There was no way anybody *could* rescue him. After all, *they* were in on it.

Dale Lantis had liked the job. It was a desk job, and it was pretty boring, but the building was nice and so were his co-workers. Dale spent most of his time going through files, analyzing and scanning documents—mostly receipts and contracts—and putting them out on a server. Easy as cake. His supervisor, Joann Bigelow, was very easy-going. She was a very hands-off supervisor. As long as he did his work, she didn't care if he spent three hours a day surfing the Internet or playing games on his computer. He got his work done and that was all that mattered.

The job paid squat, but he got free room and board. After being unemployed for so long, the free room and board were important to Dale. Of course, he had to pay for his dry cleaning and laundry, had to pay for his meals, but that was no big deal. They'd given him a room, and during his off hours he often hung out with the other staff members. They usually hung out at the employee bar-and-grill, shot the shit over a game of darts, whatever. As long as they didn't frequent the areas of the resort that was reserved strictly for the guests, it didn't matter.

Dale wouldn't patronize Bent Creek even if he *had* the money. The people that paid to come here weren't his kind of people.

Dale moved his arms in a circular motion. Whoever had knocked him out had tied him up pretty good. They'd wrapped coils of rope around him, binding his arms to his sides and tying his legs together at the thighs and ankles. The last three days of being trussed up had been hell on his circulation. His limbs had gone numb, which he'd had to address by rolling over and flexing his muscles whenever and however he could. That had worked, and little by little sensation had crept back in. One thing he *hadn't* anticipated, though, was the rapid loss of weight he experienced. They hadn't brought him any food, had hardly given him any water, and his body had begun to compensate.

Dale Lantis was what most people would call a Big Boy. Standing five foot six and weighing two hundred and seventy-eight pounds, he was a roly-poly man, all triple chins and quivering stomach and buttocks. His upper arms were ham hocks. He could inhale a twenty-ounce T-bone steak, baked potato with all the trimmings, vegetables, soup and salad, and one of those appetizer plates and *still* have room left for a dessert of cake, pie, *and* cookies. Bottom line, Dale loved to eat. He loved his food, and like his mama always taught him, he made sure to clean off his plate with each meal.

Only three days of no food and very little water had set his body against him. It had begun breaking up the fat in his system, converting it to much needed nourishment. The waste it produced left his system via his urine. His slacks had been constantly soaked with it since his incarceration; a spreading puddle of it had drenched almost every inch of him, including his short, wiry hair. Likewise, when he'd had to eliminate his bowels he'd had to do it in his trousers. At first he'd been embarrassed, and he'd cried to himself in frustration amid the rising stench of his shit as it caked onto the back of his thighs. The more dehydrated he got from lack of water, the more it turned what was left in his bowels to burning diarrhea.

And with this seeming betrayal of his body had come something else.

A rapid loss of weight.

Dale flexed the muscles of his arms. The ropes that bound his arms to his body were very slack now. He had more flexibility in his upper chest; had even more in his thighs. He'd probably pissed away twenty pounds of excess fat. Well, maybe not that much, but it sure seemed that way. It was amazing how much fat the body could use in such a short period of time. Another day or two, he might have enough room to wriggle out of these bonds.

But with no water, that wouldn't matter. He'd be dead.

Dale sighed, trying to calm himself down. He couldn't let himself get worked up. When he got worked up like this, his heart raced. Felt like he was on the way to a heart attack. He had to stay calm. Had to stay focused. Had to stay—

From somewhere close by, a door opened.

Dale froze. Somebody came in every few hours or so. Opened the door and checked on him. Whoever it was never touched him, just looked him over and left. Sometimes this person gave him small sips of water from a water bottle. Dale never caught a glimpse of who it was; the light from wherever his captor was standing in was too blinding for Dale. The only thing Dale could see was a large silhouette. Whoever his captor was, he was of average size. Maybe a bit on the pear-shaped size, but surely not grossly obese like he was. That was all Dale could tell about him.

Footsteps approached the room. Coming closer.

Dale held his breath, his heart racing. He still had no idea where he was. Surely it couldn't be Bent Creek; it didn't feel like it. The concrete beneath him was rough, and he had the sense that the room he was in was small. All he knew was that he was in a small room, with a large steel door. If Dale had to describe it, he could liken it to being in a dungeon. Or a jail cell.

The shadowy figure drew closer. Dale shrunk back, heart beating rapidly. Dressed in tan khaki's and a red polo-shirt, the figure stooped down. Dale could see the man's face, but he didn't recognize him. The man's face was round, framed by gray beard stubble and short, wispy graying hair that revealed male pattern baldness. His eyes were liquid pools of blue. Those eyes appraised him now, as he crouched over Dale.

"What..." Dale began. "What do you want?"

The man reached out and began touching Dale. His hands roamed over his body—chest, belly, the flab of his love-handles, his thighs and buttocks. They caressed the meat of his thighs and ass, then moved up to appraise his biceps. Dale tried to squirm away from the man's grasp, revolted at the sudden shock of what was going on. The way the man was looking at him, with a hungry sense of lust, seemed to whisper *sexual predator* to him. *Oh shit, is this guy one of those serial killers? Like a Jeffrey Dahmer? Is he going to keep me as his sexual slave and then kill me when he gets tired of me?*

The bonds were too tight to allow Dale much movement, so he was forced to endure the man's assessment of his flesh. "Very nice," the man said. "Very nice and supple."

A well of emotion rose in Dale. He felt his vision blur as tears sprang to his eyes. "Please," he said. "Please...don't hurt me."

The man's hand trailed down to Dale's piss-soaked slacks, lingered there. "I bet you want to get these slacks off and wash yourself off, don't you?"

Dale nodded vigorously. "Yes, I do....please!"

The man smiled. His eyes flicked toward the center of the room, about five feet away from where Dale lay trussed up on the floor. He hooked both hands beneath Dale's bulk and gently rolled him over once toward the center of the room. Dale felt his heart leap—was the man getting him in a better position to free him? Dale felt cold pee that had accumulated in the folds of his slacks spill down his leg. He flopped onto his stomach, his face a few feet away from a drain set in the center of the room. The man rose to his feet and moved behind him. Dale felt the *schtick* of steel, then strong fingers clutched his hair and pulled his head up, exposing his neck. A quick blur of a hand moving below his field of vision, a brief sting of pain in his throat followed by a sudden sense of incredible warmth flowing down his chest, and then he felt surprisingly light-headed. The sound of liquid splashing on the cold concrete below him barely registered as the feeling grew, and it wasn't until he felt his consciousness fading that he realized what had happened, and by then it was too late.

CHAPTER 7

Sixteen Months Ago

Joe Taylor had picked out the most recent and best photo of Carla he could find. He pushed it across the cluttered desk of the desk sergeant at the Casper, Wyoming Police Station. The desk sergeant's name badge identified him as Ron Keene.

"She's twenty-three years old," Joe said. "As I explained to you over the phone, she disappeared on August 7 of last year. Her last known residence was a Motel 6 on Lincoln Highway on the north edge of town."

Sergeant Ron Keene looked at Joe with a sense of weary resignation. He was close to Joe's age, with the weariness and bulk that suggested he was at the end of a long and weary career. "Listen, Mr. Taylor, I appreciate you flying out here, but you really didn't have to do that. Like I told you over the phone, there's not much we can—"

"I realize there is no evidence of foul play," Joe stated firmly. He remained standing behind the desk, putting everything he'd learned in his long career in the business world to play. "And I realize that, as an adult, Carla can choose to disappear if she wants to. After all, she and I had an estranged relationship. But she hasn't been in contact with her best friend since she was last seen, nor her mother, who she still kept in contact with. And the Motel 6 reported she'd skipped out on her bill, which is highly unusual for her."

"It isn't unusual for people living a transient lifestyle to skip out on their motel bills," Sergeant Keene said. "Especially the kind of motels that are on the low-end of the scale. Motel 6, though, is a national chain. Those places usually require payment up front, and with a credit card to guarantee payment. How was she able to skip out on her bill?"

"Carla could be manipulative when she wanted to be," Joe said. He sighed. Rubbed the bridge of his nose. "She'd managed to hold on to her laptop through her financial disintegration and was able to book this particular Motel 6 through a third-party website that specialized in motel bookings that did not require upfront payment. Some of the motels that work with this site are franchises, like this Motel 6. That's how she did it. She booked two weeks, paid a few days up front, then..." He let himself trail off.

"I see..."

"Later, I hired a private detective. He took a trip out here, did some follow-ups with Carla's last known contacts. They all report that they were very surprised when Carla disappeared."

"How do you know she disappeared?" Sergeant Keene asked, sitting straight behind his desk. "And who is this private investigator you speak of?"

"Dean Campbell," Joe replied. "He works out of Los Angeles, has an office in Pasadena, where I live."

"Who'd he talk to?"

"Carla's former co-workers, Debbie Mitchum and Beth Levine. Both still kept in contact with Carla after she was let go from Braun & Meyer's."

"I'd hardly call that—"

"Mr. Campbell reported to me that Carla skipped out on her motel bill owing a little over one week's rent," Joe continued. "Her belongings were gone; motel staff report they did not take possession of any personal belongings, which is standard OP. The manager of the Motel 6 told my detective that Carla had taken all her belongings with her. She had no bank account, but the Walmart where she cashed her payroll checks reported that the last time she was in was three days before we pinpointed her missing. Mr. Campbell even talked to the clerk that usually cashed her check. A woman by the name of Mary Rosenberg. Miss Rosenberg claims Carla's demeanor did not strike her as unusual, that Carla was talkative and was her usual self. No indication that she was planning to skip out. Plus, she would have had enough to cash to pay for her room. Dean was able to get a copy of Carla's bank receipt. She *had* the money to pay her motel bill."

Sergeant Keene regarded Joe from behind his desk. "You say you've formally reported her missing to the Wyoming State Police?"

Joe nodded. "Yes, I did."

"And you realize that all I can really do is take the info on her and put it, and her photo, out on the wire? That we can't devote any man-hours to searching for her?"

"Yes, sir, I realize that."

Keene held out his hand for the material. Joe slid the file containing Carla's photo and the information he and Dean Campbell had compiled across the desk. Sergeant Keene slid the material out of the folder and began to read through it quietly. Joe Taylor stood in front of the desk, waiting. Behind him, the sound of late afternoon traffic grew louder as the sun went down and nine-to-fivers began to head home to the outer suburbs. Somewhere, a block away, a siren wailed, then faded.

After a moment, Sergeant Keene set the material down. "I'd like for you to have your private detective contact us the next time he's in town to work on this. Just so we have it on record."

"Of course."

"What agency is Mr. Campbell from?"

"He's freelance, but he contracts with several insurance companies for fraud investigations," Joe said. He reached into his pocket and handed Sergeant Keene a business card. "Here's his card."

Sergeant Keene took the card and looked at it. "Campbell

Investigations, Limited. Good. Thank you." He made the business card disappear. He regarded Joe from behind his desk. This time, his features were sympathetic. "My apologies for being so brusque. We get fifty missing persons reports a week, and ninety-nine point nine percent of them are resolved within a few hours. People don't even wait a day to report that a loved one is missing either; I've had people report their parents missing, their wife or husband, whatever, missing after they've gone to the store and they're not back by a certain time. Usually the missing person has been stuck in traffic or simply added another destination to their schedule, which made them late. Can you believe that?"

"In this day and age, I can believe anything," Joe said. He stepped away from the front desk and waved. "Thank you, Sergeant Keene, and have a good day."

When Joe Taylor exited the Casper, Wyoming Police Station headquarters, he walked down Main Street toward the parking garage where he'd left the rental car. He was only in town for two days. He was meeting Dean Campbell later that evening, for dinner. No reason to tell Sergeant Keene that Dean was in town at this point. It was best to play this their own way for now, especially since local law enforcement had proven to be not very interested in this case. Joe and Dean had confirmed this over the course of the last few weeks with repeated phone calls to the department, reporting Carla missing, followed by calls to other local agencies. This was the third time they had tried to file a missing persons report with the county sheriff's department. Filing a missing persons report with the city and at the local level had been relatively easy.

But at the county level—Sweetwater County, Wyoming, level? Resistance all the way. Until now.

Joe Taylor thought about that. The more he turned it over in his mind, the more he didn't like it.

So the local police knew his name now. They knew Dean Campbell's name. He'd promised Sergeant Keene that when

Dean came back into town for follow-up work, he would contact the department to give them a heads-up. That was just a formality, though. Paying lip service. They were going to do no such thing.

Not at this stage.

CHAPTER 8

Wednesday

Early morning shifts were the best.

The Bent Creek Country Club patrons were usually on their best behavior very early during the breakfast shift. That was usually because they were too zoned-out from late night partying, or the caffeine had not kicked in yet. It allowed Anna to observe her customer's behavior, see the real people behind the facades they'd so carefully built up for themselves. She paid close attention, kept careful mental notes on everybody. Knowledge is power. And to know the enemy was to defeat him. Or so said Sun Tzu.

Chef Munchel usually slept in during breakfast service, handing over the duties to his *sous* chef, Diane Winters. Diane ran the staff of four line cooks and three garnish chefs like a well-oiled machine, getting orders out quickly and always prepared to perfection. There were four wait staff on duty this morning. Two more would join their ranks as the morning wore on, then there would be a lull for much of the afternoon. Anna would get a short reprieve around ten-thirty; she'd be back on duty for the four to midnight shift.

Anna delivered an order to table number five—stuffed French toast with bacon strips, fresh fruit and toasted baguette—to a middle-aged couple that were polite, but quiet.

Anna asked them if they required anything else—a refill on their coffee carafe, or fresh orange juice perhaps? The man, who reminded her of that senator from Kentucky, John Boehner, shook his head. "Thank you, but we're fine. The food looks and smells wonderful."

"Thank you very much, sir. If there's anything you want, please ask." And with that, Anna turned and was just about to head back to the pass to see if any of her other orders were up, when she saw that she had a new customer at table seven. She headed over.

When she saw who the customer was, she felt relieved. It was Bob, no last name yet (or at least none she was aware of; he'd only introduced himself to her as Bob). He'd formally introduced himself to her last night after her minor skirmish with Shane Daniels while waiting on him—the man with the movie-star handsome features. After her encounter with Shane Daniels last night, Bob had offered some kind and encouraging words to her. Anna appreciated a customer who was genuinely nice. Between him and the Ken and Barbie couple—the Johnson's—who Anna had wound up spending the night with after her shift ended, the evening had been nice after all.

"Good morning, sir," Anna said through her most genuine smile. "Can I get you some coffee or juice this morning?"

Bob offered Anna a smile. He was dressed casually in a white polo shirt, tan khaki shorts, blue tennis shoes and white ankle-high socks. Like the John Boehner doppelganger at table five, Bob had a tan. Unlike the John Boehner doppelganger, Bob was much younger—mid-forties was her guess—and much more handsome. He had longish brown hair, but not too long; barely even collar-length, giving him a youthful, boyish appearance. His face was model-perfect; finely chiseled nose and cheekbones, piercing green eyes, sensuous lips, perfect, white teeth. It looked like he partook in moderate exercise to keep in shape. He was trim, healthy-looking. In short, Bob was hot. She'd jump his bones in an instant. "Coffee will be great," Bob said. He smiled and winked at her.

"Coffee coming up!" Anna left the table and headed toward the pass. She checked on her orders quickly, found she had seven minutes until Chef Winters served up an order for one of her tables, then headed to the beverage station. She placed a carafe of coffee, a white saucer and a porcelain mug on a serving tray. Then, balancing the tray on her right hand, she headed toward table seven.

She set the tray down on the table and began serving him. As she poured his coffee, she asked, "So, do you have big plans for the day?"

Bob spread his white linen napkin over his lap. "I'll probably do some hiking."

"Very good." Last evening, Anna had casually asked Bob what his plans were after dinner and his response had been equally vague. Every client at Bent Creek gushed with details, as if they couldn't help but rub it into the faces of the wait staff that they were doing Really Great Things and Don't You Wish You Could Do This Too? Not Bob. Anna was under the impression that Bob's answers were not out of a conscious effort to be subtle, but came naturally to him, as if it was natural to not give away too many details about himself. It made her run through the list of possibilities of what kind of life he led when he didn't vacation at Bent Creek. High-level government official, perhaps? CIA or FBI?

"How about you?" Bob asked. He reached for the cup of sugar that resided in a crystal bowl and spooned some in. He was looking at her with inquisitive features. "I take it you're working dinner service tonight?"

"Yes, I am," Anna answered. "I don't work lunch service at Bent Creek."

"It gives you a few hours to relax between services. That's good." Bob splashed some cream in his coffee and stirred.

"Absolutely. It'll give me a chance to get caught up on my reading."

"What do you like to read?"

"All kinds of stuff. Currently, I'm on a gothic novel kick."

"Oh?"

"Yeah. But probably not the kind of gothic novels you're thinking."

"Let me guess," Bob said, appraising her with those remarkable green eyes as he sipped his coffee. "Something by one of the Brontë sisters, perhaps? Or Jane Austin?"

"Kinda-sorta."

"Something more obscure? Maturin's *Melmoth the Wanderer*, perhaps?"

"Closer." Anna couldn't help but crack a grin. Not only was Bob good-looking, he had a brain. "I'm halfway through Le Fanu's *Uncle Silas*. Last week it was Hawthorne's *The Scarlet Letter*."

Bob nodded as he took a sip of coffee. "I have to admit, I've never read *Uncle Silas*. Love *Carmilla*, though. That's one of my favorites. As for Hawthorne, the theme of past sins weaves through some of his other works but is more pervasive throughout *The Scarlet Letter*. It's like a driving force."

"Absolutely," Anna said. "That, and Hawthorne's disdain for the stern morality and rigidity of the Puritans is very front and center in that novel. I almost get the feeling that this is a pervading theme in a goodly portion of his work. Some of his short fiction, particularly "The Minister's Black Veil" and "Young Goodman Brown" and his novel *The House of the Seven Gables* explore similar themes just as strongly."

Bob regarded her as he sipped his coffee. "What do you *really* do, Anna?"

Anna started. The question came completely out of left field. "Excuse me, sir?"

"No, excuse *me* for asking such an abrupt question." Bob set his coffee down. "I didn't mean to surprise you, so forgive me for that, and for the nature of the question itself, but...in all seriousness, what do you *really* do? You are probably the most verbose and quietly intelligent person among the wait staff. I get the sense that this job is only filling a vacancy, that you're out of your element. Don't get me wrong, you're an excellent waitress, but I get the sense that..." Bob let the sentence trail off as he regarded her quietly.

Anna felt as if she'd been placed under a magnifying glass, or perhaps a microscope. For a brief instant, so fleeting that it was gone within a second, she felt as if she'd been caught at something dreadful. As if she'd been discovered performing some horrible, secret act. She smiled at Bob, confident he hadn't seen that very fast blip across her demeanor. "You're a perceptive man, Bob. I used to be a business analyst with Deloitte and Touche. A very successful one, and in demand, too. I got laid off from Deloitte almost a year ago."

"I'm sorry to hear that," Bob said. He took another sip of coffee. "Which office did you work out of?"

"I worked out of their Denver office, but they had me with clients all over the south-west."

"Where'd you go to school?"

"UCLA for my Bachelor's, Pepperdine for my Master's."

Bob nodded. Anna could tell he was impressed. He set his coffee cup down and reached into the left front pocket of his shorts. He drew out a business card, which he handed to her. "I have a lot of professional contacts in the greater Denver and Boulder area. Give me a call when the season's over. Maybe I can help you."

Anna gave the business card a quick glance. It was printed on a high-grade stock, with raised letters. The card identified him as Robert Garrison, owner of Garrison Enterprises, Limited. There was an Aurora, Colorado address, along with a series of phone numbers and an email address. Anna quickly pocketed the card. "Thank you," she murmured. She quickly glanced toward the pass and saw that her orders were in the process of being placed there. "I have to pick up an order, but I'll be back to take yours in a moment."

Bob waved her off. "Go on. I'll be here."

Anna nodded and stepped away from the table. As she

headed toward the kitchen, she felt a rising sense of optimism. The past thirteen months had been brutal for the job market, especially the kind of work she specialized in. She didn't like having to resort to what she was doing here at Bent Creek, but she had to survive. This waitressing job, which she'd only taken because the opportunity had been too good to pass up, and she'd needed the money desperately, was the most demeaning job she'd ever been forced to take. It wasn't the first time she'd held a waitress position; she'd had two waitress jobs in college. But waitressing here, at the Bent Creek Country Club and Resorts, was hard on both body and soul. The Bent Creek patrons were more than demeaning; most of them were aloof, uncaring, clueless, and some were downright mean. They saw her and her fellow wait staff not as fellow human beings, but as objects, servants to boss around at their sole whim. She'd known that going in, and had maintained a stiff upper lip throughout the four month-long gig. She had a good exterior shell that deflected the insults and meanness that was hurled her way.

But sometimes...

Sometimes, the cruel jabs got to her. She was only human, after all. But she never let the Bent Creek patrons see that they'd gotten to her. She never let her emotion rise to the surface when she was insulted, verbally berated and dressed down in public by some rich snob, never exploded in anger or frustration when it became too much for her to handle (except that time when the pus-filled bandages were thrust into her hands—she couldn't help reacting in the way she did when that happened).

Anna approached the pass just as Chef Winters placed the last dish up for table four's order. Anna began transferring the dishes on to the serving platter. There were only a few more days to go before the season was over. Then she could be rid of this place forever. The snooty bastards that patronized Bent Creek would never see her again and good riddance to them. She knew things were going to get better once the season was over and she was back home, and Bob Garrison's kindness had only sweetened the deal. Perhaps there was light at the end of the tunnel after all.

Thinking about this, and about Bob's generous offer of a helping hand, gave her pause. As she waited for one final entree to be brought up to the pass, her right hand dove into one of her pockets and fingered the business card Bob had given her. It was real. It was a lifeline. She couldn't stop what she was doing now—after all, she only had a few more days at Bent Creek. But when the season was over?

The pass chef delivered the last entree. With table four's order on the serving tray, Anna headed back to her station to continue the temporary work she'd been hired for, knowing that it wouldn't be long before she'd never have to do this kind of work ever again.

CHAPTER 9

When Carl White logged in to his bank account in the privacy of his suite, he felt himself go lightheaded with shock.

What the hell? This can't be!

Carl leaned forward over the cherry-wood desk in his suite, peering at the screen that displayed his account. He'd checked it the day before yesterday, and the last transaction had been a transfer of one hundred thousand dollars into his main account, where all the funds of the Lewis Project were percolating. The transfers, over an eight-month time period, had added up to seventy-five million, four hundred thousand dollars.

Over one million dollars of that money was now missing.

Carl quickly checked the link that displayed all transactions, wondering if somebody had hacked in and transferred those funds to another account. His heart took another shock when he ran his gaze down the list of transactions. All the transfers he'd made into the account were picture perfect. They all showed transfers *into* the account.

There were no transfers showing money that had been taken *out* of the account.

A tad over a million dollars out of seventy-five million was a drop in the bucket. Not a big deal. But still...it was a million bucks. He had not authorized its transfer. And if Jake, his partner, found out it was missing—

Carl picked up his cell phone and called Jake. "Jake, we have a problem."

Carl stood up and began pacing the suite. He went to the window and closed the drapes, shutting out the warm sunny day. "I just checked the account and there's money missing." Beat. "About one million point two five." Beat. "You tell me! I checked the transactions, that account only shows transfers going *in* to the account. It was set up so nothing could be transferred *out*, and it currently shows that there are no transfers out of the account. But get this...the balance was seventy-five and a half million dollars yesterday. Today it's a tad over seventy-*four* million. How do you explain that?"

Carl stopped pacing, phone held to his ear as he listened to Jake. He could feel his heart race, could feel himself start to sweat. "Does anybody know where I'm at?"

Carl listened. He felt a little better hearing Jake tell him no, his current location was unknown except to the two of them. "Maybe I should check out," Carl said. "Go home."

That brought a flurry of words from Jake. Carl listened, sat down on his rumpled bed, feeling his heart race again. He looked at himself in the mirror that hung over the dresser as Jake talked. "You think somebody here at Bent Creek set me up? Who would do that?"

Jake didn't know. And he told Carl that they had to play this carefully if they wanted to finish the job. Leave Bent Creek now, it could alert the wrong people. Carl sighed. "So what do we do?"

For the next hour, Carl and Jake made plans.

Paul Westcott was sitting in Rick Nicholson's office, getting him up to speed on the two major events that occurred this season at Bent Creek: the theft of Parker Goode's cash from his attaché case on Monday, and the disappearance of Brian Gaiman, which most likely occurred that same night.

"In my professional and humble opinion, the two are unrelated," Paul said. He was seated in one of Rick's chairs, lounging in a relaxed pose. He was tapping a pen on a white notepad. Paul was fifteen years Rick's senior, and favored dark suits and white shirts; he thought it made him look like a real law enforcement agent. Maybe the style of dress did, but Rick thought Paul looked more like a salesman. His face had that engaging look that seemed to trap you the minute you looked at him. It was an open, friendly face that always seemed to be wearing a sunny disposition. "Brian's background doesn't indicate he's capable of this type of theft despite his record. It's obvious somebody else is the thief. Probably one of Mr. Goode's friends. Somebody he plays poker with."

"But you questioned those guys, had their rooms searched, and haven't found anything," Rick said.

"True. We also questioned people Mr. Goode and his friends have been hobnobbing with. The Bakers, the Smiths, the Zuckerman's. They all checked out. One of my investigators checked out the attaché case and found evidence that the lock was picked with a sharp object, possibly a picking tool usually found in the personal belongings of professional locksmiths."

"Really?" This was something new to Rick. He sat up behind his desk to pay closer attention.

Outside Rick's picturesque office window, the Wyoming sky was a deep blue. The thermometer tacked onto Rick's office wall revealed the outside temperature to be a balmy seventy-one degrees. Quite warm for early fall. In another month, the area would begin to experience the first biting cold of approaching winter. Rick would be back home in Boulder by then, planning his next move in life.

"Yeah. Locksmiths have a picking tool that are multi-functional. They're non-destructive to the lock. An experienced locksmith or burglar can have an old fashioned lock like the kind found on older attaché cases open within seconds. Mr. Goode's attaché case bore several marks around the edges of the lock, and when Johnny opened it, he found deep groove marks in the steel; clear indication a professional had been at it.

Brian Gaiman was a smash and grab kind of guy. He sneaked into open windows, that kind of thing. He never did break into homes using tools like this."

"Maybe he was just never caught in the act," Rick said.

Paul shrugged. "Maybe so, maybe not. Man only had one count of breaking and entering, and that's when he broke into an old girlfriend's apartment to lift her stereo for drugs. He pried her basement window open and got in that way. His criminal record has counts for strong-arm robbery and assault, DUI, drug possession, and trespassing, but no other burglary offenses."

Rick sighed and looked out the window. It didn't add up. He could understand why Paul would question Mr. Goode's friends and those guests they'd mingled with at Bent Creek. It was doubtful they'd revealed to those guests that they were involved in high-stakes poker in their rooms and why Mr. Goode had all that cash. "Parker's friends weren't robbed either, correct?" Rick asked, verifying this information to himself. "You and your team inspected the cash they had and searched their rooms completely?"

"We gave their rooms a thorough inspection," Paul confirmed. "And they surrendered their money to us and that money is now in the Bent Creek safe at the front desk."

Rick nodded. Bent Creek Country Club and Resorts, like all hotels, maintained a safe accessible only to employees for the purpose of providing a secure storage place for its customer's valuables. Over five million dollars in cash had been surrendered to Paul Westcott by Parker Goode's friends yesterday, following news of the theft. One of them had complained to Rick that he was very disappointed that they would be unable to partake in what had become a dearly beloved yearly tradition.

"Okay, so let's say it *isn't* Brian," Rick said, musing aloud. "I'm still bothered by him taking off so suddenly. To me, that says he was up to something."

"I understand that," Paul said. He shrugged. "Especially

when you look into the time-line. It's estimated Parker's suitcase was broken into very late Monday night, when he was with his friends at the Roxy." The Roxy was the dance club on Bent Creek grounds. It catered to its younger clientele. "Carmen indicated she last saw Brian Gaiman Monday night around ten-thirty. Parker and his friends returned to their rooms around two-thirty on Tuesday morning. By all accounts, Parker never bothered to check his attaché case when he returned, because it was in the same spot he'd left it. Plus, there was no obvious signs of a break-in to his room. He goes to sleep, wakes up later that Tuesday morning, opens the case at nine-thirty and the money is gone."

"That means if it *was* Brian, he would have had close to four hours to break into Parker's suite and steal that money," Rick said.

"True," Paul said, holding a finger up. "*Especially* if we consider that end of suites where Parker is staying is along Brian's maintenance route. Brian didn't return to work Tuesday morning, and with Carmen reporting him missing, that would have made me suspicious too."

"But you're not," Rick said. "Why?"

"Brian would have had to have stashed that money someplace," Paul replied. "Nobody saw him leave Bent Creek grounds. Furthermore, his fellow employees never saw him in the employee wing of the building Monday night, or yesterday morning. His and Carmen's quarters were searched. No money was found."

"What did you find in your search of Brian Gaiman's room?" Rick asked.

"Nothing." Paul regarded Rick calmly from across the desk. "Not a damn thing. There was no personal effects, no clothing. If anything, it looked like Brian packed up all his stuff and snuck the hell out."

This new bit of information was surprising to Rick. "Snuck out?"

"Well, when Carmen reported him missing, what did *you* think happened?"

"I don't know. I thought he was hiding out somewhere on the grounds. Maybe he grabbed a few bottles of booze from one of the bars and snuck off somewhere to fall off the wagon."

Paul chuckled. "Sure, I can buy that. Happens a lot with these guys. I thought that too. But a complete search of the grounds shows no evidence of that. No missing liquor bottles, no signs Brian is hiding away in the stables or the workshed, or even the garage." Bent Creek maintained a fully-functioning auto shop that serviced company vehicles and those vehicles owned by some of the high-roller clients. "What it looks like to me is that Brian simply snuck off the grounds very early in the morning, before the early day-shift janitorial crew started and the kitchen crew clocked in."

"And he packed up all his stuff and took it with him?" Rick asked.

Paul shrugged again. "Looks like it. His clothes are gone, and there's no suitcase."

Rick thought about this. It just didn't make sense. "You think he trucked his suitcase two miles down the private road to the secondary road? Route 501?"

"Why not? Carmen told me that he had some dealings with some characters in Boise that could only be described as shady."

Another new bit of information for Rick. The more he learned about the work-release employees, the more he didn't like the program. Rick wasn't responsible for their hiring; that usually fell under the jurisdiction of the Board of Directors, who did all the direct hiring for that particular program. "Color me surprised," Rick said. He leaned back in his chair. "How am I supposed to know these guys' backgrounds as Director of Operations if I can't even have access to their HR records?"

"Hey, you're preaching to the choir, buddy." Paul Westcott rose to his feet and stretched. "I've complained to Wayne about this before. All he tells me is that their charter prohibits it.

Something about how these guys aren't even real employees of the company but just indentured servants or some shit. You ask me, every last one of us is an indentured servant to these bozos."

Rick cracked a smile at that. Paul smiled and laughed.

"Seriously, though," Rick said, as he rose to his feet behind his desk. Paul moved toward the door and Rick stepped around the desk to show him out. "I like to run as tight a ship as I can, and it's pretty hard to do when I'm not allowed to know the complete criminal background of these work-release guys. It would have made things a lot easier had I known Brian's background beforehand. I wouldn't have assigned him to work that section of the suites. I would've put him on common-area maintenance duty."

"I hear you," Paul said. He stopped at the door, hand on the doorknob, and paused. "I'll tell you something," he said, turning to Rick. "Brian's not the only work-release guy to skip out during the season. We've had others. Every single one of them has had something going on outside, too. A scam he's working with buddies back home, a girl he's pining for, that kind of thing. Brian's no different. When I finally got a look at his complete record, I saw he had ties with a fencing ring in Boise. You ask me, that's where he's headed."

"To Boise?"

"Why not? Boise's a real city. Unlike bumfuck, Wyoming." Paul opened the office door and bade Rick a farewell with a wave. "Don't worry about it, Rick. Brian's gone, and my team is questioning the rest of the employees over the next day or two. We'll find Mr. Goode's money."

"Let me ask you something else," Rick asked.

"Shoot." Paul hung back in the hallway. Rick stood in the threshold of his office and glanced both ways—his office was at the end of the hall; there were three other offices set up along this hallway that housed other administrative employees. They were all out to lunch, so it was just Rick and Paul. "Has there ever been a theft of this magnitude at Bent Creek before?"

Paul's features were serious. His gaze was direct. "There's never been a theft at Bent Creek, *period*."

"Really?"

"Really." Gone was the slight joking manner Paul exhibited in Rick's office. Now he was dead serious. "Not so much as an incident of pick-pocketing or petty theft. Bent Creek's clients don't play that. If any of them are crooks, they're of the high-level white-collar variety, and I'd be hard-pressed to find *any* that are engaged in that kind of activity, even if we do have a few hedge fund managers on our client list. For the most part, our clients are high-level corporate executives and lawyers, Wall Street players, or they're genuine blue bloods. They don't *have* to steal from each other. Why would they? The lowest net worth of some of them is around twenty million or more. A lot of them are worth much more than that. Quite a few of them are at the Mitt Romney level of the wealth scale, or for all I know the George Soros or Koch Brothers billionaire level. Once you have that kind of money, why would you need any more? You know what I mean?"

"Very well," Rick said. He couldn't comprehend having that kind of money.

Paul stepped away. "I'll report the result of our talks with the other employees sometime tonight or tomorrow."

"Sounds good."

Paul headed down the hall and Rick retreated back into his office and closed the door.

When he sank back into his chair, his mind was a whirling maelstrom of thoughts. Carmen had been making noise about Brian's disappearance since yesterday. She was very upset by it, and that told Rick that she wasn't involved in the theft if Brian masterminded it. If Brian had taken the money, he would've trusted Carmen with it, no question about it. Rick saw how close the two of them were, and if a search of her quarters hadn't turned up anything, her vigorous demands that management do something about Brian's disappearance was further proof. Rick still found it hard to believe that Paul had dismissed

Brian as a likely suspect in the theft of Mr. Goode's money, but it was a real possibility he had to keep open for now. The report Paul submitted to him and the rest of the board this morning was conclusive: there was no forensic evidence showing Brian Gaiman had broken in to Mr. Goode's room. In fact, there was no evidence Mr. Goode's room had been broken into at all. Naturally, that led Rick to believe it was an inside job—either somebody with Mr. Goode's key card or an employee with access to the room had stolen the money. The question was, who?

Rick tapped a key on his computer's keyboard and the screen saver disappeared. He was hungry. He clicked on a web browser to do some casual web surfing, letting his mind wander. He couldn't help but think about the theft of all that cash. Surely it couldn't be somebody on staff; everybody that worked at the Bent Creek Country Club and Resorts—with the exception of the handful of maintenance guys on the work release program—had undergone criminal background checks prior to their being hired. They'd also undergone credit checks. Those with credit scores below 700 were not hired, period. With the exception of those few employees involved in the work-release program, everybody on staff had a spotless record. So if it wasn't an employee who'd stolen the money, who did it?

The sound of chattering voices entering the hall shattered his thoughts and Rick stood up, his stomach rumbling. It sounded like Karen and Jay were coming back from lunch. He poked his head out the door. Jay was just entering his office when he saw Rick and nodded. "Hey, Rick."

Rick nodded back. "Jay. How was lunch?"

"Good. Karen, Geoff, and I went to the grill. It's pretty empty now if you want to go snag something."

"Thanks. I think I will." It was common for the office staff to come back and inform Rick that business at the grill had died down, allowing Rick to take a quick trip to grab a sandwich and head back. Rick patted his slacks' pocket to make sure his wallet was there, then he closed his door and headed out to lunch.

* * *

He wheeled the body into the cutting room on a stainless steel gurney.

This was one of four he was dealing with. Two had been dispatched and were already prepared, sitting in the freezer to await the main event. The third was tied up and would be dispatched later—probably tomorrow. This one had just been killed a few hours ago and it couldn't have gone better.

He stood over the body, breathing deeply. This specimen was young and well built, with the body of an athlete. Sharply defined chest and arms suggested he'd been a body builder. That was good. Personally, he liked body builders. He was a muscle man.

He walked around to where the head of the victim was. The body was lying on its back. He could see the bullet wound's entry and exit clearly—big hole above the right temple, large gaping maw of flesh and bone toward the rear left of the skull. He frowned. A specimen this well nourished and in such good physical shape, it was a shame the head was not intact. Apparently the client didn't care for this one's head. Their loss.

He glanced at his watch quickly. He had an hour before he had to get to work. This shouldn't take that long.

Grabbing his heaviest, sharpest butcher knife out of the sheath of his leather apron, he moved around the table and ran his fingers down the nude body. He felt his cock stir and begin to rise beneath the leather apron that covered his waist. He couldn't help that. Preparing them always turned him on.

He was quick and methodical. His first cut was precise, slicing from below the breastbone and down toward the naval. He reached in to the abdominal cavity and grabbed a hold of the muscle and skin, peeling it back from both sides. A strong smell of bile wafted up, but he ignored it. It was a smell he was used to.

He eviscerated the body, making sure to examine the liver. It was in good shape. Healthy. He put the liver in a special stainless-steel bowl. Everything else—stomach, gall bladder, spleen, intestines, he placed in a larger stainless-steel bucket. He frowned as the viscera plopped into the bucket amid great gouts of blood and tissue. Sometimes the intestines could be put to good use. He made a mental note to himself to inspect them more closely when he was finished.

When the internal organs were out of the body, he reached for the rib sheers and cut through the ribs. There was an audible snap and crack as ribs separated from the breastbone. Grunting with the effort, he set the rib sheers down, then reached his hand inside the chest cavity and grabbed the heart. It felt good. Nice and strong. A few quick slices with a scalpel and the muscle was free. He examined it, noting that it was as healthy as its former owner's exterior self had been. Nice.

He placed the heart in the same bowl as the liver and continued.

He set the scalpel down and reached for a second knife, this one sharper, with a heavier blade.

The head came off at the second and third neck vertebra. The torso was bisected between the twenty-third and twenty-fourth lumbar vertebrae. He performed a thorough inspection of both halves, breathing heavy now and rubbing his engorged cock occasionally through the leather apron that concealed it. When he was finished here, he would play with himself, but not now. He had work to do.

The limbs were separated at the shoulders, hips, elbow and knee joints, and the feet and hands were removed. He picked up the left thigh, inspecting it, his stomach fluttering with anticipation as he poked the nimble flesh. So nice! And *supple*!

Then, humming a tune, and trying to keep his lust in check, he started to carve flesh from the leg.

When he was finished with that leg, he started on the other one.

CHAPTER 10

Fifteen Months Ago

"So what did you find out?" Joe Taylor asked. He was on the phone with Dean Campbell and had taken the call in his living room. He muted the sound on the television with the remote control and picked up a pad and pencil to take notes. Outside, spring was in full bloom. Down the street, he heard the neighborhood kids begin some kind of game in somebody's backyard basketball court.

"It's official," Dean said. "I traced her to Casper, Wyoming. She was very careful to not leave a paper trail. She didn't use a credit card or a debit card, but she did open a bank account and she rented an apartment. The landlord says she moved out four months later, after she lost her job at Braun & Meyer's."

Joe nodded. He'd asked Dean to make the investigation thorough and official. He was operating on the assumption Carla had moved to Casper, based on the conversations he'd had with her friend, Danielle. Those conversations had been backed up by Human Resources representatives at Braun & Meyer's, who would only confirm Carla's hiring date and the date she'd been terminated. Everything else was hearsay. Joe wanted concrete evidence. "I see," he said. "Anything else?"

"I talked to her supervisor at Braun & Meyer's" Dean said. "A guy named Allen Davidson. He said he was very sorry to let her go, but he had no choice. He was directed by his superiors to cut staff, starting with those that had less seniority. He had ten staff members that fell under this category. Out of those ten, he told me he went to his director and appealed to him that he wanted to make an exception for Carla. Apparently, your daughter had become a very strong asset to Mr. Davidson's team and he didn't want to lose her."

Joe smiled at this, but hearing this bit of information didn't make him feel better. "That's my girl," he said. That was just like Carla. When she wanted something, she put everything she had into it.

"It sounds like she was very well-liked there," Dean continued. "I talked to a couple of her co-workers. They all liked her. Despite that, she'd made few friends at the job. Everybody I talked to said she was extremely sociable and likeable, but she didn't make a lot of strong friendships there save for a few. I'm going to talk to those people tomorrow."

Joe Taylor nodded. He jotted down a few notes. "Her boss, this Mr. Davidson...did he tell you what his director told him when he appealed Carla's layoff to them?"

"Just that he was denied the request," Dean answered. "That they were very hard-lined about it. No exceptions."

Joe sighed. That was a very corporate thing. When it came time to cut staff, the trend was to cut the correct percentage regardless of how valuable those employees were to the organization. Decisions like that almost always wound up costing the organization more money in the long run than they would have saved, since the valuable employee was no longer an asset. When faced with similar decisions at the various companies he sat on the board for, Joe was always in the minority opinion—sometimes employee cuts *were* necessary, but Joe didn't believe in such drastic cuts in staff without any regard to *how* such cuts would affect the company, much less the personal lives of those employees. "Did Mr. Davidson give Carla a recommendation for her next job?"

"Absolutely," Dean said. "He told me he talked to her perhaps four or five times in the months that followed. He was dismayed to hear she could not find a comparable position."

"And the few people she formed friendships with at Braun & Meyers," Joe continued. "They still kept in touch?"

"It sounds like it. I'll learn more tomorrow."

"Good. Keep me posted. Give me a call after you talk to them."

"I will."

When the call was ended, Joe finished taking notes, then read them over. Whatever game had started down the street had been joined by even more kids. Their squeals of play were background noise, taking him back to his own childhood, to Carla's childhood when he and Nina were married and struggling to raise a family and forge ahead in their careers. It brought him back to those days when he would come home from the office on a late Friday afternoon, completely exhausted from the week, and recline on the living room sofa, listening as Carla and her brother, Robert, played outside with the neighborhood kids, not even aware of what their father was going through to make their lives better. It had been important for him to shield them from all that. He'd wanted to give his kids the childhood he'd never had.

Joe looked out the living room window.

Nina wouldn't talk to him. She'd been increasingly hostile and uncooperative since the divorce, but she was downright cold to him now that Carla was gone. They communicated through their attorneys. He was on good terms with Robert, but he had a feeling that his son was wary around him, as if he was being careful about what he said around his father. He also got the feeling that Robert was feeding information to Nina. Every time he saw Robert, Lester Connolly, Nina's lawyer, would contact Dennis Lawson, his attorney, and ask for clarification on certain things pertaining to the terms of their divorce, which had been finalized three years ago. Nit-picking things; was the Henderson fund yielding proper returns and, if so, Nina required her portion since, as per the terms of their divorce, she was entitled to half of everything he earned for assets accumulated during the years of their marriage. Joe played the game, but lately he'd been too distracted to engage in it vigorously with her. His complete focus was on finding their daughter. On making amends. On setting things right.

Joe set the note pad and pen down on the coffee table. It was comforting to know that Carla had started to make connections in her new life. That was important. He was hoping that Dean would elicit valuable information from her new friends. It was quite possible she had confided in them, that she'd shared things with them she would not share with Danielle. If this was the case, it was quite possible they would know where Carla had gone.

The clock over the mantle on the hearth read four-fifteen. Joe stood up, and headed to the kitchen to prepare a light meal for this evening's supper.

CHAPTER 11

It was two hours into dinner service, and Anna was at it in full force, taking orders, delivering entrees and appetizers, serving drinks. Service so far was going well. There appeared to be a festive mood in the air. It was the last night of the season; a quarter of the quests had checked out earlier in the day, but the vast majority of them would not leave until tomorrow. Unfortunately, Shane Daniels and his wife, Jackie, were not among those who had left. They were seated at her station and were not as annoying to her as they usually were. Instead, Shane appeared to leer at her in a subtle way, his eyes roaming over her in full view of Jackie, whose smile seemed to conceal a secret joke. Anna ignored it, realizing she probably should have talked to Rick about them, but she was on strained terms with Rick now, especially since she'd been avoiding him following the evening she'd spent in his suite five nights ago.

Well, he did *come on to me.*

Anna put in her latest orders at the pass and checked to see if anything had come up. Nothing so far. She surveyed her station, mind racing briefly on Rick and her feelings. She hadn't meant to lead him on, had tried to be brutally up front with him during the heat of their passion, but he hadn't taken the hint. Sure, he was subtle about it—he obviously knew every trick in the book about not coming across as a sexual harasser in the work-place. For her part, Anna simply wanted to keep her head down and get through the next few days. What they'd had five nights ago had been nice, and it had served her purpose, and that was the extent of her feelings toward it. To go to Rick about the Daniels couple really would be fruitless at this point.

Just one more night. She'd been expecting more catcalling, more verbal and physical harassment, but none of that happened. If anything, Shane and Jackie were aloof, like wolves watching over a flock of sheep.

Alex Lillywhite was on hand at this evening's dinner service as well, roaming the dining area, talking to the guests, greeting them as they arrived. He made his presence known in the kitchen as Chef Munchel and his crew prepared high-quality meals that would cost astronomically in most five-star restaurants. Anna had never eaten Chef Munchel's food—like the rest of the lower echelon staff, she was forced to eat at the bar-and-grill on the other side of the Bent Creek grounds—but the presentation and aroma of the dishes he prepared was mouth watering. The fact that she had to serve it would have been torture on an empty stomach.

Entrees for table number five came up, and Anna brought them out. She was serving them—two couples, a pair of Wall Street bankers and their wives—when the hostess seated a new couple at table number seven. Anna approached table number seven with a smile, noting it was Mitch and Cindy Johnson. They were well-dressed tonight, Mitch in a three-piece black suit, Cindy in a matching wine-colored evening dress, her blonde hair cut and styled to flow naturally across her shoulders.

"Good evening, Mr. and Mrs. Johnson," Anna said with a smile. "Can I get you anything to drink?"

Mitch and Cindy smiled at her. "A bottle of Cabernet would be wonderful," Mitch said.

"Very good." Anna bowed slightly and left.

She could feel Mitch and Cindy's gaze on her as she left the table. Last evening, after dinner service, the Johnson's had invited Anna to their suite for a few drinks. They'd made the offer casually, discreetly, as if they were aware of the rules that Bent Creek employees were not allowed to socialize with the guests, even during their off hours, on their own time. Anna had been a little taken aback by it, but Mitch had been persistent. Mitch Johnson was an incredibly handsome man, tall, well-built, with a sunny disposition that gave his handsome features a slightly boyish look. Cindy looked like she could step out of the pages of a *Playboy* centerfold. She'd wondered if that interest from them was sexual in nature. It wouldn't be the first time she'd gotten strong, subliminal sexual messages from clients at Bent Creek, or anywhere else for that matter; she knew the signs, had followed up on them in the past when the mood struck her. Like with Rick.

Last night had been no exception. Only she hadn't allowed the Johnson's to seduce her.

She'd seduced *them*.

The Johnson's were doing a fine job of being inconspicuous about last night's ménage `a trois. They'd barely glanced at Anna during breakfast service today, and now, during dinner service, their demeanors showed no overt signs that anything had occurred between the three of them last night. Anna kept a poker face as she bustled through dinner service, her mind a whirlwind of thoughts as she smiled, chatted amicably with the guests, and took orders.

Anna called the Johnson's wine order out to Martin. When he delivered the bottle and the wine flutes, he asked, "What are you smiling at?"

"The thought that tonight's our last night here," Anna said. Martin chuckled at that as Anna lifted the Johnson's drink order on her serving tray and headed back to their table.

* * *

Another late night.

Rick sat slumped behind his desk in his office, his mind racing. His fingers drummed on the desk in nervous anticipation.

It was the last night of the season. Tomorrow the majority of the guests would check out, leaving a handful of the very high-rollers left, who had paid for use of the grounds for their private party, for which they'd retained the services of Chef Munchel. Tomorrow would be a day off for Rick, but the skeleton crew staff, hand-picked by Wayne Sanders, would be on hand for clean-up. Two days from now, Friday night, would be the inaugural kick off of the private event, which was to last four days. The private party would leave Tuesday morning and Rick and the staff would depart with them, leaving Wayne Sanders and the board members to shut down the premises until next season.

That gave Rick at least one full day to himself. There was nothing in his contract that called for him to remain on Bent Creek grounds during that day, either. He'd been reading over his contract all afternoon to make sure. The terms did not specifically prohibit him from taking his day off on company property, but neither did it state he had to stay.

It's a six hour drive, he thought. *I can snag a few cans of Red Bull, leave tonight before the season's dinner service ends and be home by dawn. I can take care of my business in town later in the morning after a short nap, then be back on the road to Bent Creek by late afternoon.*

It was a good plan.

And it would give him time to think about other things.

Rick glanced at the manila file folder on his desk, the one Paul Westcott had given to him earlier that day. The file contained information on the Brian Gaiman case. Rick picked the file up and leafed through it, frowning. He was still bothered by the missing money, by Brian's sudden disappearance. During last year's season, the staff had worked like a tightly-wound watch; everything had ticked by accordingly, on time, like a metronome. This season...well, it was shambles compared to the previous year. Rick took great pride in his work. To have such a brazen theft conducted under his watch and then to have an employee disappear within the same time frame, was a serious blow to how he managed employees and ran the operation. He was afraid this mishap would reflect badly on his performance bonus—that money was greatly needed by Rick. He'd been using most of his income to help his mother, who was sick from cancer, and which medicare was not providing adequate coverage for her treatment. Rick was in a serious financial hole because of it, and the performance bonus would shore it up, plug up the leaks.

Of course, the theft would affect Paul Westcott's performance bonus too. But Paul Westcott was the least of his worries.

I have to operate on the assumption this will affect things, he thought as he closed the file, opened one of his file drawers at his desk and found a spot for the documents. *If that's the case, I need to leave tonight, get to Denver by dawn, get a few hours sleep, then start calling in some favors. Then I can head back up here, finish my duties, and be done with this place by this time next week and never come back.*

It was a plan. It was solid. The more Rick thought about it, turned it over in his mind, the better he felt.

He thought about Anna briefly, then put her out of his mind. Anna had been a mistake. She was wise to not respond to the vibes he'd put out to her after their one-night stand. It never should have happened, but she was attractive. And, he thought, she'd been attracted to him. She'd certainly been friendly around him during department meetings, and the few times he'd sat with her and a bunch of the other wait staff in the bar-and-grill, she'd seemed gregarious, friendly. The kind of girl he liked.

But then five nights ago, one thing had led to another in the employee lounge, and they'd managed to discreetly get away from their fellow employees and wound up in his suite. Anna had told him even then as they wrapped themselves together that she wasn't serious about him—she was just looking to have some fun. Blow off steam. Part of him was into that as well. But then another part of him wanted a bigger connection, something more. It was that smaller part that had tried to follow up with her in the days that followed, only to be subtly rebuffed. The more Rick thought about it, the more he realized it was for the best. With everything going on in his life, he simply didn't have time for a relationship. And he finally realized that Anna probably didn't have time to pursue one, either.

That decided things for him. Rick shut his computer down, then turned the lights off in his office and closed the door behind him when he left. He made his way to the executive suite of the employee area of the resort, confident that things were going to work out.

It didn't take Rick long to pack a quick over-night bag. He stuffed underwear, clothing for tomorrow, and his toiletries into his small duffel bag. He'd already changed into faded blue jeans, a tan polo shirt, white socks and tennis shoes. His Blackberry was charged up. He had his eye-glasses, which he wore for driving at night. Now all he needed was some Red Bull for the road.

His car was in the lot adjacent to the employee executive suites. The closest kiosk where he could buy Red Bull was at the employee gift shop, which was in the opposite direction. Rick pocketed his key card and exited his room.

When he reached the kiosk he headed straight for the soft drink section. He picked out four cans of Red Bull and paid for them with cash. The cashier, a bored-looking Hispanic woman, snapped at her chewing gum. "Last night, Mr. Nicholson."

"Yep," Rick said. "How's things going, Jen?"

"Kinda slow."

"Be sure to keep things open until two a.m.," Rick reminded her.

"I will," Jen said. "You working that private thing?"

"Yeah. I wish I was going home tomorrow like you, though."

Jen laughed and smacked her gum. "You want to sneak out tomorrow morning, I'll give you a ride."

Rick laughed with her. "Any other time, I'd take you up on that offer. But duty calls."

"That's why you make the big bucks."

"So they tell me." Rick stepped away from the counter. "Have a good one, Jen."

"You too, Rick. You coming back next year?"

"Probably." It was best to keep future plans vague, giving everybody the sense that he'd most likely be back. "You?"

"Of course. Money isn't bad, and I get free room and board for the summer. You know what I'm sayin?"

"I do. See you, Jen. Take care of yourself."

"You too, Rick."

Rick exited the kiosk just as Wayne Sanders was entering it. Both men stopped in their tracks. Rick was surprised to see Wayne in the employee wing of Bent Creek. He'd never known the board of directors to venture where the commoners lived. "Wayne!"

"Just the man I was coming to see," Wayne said. The sudden surprise at running into Rick was gone from Wayne's face. "I've got something I need to talk to you about."

"Sure," Rick said, feeling a momentary sense of trepidation. He didn't want to invite Wayne back to his suite—if the CEO saw the packed duffel bag, he might ask questions. "What's up?"

Wayne hadn't even bothered to look at the brown paper bag Rick was holding. His attention was directed wholly on Rick's face. "There's been another theft," Wayne said, his voice low. "Three hundred thousand in cash."

Rick felt dumbstruck by the news. A worm of unease began to gnaw at his stomach. "What? This is...this is *insane*!"

"Paul alerted me to the theft thirty minutes ago," Wayne said. His gray eyes were narrow flints as they focused on Rick. "Once again, it was a theft from one of the rooms. A Mr. and Mrs. Westlake. They were going to use the cash to buy a rare piece of art in Casper tomorrow. They'd just checked the money out of the hotel safe this morning and it was sitting in an envelope on a desk in their suite. They went out riding this afternoon, then ate dinner at the roadhouse in town." The roadhouse was a high-class steak-house outside of Bent Creek grounds. Many times, clients who were into horseback riding ate at the roadhouse more for the atmosphere than the food, which was really pretty good. Rick had eaten a meal there himself a few times. "When they returned from dinner at nine, they noticed the envelope was missing."

"What do you want from me?" Rick asked.

"Their room is being searched now and they've been questioned," Wayne said. "I would like you to communicate to your direct reports that *nobody* is to leave until Paul's team has questioned the entire staff and searched their rooms."

"You really think an employee is responsible for the theft?"

"It *has* to be somebody in housekeeping with key card access," Wayne said. He looked grim. "We're not taking any chances, though. It could be anybody on staff.

Rick nodded. "I agree. I'll put out the word now." He began to head in the opposite direction, toward the Administrative wing.

"Mr. Nicholson?"

Rick stopped. "Yes?"

"I apologize for putting a dent in your night off," Wayne said. His features were unreadable. His bald pate shined beneath the florescent lights that lit the hallway. "I'd appreciate it if you could assist in the supervision of the questioning of your direct reports' staff members."

"No problem," Rick said. He hefted the bag to get a firm grip. "The Red Bull I picked up for my office fridge will come in handy tonight."

Wayne nodded. "Very good. I've arranged for a quick meeting at ten p.m. in the conference room to provide updates."

"I'll be there," Rick said.

As Rick headed down the hall toward the Administrative wing, his spirits soured. This was going to destroy his plans. There was no way he could wiggle out of this one. Worst case scenario, he would be up until the early hours of the morning dealing with this. There was no way he'd be up to a five-hour drive home to Boulder. He wasn't even sure he'd be able to sneak off the grounds and be back in time for the preparation of the private event. He was stuck at Bent Creek until the board of directors shut down the facilities.

I can call them tomorrow, Rick thought as he walked down the hall. *I can call the key people I need to speak with, maybe try to arrange some kind of meeting or conference call. That can at least get the ball rolling.*

Rick turned this over in his mind as he headed toward the Administrative wing, knowing he had to stay on top of this crisis if he wanted to avert the very personal one that was beginning to destroy his personal life.

CHAPTER 12

Thursday, Eight A.M.

Anna King trailed her roll-away suitcase behind her as she approached the lobby. She had dressed lightly but comfortably in baggy jeans, a loose-fitting blouse, and tennis shoes. Her hair wasn't bound up in a pony-tail per service regulations, but was spilled over her shoulders. She was wearing a baseball cap. She clutched a small purse in her left hand. She was carrying a black backpack that contained her laptop, notebook, and some of her other things. She'd entered Bent Creek grounds with the same amount of personal stuff she was exiting it with. No sense in leaving with more than you arrived with. Anna didn't believe in saddling yourself with unnecessary vacation trinkets or souvenirs. What was the point?

Anna stood outside the bank of elevators that had deposited her on the first floor. She looked up and down the marble-lined hall and lobby. Between the elevators and the front desk, which was set in an alcove-like area to her right, a door led to the Administration area of Bent Creek corporate. Anna doubted anybody was at work this morning; all the big-wigs had been up until the wee hours of the morning, assisting with the mass questioning of the employees regarding a theft. Beyond the entrance to corporate lay the front desk of the hotel. Two desk clerks manned it. Standing in front of the desk were two guests, a middle-aged couple, checking out. The man was replacing his wallet in his coat, his wife picked up a bag and placed it on the luggage rack. A bellboy stood waiting to cart the luggage outside. The lobby's lounge was empty—nobody sat in the chairs reading newspapers, sipping coffee, making small talk. Anna thought at the very least a few of her fellow serfs would have tried to get a jump on leaving early, but it had been a very late night for all of them. Last night of the season meant the guests had pushed things to the limit. The bars, dance club, and restaurants had stayed open until two a.m., and after closing, those that had not been subject to questioning of the theft had to take a trip to Paul Westcott or Rick Nicholson's office to talk to security. Many had been forced to wait their turn outside the Administrative area. Anna had been questioned by one of Paul's security team in a small conference room at close to four a.m. She'd stayed awake and alert by drinking coffee. By the time she got back to her room and crashed, she'd been too wired mentally to fall asleep. Her body screamed for sleep, but her mind kept her awake, racing with the implications and possibilities of everything—her services last night, the brazen theft, dealing with Rick, the questioning, her anxiousness at finally leaving this place and awaiting her final check—it all swam inside her mind, each item demanding her attention.

At some point she must have slept because the next thing she knew her alarm was buzzing; she'd set it for six-thirty. She sprang out of bed and, after a quick shower and change of clothes, she hurriedly packed her belongings and slipped out of her room. Following the close of dinner service, she was technically off duty. She wasn't working the private party—she would have been alerted late last night by Alex at the close of her shift and that hadn't happened—so she was out of here.

With the coast clear, Anna began heading toward the lobby. She heard the ping of the elevator behind her and she kept going—it was probably a guest checking out. Staff members didn't have to check out, so Anna did not need to stop at the front desk. The elevator opened behind her and Anna was almost at the end of the elevator bank when she heard Bob Garrison's distinctive voice call her name.

Anna stopped and looked back. Bob had just exited one of the elevators. He was dressed in a pair of tan shorts and a white polo shirt, white socks and tennis shoes, as if he were out for a morning game of tennis. He smiled at her. "I was hoping I'd see you before you left," he said. "I'm sorry we didn't get much of a chance to talk during dinner service last night. It was pretty hectic in there last night."

"Yes, it was," Anna said, recovering quickly from her surprise. She warmed up to Bob, returning his smile. "I'm sorry, too, but it really was a busy night. Did you enjoy your last evening?"

"Very much so." Bob stopped in front of her and gestured toward the front desk. "I was just coming down to give the front desk my payment for the private event. I take it you aren't working it?"

Anna shook her head. "No, I'm not. Chef Munchel didn't pick me. Lucky me, I guess."

Bob smiled. "After the night you had, you deserve a break. You still have my card?"

"I do, yes."

"Good. Give me a call next week. We'll meet for lunch. Maybe I can help you land a position with one of the companies I work with."

"That would be great, Mr. Garrison."

"Please, call me Bob."

Anna smiled. "Okay, Bob it is."

Bob reached out and took her hand in a farewell handshake. He motioned to her luggage. "You're taking off early, I see."

"Oh, yes. Well, my father called me last night during my break and said my brother is really sick. I wasn't going to leave until this afternoon after I'd gotten a good night's sleep, but when I got my father's call..." She shrugged.

"Of course," Bob said. "Duty calls when it comes to family situations like that. I hope it isn't serious."

"I don't think it is," Anna said.

"Give me a call when you're ready. And if you need to get in touch with me before then, feel free to get in touch with me at my cell number."

"I will. Thanks, Bob."

"Thank *you*," Bob said. He gave her one last smile and then made his way to the resort's restaurant, which was just off to the right of the elevator banks.

Anna sighed, then reached down to grasp the handle of her luggage. Her purse slipped from her grasp and fell to the marble floor. She cursed silently, reached down and scooped it up. Once she got a firm grip on it, she grabbed the handle of her suitcase and began heading toward the front door. No sooner did she breach the entrance toward the corporate offices than the door opened and Paul Westcott stepped out.

Anna stopped, momentarily startled. Bob was already a dozen yards ahead of her and she could barely see him as he moved into the slight alcove-like area to the front desk. At first glance, Paul appeared to be just as surprised by her appearance, but he quickly recovered. "Where do you think you're going?" he said.

Anna was startled by the question. "Home. Where else would I be going?"

"Home?"

"Yes, home." Anna frowned. "Why?"

"Didn't Alex tell you?"

Anna felt a tingling in her spine. "Alex didn't tell me anything. What's going on?"

Paul held the door open and gestured for her to come inside. "Come on back here. We need to talk."

Anna looked around. She was still holding on to her suitcase.

"The concierge will make sure it stays at the front desk," Paul said. "Come on."

Anna glanced at the front desk clerk, who nodded, affirming he'd heard what Paul said, then without a backward glance, she entered the Administrative area after Paul.

"Checking out, sir?"

The front desk clerk was smiling and affable as Joe Taylor approached the front desk. He'd intended to head to the restaurant for a quick breakfast when a nagging feeling made him stop and head back toward the front desk. Joe smiled back, reaching for his wallet that contained Chef Munchel's business card and the hand-written code number he'd jotted on it a month ago when the Chef invited Joe to partake in the event. "Actually, I'm not," he said. He leaned against the front desk. "I'm checked in to Suite 408, under the name Robert Garrison. Chef Jim Munchel invited me at the last minute to participate in the private event taking place this week. I've already put down my security deposit and was told I could remit the remainder this week during my stay."

"Very good, Mr. Garrison." The desk clerk was in his mid-twenties, with pleasant features and short-cropped brown hair. He was wearing an impeccable blue suit with a white shirt and black tie. "Were you given an event code?"

"Yes." Joe took his wallet out and plucked Chef Munchel's card out just as a whisk of movement and a scraping sound behind him attracted his attention. He turned around.

Anna King's suitcase lay on the marble floor fifteen feet away from where he'd just spoken to her. Anna was nowhere in sight.

Frowning, Joe moved away from the desk toward the hall. Was that a doorway that was closing just past the elevators?

"Is everything all right, Mr. Garrison?"

Joe stopped, turned to the front desk. The desk clerk was looking at him curiously. Joe motioned to the luggage on the floor. "There was a young woman back there a minute ago. I was just talking to her. Did you see her?"

"Yes, I did, sir. She was called to a quick meeting. Don't worry about her baggage. When the concierge returns, I'll have him retrieve her suitcase and place them behind the front desk."

"Very good, thank you," Joe said, returning to the front desk. Despite the desk clerk's strict professionalism and calming tone of voice, something didn't sit right with Joe. Anna had seemed pretty anxious to leave Bent Creek so early.

The desk clerk's fingers were poised over the computer's keyboard but his gaze was centered on Joe. "Your code, Mr. Garrison?"

Joe read the code to him. The clerk typed it in to the computer, verified his name. Then he asked for his ID. Joe handed over the Colorado driver's license that Dean Campbell had made for him with the Bob Garrison pseudonym. The desk clerk examined it quickly, nodded, then typed something else in. "Do you wish to complete your transaction with a major credit card or with cash?"

"I'll pay cash," Joe said.

"Very good, sir."

Joe reached into the front pocket of his shorts and extracted a white envelope containing two hundred and fifty thousand dollars in large bills. He handed the envelope over to the desk clerk, who counted it discreetly and placed it in the side compartment of the hotel's cash drawer. His fingers flew across the keyboard. "I'll have your receipt in a moment, Mr. Garrison."

"Thank you," Joe said.

The lobby doors opened and the concierge returned with an empty luggage cart. Without looking up from the computer terminal, the desk clerk called out to him. "Eric, can you retrieve the luggage on the floor and bring it around behind the front desk, please?"

The concierge nodded. He parked the luggage cart near the entrance, then retrieved Anna's suitcase from the floor. The whir of the laser printer behind the front desk sounded and the desk clerk smiled at Joe. "Don't worry, Mr. Garrison, we'll take care of her luggage." He lifted the receipt out of the printer's tray and slid it across the marble counter-top at him. "And here's your receipt. I hope you enjoy the remainder of your stay."

"Thank you," Joe said, nodding. He folded the receipt in half and placed it in the front pocket of his shorts next to his wallet. He stepped away from the front desk and headed outside.

When he stepped out to the front receiving area of the hotel, he kept his sunny disposition on his face. He looked out at the circular driveway, at the rolling expanse of greenery that made up the estate. The air was brisk, slightly cool, but the sun was out and there wasn't a cloud in the sky. It was going to be a nice day, weather-wise.

You can't attract attention here, he said to himself. *Take a walk. Give them the impression you're not concerned for the girl.*

And even though Joe Taylor was growing very concerned for Anna King, he took his own advice. He headed out for a walk.

CHAPTER 13

Fourteen Months Ago

He met Dean Campbell at a greasy spoon in downtown Casper, Wyoming. As he slid into the booth, Dean slid a menu across the table to him. Beneath the menu was a tan manila folder. "I ate dinner here last night and the food is amazing," Dean said. "Go ahead, order up."

"I'm not hungry," Joe said.

"You are today," Dean said. He took a sip of water.

"I am?"

Dean shot him a look that was so subtle it would have been impossible to notice if Joe wasn't seated exactly opposite him. That look seemed to say *we might be under surveillance, so act normal.*

Joe took a look at the menu. It was standard diner fare. Different kinds of sandwiches, hamburgers, chicken dishes, pastas, steaks, salads, seafood. Joe had worked as a line cook in such an establishment a long time ago, when he was a far different person. He quickly zeroed in on a selection that appealed to him—grilled flounder on a bed of rice pilaf. A middle-aged waitress took their order and, after she delivered a pot of coffee, Joe deftly moved the envelope down to the seat and stuck it in his front slacks' pocket while Dean started feeding him information. "She lived on Unemployment Insurance for about a month and was looking for work. She broke her lease at the apartment she was at and moved into a series of motels, the last one about a block from here."

"Were the other motels within walking distance of this place?"

Dean took a sip of his coffee. "The first three weren't. The last two were."

"And this was *after* she lost her second job?"

"Well, yes, if you count job-jobs," Dean said. "Remember, she kept the apartment during her stint as a consultant. She only resorted to the retail type jobs because the economy turned so shitty."

"Right." Carla could have had a good position with any of the four companies Joe sat on the board for, no questions asked. All she had to do was come home. Carla had proven to be as stubborn as he was at that age.

"Anyway, nobody saw her leave the motel around the time of her last job interview. And her car was never found. The cell phone number she had, that's a dead end from a legal standpoint. To get a trace on the phone through her carrier would require a court order, and we can't do that without evidence of a crime."

"Not even with her listed as missing?"

Dean shrugged. "There's no evidence of foul play. Far as the police are concerned, she just took off in her car for parts unknown."

"But that's bullshit!"

"I know that and you know that. But according to Joe Law, that's where shit stands now."

"You talked to the police?"

"I have."

"What do they say?"

"I got a little bit farther than you did. Got one detective who expressed somewhat of an interest in Carla's disappearance. With his help, I was able to talk to her former employer, some of the friends she made. Everybody I talked to is surprised she up and disappeared like that. One of her friends, a lady named Gabby, who worked with her at Braun & Meyers, says Carla wasn't the type of person to just suddenly drop out of sight."

Joe took a sip of his coffee. The diner was half-full. Dinner service was another hour or so away. Out on Main Street, traffic was brisk. "So we're at another dead end."

"Not quite. I did get Gabby to remember an important detail."

"Oh yeah?"

Dean nodded. He poured himself some more coffee from the metal carafe. "Gabby couldn't remember all the details, but she said the last time she spoke to Carla, maybe four days before anybody last saw her, she claimed Carla told her she had this face-to-face job interview. Gabby couldn't remember the name of the company, or what kind of job it was, or in what part of town. All she could remember was the name of the man Carla was supposed to meet."

"What was it?" Joe asked, curious. He thought it was odd for Carla's friend to remember something this miniscule.

"Bill Richards." Dean regarded Joe from across the table. Something in the private detective's features sparked something in his instincts. *This is important*, he thought. He'd never seen Dean look so excited, so encouraged by this bit of news. "You might wonder why Gabby would remember the man's name but not the company or any other detail, and I can't tell you, Mr. Taylor. The way the brain works, the way people recall things when they're trying to remember it…well, I've had clients give me explicit details on the most trivial things that most people would forget: what they had for breakfast two weeks ago, what slot they parked their car in at the grocery store parking lot the previous Saturday, all sorts of nonsense. Gabby said that Carla told her about this job interview a few times. The first time Carla told her about it, she sounded excited. Gabby told her she would be happy to be a reference for her. She was pretty certain it was some kind of financial job again, but she couldn't remember the name of the company. She kept telling me that things like that, company names, they always slipped her mind. The second time she talked to Carla, Gabby said she was just brimming with happiness. She'd had a very good phone interview with this Bill Richards guy, and she told Gabby he'd sounded nice on the phone, that he asked the right questions and the two of them seemed to really connect professionally. I could relate."

"So Gabby remembered Carla doing the interviews, but not the name of the company?"

Dean shrugged. "She said normally she wouldn't remember details this mundane, but this one was different, and it wasn't because Carla had been under-employed and desperate for so long, too."

"Oh?"

"Yeah. Carla told her she'd had to undergo a background check and drug screening *prior* to her second interview."

Joe frowned.

"I know," Dean said. "I thought that was unusual, too. Employers usually don't bring the whole background check and drug testing thing into the equation until after the second interview, sometimes after the third, when it's evident they're going to hire you."

"Some high-end positions will require background checks before a second interview," Joe said, his thoughts racing. "Especially if the candidate is going to be working with sensitive financial data. You know, stock-broker, that kind of thing."

Dean nodded. He took a sip of his coffee. "Sure."

"What else did Gabby say?"

"Carla told Gabby a week later that Richards had called to arrange a face-to-face. She came away from that even *more* impressed. Gabby is certain Carla told her the name of the company, but she can't remember it. She said it had a very bland sounding name."

"It wasn't Corporate Financial, was it?" Joe asked, a worm of unease spiking in his abdomen. When he'd learned Carla had been at Corporate Financial for a brief stint, he'd been worried, but she hadn't been there that long.

"No, it wasn't them. But something similar. She said they have a small office, north west side of town, but that's about all she told Gabby."

"But she remembered this guy's name, Bill Richards."

"Yeah." Dean took a sip of coffee.

Joe leaned back on his side of the booth, his thoughts racing. "Did she give Gabby a physical description?"

Dean shook his head. "She didn't."

"Where does that leave us?"

"I call every financial firm, accounting firm, bank, and stock broker in this city and ask for a Bill Richards," Dean Campbell said. "He's bound to turn up after a few days of cold calling. Somebody's got to know him."

Joe nodded, agreeing with the plan. If they could find this Bill Richards guy, he might be able to tell them key information about Carla. Was she nervous at the interview? Behaving strangely? Joe would think that if Carla had been looking forward to this interview, she would have been behaving quite the opposite, actually. If she'd been planning to make a break for parts unknown, why would she have agreed to a final interview anyway?

"Did Carla tell Gabby..." Joe asked, groping for the right way to phrase the question. "Did she give any indication that she was even *thinking* about... making a break from Casper and just relocating somewhere else?"

"I asked Gabby this," Dean said. He looked at Joe with a sense of resignation, of puzzlement. "And she was adamant that Carla was determined to stay in Casper. She was determined to find a position, to make the area her home. In all the months Gabby knew her, even after Carla was laid off, your daughter never said a word to her about packing up and leaving."

"Not even offhandedly?" Joe asked.

"Not even offhandedly."

The waitress delivered their meals and they paused in their conversation. Joe thought about this as they dug into their food. What Dean revealed sounded like Carla. It also dovetailed with what Danielle told him. How many times had Carla told Joe, in a very determined tone of voice, that she was going to do something and she stuck to her guns? Every single time. Joe considered the complications as he savored his dish, which was prepared to perfection.

"I think your next move is sound," Joe said. He was digging into his grilled flounder and enjoying it very much. "But I have two questions for you."

"Shoot."

"Why did you insist that I fly up here to meet you?"

Dean didn't look up as he dug into his meal. "It's much more secure to talk to you face-to-face. Cellular communications can be hijacked, encrypted email can be intercepted."

"That leads me to question number two," Joe said, trying to be as casual as he could without being overly conspicuous about it. He hadn't noticed anything abnormal about the other restaurant patrons at all upon arrival, but during their time here Joe had snuck casual looks around. They were well out of eavesdropping range, and Joe was certain Dean wouldn't have said as much if he knew their booth was bugged. "You gave me the impression earlier that we might be a topic of interest. Is that true?"

"I'm not taking chances," Dean said.

"Why not?"

Dean paused. He held a half-eaten French fry in his hand. "Let's just say that I have the sudden instinct to play this very, *very*, safe."

CHAPTER 14

Anna's mind was racing as Paul Westcott led her down the hallway to one of the rear conference rooms at the end of the hall. She had her purse slung over her right shoulder, her backpack was strapped to her back. Only her suitcase had been left at the front desk, and she was confident the front desk would keep careful watch over it. So why was she so nervous?

Two other security guards came out of the conference room they were heading toward and Anna felt her stomach lurch. As they approached Rick Nicholson's office, he emerged in the doorway. He was still wearing the clothes he'd had on last night and he looked exhausted. She heard him ask what was going on as Paul led her through the door to the conference room.

Anna took a deep breath to calm herself down as Paul and the two security guards entered the room. "What's this all about?"

A third security guard entered the conference room. He was wheeling in her luggage. As he lifted the suitcase onto the conference room table, Anna blurted, "What the hell is going on here?"

"Trying to sneak out while still on duty?" Paul asked. He was regarding her from across the conference room table with suspicion. "Got something to hide, Ms. King?"

"Something to hide?" Anna felt a flush of fear rise in her, but she quickly got it under control. "I don't know what you're talking about. What's going on?"

Rick stepped forward. He looked nervous. "Paul, let's..."

Paul held his right hand up to stop him. He didn't remove his gaze from Anna. "Why are you leaving?"

"Because last night was the last day of the season." Her stomach was rolling. She tried not to appear so nervous.

"You didn't tell your shift supervisor you were taking the day off, and Rick wasn't aware of it. This is serious business, Anna."

"Taking the day off?" What was Paul Westcott talking about? "My last day of employment was yesterday. What are *you* talking about?"

Paul and Rick traded a glance. Rick appeared to visibly deflate. He looked embarrassed. He ran a hand over his face and when he looked at Anna he wouldn't meet her gaze. "Alex should have told you yesterday afternoon that you were tapped to work the Private Event this week."

"*What*?" Now it was Anna's turn to be confused. Alex hadn't said shit to her. "Alex never told me anything about staying on for another week."

"Miscommunication," Paul muttered. "Ain't that a bitch!"

"You're telling me I've been tapped to work dinner service for Chef Munchel for this private event?"

"Yes, that's what's happening," Rick said.

Anna felt herself wanting to relax, to laugh at the absurdity of it, but she couldn't. She shook her head, the unease and nervousness deflating as suddenly as it had come over her. "Oh my God!"

"I apologize for the miscommunication and the sudden surprise," Paul Westcott said, his demeanor very different now. "As you were told at orientation, you will be *very* well compensated for your service this week and—"

"That's all fine and good," Anna said, overriding him, "but I can't stay."

"Why not?"

"I have things to do," Anna said. The minute she said it, she realized what a lame excuse it was.

Paul Westcott was sharper than he looked. His demeanor changed back again to its previous state: suspicion and anger. He nodded at Glenn. "Open her suitcase."

"You're not opening my suitcase," Anna protested.

"Yes we are."

"What for?"

"I don't like the way you're behaving," Paul said, his eyes locked with hers. "I don't like the fact that we have a Bent Creek employee getting out of dodge only hours after being questioned about the theft of over three hundred thousand dollars in cash from one of our guests. A Bent Creek employee who, I might add, was stopped while trying to sneak off the premises."

"I told you, Alex didn't tell me anything about staying on!"

Glenn ran his fingers over the suitcase locks, fumbled with them a moment, then turned to Paul. "Lock has a combination," he said.

Paul Westcott turned to her. The room grew silent as all eyes fell on Anna. She knew that look very well. She was being accused of the theft.

"You understand that you have no legal right to search my suitcase," Anna said.

"Of course," Paul Westcott said. "And you also understand that if you *don't* open this suitcase and let us search it, I can have the police here in less than fifteen minutes. They're quite aware of the thefts that have been going on here, and they will be happy to work with us in getting to the bottom of them. You will be their most likely suspect, too, I might add. So, if you don't have anything to hide, tell Martin the combination and let him open your suitcase."

"Fine, call the police," Anna said, her heart pounding. This was bullshit! "I know my rights. My employment ended here last night. Technically I've been a guest since two a.m. this morning. You detaining me constitutes kidnapping."

Paul sighed and turned to Rick. "Call the police, Mr. Nicholson."

Rick nodded and headed toward the conference room door.

Everything was spiraling downward very fast. If the police showed up and detained her further, her plans were spoiled. There was no telling how long the police would keep her.

"Okay, okay," Anna said. "I'll open it. I just want to get the hell out of here and be on my way."

Paul Westcott raised his right hand again at Rick, who stopped. Paul hadn't broken his gaze from Anna. "Excellent! You can start by giving Glenn the combination."

"I'll open it myself," Anna said. She stepped up to the table and Glenn moved out of her way. Anna flipped through the combination quickly, getting the numbers in place by rote memory. She flipped the latches back and raised the lid to the suitcase, keeping her body positioned in front of it for a moment as she prepared herself quickly for what was to come. She took a deep breath, composed herself. "Here you go. Knock yourself out."

Glenn and another security guard stepped in and began rummaging through the suitcase. They were very thorough. Paul and Rick stepped closer to Anna and watched as the suitcase was searched. Her clothes were removed and patted down. The mesh partition she stored her undergarments in was emptied, and she remained stoical as they pawed through her panties and bra, daring them to look at her. Glenn patted down the side compartments, emptied them of their contents—toiletries in one, Kleenex and wadded tissues in another—and the other security guard emptied out the zip-lock bag that contained the last two nights worth of laundry. When they were finished, the entire contents of her suitcase was piled on the conference room table, a haphazard of slacks, blouses, T-shirts, pajamas, underwear, bras, socks, and several pairs of shoes. When the guards were finished with the interior of her suitcase, one turned his attention to the exteriors' various pockets and zippered compartments while Glenn turned his attention to her purse. Anna said nothing as he began removing items from her purse—a packet of tissues, her change purse, which he opened, spilling loose change and a roll of bills onto the tabletop. Other items from her purse were also deposited on the table—a bottle of Anacin, a roll of Antacids, her birth control pills, some extra tampons, a stick of spearmint chewing gum, a packet of breath fresheners, her iPod Touch and a pair of ear buds, her iPhone. Glenn patted the inside of the purse to insure there was nothing stashed in any of the zippered pockets. The other security guard completed his search of her suitcase and thumbed through the bills amid the loose change: two twenties, a ten, a five, and three ones was all that comprised of the petty cash Anna was carrying.

Glenn motioned to Anna. "Take off your backpack."

Anna rolled her eyes and slipped the backpack off. She set it on the conference room table and unzipped one of the compartments. "My laptop and power cord," she said, halfway pulling out a MacBook Pro. She slid the laptop back in, opened another compartment and slid a notebook out. "My notebook and pens. Some paperbacks." She opened this second compartment more fully—several paperback novels lay inside. "That's all."

"I'll be the judge of that," the guard said, reaching out for the backpack.

Glenn finished searching her suitcase and turned to Paul. "Suitcase and purse are clean."

"Satisfied now?" Anna asked Paul.

"Get Karen in here so she can give Anna a physical pat down," Paul told Glenn. The guard who had grabbed her backpack was pawing through, taking things out.

"What? A pat down?"

Paul regarded Anna, that mistrust still in his eyes. "How do I know you aren't hiding anything in the pockets of your jacket?"

"You've gotta be...okay, fine!" Anna reached both hands into the pockets of her leather jacket and pulled them inside out.

Everybody stopped what they were doing and watched her. "Here you go. See? Nothing in my pockets, nothing up my sleeves. I'll show you myself."

With that, Anna peeled off her jacket and handed it to the guard who was rummaging through her backpack, who took it wordlessly (but she could detect he was a little surprised by her willingness to give it up so quickly). He stopped searching through the backpack as she proceeded to turn the front pockets of her jeans inside out. "Nothing there either," she said. She turned around. "And if you want to look at my ass, check out the back pockets. No big wad of bills stuffed in my back pockets. Nothing stuffed down the front either."

"Paul," Rick said, "I think after seeing this, we can safely rule out Miss King as being a suspect in—"

"Not now," Paul said, once again raising his hand to stop Rick in mid-sentence. Paul continued to pay close attention to Anna, who kept her own gaze locked with him. By contrast, Rick appeared uncomfortable. It looked like he didn't want to be here, either.

"Okay," Paul said, his eyes roaming over her, visually assessing her. "You aren't wearing the type of clothing that can successfully hide that much cash, and the money wasn't in your suitcase, backpack, or your purse. My apologies for jumping to conclusions."

Anna didn't answer him. She reached out for her jacket and backpack and began reassembling things. Both security guards looked to Paul for guidance. "Now that we're finished, can I pack up and get the hell out of here?"

"Did you misunderstand what I said earlier about you being tapped for dinner service this week?"

"No, I didn't. Did you misunderstand *me* when I informed you that nobody told me, and I can't do it?"

Paul Westcott smiled. It was the first time Anna had seen the Security Director of Bent Creek Country Club and Resorts smile. "Come on, Anna, let's not be difficult. This really *is* your lucky day. I apologize if Alex didn't properly communicate to you last evening that Chef Munchel personally selected you for service; I will have to deal with his insubordination at another time. Let me be the first to congratulate you and encourage you to stay on board."

"And I told you, I can't stay," Anna began. "I have—"

"Things to do. Yes, you told me that. But if you'll remember from orientation, those who are selected to work the Private Event will receive a ten thousand dollar bonus."

Anna stopped arguing. To do so would only cause further suspicion. Most people would jump at the chance to earn that kind of money for only five days of work. She had to think this through carefully.

"I might further add," Paul Westcott continued, "that working the Private Event, if selected, is a condition of your employment contract with us." Anna let that sink in as the room grew silent. "I'd hate for you to be the first Bent Creek employee Rick has to take to court for violating their contract."

Anna sighed. "Okay, fine. Color me surprised that Chef Munchel selected me."

"Why don't you get your things together? I'll have the concierge in to have your belongings transported back to your room. Then maybe you can get that sleep you wanted."

"Yeah, sure," Anna said. The more she stayed here, the more uneasy she was becoming. She needed to get back to her room to rethink this. Reschedule her plans for the week.

Paul nodded at her, then nodded at Glenn and the other two security guards. "Why don't we let Miss King gather her things? Glenn, will you inform Guests Services to have the concierge bring a luggage cart to the conference room?"

"Yes, Mr. Westcott," Glenn said. He and the other two security guards left the conference room.

"Very good," Paul said. He smiled at Anna. "And let me be the first to congratulate you on being *personally* selected by Chef Munchel to serve our guests at this week's esteemed private event!"

CHAPTER 15

The meeting with Anna King had been wrapped up thirty minutes ago, and Rick Nicholson was still trying to tie things up so he could go upstairs to his room and get some sleep.

He was at the front desk collecting the print-out of a report the front desk supervisor had run for him. Front Desk Services was getting a steady upstream in business as Bent Creek guests began to check out. Rick avoided eye contract with them as he darted in the back to Hal Green's office to collect his report and confer with him, then he was back at the front desk, waiting for another report to print out.

Rick had been up for almost thirty-two hours. Last night had been horrendous. The theft of a quarter of a million dollars in cash was bad enough. Staying on duty to be on hand for the questioning of every Bent Creek service employee, from the wait staff and kitchen staff, to maintenance, guest room services, to those employees that manned the gift shops and entertainment services, had been trying and drawn out. And it wasn't over, either. Security had arranged to question the final wave of exiting employees, with two teams handling the actual questioning and another team conducting a search of their rooms. This tactic had been employed last night with those employees who were working. Rick had been present at Anna King's questioning, and he'd seen the report on the search of her room, which had come back clean. Her questioning had raised no red flags, either.

Rick frowned as he went over last night's events and the encounter with Anna an hour ago. Why Chef Munchel tapped her for dinner service was beyond him, considering this morning's performance. According to her performance reviews, Anna had mixed reviews from the customers; some praised her highly, others went out of their way to make her supervisors know that she was unworthy of future employment at Bent Creek as a waitress. This was common par with somebody with Anna's professional background being out of their element, especially when they were expected to work a service job that catered to people that could be downright snobs. To be fair, every waiter and server on staff received negative comments. It was common when working as a guest services staff member at a place that catered to the rich and pampered.

"Here you go, Mr. Nicholson." Tony Bunn, the lead desk clerk handed the last report to Rick, snapping him out of his thoughts. "Anything else you need?"

"Nope, this will be fine." Rick gave Tony a smile, then headed around the front desk and began to weave his way past the loose throng of guests congregating in the lobby to check out.

As he made his way through the lobby, he nodded at those guests he recognized. Some nodded back. Only one acknowledged him by name. "Good morning, Mr. Nicholson."

"Good morning," Rick said. The guest held out his right hand to be shaken and Rick stopped. He regarded the man as he shook hands with him. His name came to him instantly. "Bob Garrison, right?"

"Yes, sir," Bob said, smiling. Bob Garrison had come to Bent Creek by himself three days ago and had made small talk with Rick on the few occasions they came into contact with each other. He was instantly likeable. Rick believed he was involved in hedge funds. "You'll be around this week, right?"

"Of course," Rick said. "Duty calls. Where you off to this week?"

"I'm staying on," Bob said. "Decided to at the last minute after giving it some thought and really enjoying myself the past few days."

"Really?" This was news to Rick. He had a manifest of all the guest names who had paid for the private event and Garrison's name wasn't on the list. "I didn't know that."

"Chef Munchel invited me a month ago," Bob said, his face open and affable. "He's prepared dinner for several private functions I was involved with and we got to talking. He told me about this event, extended the invitation, and I came out to see for myself."

"You remitted your payment?" Rick asked. Rick knew the price for the private event was very steep—half a million dollars per person.

"I gave Chef Munchel a down payment last month and remitted the rest of it this morning at the front desk," Bob said. "They even gave me a receipt. Do you want to see it?" Bob began to reach into the front pockets of his shorts for his wallet.

"No, that won't be necessary," Rick said, his thoughts racing. He would have to double-check the database once he returned to his office. "I guess I'll be seeing you this week, then."

"It'll be my pleasure," Bob said. He flashed another smile, clapped Rick on the shoulder and left.

Rick Nicholson watched the taller man weave his way through the crowd, heading toward the elevators. Wistfully, he turned and headed toward the corporate offices.

Once back in his office he slumped in his chair and set the reports down on his desk. His mind reran the encounter with Bob Garrison again, then he turned to his computer and called up the database. His fingers flew across the keyboard as he typed in a search query for Bob Garrison.

The only information that came up on Garrison was that he had been a registered guest since Monday, three days ago.

There was no key indicating Garrison was in the system for the private event. Rick double-checked the second database, though, just to be sure. He quickly went through the list of fifteen names of those guests who had paid to be in attendance at the private function. Garrison wasn't listed.

Rick frowned. He picked up the phone and dialed Paul Westcott's extension. Paul picked up on the third ring.

"What's up, Rick?"

"Not much," Rick said. "I just grabbed the last of the reports from guest services and I'm gonna go upstairs to get some sleep. I ran into a guest in the lobby. Guy by the name of Bob Garrison. He said Chef Munchel invited him to the private event a month ago and that he paid up, but he's not in the system. You know anything about that?"

"He should be in one of the reports you printed out at guest services," Paul said. "Look there."

Curious, Rick thumbed through the reports on his desk. He found one titled PRIVATE EVENT GUEST LIST, and quickly ran his index finger down the columns, searching the names carefully. Bob Garrison's name was sandwiched in between Stan Fitzgerald and Clive Henderson, two long-time clients of Bent Creek. "He's there," Rick said, looking down the row to check the dates. "This report says he paid up this morning."

"So we're good then?"

"Why isn't he in the main database?"

"I don't know. But if the man paid for it, and Jim vouched for him, that's good enough for me."

Rick felt like he was on the brink of exploring uncharted territory. He wanted to ask Paul Westcott more about the private event. What exactly did these highest of the high rollers do during the four days they were here at Bent Creek? What was so special about this event that required such layers of security? Rick was on duty last year during the private event, and his initial thoughts regarding this were due to the high-ranking congressman that was in attendance and the Saudi Arabian prince that had flown in for the event. This year the congressman was back, but the prince had elected not to fly in this year. In his place was the CEO of Kaiser Development Systems, a leading Technology company that created and maintained technology for the healthcare industry. All fifteen of the guests stayed in the high-roller suites; they had access to the gym, the pool and sauna, and the grounds during the day. As far as Rick could tell, they received the same level of pampering as the other guests did during the season, with one exception: management turned the other way when it came to drugs and prostitution. Last year, Paul told him that some of these high-rollers brought in very expensive call girls during their four day visit. The call girls usually stayed on grounds, in the private suites, even during dinner. Surely the private event wasn't entirely of the benefit for providing extra discretion for extra-marital liaisons.

"So are we good?" Paul asked.

"I guess so," Rick said.

"Listen, don't worry about it," Paul continued. "I know Mr. Garrison has to be in both systems. That's my rules, and I'll handle that. I just didn't have any advance warning on this one."

"I didn't either."

"I'm going to talk to Wayne about this tonight. I'd like to think he knows about Mr. Garrison. I get the impression he's seen that Jim is...well...not himself lately."

"What's that supposed to mean?"

Paul sighed. "Look, Chef Munchel's a good guy. I've known him for twenty years. Lately, he's been under a lot of strain. His mom died last year, and he's been under a lot of stress with several new restaurant openings and a guest spot on one of those Food Channel shows. He almost cancelled the private event this year, but Wayne insisted. This *is* Wayne's show, after all."

"It is? I didn't know that." Rick's impression was that the private event was partly Chef Munchel's chance to make a lot of extra money by preparing exotic and expensive dishes for his wealthy clients. He'd heard about some of the dishes he prepared at Bent Creek—stuff that sounded mouth-watering and prohibitively expensive, made with ingredients that were imported from countries with unpronounceable names.

"Don't tell anybody I told you that," Paul said. He chuckled slightly. "I wouldn't have found out myself if Wayne hadn't told me a few years ago. This little party is all his. Well, his and the other board members'."

"Interesting." All Rick knew about the Bent Creek board members was from their brief meetings during the season. The board was comprised of six men and two women, all who sat on various corporate boards and were involved in very high-end business dealings around the world. It was all clear to him now: he'd thought this event was Chef Munchel's show, but the chef was working for *them* this week. Rick wondered how big Jim's paycheck was for this private event.

"Get some rest," Paul Westcott said. "I'll see you tonight at the meeting."

"Okay. How's Anna King doing?"

"Sleeping like a baby in her room. As far as I'm concerned, she's clear. My staff is still searching rooms and questioning the remaining employees."

"Okay," Rick said. "Give me an update tonight. I'll talk to you later."

After he hung up, Rick sat at his desk for a moment, looking down at the report. He thought about Chef Jim Munchel's personal invite to Bob Garrison. Surely that invite would have had to be verified by Wayne Sanders and the board members, correct? Maybe not, especially if Wayne and the rest of the board were paying Chef Munchel for his services. It was possible Chef Munchel had come across another high-roller during the off season and simply extended the invitation to him at that time, knowing he was a man who could afford his services. Chef Munchel seemed to be pretty tight with Wayne and the rest of the board, too. He'd probably run the idea of inviting

Bob Garrison by them, and Wayne had simply forgotten to tell Paul Westcott to put Garrison's name in the system.

That's it, he thought. *Don't worry about this shit. You just work here.*

With that thought, Rick Nicholson exited his office and headed up to his room to get some much needed sleep.

CHAPTER 16

Thirteen Months Ago

When the front doorbell rang, Joe was quick on his feet to answer it. He opened the door and beckoned for the young man standing on his front porch to come in.

The young man stepped inside the entry hall tentatively. He was nervous, and with his thin stature, large framed glasses, and mussed-up hair, he gave Joe the impression of the geeky college nerd that is too smart for his own good. "I ran the check like you asked and pulled some numbers," he said after Joe closed the front door.

"Did you find anything?" Joe asked.

The young man reached into his jacket and pulled a sheaf of papers out. He handed the papers to Joe. "That's all of them. Everything I could get."

Joe glanced at the papers and nodded. He placed the sheaf of papers on the credenza in the entry hall and reached into his own pocket for the white business-sized envelope. He handed the envelope to the young man. "Thank you very much."

"No problem," the young man said. He stood there awkwardly, looking nervous as he took a peak at the thick wad of bills in the envelope. He looked back up at Joe. "Listen, um...if you need anything else...you know where to find me?"

"Absolutely." Joe steered the young man to the front door. "You'll be the first person I call."

The young man smiled. He stuffed the envelope in his front jeans pocket and stepped outside, turning briefly to Joe. "That's great! Talk to you later." He turned and started heading down the concrete walkway to a lime-green Toyota Tercel parked at the curb.

Joe Taylor closed and locked the front door. He picked up the sheaf of papers from the credenza on his way to his office off the entry hall and slid behind his desk. One move of the mouse and his iMac woke up from sleep. Joe opened up his FileMaker Pro database, consulted the numbers on the sheaf of papers the young man had sold to him, and began the task of cross-referencing them in his own database.

CHAPTER 17

"So when will you be back?"

Anna thought about what to tell Mark without worrying him. "Today is an off day," she said. She was reclining on the king-sized bed in her room, still dressed in the clothes she'd been wearing earlier that morning except for her shoes, which she'd slipped off immediately upon locking the door. "I'm on breakfast duty tomorrow, then dinner service that night. I'm told that after cleanup five nights from now, I'm good to go."

"You want me to meet you at the drop-off?" Mark asked. All Bent Creek employees had to be ferried to the grounds by a private bus that transported them through five miles of forest to the large gated complex. Those that drove their own vehicles had been allowed to park them in the employee parking lot at the end of the long, dirt road that led to the country club. They'd had to leave the keys to their vehicles with front gate security, who made sure the vehicles were maintained in anticipation of their departure the last day of work. Mark Copper had dropped Anna off in his vehicle on her first day of employment, and had been waiting for her early this morning when she called and told him she was staying on for another five days.

"Yeah, meet me at the front gate," Anna said, her mind racing. "I'll take the first shuttle bus out Wednesday morning." She assumed the same private bus company would be on hand again after the private event.

Mark was silent for a moment. Anna knew he was worried. She also knew he was trying to be careful about what to say. Cellular phone conversations could be easily intercepted. "I know you want me to come home, and I want to be home with you too," she quickly said. "But...well, it's a lot of money, Mark. Not only that, but if I quit now, they can sue me for all of my back wages. It's in the contract I signed."

"What bullshit," Mark muttered.

"The only thing bullshit about it is their failure to give me more advance notice. Like I said, Paul and Rick seemed embarrassed and apologetic after they learned Alex never told me Chef Munchel had tapped me to work dinner service this week. And I'm sorry I gave you the impression I was coming home today. If I'd known about this earlier, I would have told you."

Mark sighed. "Yeah, I get it." She could tell Mark was trying to be subtle about the conversation. "So what now?"

"We get through the next five days and you'll see me Wednesday morning."

"I can't wait." The tone of anticipation in Mark's voice was perfect.

"I can't either. I love you."

"Love you too. Will you call me tomorrow after dinner service?"

"Absolutely."

"Okay. Don't work too hard."

Anna laughed. "I won't."

"And don't let those rich, smug bastards get to you."

"I'll try not to."

"Okay." Beat. "Talk to you later, babe."

"'Bye."

Disconnect.

Anna King sat on her rumpled bed, cell phone in hand, and thought about the five days ahead of her.

It had been hard to get to sleep earlier. Her mind was still a whirling mass of emotions—anger, fear, nervous anticipation.

She'd played through the confrontation with Paul and Rick a thousand times and each playback elicited the strong notion that she had done well under the circumstances.

She'd wound up taking a Nyquil just to get to sleep.

And now it was closing in on five p.m. and she wasn't scheduled to be back on duty until tomorrow morning for breakfast.

Anna looked around her room. It was small, with a king-sized bed, a long dresser with four drawers (now holding her clothing, which she had refilled upon arriving back in her room), a TV that rested on one side, a writing desk and chair, and a nightstand. Her suitcase was resting on the luggage rack, and she'd hung her shirts and blouses up in the closet. She'd set her laptop back up, but had not opened it. She had the rest of the day and the night to kill. A quick trip to the one remaining guest kiosk might yield reading material—the paperback rack was largely confined to *New York Times* Bestsellers, which was mostly fluff, but the latest F. Paul Wilson Repairman Jack novel was in stock. She hadn't read that yet; tonight would provide ample opportunity.

Anna rose from the bed and looked in the mirror over the dresser. Despite the four hours sleep she got, she didn't look bad at all. She grabbed her wallet and room key, then headed out the door to the guest kiosk to snag the paperback.

Brian Gaiman had been working at the bonds that held his wrists in place and was almost free.

Brian didn't know where he was. He had no concept of how much time had passed. Time had meant nothing to him in this place. All he knew was that he'd woken up in a dark room, his back propped up against a steel wall, his wrists bound together behind his back, his ankles lashed together, a cloth gag tied around the back of his head that muffled his screams.

Brian knew screaming was useless anyway. It made his throat hurt. And it made him thirsty.

Wherever he was, it was cold. But despite that, Brian had worked up a sweat.

He used the sweat to his advantage, working his wrists through the nylon rope that held his wrists in place. The abrasions he wrought on the skin of his wrists and forearms dulled to a deep throb as he worked it. The wounds bled, then scabbed over, then were reopened again on each subsequent attempt to work his way out of the bonds. Patience was the key. A little bit of effort each time, then rest. He could feel that his tactic was making progress. Each time he worked the bonds, he felt his wrists slip out of the nylon rope a little bit more.

He was certain Carmen was worried about him. She'd probably reported to management that he was missing. Would management report his disappearance to the police? He'd like to think so. After all, he was in the work-release program. If management thought he skipped out, they'd contact the police and his parole officer. Somebody would be looking for him by now.

While he had no concept of time, he was certain he'd been held captive for more than two days. During that time, somebody had entered the room every so often to give him a sip of water. Brian didn't know who it was, and never got a good look at him—the bright light that stabbed into the room from outside always blinded him, making the man who offered him the water seem dark, his features hidden by the shadow of his bulk. The first time the man had stepped in to give him water, Brian had thought he was coming to kill him. When he realized what was happening, he'd tried communicating to his captor by talking through his gag. The man had ignored him, insisting Brian take a few sips of water. Then, he left.

By Brian's count, the man had come three times. Between each visit, Brian would rest for a bit, then work at freeing his wrists. Shortly after the second visit, Brian immediately guessed the man was coming every eighteen hours or so. Which meant he'd been held captive around three days.

Gritting his teeth with the pain and exertion, Brian moved his wrists in a counter-clockwise motion. He could feel the fibers of the nylon rope grinding against the recently opened wounds in his wrist as he worked them, feeling them slip through a little more now. His body was completely oiled in sweat. Brian had been working himself up into a sweat the last eight hours. Despite the coldness of the room, he'd worked up a sweat by constantly moving—rocking back and forth, flexing the muscles of his arms and legs. Despite his limited means of movement, his efforts eventually paid off. Using the sweat that beaded along his arms and wrists, he used it to lubricate the bonds, to work them over and over, using the blood that ran down his wrists to drip on the floor to further lubricate the skin so he could slip his wrists through the bonds a little more each time as the pain allowed. Time sped by as he concentrated on freeing himself—his entire focus was centered on freeing his wrists. Once his wrists were free, he could untie the ropes that bound his ankles and get out of here.

The wounds in his wrists had been opened and reopened half a dozen times during his efforts to free himself. He was just thinking that he would probably be at this for another day when he received an unexpected surprise. As his right wrist made one of its umpteenth counter-clockwise movements, he felt the nylon rope slip over his thumb, freeing most of his hand.

His heart almost stopped in his sudden surprise. He moved his right thumb, feeling elated at its new-found mobility. An excited whine of glee escaped his throat, muffled by the gag.

With this new-found excitement, he pulled his hand back. His knuckles met resistance, but with some more wriggling motions, he was able to slip his fingers through perfectly.

With racing heart, he had his right hand out and flexed his fingers. They tingled as the circulation entered and adrenaline flowed. He took a deep breath as he used the fingers of his right hand to pick at and hold the bonds that held his left wrist. He knew the patterns of the rope his captor used to tie him—despite his right hand being free, both arms were still tied behind his back, lashed by a series of intricate knots of rope around his abdomen. Brian concentrated, grasping the complexity of the knots, and within ten minutes his left wrist was free. Two minutes later his arms were free, and he was rotating them, getting the circulation flowing into both limbs.

His eyes darted around the dark room. All his senses seemed to be on high alert, carefully attuned to everything. He could smell dampness and sweat, along with the acidic scent of his urine. The only sound was his harsh breathing—there was no sound coming from outside his prison.

Brian reached up and untied the cloth gag. Once he was ungagged, he took in a great lungful of air and silently wept. *I'm free, I'm getting out of here...*

But he couldn't count on victory yet. He still had to get his ankles free, and then—

Brian leaned forward and began picking at the bonds that lashed his ankles together. His fingers flew across the knots in the darkness, and he silently thanked God that his captor used the same knots on his ankles. He knew their familiar patterns now, and within five minutes the ropes lay on the floor and he was rubbing his ankles and legs, trying to restore better circulation into them.

His legs tingled with numbness, and for a moment Brian didn't think they'd wake up fully. As he sat on the floor, in a position more relaxing than the one he'd been stuck in for the last three days, he had a sickening thought—suppose his captor returned unexpectedly to deliver his sips of water? When was the last time he was here? Brian couldn't remember. In his excitement, he wasn't sure if his captor was last here yesterday or eight hours ago. And the way time seemed so elastic, it was hard to tell if an hour had passed or a day. Time was irrelevant here.

Don't worry about it, he thought. *If he comes, he comes. Deal with it then. Right now, I need to get my legs in working order and get the hell out of here.*

Brian re-shifted his body so that he was on all fours. A sensation of warmth seemed to spread along his lower body and legs. Brian recognized the feeling as renewed strength and sensation. He moved each leg, bending it at the knee, flexing it. He did this with the right leg, then the left, rotating his ankles as well, all in an attempt to restore feeling in his legs. As feeling and strength returned, his mind registered that the floor was cold steel as well. He needed his legs to be able to withstand his weight, needed them in good working order in case he needed to sprint. Or run.

He reached out with his right hand, groping blindly. The door to his prison was just ahead of him. His fingers brushed it—cold steel—and he crawled forward, moving his hand along the door, the wall, feeling his way around. Now that he had a sense of where he was, and using the wall as a guide, he slowly rose to his feet, making sure his left hand was supporting his weight.

He stood there for a moment, holding his breath. Then, he stepped away from the wall.

And did not fall.

Is the door locked? he thought. *Of course it is. It has to be.*

Tentatively, he reached out and groped for the door handle. His fingers grasped it, not recognizing it as a normal door handle. Curious, he leaned forward, pressing his right ear against the steel door and listened.

There were no sounds from outside. No sense of movement.

Brian listened for several minutes. When he was pretty sure there was nobody outside, he moved the latch on the inside of the door, fully expecting it to be locked from the outside.

There was a whispered click and the door eased open.

Heart pounding, Brian peered outside.

The area outside was dark, but not the way it had been in his prison. Brian waited for his vision to adjust to the slight variation, then he eased the door open more, cautiously stepping out. He slipped to the side of the door and eased it shut, making sure it closed softly to not attract unwanted attention.

Then he stood with his back against the wall, his mind racing, wondering what to do next.

I don't even know where I am, Brian thought. He looked around, craning his head up at the ceiling. He was in a thirty by forty foot room with bare concrete walls. To his left was the door that led to his temporary prison. As he looked at it and the other door next to it, he realized where he'd been kept—inside a large, metal freezer.

Why was I kept in a freezer? Where the hell am I?

As Brian stood there contemplating this, his mind raced back. He remembered walking to the utility shed on the northwest side of the Bent Creek grounds on the morning he was abducted. He had a faint memory of being inside the utility shed, then of being behind it because he'd heard something back there. After that, his next memory was of being tied up, the smell of gasoline very heavy in the air, and the sense of movement. He had the fleeting thought that he was in the trunk of a car. He felt nauseous, then he'd blacked out. His next memory was of coming to consciousness tied up on the floor of an unknown prison that he knew now was a large walk-in freezer.

Brian looked at the two walk-in freezers. The one that sat next to his beckoned him. Was there another captive in there, also tied up? Brian stood there for a moment, unsure of what to do. Then he reacted quickly. He reached out, grasped the metal handle of the second freezer's door, and pulled it open.

Cold air wafted out at him. The hum of the freezer was very audible, and Brian's first thought was, *this one is turned on. It's in use. Thank God the one I was in was either turned off or broken or I would have frozen to death.* He took a step inside then stopped suddenly, his heart lodged in his throat at what he was seeing.

The freezer was lined with metal shelves two and three feet

deep. Stacked on all the shelves were human body parts. Severed arms and legs, torsos. The severed head of a man stared at him from the shelf to his right, his eyes half-lidded, mouth slightly open. He recognized this man. He didn't know his name, but Brian had seen him around the Bent Creek grounds. He was an office worker of some sort, worked in the administrative area; he was a big guy, a fat guy, to be more accurate. And here he was, his severed head sitting on the metal shelf to his right, the rest of him probably among the other severed body parts on the shelves.

Brian's eyes darted around the freezer, his blood freezing in his veins at the sight, then he took a step back and shut the freezer door a little harder than he intended. There was a more audible clang as the freezer door slammed shut.

Holyshitwhatthefuck?

Instinct propelled him to flee and he took three running steps toward the door he saw in the corner of the room. He stopped at the door and forced himself to stay calm. *Take this slowly*, he thought. *Be careful.*

Brian put his ear to the door and listened.

Silence.

He looked back at the freezers. A third door sat catty-corner from the freezers, one he hadn't noticed before. Where did that one lead to?

Brian crossed the room slowly. He stopped at the door and paused, holding his breath. He stood there, listening for any sound, but could hear nothing.

Which door do I choose?

Brian glanced around the room quickly. The twin freezers were stacked against the far wall. A large stainless steel table sat opposite the freezer. There were dark stains on the table and along the floor. Metal shelving units ran along the opposite wall. The shelves were bare. A long-handled mop and a bucket sat in the corner.

Heart pounding, Brian contemplated his options. Surely

one of the doors had to lead somewhere and would get him out of here. But which one?

Brian turned around and surveyed the room. The placement of the steel table and the freezers suggested that the door he was at might lead to another room. But the other door, the first door he saw upon freeing himself and exiting the freezer—

He had the strong feeling that door opened to the outside.

The question was, would anybody be waiting out there when he emerged?

Brian walked back across the room and stopped at the door. He stood there for two minutes, breathing slowly and silently, straining to listen for any sound.

Nothing.

He reached out and grasped the door handle. His mind went back to his confinement, trying to remember key details of when his captor visited him. He didn't remember hearing another door open. He just remembered the door to his freezer opening and the man suddenly being there, offering him a sip of water from a plastic bottle. There was no telling from which door the man entered and exited the room.

Brian took a deep breath, weighing his options. Satisfied he was making the right choice, he slowly turned the knob, expecting it to be locked.

The knob turned and he pushed the door open slowly.

Sunlight streamed into the room. Brian winced against the sudden light and closed the door quickly, breathing heavily. His heart pounded. It was still daylight outside, but it also appeared that it was late afternoon. Should he wait a while longer for the sun to go down? No. He couldn't afford the luxury. He had to get out of here *now*!

Gritting his teeth, Brian cracked the door open again. His eyes closed in reaction to the light and he turned his face away. The door was only open a crack, surely not enough to attract unwanted attention from outside, but it was enough to tell him that beyond the doorway lay grass.

Brian looked at the grass for a moment, letting his vision adjust. His body was tense, and any minute now he half-expected his captor to come slamming through, pushing him back to the floor. Brian was tense, primed for a fight, but it never happened. If anybody was outside the building, they did not notice the door was open a crack. And as Brian's vision slowly adjusted, he moved his eyes up and took in the scene outside.

The doorway opened up to a large grassy area. Beyond that lay thick woods. There was no sign of anybody.

Brian eased the door open wider and looked around. By craning his head to the right, he saw that the building ended about twenty feet away. There was a small gravel parking lot. The lot was empty.

The door was open almost six inches and Brian thought, *fuck it*, and opened it even wider, slipping outside. He eased the door shut and stood with his back against the wall, trying to calm his racing heart down.

I made it! I got out!

Okay, first things first. Get the fuck away from here. Dart into the woods, seek cover. Hide!

Brian looked to the right. He had a better view of the lot now. It was empty. Beyond the lot was a series of buildings. He frowned. The buildings looked very much like the style and structure of some of the Bent Creek buildings.

Where the fuck am I?

Who cares? Just get the fuck out of here!

And with that, Brian heeded his own advice. He took a glance to his left, saw nothing but woods and green grass, the building continuing on his left, the windows appearing dark and shaded, and he fled. He ran away from the wall and made a beeline for the woods, darting between the trees and putting them between himself and the blue building behind him.

CHAPTER 18

Twelve Months Ago

He was on the phone with Nina, letting her verbally abuse him.

If it made her feel better, so be it.

"You're a fucking bastard," she said, her words slurring. "You're a fucking *douchebag*! This is all your fault! Everything that has happened is *all* your *fault*!"

"Okay," Joe said. He was sitting at his end of the sofa. Funny how he never got around to sitting on her end of the sofa after she left. Joe had always loved sitting on the far right side of the sofa, but Nina had claimed that spot as hers years ago. Joe didn't care either way—he'd take the far left side, no problem. But he did love the right side, since the angle from that position was better when he was watching TV. He'd always sat on Nina's side of the sofa when she wasn't home, and he thought he would claim that spot as his own when she'd finally packed her bags and moved out of the house, but he hadn't. He'd grown so used to his spot on the left side, that he gravitated to it every afternoon after work. He'd become so used to it, that he moved the phone and the television and DVR remote controls to the end table on the left side of the sofa.

"What the hell did you think would happen when you resisted her?" Nina continued. Judging by the sound of it, Nina had been drinking steadily all morning. It seemed that's all

Nina did these days was drink. She'd taken the Newport Beach house and the dogs—pure bred Shih Tzus—as part of the divorce settlement, and from what Joe could tell from the few times he'd seen her, she was living the perfect Real Housewives of Orange County lifestyle. "You knew she would do what she always does—fight you. That's what Carla does. When she wants something and we tell her no, she fights us."

"I know that," Joe said. "And I was trying to reason with her. I showed her the material on *Al Azif* and the dangers involved—"

"You drove her right *into* danger!" Nina sputtered. "You drove her *away* and *now* look! She's *gone*!" There was the faint sound of liquid gurgling in a bottle. He wondered if Nina was back to swigging The Macallan straight from the bottle. "Some father you are. *Asshole* father is more like it."

"If it feels good to verbally abuse and demean me, you go ahead."

"It *does* make me feel good, you cheap prick." Nina's voice was gritty and for a moment it lost its slur. "I didn't like you when we split up, but now I fucking *hate* you for what you did to our daughter."

"I didn't do anything to Carla."

"*You drove her away*!" Nina roared. Joe winced slightly and pulled back from the receiver. "You drove her away and now she's *gone*! Nobody has seen her or heard from her in *a year*! What the *fuck* do you mean you didn't do anything! You did *plenty*!"

Joe sighed. A throb of pain was starting between his eyes. He couldn't lose it on Nina now. She had every right to feel this way. To tell her she was directing her anger in the wrong direction would be futile. In her mind, Joe was the cause of all this. If he'd not fought Carla so much on the job offer from *Al Azif*, she'd be okay in Nina's mind. And maybe she would be. But Joe knew the risks were much greater for a young twenty-something Caucasian American woman to be kidnapped and sold into white slavery in an Arab nation than it was for the same thing to happen in the U.S. He was still convinced Carla had pulled up stakes to escape her creditors in Wyoming. He wouldn't put it past her to lie low, live and work under the radar. She'd done it during her first year of college—lived rent free in a nicely furnished apartment and worked a stand at the local flea market pulling in a couple thousand a month, all under the table. He'd warned her about the consequences, told her what to look for when it came to IRS meddling, and she'd skated by that one. He wondered if she'd used her knowledge and resources to go underground again, to escape the credit card companies and her landlords. Dean Campbell would find out soon enough.

"I suppose I did," Joe said. "And I'm sorry. I have somebody looking for Carla now, and we're getting very close to—"

"You said that last week!" Carla blurted. "You say that *every* week. I don't even think you believe she's going to be found."

"That's not true," Joe began. "I've been very—"

"You don't know shit!" Another gurgle of the bottle. When Nina came back on, her voice was cracking. It sounded like she was crying. "She's gone and there's nothing you can do. She's probably...oh God, she's probably...some pervert probably took her...killed her...and now she's lying buried somewhere and we'll never find her."

"That's not true!" Joe said. He felt his throat tightening up.

"How do you know?"

"We can't resort to giving up," Joe said. "I'm doing everything in my power to find her and bring her home."

"Well, you should have left it alone in the first place. If you hadn't been such a fucking bastard about her job offer in Saudi Arabia with those fucking sand niggers, she wouldn't be—"

Joe calmly hung up the phone.

He sat on the edge of the sofa, staring at the blank TV screen, waiting for his anger and anxiety to pass. He closed his eyes for a moment and breathed slowly, clearing his mind, trying to settle himself.

The phone never rang once while he was trying to center himself.

When he felt better, he opened his eyes. The afternoon sun cast long shadows on the hardwood floor. Joe took a breath, letting the stillness of the house comfort him. Then he rose to his feet and headed to the kitchen to see what he could prepare himself for dinner.

CHAPTER 19

They were sitting in Paul Westcott's office talking about the brazen thefts with one of the members of the board, Emily Wharton, and Rick couldn't help but think things were going to get worse.

Emily had taken it upon herself to venture down to the corporate offices to have a chat with the head of security. Rick had never dealt with her personally, but he saw her at the board meetings. She gave him the impression that she was very no-nonsense, an alpha-female in a pack of high-level suits that was largely comprised of alpha males. The only other female board member, Gail Scott, was practically invisible during the meetings. Where Emily probed the executive staff members with insightful questions during the meetings, Gail remained silent and took notes, absorbing everything, watching, observing. Where Emily grew stony and became tenacious, Gail became agreeable and soothing. They played a fair good-cop/bad cop.

Today was the first time Rick felt Emily was paying attention to him. She kept a watchful emerald gaze on him and Paul as the Head of Security brought her up to date on the thefts. Rick had downed a can of Red Bull and a quart of coffee this morning and was still feeling drowsy. The scrutiny he felt from Emily's gaze wasn't helping.

"Rick and I have worked tirelessly with our staff to uncover who might be responsible for these thefts," Paul said. "We've searched all the guest rooms, as well as the staff living quarters, and haven't found anything incriminating. We're meeting today with our departments heads to—"

"Have your department heads' living quarters been searched?" Emily asked.

"No," Paul said, and Rick detected that the question had caught him off guard. "Not yet. We're going to—"

"Have the department heads been questioned?"

Another stumbling block. "Ah, no, but like I said, we're going to—"

"If the lower-level staff's living quarters have been searched and nothing was found, they've been questioned and you've detected nothing suspicious in their answers, you need to look at your direct reports." Emily's tone was direct, matter-of-fact. *You will do this, or else.*

"I understand, Ms. Wharton," Paul said. Rick could tell that Paul was putting on his best air of diplomacy with Emily. He had no idea what company she ran in the outside world, but she carried herself with the air of a powerful woman who could bust your balls simply by looking at you. Rick felt emasculated being in the same room with her. "To be truthful, it is my top priority to recover the missing money. I have every reason to believe these thefts have been carried out by somebody on staff. Perhaps even more than one staff member."

"If that's the case, why have most of the staff been let go?" Emily asked.

"Legally, we couldn't hold them. You know that."

Emily nodded. "True." Her gaze swept to Rick. "What do you think, Mr. Nicholson?"

With the spotlight turned on him, Rick instantly perked up. "It's obviously a staff member," Rick echoed Paul's theory. "My guess is it's somebody from housekeeping."

Emily regarded them with a look that seemed to say, *do you think I'm stupid? The wait staff? Really? And why would you think that*?

"They have access to all the rooms," Paul said, as if he were answering the question she seemed to be silently asking with her gaze. "One of the housekeeper's, Carmen Hernandez, struck up an affair with a maintenance worker named Brian Gaiman, who was part of the work-release program."

"Carmen even came to my office to report him missing," Rick said, trying to inject some confidence in his tone and pose. "I admit, she sounded very convincing. We'd already had the first theft when Brian went missing. He became our chief suspect immediately."

"And you've searched their rooms?" Emily asked.

"Yes," Paul said. Rick nodded.

"And?"

"We didn't find anything in either room."

"Is Carmen Hernandez still employed with us?"

"Yes."

"Have her activities been monitored since Brian's disappearance?"

"Most certainly," Paul said. "We've traced calls she's made and received from her room. She hasn't been in contact with Gaiman at all since he disappeared."

"Hmmm." Emily appeared to think about this. "According to the report I read this morning, neither Mr. Gaiman nor Ms. Hernandez have the background that suggests they're capable of such brazen thefts. In fact, Ms. Hernandez has no criminal record whatsoever, and she passed our entrance polygraph exam with flying colors."

"Polygraph tests can be fooled," Paul stated.

"True. But what about their technical background? Neither seems to possess any."

Paul frowned. "Technical background?"

"I'm referring specifically to the theft from Carl White's bank account," Emily said. Sitting across from him in her crisp, beige business attire, Emily looked more like a prosecutor than a rich businesswoman. "It takes somebody with a deep knowledge of network security and computer hacking to be able to penetrate a financial system's database and move the funds from one account into another one, then erase all signs of the transaction, which is obviously the case there. Do you agree?"

Rick glanced at Paul. They'd talked about this briefly. The financial institution that Carl banked with reported no logs in their system that recorded any network breach. The firm's network security chief was currently performing an audit on their system for the time-line in question, trying to find where a computer hacker might have breached the system. If they could find anything, even a blip of an IP address—

"Well?" Emily bore the look of impatience. Dealing with the commoners.

"I agree that Gaiman and Hernandez do not seem likely candidates for the theft of Mr. White's funds," Paul said.

"So where does that lead us?" Emily asked. She was directing this question as much to Rick as she was to Paul. "If Gaiman and Hernandez are involved at some level, we'll find them. We have resources in place to locate them. I believe your next step is to question your direct reports and have a search conducted of their living quarters."

Would that include us? Rick thought.

Emily turned to Rick, as if sensing he had something on his mind. "Anything you'd like to share, Mr. Nicholson?"

Rick recovered quickly. "I was just thinking that if all the employee's rooms were searched and they were questioned by Paul's team, what about the thought of a fellow guest who bore a grudge against the victims?"

Emily looked like she hadn't considered that option. Her features were poker-face. "Have our guests been quarrelling? Is there anything you might have heard during the season to suggest this?"

Rick shrugged and looked at Paul. "He has a point," Paul said to Emily. "For the most part, our direct reports should be considered suspects just as much as the lower-level staff. But we never once considered the *guests* suspects. There's really no reason to."

Emily applauded lightly, the tone of it sarcastic and mocking. "Brilliant! A brilliant deduction, Watson! In fact, it is *so* brilliant, that any student of criminology will look at it and instantly deduce the same thing! Why would a guest at a vacation resort with a net worth of twenty million dollars resort to stealing a combined total of two million dollars from three different guests over the course of his or her time with us? It makes no sense! But an *employee*? Well, why *not* an employee!"

"Look, I understand your concerns," Paul said.

"Do you? I don't think you do, Mr. Westcott. In fact, it seems to me that your refusal to not even consider the questioning of your direct reports suggests you're trying to protect somebody."

Rick cut in before the exchange could escalate. "There's a guest here named Shane Daniels. He and his wife, Jackie, have ruffled quite a few feathers with other guests."

Emily dismissed this with an impatient wave of her hand. "Shane Daniels. He's no more capable of a theft this grand than finding his own asshole with a flashlight."

"Maybe not Shane, but Jackie used to be the Chief Technology Officer at Motorola," Rick continued. "In fact, her specialties were network security and financial databases."

This news was met with stunned silence. Emily and Paul regarded Rick with a sense of disbelief, as if this information was completely new to them. Paul appeared to be on the cusp of asking, *how do you know this?,* when Rick beat him to it. "Jackie told me this one night," he said quickly. "Bragged about it, actually. Both of them brag a *lot.* It's their very bragging to the staff and to the other guests that have made them very unlikable among staff and other guests."

For a moment, Rick wasn't sure if Emily Wharton was going to buy this. She sat in her chair, body posture straight. If she was considering this information, it didn't register; that's how poker-faced she was. "Tell me more," she asked Rick.

Rick settled back in his seat, both as a way of assuming a more comfortable position and as a way to quickly gather his thoughts. He decided to start at the beginning, with his first season at Bent Creek. "Last year, Shane and Jackie made enemies with another couple," Rick began, the memory spilling out all at once. "A computer software tycoon and his wife. I'm not sure what you know of Shane and Jackie's background—"

"I know enough of it," Emily said.

Rick nodded. "Then you know Shane made his money through corporate sabotage."

Emily frowned. "Corporate sabotage? Explain."

"His words, not mine," Rick said, then quickly outlined a conversation he overheard in the lounge between Shane Daniels and the aforementioned software tycoon last year. Shane had been drunk, and aside from needling the software tycoon about his "piss-poor product that couldn't perform worth a shit", he'd bragged to the same tycoon that he'd risen to stature in his company—a global metal product corporation—through ass-kissing and sabotaging the work of his corporate rivals. "He'd take on projects he wasn't suited for, then carefully lay explosive trip mines that would cause either his fellow team members or those who were ahead of him on the corporate ladder to trip over and back fire on them, enabling him to either fix things and save the company, or would make them look bad so he could come in later and offer solutions. Because he was already tight with the people he was trying to impress, Shane's tactic worked. He pulled the same strings for Jackie. Ever since he became CEO of MetalWorks, he's pulled in over ten million in salary, bonuses, and he's sold his stock options prior to the company's nose dive."

Emily took this news with great interest. She nodded. "I see. Tell me about his argument with this software tycoon. Would that be Gilbert Manning?"

"Yes." Gilbert Manning was the owner and CEO of Manning Software, which was a financial services company. "Manning's combined net worth is around half a billion. He acquired this money quite quickly, I might add. Shane Daniels, on the other hand, has a net worth of around twenty million. Shane made it very clear to Manning that his number one goal in life was to be a billionaire and that he was going to do anything and everything to obtain that goal. He pretty much told Manning that the only reason he came to Bent Creek was to hobnob with the rich and successful so that some of their riches would rub off on him."

"I see," Emily Wharton said. Her mood seemed to darken.

"This season, Shane and Jackie were more abusive and degrading to my staff members than usual," Rick continued. "They were also more obnoxious with the other guests. They acted like they were more privileged, as if they deserved to be here more than them. Jackie got into a heated verbal argument with Parker Goode early on in their stay, and their altercation with Carl White came a few days before the theft of funds from his account."

"Did either Mr. Goode or Mr. White ever file a formal complaint against Shane and Jackie?" Emily asked.

"No," Paul confirmed. "But other guests did."

"So...?" Emily made a *is that the only evidence you've got?* gesture with her hands. "If you're trying to convince me that Shane and Jackie are involved in these thefts, you need to do better than that. They've always been good clients."

Rick was about to try another tactic when Paul jumped in. "Last season, a young woman filed a complaint with me against Jackie. She said Ms. Fox made unwanted sexual advances to her." Paul fixed Emily with a serious look that was uncompromising. "I interviewed her. She was very disturbed by it. It was..." Rick watched the exchange between Paul and Emily, his breath held as the Chief of Security's features became grim, his eyes locked with Emily's. "...it was disturbing to the point that if Jackie had tried something like this outside, she'd be in very, *very* big trouble. If you know what I mean." Paul's gaze remained locked with Emily's.

"Yes, I think I know what you mean," Emily said. Her once hard, poker features seemed to slacken, as if she'd just received a bad scare. She quickly recovered and nodded to Paul in understanding. Paul nodded back. Rick remained slouched back in his seat, pretending to wait for the exchange to end but giving it rapt attention. *If I were the paranoid type, I'd think they were having a subliminal conversation*, he thought. *Something about the way Paul looked at Emily when he related Jackie's sexual advance to the female employee from last year, the way he said it could have gotten her into very big trouble on the outside...and Emily getting the message. What the hell did* that *mean*?

As quickly as Emily appeared to be shocked, she recovered, regaining her composure. She turned her attention to Rick, once again no-nonsense and direct. "Do you think it's possible for Shane and Jackie to have committed these crimes?"

"I think it's possible one of them could have persuaded a housekeeping staff member to grant them access to the rooms in question," Rick said. "It wouldn't have taken much. A couple thousand dollars in cash to the housekeeping staff is like winning the lottery to them. The Daniels couple were sociable enough with much of the guests and staff that both of them, working together, could have conspired to steal the money from Mr. Goode and the Westlake's for the purposes of embarrassing them and wounding their egos, not for their own personal financial gain."

"The Westlake's had trouble with Shane and Jackie, too?"

Paul nodded. "Yes, several. They made it a point to avoid the restaurant, even though they've professed to love Chef Munchel's food. They took most of their meals at the Roadhouse and other restaurants in Green River." Green River was the closest town to Bent Creek, and despite a population of around twelve thousand, boasted a number of good dining spots.

Emily nodded. "Okay. What about the theft of the money from Mr. White's account?"

Rick shrugged. "Jackie has the technical resources. She either did it herself, or had somebody do it for her. Of course, I can't prove it, but of the three victims, Carl White openly despised them and was causing them trouble with management, namely me." Rick offered Emily a pensive smile. "He was lodging complaints against them from his first night with us, nearly two weeks ago. Some of Paul's security staff had to intervene a few times in the lounge and the restaurant when their arguments went from heated to on the verge of full-fledged blows."

Emily turned to Paul. "Have they checked out yet this morning?"

"As of twenty minutes ago, they haven't." Paul moved toward his desk and accessed his computer. His fingers flew across the keyboard as he accessed the guest check-in database. "The system shows they haven't checked out yet. They're probably still sleeping off last night's big party."

"Have Shane brought in for questioning, but be careful with him. I want to explore this as quietly and as discreetly as possible."

"What about Jackie?" Rick asked.

"I think it would be best to have them questioned separately," Emily said. "First Shane, then Jackie. Don't let either of them know they're under suspicion. Is this more or less standard security protocol?"

"It is," Paul said. He reached across the desk and picked up his phone. "Let me see what I can do." He dialed an extension, waited a moment and then, with his eyes on Emily, said, "Glenn, I've got an assignment for you. Locate Mr. Shane Daniels and escort him to the West Conference room. Be as discreet as possible, and if Jackie is with him, don't give her cause for worry. I don't want either of them to think they're in trouble." Paul was silent as Glenn said something. "Yes, have Jackie watched while Shane is in our custody. Report back to me if she returns to her room, or does anything suspicious." Beat. "That's right, don't make it an issue. If you need to do some stroking of their egos, do it. There'll be a giant bonus for you at the end of all this. I'll buy you buckets of beer and all the wings you can eat."

Rick smiled at this as he heard Glenn's voice come in over the line, tinny in its sound, but ultimately happy. "Thanks a lot, Glenn," Paul said. His eyes met Emily's and he nodded. "I owe you one." Paul hung up. He regarded Emily and Rick from across his expansive, but cluttered, oak desk. "Glenn and Pete Atkins will bring Shane. Glenn said he'll have Scott Baker watch Jackie. When we're finished questioning Shane, I'll have Scott escort Jackie back here and, depending on how I feel about Shane's answers to my questions, I'll either have him transferred to an empty office and have somebody watch over him, or I'll have him escorted back to his room through another route so they don't cross paths with each other."

Emily Wharton rose to her feet. She smoothed her skirt down. "Excellent. I'll be waiting for your call. Two hours?"

"Two hours should give me enough time." Paul rose to his feet as well. "Final checkout isn't until four and it's barely noon now. We have plenty of time."

Rick got to his feet as Paul saw Emily out the door. No sooner had she left than Paul sighed. He looked like he was relieved to be out of Emily's presence. "Man, am I glad *that's* over with."

"Tell me about it," Rick said. As tired as he was, Rick couldn't help but feel on edge.

Paul shook his head as he moved back behind his desk. "Wharton's always been a ball breaker, but she's smart as a whip. Sometimes I think *she* runs things around here instead of Wayne."

"I can see how it would seem that way," Rick said. He stood by the door, uncertain of where things were going to go now. He'd originally come to Paul's office to tell him he was taking the day off. He was literally jumping out of his skin in anticipation. If he could get off the grounds, get back home and do what he had to do and see his mother, he could return to Bent Creek in record time for the private event tomorrow night.

"Listen, Paul," Rick began. "I've been trying to find Wayne all morning and I understand he's out of commission until tomorrow night. Do you have any way of getting in touch with him?"

Paul looked at Rick as he moved a file out from under a sheaf of papers. "No, I don't. Why?"

"I need to talk to him about taking a day off. Just the rest of the day and tomorrow. I'd be back by tomorrow night."

"I think Wayne would be just fine with that," Paul said. He was smiling at Rick, his gray eyes containing a twinkle of knowledge. "In fact, Wayne just gave me the go-ahead to offer you a permanent position with the firm."

The news came as a surprised shock to Rick. For a brief moment, it felt like he'd had the wind knocked out of him. He blinked. "Are you serious?" He couldn't think of anything to say, he was so blindsided by the news.

"Yes," Paul said. His smile was broad, genuine. "And may I be the first to congratulate you. I assume you'll accept the position, correct? I mean, you've expressed more than enough interest in becoming a full-time permanent employee, and you've proven to be an exceptional leader. We could certainly use you."

The surprise and shock enveloped Rick like a warm blanket. Everything he'd been working for, everything he'd been striving to achieve since discovering his love and talent for running a business, was finally paying off. "Yes," he said, the words coming out in a rush. "Yes, of course I'll accept. Thank you!" He reached across the desk and took Paul's hand in a vigorous handshake.

"No, thank *you*, Rick," Paul said, his grip firm and strong. "You've earned it."

A thousand thoughts were racing through Rick's mind. What to do; how to reorganize his life, his savings, his financial and personal goals. What he could do to help his mother. "My mother," Rick said, her image coming and the reason for originally seeking Paul out coming to mind. He looked at Paul. "I told you she's got cancer, right?"

Paul nodded. "Yes, you did. How's she doing?"

"As well as she could be. The reason I wanted to bug out for a day is to drive down to Boulder to see her. Make sure things are okay at home."

"It's okay with me," Paul said. "To tell you the truth, trying to get an appointment with Wayne between now and tomorrow night is going to be next to impossible due to the meetings the board members are having and all the preparations they're doing for tomorrow's event, but what Wayne doesn't know won't hurt him."

"Thanks, Paul. I really appreciate this."

"I'll be fine running things until tomorrow night. Go on, do what you need to do." Paul ushered him out the door. Rick thanked him again and left the office.

He stood outside Paul Westcott's office, giddy with relief and excitement. No need to pack a bag. He had his wallet and keys. All he had to do was head out to the employee parking lot, get in his car, and get going.

As Rick left the corporate area and made his way through the grounds and to the employee parking lot, he tried to subdue his sense of eagerness, trying not to appear that he was giddy with excitement.

No sooner was Rick out the door than Paul was back at his desk, calling Glenn on his cell phone. He kept an eye on the door to his office, his ears attuned to any sound from outside in case Rick decided to come back, but he was lucky. He heard Rick move down the hall and out the corporate area just as Glenn picked up. "What's up, Paul?"

"Change of plans," Paul said. "You locate Shane and Jackie yet?"

"Doug and I are enroute to their suite now."

"Get Mike in on this too," Paul said. "And listen to me carefully..."

CHAPTER 2

Eleven Months Ago

Joe Taylor was in Casper, Wyoming, at the County Deeds office at City Hall, doing some research.

He'd flown to Casper the day before and stayed at the Courtyard Marriot. After dinner, he'd done some research in his hotel room utilizing the material Dean Campbell had found. It hadn't taken much to see the pattern in the reports Dean had submitted to him, and after getting all his notes in order, he'd called it a night and gone to bed.

This morning, after coffee and room-service breakfast, he'd showered, gotten dressed, and drove his rental car to City Hall. Once there, he asked the front desk clerk if he could have access to the County Deeds records for some real-estate research. The clerk, a young Native American woman, directed him to the County Deeds office and introduced him to the clerk who manned it, a bored-looking older man named Roy Jenkins.

"County records for the time periods you're interested in are stored along that far wall." Jenkins indicated the area with a sweep of his arm. His craggy face was weather-beaten, giving him a tired appearance. He was wearing tan slacks and a white button-down shirt. Stick him in a cowboy outfit and he'd fit right in with the Old West stereotype. "Photocopying machine is in the little cubicle by my desk. Need anything, just ask."

Joe Taylor thanked him, then got to work.

Riffling through the records hadn't been as tiresome or as tedious as he thought. It took fifteen minutes of diligent searching to find what he was looking for. When he did, he pulled out the deed in question and looked at it, frowning. He consulted his notes, checked a few things off, jotted down some other notes, then placed the notepad in his back jeans pocket along with the pen. He fingered the deed, debating on if he wanted the photocopy. He glanced at Jenkins reclining behind his desk, reading a magazine. The cubicle that contained the photocopying machine was out of sight's way. The caretaker would know he was making a photocopy and nothing more. Joe closed the drawer where he'd found the deed and headed to the cubicle, the deed clenched in his right hand.

Five minutes later, with a copy of the deed in his briefcase and the original back in the drawer where he'd found it, Joe Taylor headed back to his hotel room, his mind racing, feeling a sense of dread.

CHAPTER 21

Shane Daniels' head hurt.

He stood at his bed eyeing the half-packed suitcase, feeling unmotivated. Jackie's crap was still all over the place. The room looked like her closet had exploded. Why did women insist on taking their entire wardrobe with them on vacation? Shane never understood that particular aspect of the female animal. Actually, there wasn't much of anything he understood about women except they liked clothes and shoes the way he liked football, money, and pussy. And they were goddamn moody when it was their time of the month.

Jackie's time of the month had come three days ago, and she'd become intolerable. Unfortunately, because she never self-medicated when she was on her period, she wouldn't leave him alone, either, which meant Shane had to drink that much more just to tune her bullshit out. Now he was feeling the effects of it. Last night's shindig at the Bent Creek lounge had been a rip-roaring success. That Parker Goode asshole had been there, eyeing him from the bar like he was ready to start something, but Shane had ignored him. He'd been too busy trying to cement his new friendship with Alton Hawthorne, who sat on the board of a major energy company. Alton was at Bent Creek with his wife, celebrating their thirty-fifth wedding anniversary. Mrs. Hawthorne had retired early, but Alton had stuck around to have some fun. Shane had spent the evening with him at a table with three other people: Blair Jackson, David Sterling, and Bruce Roth. Sterling and Roth were bankers, Jackson was simply a rich kid who'd inherited his daddy's money. They were all good guys, though; they liked to have fun. Having fun was what Shane was all about.

Well, that, and some serious networking with the end goal of boosting his total net worth. Mustn't forget that.

Shane rubbed a hand over his face, contemplating what to do next. Check-out was in four hours, but he wanted to hit the road now. They had reservations at the Hilton Garden Inn for the evening. They would take a shuttle to the airport the following morning. Shane wanted to get there before the sun went down. But the way Jackie was dragging her fat ass, they wouldn't make it out of their room until shortly before check-out time.

"I'm gonna finish packing and take my suitcase down to the concierge," Shane said.

"Why can't you just wait?" Jackie was in the bathroom, applying her makeup. She'd been applying her makeup for the past hour. Maybe it was a good thing it was her time of the month. If not, she'd be stoned on Oxy and would still be in bed. "I'm almost done, and then I can get my stuff together and we'll both go."

"You've still got stuff in the closet," Shane said.

"What's that supposed to mean?"

"It means you've got shit all over the place."

"Fuck you!"

Shane flashed his middle finger in her general direction and stepped away from the bed. He looked around at their suite. Jackie's clothes spilled out of various drawers; the closet was still filled with blouses, shirts, coats; her shoes were still on the shoe rack in the corner. The three suitcases she'd brought were mostly half empty and lay in the corner of the entryway. He knew if he offered to help her pack, she'd only yell at him. His shit was already packed and ready to go. So what could he do for the next few hours?

"I'm gonna go down to the lounge and have a drink," he said.

"You go do that," Jackie answered from the bathroom.

"I will." Shane grabbed his wallet and the room key card. He paused for a moment. Jackie was still in the bathroom, applying her makeup. She'd probably applied different layers already and then wiped it all off in a pathetic attempt to start over. Whatever. Let her amuse herself. She knew that if they didn't leave in the next hour, he would make things extremely difficult for her. They'd had this conversation before, during past trips. Those hadn't ended well for Jackie, either.

Unlike most hotels, five-star or otherwise, the suites at Bent Creek were built more like small luxury apartments. The entryways into each suite were just that—entryways, with a small alcove for storing empty suitcases. Beyond the entryway was a living room furnished with a sofa, two easy chairs, and a small coffee table. The kitchen and a breakfast nook lay to the right; the breakfast nook was furnished with a table that seated four; the kitchen was stocked with a refrigerator, a four-burner electric stove, the drawers and shelves stocked with an assortment of pots and pans and various utensils for those guests who wanted to prepare meals in the privacy of their suites. Beyond the breakfast nook/kitchen was a doorway that led to the bedroom on the left, and a large bathroom on the right. Shane looked toward the entryway and said, "I've got my cell phone with me. Give me a call when you're ready to get going."

"I will," Jackie said from the bathroom.

Shane started making his way to the door when there was a series of sharp raps on it. Visitors.

Frowning, Shane continued to the door and peered through the peephole. Standing in front of the door was Paul, the head of Security. Shane didn't know his last name—why should he know the last name of every Tom, Dick, and Harry that worked here? Paul was with another guy, probably his partner. The first thing Shane thought was this had to do with that hot little tart that worked at the restaurant, that waitress, Anna Something.

Shane and Jackie had ridden her ass hard the entire time they were here, and he knew the little bitch had complained about them to some of the higher ups at Bent Creek. The girl was a worthless piece of shit. Thought she was better than everybody. You didn't play that with Shane. It was best if you knew your place in life. You knew your place, you did just fine. If you didn't, you deserved everything you got. Shane and Jackie had dished it out to Anna, but it was well deserved. It pissed him off that the little bitch would complain to her superiors. In past years, Shane had gotten more than a few wait staff and maids fired for that.

Shane paused at the door, his mind racing. Bent Creek hadn't fired Anna, but he knew they'd come close. The only other reason he could think of why Paul would be up here was the ruckus he'd helped cause last night at the lounge. Was Security here to escort he and Jackie out? They fucking better well not be. Putting on his best smile, Shane opened the door. "Hey there," he said, taking a slight step into the hall. "I was just heading out."

Paul and the other guy took a step forward, forcing Shane back and he realized there were actually *four* security guys here—the other two had been standing out of range of the peephole. Before Shane knew it, one of the other security guys was on him. He drove his fist into Shane's mid-section, doubling him over. Shane felt the breath whoosh out of him and he crumpled to the floor, curled up in pain. He couldn't breathe, couldn't say anything, even as Paul hoisted him to his feet and his partner applied a vice-like pressure to his shoulder, and then he was out like a light.

Brian Gaiman had circled around the Bent Creek grounds and was standing well within the shadows, watching the east end of the employee suites, wondering if he should risk sneaking back onto the property in an attempt to find Carmen.

Since escaping the north end of the property, Brian's first

instinct had been to get as far away from his former prison as quickly as possible. He'd run deep into the woods, not knowing where he was going, totally off course, his internal compass completely turned around. He'd been panicked, and he'd had to force himself to stop and survey his surroundings, try to get a sense of where he was. All he knew was that he was in the woods. He still had no idea he'd been held on Bent Creek grounds—he was operating on the assumption he'd been taken off the property and was being held somewhere else. With that in mind, he was sure there was a road somewhere, even a path that led to his former prison. He had to find it.

This had led Brian to head back through the woods. He had to get a better look at the building he was held captive in. He made his way through the woods slowly, aware of every sound, the chirps of the birds fluttering through the trees, the soft crunch of leaves and twigs as he stepped through the lush forest. As he drew closer to the edge of the woods, he became more cautious. He peered through the dense foliage, getting a better glimpse of the buildings, and he watched it silently for a while to make sure nobody was there. There was no sign of activity, so he drew closer until he was about twenty feet from the edge of the forest. He found a large moss-covered tree and darted behind it. Only then did he take a good look at the building he'd just escaped from.

From this angle he had a good view of the building and the surrounding grounds. What he saw shocked him.

He recognized it instantly. It was the north-east corner of the Bent Creek Country club grounds.

Brian Gaiman watched the area with bated breath, his mind racing. He'd been abducted on the opposite end of the grounds, near the employee quarters. Whoever had taken him had then driven him six miles around the circumference of the property, ushered him in that building, tied him up and gagged him, then thrown him into that empty freezer, next to a running freezer with dismembered human remains.

What the fuck is going on here? Brian thought. He had no idea what purpose this building served. He'd seen it before; it stood apart from the main section of the country club, which was where the restaurant and one of the bars was located. Brian had watched the area for thirty minutes but nobody showed up, not even a staff employee performing some maintenance duty. After a while, Brian eased back into the woods and thought about what to do next.

He had to get out of here. That was paramount. But he also had to find Carmen and warn her. He'd only gotten a glimpse of the bodies in that freezer, and he hoped Carmen wasn't among those that lay butchered like slabs of flank steak. If she was alive, he had to find her and get her out of here.

The thought of the human bodies in that freezer made him wonder whose remains they were. He'd recognized one of them—that fat office worker guy. But the others? He was pretty certain there had been more than one set of human remains in there. Was there a serial killer operating on Bent Creek grounds? If so, who? It had to be a fellow employee. Brian wondered if it was somebody from the kitchen crew. There were two sets of crew that manned the kitchens; Chef Munchel oversaw both, one which catered exclusively to the guests, the other which was the employee bar-and-grill on the south-east corner of the grounds, almost the opposite direction of where Brian had been imprisoned. The employee bar-and-grill was manned by a guy named John Lansdale, a pretty good cook who would grill a mean steak. Brian had been in both Lansdale's and Munchel's kitchens plenty of times to perform various maintenance duties and hadn't seen anything weird or out of the way in either man. Both kitchens contained their own freezers in their respective storage areas, and the area Brian had escaped from definitely wasn't either of them. The room with the two freezers was contained in a small building catty-corner from the main structure. When Brian had first started, he was told by Paul Westcott that he did not have to concern himself with maintenance duties in that building, so Brian hadn't given it much thought. When he'd escaped, he realized the door had been locked from the outside. That told Brian that a staff member was responsible.

Brian's first thought was that it was Wayne Sanders. He'd met the Board Director half a dozen times, and the man gave him the creeps. While he was always dressed in a crisp, stylishly cut suit, he had all the grace of a stalking praying mantis. Wayne wore wireless glasses that perched on his beak of a nose, and his bald pate gave off a shiny veneer. His finely chiseled features gave him the impression of something sinister. If Brian was a casting director for movies, he'd have cast Wayne as Hannibal Lector in *The Silence of the Lambs*. He had that aura about him; highly intelligent, calm, a man that commanded respect, one who was a leader. But beneath that there was something dangerous.

Okay, Wayne is pretty creepy, Brian thought. *But let's not get sidetracked. Your first point of business is to find out where Carmen is and, if she's here, get her and yourself the fuck out of this place. Worry about Wayne later.*

With that mission in mind, and with his sense of location now established, he set off to traverse the perimeter of the country club to access the employee living quarters.

And now he was here, trying to come up with a good game plan.

Brian had kept well within the shadows of the woods on his journey to the south end of the property. He'd noticed the shuttle bus ferrying people down the long, winding drive toward the front gate, more so than usual. That meant today was check-out time. He'd been held captive for almost three days.

Was Carmen still here? Brian liked to think so. Maybe she'd already left on a shuttle bus with the other employees, worrying sick and wondering what had happened to him. While that was the most likely scenario, Brian had to be sure. His maintenance partner, Charlie Thompson, would still be on the grounds. Charlie had worked the private event last year and was pretty sure he was going to work it again. If so, Charlie would be in his room, pounding back some brews and watching TV. Charlie probably thought he'd either skipped out or had been let go. If Brian could sneak onto the grounds, get into the employee wing and find Charlie in his room, he'd ask if Carmen was still on the grounds. Maybe Charlie would help him. Surely he'd wonder what had happened to him.

With that thought in mind, he crept toward the outer perimeter of the woods. He scanned the buildings and noted the security camera mounted on the roof. He looked around for another one; the closest was about fifty yards to his right, but it was pointed in a different direction.

Brian watched the camera closest to him and decided that if he jogged about ten yards to the left, he'd be out of the camera's range. There would be another camera beyond that, at the corner of the property, but it would be trained on the south-east end. With that in mind, he set off in a mad sprint toward the employee wing.

He reached the building and flattened himself against the wall. Charlie's room was on this side of the building. Brian's key card was among the items missing from his pockets, so he couldn't use it to access the building. He would have to creep along the wall, find the window to Charlie's room, and knock on it, hoping Charlie was there. If Charlie wasn't there, maybe he could get the window open somehow and climb in.

With that plan in mind, Brian began inching his way down the building. He counted down the windows as he went past each one, and when he got to Charlie's he paused. He mentally tracked down each window to make sure he was at the right one, then he knocked on the pane of glass with his right hand.

CHAPTER 22

Ten Months Ago

Joe Taylor was seated at the bar at the Crescent Country club in Kansas City, Missouri, enjoying a martini when he felt the presence of somebody approaching him from behind. Joe turned around and nodded as a blond-haired man in his late thirties dressed in a tan suit with a white shirt smiled at him and stuck out his hand. "Bob Garrison?"

"That's me," Joe said, taking the guy's hand. Dean had secured the Bob Garrison identification for him two months ago and Joe had spent hours perfecting the details of his alter-ego, including learning how to respond to his new name. *It has to come to you naturally*, Dean had said during one of their training exercises. *You have to* become *Bob. You have to respond to that name when someone addresses you as Bob*. Joe had been a good student, and had employed earlier lessons he had taken in high school drama classes. Method acting worked well in business situations, too. "You're George Spector."

"Yes," George said. His grip was firm. Confident. "Good to meet you."

"You too. Have a seat."

George took the barstool next to Joe and signaled the bartender. "I'll have what he's having."

The bartender nodded and got to work.

"How was your flight?" George asked.

"Good. I'm down here every few months anyway, so it's like second nature to me."

George was nodding. "Yeah, I hear you. I fly between New York and Los Angeles every four months."

"Where do you stay when you're in Kansas City?"

"At the Crowne Plaza."

Joe nodded, sipped his martini. "I'm at Sheraton."

They made small talk as the bartender brought George his martini; where they went to school, their current status in their respective industries, the trends and uncertainties of the marketplace each industry was facing in the rapidly changing global business world. The conversation segued into the heart of what Joe wanted to meet George about quite naturally. "I can see why you would want to invest in cloud computing," George said. "That's where everything is going. The market is very small now, but it's expected to grow by—"

Joe nodded and listened, and the conversation flowed naturally. He was keenly interested in what George had to say about the company he represented. After all, Joe *was* a serious investor. He sat on several boards for different companies. He knew the business world. Last year, he'd made forty-three million dollars from his stake in the world of finance and technology, most of it coming from Capital Gains and Dividends. This year would be no different. But he had another agenda too, one George wasn't aware of. One he *wouldn't* be aware of, and might not learn about at all until everything was over.

For now, Joe Taylor played the role of Bob Garrison. And when the evening was over, the two men shook hands outside under the awning of the Crescent Country club. An agreement was made.

Joe Taylor was on a mission.

CHAPTER 23

When Emily Wharton's cell phone rang, she was expecting Paul Westcott's name to appear in the LED readout. Instead, she was surprised to see the call was coming from Jim Munchel.

She picked up on the third ring. "Yes?"

"We have a problem."

"What?"

"Gaiman is missing."

Emily felt a worm of unease roll through her belly. She'd returned to her suite to await Paul's phone call and was wrapping up board member business on her laptop. She leaned forward over the desk, her work forgotten now. "What do you mean he's gone?"

"I followed your instructions. He was tied up and gagged, very securely I might add, and he was placed in the freezer next to the others. Somehow, he slipped his way out."

Emily's first instinct was to explode in anger; the way the Chef had said, *I followed your instructions* suggested he was laying blame on her. Emily quickly dispelled her anger and went into full *I have to take care of this problem* mode. "You just found out?"

"I'm at the storage facility now."

"When was the last time you checked on him?"

"Yesterday afternoon."

"And you couldn't tell he was trying to escape? You didn't *notice*?"

"I was on dinner service last night," Jim said. She could tell the chef was trying to hold back his emotions too. "Last night of the season, first night I had to begin preparations for your event. I had a lot on my plate. He looked completely secure."

Obviously, he wasn't, Emily thought, but held her tongue. She closed her eyes, trying to think this through. "He could still be on the grounds, then," Emily said. "Have you called Paul yet?"

"No. I wanted to tell you first. Wayne is holed up in his suite, completely unreachable. I couldn't find Mr. Westcott. You're the first person I—"

There was another call coming in. "Hold that thought for a moment," Emily said. Without waiting for a response, she checked the LED screen of her cell phone. It was an incoming call from Paul Westcott. "Paul's calling me right now. Let me get this." Emily answered the incoming call and didn't even wait for the Security Director to begin speaking. "We have a problem. Brian Gaiman escaped."

Whatever Paul was going to tell her crumbled away. "What?"

"We need to move on this," Emily said, quickly taking control. "Do you have Mr. and Mrs. Daniels?"

"Yes. We have them in their suite now. Glenn and Pete are securing them for transport."

"What about Scott?"

"He's here."

"Have Scott make the transport. I need you and the others to supervise the check-out of the other guests and find Brian Gaiman. He probably headed into the woods. For all I know, he's halfway to Highway 191 by now."

"*Shit!*" She could tell Paul sounded frustrated, scared, and angry. "*Goddammit!*"

"I'll alert Wayne," Emily said. "And I'll take care of Mr. and Mrs. Daniels. Have Scott bring them to Chef Munchel's kitchen by the back way."

"Okay, I'll get on it."

"Oh, and Paul?"

"Yes?

"Find him. Use every method available. Shoot him if you have to."

"But I thought that you—"

"I said, *shoot him if you have to*!" Emily raised her voice in frustration and anger. "Change of plans, my dear. One got away. I can try again next year. But if there's to *be* a next year, I need *you* to bring Brian back by any means possible, and that includes *dead*. You understand me?"

"Yeah," Paul said. "What about Carmen Hernandez?"

Emily started; she'd completely forgotten about the maid. "Have Geri inform Carmen that her services are no longer needed," Emily said. Geri Graves was the supervisor of housekeeping. "Have one of your guys and Geri escort Carmen to her room to collect her things, then escort her off the property. Make sure she's picked up. And make sure Geri has HR cut her a final check before she leaves."

"Okay." Paul sounded like he was overwhelmed.

"Are we good? You sure you can handle all this, Paul?"

"Yeah, yeah, I'm sure."

"Good. Give me an update in thirty." She disconnected from Paul and went back to the other line to bring Jim up to speed.

"Tell me about Mr. and Mrs. Daniels again," Chef Munchel said. Emily had given him the cliff notes version of her meeting with Paul and Rick Nicholson this morning via email.

"I instructed Paul to have them brought individually to his office for questioning as a ruse to Mr. Nicholson," Emily said. "Wayne's been keeping an eye on Rick. He'll make a perfect Igor because he has such blind faith. Paul was going to tell him he's on board full time, with full benefits, and was to give him the rest of the day and tomorrow off. He'll be zoning out in his suite. Paul knows the protocol for breaches like this, though, especially when they're made against a member of our collective."

"They stole how much from Carl White?"

"A tad over a million."

"And Rick thinks they did it out of some kind of petty spite?"

"Rick's very observant. He's been an incredible asset to the team. And I must admit, I've heard my share of rumors regarding Mr. and Mrs. Daniels as well, none of them flattering, I might add. Mr. Daniels, especially, strikes me as the kind of childish, immature type who would resort to such petty activities. Yes, I do believe they're capable of this."

"Suppose they aren't, though?" Jim asked. "Suppose they're just the complete assholes everybody says they are, but they have nothing to do with the theft of the money?"

"We'll find that out very shortly, won't we," Emily said. Her mind was racing on devising the best way to extract a truthful confession out of them. Once Paul's team had access to any computers Shane or Jackie might have, it would be easy to have Glenn run some tests and perform some quick forensics to determine if they were responsible for the theft of Mr. White's money. Scott or Glenn could conduct a search of the room. And, of course, she and Paul would question Shane and Jackie, too. If they confessed, they had their thieves. If not, and if no evidence was found, they'd deal with that.

She relayed all of this to Jim, who listened silently. When she was finished, he sighed. "This is beginning to get too big, Emily. You know how I feel about safety in numbers."

"I know."

"And I was perfectly fine with working for you and the other seven members of the board," Jim continued. "I trust Wayne explicitly, and you and I have become good friends. I like the other board members very much. But I've always been uneasy about opening the collective up to others unless Wayne or I have vetted them, even if they can afford—"

"Mr. White is completely discreet," Emily said. "He and I go back a long ways."

"It's not Mr. White I'm worried about, and you know that," Jim said. "Had news of the theft of his money attracted the attention of his financial institution, the authorities would want to know about every transaction he's ever made. And that could only lead—"

"And that is why we're delivering Shane and Jackie to *you*." Emily couldn't help but grin. "In fact, I think Carl will be very interested in this bit of news, don't you think?"

There was a pause on the other end of the line. Then, "You know, as appealing as that is, I have to encourage you to be cautious about this."

"I will be," Emily said. "And Paul will be too. He's as much a part of this as any of us. He'll be able to use his resources to make things right."

"I hope so." Jim paused again. "Should I prepare for their arrival?"

"I think you should. I'll alert Mr. White, as well. I think he needs to be present when we question them."

"Very well," Jim murmured. "I'll see you shortly." Jim hung up.

Emily set her phone down. The screensaver on her MacBook Pro had started. She backed away from the desk, at a crossroads. What to do?

Whatever the decision, she knew how the final outcome would be regardless. Thinking about it made her smile. They would get through this. They had a good team in place. She would inform Wayne what was happening. He would get other members of the board involved—they were all on site anyway, holed up in their suites, waiting for tomorrow night's festivities to begin. They all shared the same goal, the same interests, the same concerns. Working together, they would fix this problem.

Emily stood up. Time to take care of the problem.

Besides, her stomach was rumbling. She was getting hungry.

Emily quietly left her suite and headed down to Chef Munchel's kitchen.

* * *

Paul gave them their orders in the entry hall. He spoke in hushed tones. He'd already instructed Scott to get a service vehicle and drive it around to the back entrance of the D wing. Paul had called the front desk and casually asked the clerk what the status was on guest check-outs for those staying in the D wing. The front desk clerk confirmed that all guests except for Mr. and Mrs. Daniels had checked out, most of them days ago. Since there was no direct view of the entrance from any other rooms from this section of the resort, Scott could work in relative privacy in transporting them. Paul explained this to him, making sure Scott understood it. Scott nodded, his features grim, determined. He was a good kid. Paul had liked him the moment he interviewed him four seasons back. He'd liked him so much he'd hired Scott for some freelance gigs during the winter months. The kid was reliable, discreet, and loyal. Paul made sure he was well taken care of financially in return. That's all the kid wanted. To be respected. To have his financial needs met. It was a symbiotic relationship.

It was all any of them wanted, really. Pete and Glenn were motivated by the same things Scott was, and Paul had put them through more intense things this season due to their length of tenure and experience. Last year, Glenn had single-handedly chased after and caught somebody that tried to get away during an abduction, risking his own neck to do so. That had been an intense moment that had taken place in downtown Minneapolis. Paul had been supervising the operation himself. Two other guys were working the abduction with them. The abduction itself had gone smooth, but the subject had not been rendered unconscious fully. He'd come awake as Glenn had paused to grab another coil of rope, and within seconds the subject was up and sprinting out of the van, running down the street toward an alley. Glenn hadn't thought twice; he'd raced after him. Paul had scrambled to get the door to the van shut, then Pete had swung the vehicle around the corner and followed the pursuit while Paul watched out for the police. Luckily, the chase hadn't lasted long. Glenn had tackled the subject at the end of a long alley. Pete had pulled in and they'd gotten the subject back in with no trouble. There'd been no witnesses, either. It had been a late night, in a bad part of town. Nobody had been out to see anything.

"Once Scott gets back, he'll get these two over to the exit of the building and transport them to the north end of the grounds. He'll assist Chef Munchel in getting them to the storage area, where they'll wait for me to arrive with Mr. White. In the meantime, while this is happening, Pete, Glenn, and myself will fan out and hunt down Mr. Gaiman. There's no sense in splitting up since time is of the essence. The three of us will start where Mr. Gaiman was last seen and we'll look for any signs of where he may have gone. If it looks like he reached the main road, we'll call the search off and regroup."

"What if he went deeper into the woods and we can't find him?" Pete asked. Like Scott and Glenn, Pete was an ex-cop who was completely loyal to Paul. Paul provided him with a very good six figure salary. Pete had never disappointed him yet.

"We'll cross that bridge when we get to it," Paul said. Truth be told, the possibility of that scared the crap out of him. He tried not to let his worry show, but he could tell his team could detect his unease.

Glenn fingered the butt of his handgun, which sat in a holster he wore around his waist. His shirt usually concealed the weapon, but now it rode in full view. "We've got plenty of hours of daylight left," he said. "We should be able to find him."

Pete nodded. "And he wouldn't have been able to hitch a ride on a shuttle. We'd've heard about that by now."

That was something Paul hadn't thought of. Pete was right. Had Brian stumbled on to the main and only road to the resort, the shuttle bus driver would have called it in. He hadn't gotten a call. Which meant Brian was either deep in the woods, hiding out, or he was somewhere close to the grounds. "You've got a good point there. I just wish I had more men to help with this search."

There was a sharp series of raps on the door, three fast ones, followed by two long ones. Scott, returning. Paul verified it was Scott through the peephole and opened the door. "Van's pulled up to the back," Scott said, shouldering his way in. "Shall we get going?"

Paul nodded. He regarded each of his team members. "Yeah, let's get this show on the road."

And with that, they set out on their plans.

CHAPTER 24

Shane Daniels woke up to an extremely painful headache.

He opened his eyes and the harsh light blinded him. He squinted and tried to raise his right hand to shield the glare, but he couldn't move. There was extreme pain in his shoulder and he winced. As consciousness hit him more fully, he blinked rapidly, trying to get used to the light. He tried to move his limbs. Aside from his right shoulder, which hurt like hell, everything else was fine. He just couldn't move his arms. Or his legs.

He was lying on cold steel. He turned his head to the side and opened his eyes. The light wasn't as harsh from this angle, and as his vision adjusted he made out the details of the room. There were metal shelves against the wall holding kitchen utensils—large mixing bowls, boxes of dried goods. He licked his lips—he wasn't gagged, but he could tell he was tied down to the steel table he was lying on.

He slowly moved his head up, wincing at the harsh light. He turned to the right to get a look at that end of the room and that's when he saw Jackie.

Jackie was lying on an identical steel table beside him. She, too, wasn't gagged. She was conscious. She turned her head to Shane and he could see the confusion and fear in her eyes. "What's...what's going on? What happened?"

"I don't know," Shane said. His throat was dry. He licked his lips, gathering his strength. His eyes darted around the room.

He had no idea where they were, but somebody was going to fucking hear about this. Yes, sir.

"Did they...are we...?" Jackie's tone of voice mirrored her confusion. She was looking around the room, slow realization dawning on her features. "Are we being held prisoner?"

"*Hey*!" Shane yelled. "Hey, what the hell's the meaning of this! Let us out of here!" He tugged at the ropes that bound his arms and legs to the table. They were securely tied down. He felt them barely give. Shane's breathing came fast and heavy. His heartbeat started to race. They were in a very bad spot.

A door opened and Shane's gaze darted to the far side of the room. Chef Munchel and Carl White stepped inside. The minute Shane saw Carl, his eyes narrowed in hatred. "Can't take a joke, Mr. White? You cheap prick!"

Carl White said nothing as he approached the stainless steel tables where Shane and Jackie were tied up. He was grinning. Chef Munchel, who was dressed in a red long-sleeved T-shirt and blue jeans, was hiding a grin of his own. Munchel was of medium height, his body pear-shaped, but not overly so, with short graying hair that was balding at the top. He always seemed to be grinning in merriment and it gave his demeanor a joking, happy-go-lucky sense of mischievous. His gray eyes twinkled with some kind of hidden joke.

"What's the meaning of this?" Shane barked. "Fucking untie me *now*!"

The door to the storage room opened again. A woman entered. Late thirties, short, plump but curvy, long dark hair, tan skin, wearing glasses, dressed as if she were about to attend a board meeting. Nice-looking. Shane didn't recognize her. "Who the fuck are you?"

"I'm one of the owners of Bent Creek," the woman said. "Emily Wharton. You're Shane Daniels, and your bitch is Jackie."

Shane gasped. These people were really crossing the line. "Untie me, *now*!"

"I plan to," Emily said. "I just have a few questions to ask you first."

"I'm not answering any questions. Your security team barged into my room, assaulted my wife and I, and—"

"You'll be well compensated when this is over," Emily said, overriding him.

At the mention of being well compensated, Shane shut his trap. He regarded Emily, Chef Munchel, and Carl White. Only Carl seemed overly eager about something. He could hardly contain his grin. "What the hell are *they* doing here?"

"They have a purpose here," Emily said. "When it is time for them to speak, they shall. Until then, forget about them. Your audience is with me." Emily shot a glance at Jackie, who was watching all of this with bated breath. "That goes for you too, sweetie. Okay, ready for my version of twenty questions?"

Shane said nothing, his jaw set, eyes glowering. Despite his predicament, he was more angry than scared. Fine. He'll play their bullshit game. When it was over, he was going to get to the heart of the financial incentive Emily had teased him with. Then, when he and Jackie were free, they were getting the fuck out of here and never setting foot on Bent Creek property again. *This is probably just some fucked up, sick revenge fantasy Carl paid them to set up*, he thought. *Guy's got so much money falling out of his orifices, I've heard he gives some of it away to crack addicts every Christmas. He probably paid Emily to set this all up. Long as Jackie and I get our share.*

"Question Number One," Emily began, taking a casual stroll around the table out of Shane's line of vision. "Mr. Parker Goode."

Shane waited for the question. Emily moved over to Jackie's side and paused, standing directly at the head of the table Jackie was secured on. "Yeah?" Jackie asked.

"Hmmm. Name doesn't ring a bell, does it?"

"Should it?"

"That leads me to question Number Two. Mr. and Mrs. Glen and Olivia Westlake."

"Who the fuck are they?" Shane barked.

Emily was moving down Jackie's side of the table. She was watching them closely. Shane craned his head around so he could watch her. Emily didn't react. "What about you, Jackie? Olivia Westlake? Ever meet her?"

"I...I...no...I don't think so." She looked at Shane, confused. She looked back at Emily, who was making her way around the two tables and back to Shane's left side. "Why? Should I?"

"Question Number Three," Emily said, ignoring her. She directed her gaze to both of them. "Cititrade Group Account number 458723, two days ago. Ring any bells now?"

Now Shane was becoming confused. What kind of game was this? "I don't know what you're talking about."

"Neither do I," Jackie said. Her tone of voice told Shane she was as much in the dark about all this as he was.

"Hmmm." Emily stopped. She was at Shane's left side again. "I was afraid of that." She turned to Carl White. "Sorry, Mr. White."

"That's okay," Carl said. He took a step forward, that grin still on his face. "It's nice to have Shane and Jackie here anyway, all tied up and helpless. Makes things more *spicy*!"

Shane ignored Carl's comment and addressed him directly. "Look, I don't know what this is about. If I offended you, I'm sorry. Let's just get...let's just cut to the chase here." He directed his attention back to Emily. "You mentioned a financial incentive to this...this game, or whatever it is. Okay, let's hear it. What do you want from us?"

"You can't be upset at Shane because of that silly argument we had at the lounge," Jackie said to Carl. She was regarding Carl from her position on the table she was tied to. Her confusion was giving way to a slow dawning. "Is that what this is? Shane embarrassed you that night, so this is your idea of revenge?"

"How much did he pay you?" Shane asked Emily. "Tell me."

Emily chuckled. "Mr. Daniels, Mr. Daniels...Mr. White didn't pay me a cent."

"Then what the hell is this all about?"

Carl White was looking at Shane with an intense gaze. He looked at Jackie, letting his gaze linger for a moment. "I don't know. They were pretty quick on all three denials. Of course, they could have rehearsed it all, too."

"Rehearsed *what*?" Shane exclaimed. "What are you accusing us of doing? Just spit it out!"

"Two nights ago, Mr. White's investment account with Cititrade was hacked into," Emily related. Her tone was direct, business-like. "A tad over one million dollars was transferred out of his account, its whereabouts are currently unknown."

"And you think *I* had something to do with it?"

"Either you or Jackie." Emily's eyes darted to Jackie. "I understand you're quite the techie. You have a pretty good knowledge of financial systems and their databases."

"There's no way I could have broken into Mr. White's account," Jackie protested. "Those kind of electronic transactions are...well, they're extremely difficult to pull off. There's encryptions to break, network firewalls to get past. Why would I risk something like that?"

"To embarrass Mr. White?" Emily suggested. "To get back at him for embarrassing your husband? The two of you certainly possess that sense of pettiness that goes hand in hand with schoolyard bullying and general immaturity."

It suddenly became clear what this was all about. Shane looked at Carl. "You're pissed at me because I made you look like an asshole that night at the lounge," he said. "When we had that discussion about the history of the gold exchange and—"

"I'm not upset at you about that," Carl said. "I don't hold grudges, Mr. Daniels. I took your behavior that night for what it was. A silly and immature attempt by you to play the big dog. You're nothing but a buffoon, a consummate loser who feels he has to bully others and intimidate everybody around him to get what he wants. And when someone isn't paying attention?" Carl shook his head, that grin still on his face. "Then widdle Shane throws a widdle temper tantrum. Isn't that right?"

"Look, this has gone far enough!" Shane barked. "If I offended you, that's one thing, but you don't have to resort to criminal acts to—"

"I don't think Shane and Jackie had anything to do with the theft of your money, Mr. White," Emily said, regarding them with a quick once-over. "And I'm sure Paul would agree with me if he and his staff weren't tied up with another problem. I'm convinced." She looked at Carl. "Sorry."

Shane couldn't believe what he was hearing. This bitch had he and Jackie overpowered by her security goons and taken to this storeroom, which looked like it was near the kitchen, just to confront them in front of Carl White? Did they think they were above the law? These people were so going to need a team of lawyers when he got out of here, it wasn't even funny. Shane held his anger back, his mind working on overdrive. First, he had to get out of here. "Okay," he said. "You believe us. Jackie and I didn't steal your money. And why would I? I have no use for your money. It's something I wouldn't do even as a form of petty revenge. Now can you untie us?"

Emily nodded at Chef Munchel and Carl. "I'll put in a call to Paul and give him an update. Will you handle them?"

Chef Munchel nodded back. "Of course."

Without a backward glance, Emily exited the room. Chef Munchel and Carl approached the table. Carl's grin grew wider. "I am so looking forward to this," he said. His fingers lingered over the ropes that bound Shane's right wrist to the steel table.

Shane felt his stomach plunge; it felt like that time-honored cliché of plunging down an elevator shaft. His skin felt warm, tingly. His mouth was suddenly bone dry. "Listen, Carl," he stammered. "I'm sorry for those things I said and how I made you the laughing stock of the lounge that night, but—"

"You didn't make me the laughing stock," Carl said. He turned to Chef Munchel. "Should I untie his hands first?"

"Yes," Chef Munchel said. He was out of Shane's range of vision. Shane could hear him rustling with some tools in the background. "But first, let's wheel him in to the other room."

"Okay." Carl moved to Shane's head and Shane saw that Munchel had already commandeered Jackie's table. He noticed for the first time that both tables were on wheels, like rolling gurneys. His pulse began to pound as he felt the table he was on being pushed out of the room, after Jackie, which was being pushed by Chef Munchel.

"Where are you taking us?" Jackie asked. There was a hint of fear in her voice.

"This will only take a moment," Chef Munchel said. They stopped in the center of the room and Shane tried to get a good look at it. It was completely bare. The walls and floor were solid concrete. The floor had a very large stain and what appeared to be a drain in the center of the room. Directly over them was a large overhead light powered by a high-wattage bulb. Dangling from the ceiling were two heavy chains with large hooks at the end. Chef Munchel picked up the rope that bound Jackie's ankles together; the end of it had been turned into a granny knot. Chef Munchel slipped it through one of the hooks.

"Hey, what are you doing?" Shane barked.

"Like this?" Carl asked Chef Munchel, completely ignoring Shane and Jackie. He grabbed the end of the rope that bound Shane's ankles together and slipped the granny knot through the second hook.

Chef Munchel nodded.

"Look, Shane said he was sorry for insulting you," Jackie said, and Shane could really hear the fear in her voice now. Her voice quavered, crackling in its intense fear. "We've learned our lesson, really..."

She sounds like a goddamn wuss, Shane thought briefly. This whole escapade, to be reduced to sniveling and begging to not be strung up upside down, which is what it appeared Chef Munchel and Carl White were going to do, was making him angry. "Okay, I get it," Shane said. "I insulted you and now you want to insult *me* by stringing me upside down. You'll probably bring a few people in here that I've insulted this week and you'll all have a grand old time calling me names, maybe you'll even whip out your wankers and pee on us. That'll make you feel better, right?"

Chef Munchel had moved to the far wall where there was a hand crank. He began working the crank. Jackie's legs began to rise up. She started to protest. "Hey! No, please don't do this!"

As Chef Munchel continued with the crank, raising Jackie up, her body becoming more vertical by the moment until she was finally upside down and completely suspended over the table she'd lain on. Carl leaned over Shane. Something about that smile...

"This isn't about revenge, Shane," Carl said.

Shane's eyes darted from Jackie, dangling upside down and sobbing, to Chef Munchel, who began working the second crank. Shane felt the pull on the chain as it dragged his legs up. Shane turned to Carl, not caring how desperate he looked or sounded. "Then if it isn't about revenge, let us go!"

Chef Munchel grinned as he worked the crank, drawing Shane's body up, higher and higher.

"Please! Don't do this!" Now Shane's body was completely vertical. The weight and suspension of his body made his arms fall below his head. He was upside down, dangling over the metal table. Both tables were pushed away and for a moment Shane saw another drain in the floor, surrounded by another large stain. *Is that blood? That looks like blood! Holy fucking Christ—*

And as the realization that he was going to die flitted through Shane's brain, Chef Munchel stepped in front of him. Shane saw the huge butcher knife gripped in the chef's right hand. He opened his mouth to scream, but the knife flashed below his field of vision and a line of pain erupted across his throat. His face was bathed in warm blood and he couldn't speak. He could only hear air escaping amid a wet open wound. And as Shane Daniels watched his life's blood spill onto the floor to pool down the drain, he tried to think of something, *anything*, to fight back, but darkness quickly came upon him, and he heard Jackie scream, and then darkness claimed him.

CHAPTER 25

Nine Months Ago

They were having dinner at the Pinnacle in Newport Beach, California, at the tip of Balboa Island. Their table seated four—Joe Taylor, George Spector, and the two men George had promised Joe he would meet: John Lansdale, and Earl Sanders. Lansdale and Sanders sat on several corporate boards together, among them Motorola, Valuemax Metals, and Cases Unlimited. Joe could tell that the three men were tight; they had that casual air about them that, as an outsider, was hard to penetrate. The three of them were languid around each other, relaxed, but when it came to business they were also very straight up with each other, and with him. Joe was trying to penetrate their veneer under the Bob Garrison alias. He'd been in contact with George Spector since their dinner meeting at the Crescent, in Kansas City, a month ago.

Upon arrival at the Pinnacle, Earl had given the maitre'd his name. The maitre'd nodded, and escorted them to a table in a private alcove, completely separate from the rest of the dining area. It was like a private room. Once ushered through the alcove's door, the maitre'd closed it off with a sliding door Joe hadn't noticed. At the other end of the alcove was another door that probably led to the kitchen. *Private banquet room*, he thought. *Nice. Being that this is the type of place Nina would dine at, I hope she doesn't show up when we're leaving. That could spell trouble.*

"I'm friends with the owner and head chef here," Earl had told Joe once they were seated. "He owns another restaurant in New York."

"He gives us five-star treatment all the way!" John Lansdale said.

And five star treatment they got. They had a private waiter and server who took and delivered drink and appetizer orders. Joe found the menu completely tantalizing. There were no prices listed on the menu, but that was okay. Earl Sanders was picking up the tab on behalf of the other three partners. It was Joe's hope that the evening's dinner meeting would be successful and would lead to him being taken very seriously as a potential investor in their start-up venture—Price Mutual Funds, Ltd.

After some serious deliberation, Joe made his dinner selection. For the first course he ordered Sautéed Nantucket Bay Scallops which were served over Asian Cabbage Salad, crispy rice sticks, pea tendrils and pickled ginger vinaigrette. For his second course he ordered the wood-oven roasted devil's gulch ranch rabbit loin which was served with herb brioche and golden raisins stuffing, bacon, black trumpet mushrooms confit shoulder pastilla, chestnuts and natural juice. Earl ordered the wine, two bottles of Nun, Xarel-lo, 2006, from Spain. For dessert, Joe ordered a cup of French Vanilla coffee and a chocolate soufflé.

During the various courses of the meal, business was discussed. Because mutual fund investing was Joe's area of expertise, he had a deep knowledge and understanding of the entire spectrum of this particular field of finance. As Earl Sanders and John Lansdale distributed two comb-bound reports, Joe put his reading glasses on and read through them. Impressive. He asked the right questions. Listened with great interest. He had his own business plan at the forefront of his brain and could retrieve and quote from it at length, which he did as he crunched the numbers in his head during the discussion. As the various courses of the meal commenced, Joe participated in the discussion: what was his opinion of the plan? Did he see a strong market value in the various funds they were trying to package together? What was Joe's (rather, Bob's) long-term financial and business goals with his own company? What were his short-term goals? What kind of connections did he have with various brokerage and high-level banking institutions? Joe had already provided George Spector with a list of his references, which had been carefully selected by Dean Campbell and included no less than half a dozen names, all of them close friends and business associates of Joe's who had been vetted and prepped by Dean and Joe for months and who had shared Joe's anguish and pain when Carla had gone missing. All of them had pledged their own private equity and resources in helping to bring his daughter home safe. They were all on board with this plan. One of them, Lyle Henderson, had even volunteered to go undercover with Joe in this clandestine effort to locate Carla Taylor. Joe had politely turned him down. "I love you like a brother, Lyle," he'd said. "But if this is as big as I think it is, I don't want you in any danger. You're providing a tremendous help to Dean and I by providing the kind of backup I need, and I thank you for that."

Lyle had called Joe two weeks ago to tell him one of Earl Sanders's underlings had inquired about him. Just a simple verification process, checking references. The other men on Dean's hand-picked list of references had also chimed in over the next day or so to verify they'd been contacted too. The ruse had worked. George Spector had called him last week to invite Joe to an exclusive dinner at the Pinnacle, a swanky five-star restaurant in Newport Beach, to discuss the details of their impending merger. Joe had only been too eager to accept.

And now the meeting was concluding as dessert wound down. Joe dabbed at his mouth with a white, heavy, cloth napkin. The meal had been excellent, one of the best he'd ever had, and he was even more pleased by the progress of the meeting. Earl Sanders seemed downright giddy. Joe nodded at Earl. "I'm very impressed," he said. "I'm even more excited that we can bring our mutual strengths together and create something of long lasting and high yielding value."

"I'm excited about the possibilities myself," Earl said. He set his napkin aside.

"How'd you enjoy your meal, Bob?" George asked.

Joe groaned, rubbed his stomach in mock display of fullness. "It was just...words can't describe it. I have never had rabbit that was just so mouth-watering."

George grinned. "Chef Munchel has a way with exotic dishes."

"I bet he does a great duck, and an even better pheasant."

"Oh, he does," John said. He was packaging the reports up in his slim briefcase. "His specialty is exotic dishes and the outré. What he offers on his menus at his restaurants is just the tip of the iceberg of his specialties."

"How about if we introduce you?" George exclaimed. He'd put away a little bit more wine than the rest of them, and had grown more chatty and outgoing as the meal, and the meeting, had progressed.

"Sure," Joe said. Why not? Wasn't meeting and complimenting the chef on an excellent meal common courtesy?

John shrugged. "Can't hurt anything." He turned to one of the servers, a slim Asian man in his twenties. "If Chef has a moment, ask him if he could come out and meet our guest."

"Yes, Mr. Lansdale." The man nodded and removed John's empty dessert dish from the table.

Joe gathered his reports together as the dinner wound down. There was some small banter. When was Bob leaving to head back home to Aurora, Colorado? Was he going to take in some of the sights in Newport Beach tomorrow? Joe explained that he was thinking of buying a place close by. John mentioned a realtor he worked with, and was searching for the realtor's business card when the Asian waiter returned from the side door with Chef Munchel.

Chef Munchel appeared to be in his late forties or early fifties. Dressed in chef's whites, he was a bit on the portly side, standing about five foot nine. His close-cropped graying hair was receding from his forehead, but his features were those of a child engaged forever in mirth; his eyes twinkled in amusement, his lips curved up at some silent joke. He was very disarming and pleasant. "Mr. Garrison, I presume?" Chef Munchel said, stepping forward and holding his right hand out to be shaken. His grip was firm, his voice melodic with an inflection of merriment and humor. Joe nodded. "I surely hope you enjoyed your meal," Chef Munchel said.

"In a word, it was fantastic!" Joe said.

Chef Munchel's grin widened. "Wonderful! So good to hear." His eyes fell on Earl Sanders and the rest of the group. "And I take it your meals were all to your satisfaction?"

"As always, Chef, you're Number One!" John said. He was standing up now, smoothing down his shirt, prepping himself for the walk through the main dining room to their waiting vehicles at the valet.

"Very good," Chef Munchel said, bowing politely. "I take it the facilities were to your liking to conduct business?"

"Very much so," George said. He was buttoning his sport coat and gathering his briefcase. He nodded to Joe. "We had a *very* good meeting."

"Ah! Wonderful!" Chef Munchel turned to Joe. "I take it I'll probably see more of you, then?"

"You probably will," Joe said. He smiled.

"Good! Good!" Chef Munchel exclaimed. "Well, if you men will excuse me, I really must get back to my kitchen. Mr. Garrison, it was a pleasure." Chef Munchel bowed slightly.

"Nice to meet you, Chef Munchel," Joe said.

Chef Munchel addressed Earl Sanders. "I suppose I'll see you next week for your other dinner meeting, Mr. Sanders?"

"Yes, you will," Bill said. He stopped to talk to Chef Munchel as Joe exited the private dining room with John and George. As they left, he heard Earl say, "John will be joining us, but George has to fly to Atlanta for business. He'll be—"

The rest was drowned out as Joe weaved his way through the dining room, following John and George. His mind was racing as they exited the restaurant and stood under the awning that shielded the entryway from the elements. An older man dressed in a suit was waiting for them outside, standing near the valet station. "The valets are bringing your vehicles, gentlemen," the man said.

John nodded at the man and slipped him a fifty-dollar bill. The man made the bill disappear. And as Joe stood under the awning, talking to his new business partners, he hoped he didn't come across as too eager to escape their company and head back to his hotel. He wanted to get back to the privacy of his room and call Dean Campbell to tell him the meeting had gone as perfectly as they'd hoped it would.

CHAPTER 26

It was a little after one a.m. and they'd taken the suite apart in their search for the missing money. Scott Baker stood in the middle of the living room, tired, frustrated, and at wits end. He regarded Pete Atkins and Glenn Cunningham, who had just finished a second search of the master bedroom. "We've gotta face the fact that the money just isn't here," he said.

Glenn nodded. He crossed the room and slumped down in the large sofa. The sofa had been taken apart completely; the cushions had been opened, the stuffing gone through, the frame beneath it searched, the back torn up and inspected. Pieces of the sofa lay on the floor. Likewise, the easy chair had been taken apart and the entertainment center had been unpacked and inspected. Shane and Jackie's belongings had been removed from their suitcases and gone over completely at least twice. The kitchen, bathroom, and the bedroom had been searched. The rug had been pulled up in places. They had spent three hours in this suite alone searching for the missing money. It just wasn't here.

Pete was standing in the kitchen. "So the money isn't here, and it isn't in Carl White's suite or in the suites of the other victims."

Scott nodded. "Exactly." They'd conducted similar searches of the rooms of the theft victims themselves after Paul suggested maybe they'd made false claims against Shane and Jackie.

Not that making false claims mattered at this point with Shane and Jackie dead, but Paul was thorough like that.

"So where the fuck is it?" Glenn asked. "I doubt the Westlakes or Mr. Goode would make shit up."

"No, they were serious about it," Scott said. "I was there with Paul when Parker Goode filed his complaint. Guy was livid. Who wouldn't be pissed off at half a million bucks disappearing from your hotel room?"

Pete nodded. "Yeah, that would piss me the fuck off, too."

Scott was frustrated. To have two well-paying guests make theft claims like this in such a short period of time meant something fucked up was happening. The Westlake couple and Mr. Goode had been contacted by Paul via cell phone earlier in the evening and questioned about their relationships with Jackie and Shane. Neither victim thought Jackie and Shane were the culprits, but did admit to butting heads with the couple numerous times during their stay. Parker Goode had even mentioned Shane bragged that he could "clean his clock financially" when it came to gambling. When Mr. Goode had responded with a flippant, "Okay, hot shot, you think you can clean me out this week. You go for it." Two days later, the cash in the suitcase earmarked for his yearly poker games with his friends went missing. The only reason Parker didn't suspect Jackie or Shane was that during the time it was believed the money was stolen, he was in the lounge with the couple the entire evening. A dozen people had been able to verify this.

So if Shane and Jackie hadn't stolen the money, who did?

"Something's fucked up," Glenn said.

"Yeah, it is," Scott said. He was tired, but he couldn't stop thinking that something just didn't add up. He looked at Glenn and Pete. "And it sounds like you guys are thinking what I'm thinking."

"Jackie and Shane didn't steal the money," Pete said.

"Yeah, it looks like it." Scott sighed. He pulled his cell phone out of his pocket. "I'm gonna wake Paul up and tell him."

* * *

Paul was sitting up in bed with the drapes to his suite closed, phone to his ear, listening as Pete gave him a rundown of their complete searches of all four suites in question—Jackie and Shane's, Mr. and Mrs. Westlake's, Parker Goode's, and Carl White's. Carl had been moved to an entirely new suite, recently vacated by a regular seasonal guest, and wasn't aware his old suite was being searched. According to Emily Wharton, he hadn't seemed too concerned that Jackie and Shane probably hadn't stolen his money.

Paul sighed. "Okay," he said. He'd been in such a deep sleep he almost hadn't heard his phone ring. He'd had to grope for it like a blind man in the dark, and had knocked the instrument off his nightstand. "I guess we need to do something about this."

"Yeah, we do," Scott said. "We searched all the guest's rooms last night, and we also searched the employees'. What next?"

"I really don't want to do this, but I see no other choice." Paul rubbed his face, for the first time feeling nervous. "I think the next step is to search senior staff members' rooms. Start with Rick Nicholson's suite since he's not due back until tomorrow. Report back to me on the results. I'm positive you won't find anything in Rick's suite, but report back anyway and continue on with Mark Robinson's and Pete Pellegrino's suites."

"Okay, will do," Scott said. "Mind if I give my guys a few hours of sleep first?"

"No," Paul said. "Go ahead. Any word from the local police yet on Gaiman?"

"None." Out of desperation, Paul had contacted the head of the local county sheriff earlier that afternoon to report Brian Gaiman as an escaped ex-convict. The local authorities were well aware of the work-release program at Bent Creek, and Paul further informed Sheriff Stephen Brady that Brian Gaiman had psychiatric problems. "He's paranoid," he'd told Sheriff Brady.

"He's a tweaker and is convinced everybody is out to get him, from the government, to aliens from the planet Neptune. He's also convinced there's a race of cannibals that live in the woods beyond the Bent Creek grounds. We were in the process of getting his parole officer here and having him removed from his duties when he went AWOL on us. I've had my guys searching the woods and the surrounding properties and we've been unable to find him."

Sheriff Brady had assured Paul that his men would be on the lookout for him and that he would be held for Paul and his team when he was picked up. "I'm going to contact Sheriff Brady in a few hours," he told Scott. "Get some rest, then start with Rick's suite. I'll talk to you at eight o'clock."

"Yes sir, Mr. Westcott," Scott said.

When the call was over Paul sat up in bed, his mind running in a thousand directions. If he were running this show, he'd call this year's event off entirely. Wayne Sanders wouldn't have it though. He could probably convince Emily and a few of the other members, but Wayne would be a hard nut to crack. He would stubbornly insist that things go as planned and expect Paul and his team to handle security and provide that buffer they needed. Paul could do it—he definitely had the resources and skill—but with so many holes and dents in the armor now, from Brian Gaiman's escape, to the three brazen thefts, and the sudden decision to eliminate Shane and Jackie, there were just too many distractions. If he could direct the efforts of his small crew in searching the executive suites, Paul could get to work on providing alibis for Shane and Jackie's disappearances. They would probably be reported missing in a few days. As far as he knew, their car was still in the guest parking lot. That car would have to disappear, and the database records would have to be updated to reflect that Shane and Jackie had checked out promptly. A quick call to Mark Robinson, Bent Creek's IT Director, would have to be made tomorrow morning as well. Mark could make those changes remotely without question.

He jotted this down as a reminder to himself on the notepad he kept by the nightstand.

Feeling better that he had some semblance of control back, Paul Westcott laid back down in his king-sized bed and tried to get back to sleep.

But his sleep was fitful, and his dreams were nightmarish.

CHAPTER 27

Friday

When Rick Nicholson arrived back at Bent Creek that morning at eight a.m., he felt relieved, but he was still on edge.

His key card had let him in through the front gate. He piloted his car through a second set of security gates and parked in the executive lot in the rear of the administrative wing. *I guess it wasn't a dream then*, he thought as he headed to the rear entrance of the building. *They haven't deactivated my access. I guess Wayne really* does *want me as a full-time permanent employee. This is good.*

Rick was still on an emotional high from yesterday. He couldn't help but blurt the news out to his mother yesterday, at her apartment, when he arrived to check up on her. Mom had been happy for him, but he could tell that beneath her happiness, she was tired, worn out. Rick had pretended not to notice, but he could tell Mom knew he was faking it, and he cut his visit short. After making sure she had enough money to get by for the next week, and that her utilities, medical bills, and rent were taken care of for the next month, he'd stood at her front door talking to her for a few minutes. She could sense he was eager to get back to Bent Creek, and ushered him out. "Go on," she'd said, shooing him out. "I'll be fine. I've got my pain meds, and I've got my vitamins, and I've got plenty of books to keep me occupied. Got plenty of food here, and Ms. Ellis down the hall stops in every day on her way home from work to check in on me." Ms. Ellis was a thirty-something spinster who lived at the end of the hall in Mom's building. She was a reasonably attractive woman, but she seemed to live for nothing else but her cats and providing diversion and entertainment for Mom; she regularly stopped in to bring things for Mom, making Rick feel like a good-for-nothing son. He'd complained about this to Mom once and she wouldn't have it. "You're in a bad spot right now," Mom had said. "And you need to get on your feet. You're working at this, and all that hard work you do helps me. Believe me, Ricky, you do plenty for me. And I thank you and love you for it."

Rick had given Mom a kiss and left the apartment. He'd swung by his own apartment where he took a quick nap, a shower, and changed into fresh clothes. He'd done a few other errands, called Gary Thompson at his office to make sure things were still in place for next week, and casually told him about Bent Creek's offer. Gary offered a cautious congratulations. "Tread lightly, brother," Gary had said. "Something that sounds that good probably has certain conditions attached to it."

After assuring Gary he would scrutinize the offer closely once he had it on paper, he locked up the apartment and headed out. He stopped at a roadside diner for a late dinner, then headed north into Wyoming. His goal was to get back to Bent Creek by eight or so, check on things, then go to his suite to sleep and get rested fully in time for the private event later that afternoon.

He'd thought about everything during the four hour drive: the job offer, his mother and her illness, the things he'd had to do to keep himself afloat and keep a roof over Mom's head and her healthcare maintained. He wasn't proud of some of it, especially the stuff that went on at Bent Creek, but he had no other choice. That's why he'd started making these other arrangements with Gary, who was prepared to follow in Rick's footsteps and leave the law firm. All he had to do was get through this week, get back home to Boulder, and he and Gary could get back to business. If what they were planning bore fruit, he might not have to take the position at Bent Creek.

Once inside the building, Rick headed to his office. The neighboring offices and cubicles were empty and dark, the absence of the staff providing a welcoming calm. Rick turned on the lights, set his duffel bag on the chair in front of his desk, and sat down. He turned his computer on, and as it booted up he thought about the past twenty-four hours. He felt good about backing up Carl White's suspicions about Jackie and Shane Daniels being responsible for the theft of his money. Part of the reason for backing up those claims was his severe dislike of the couple, especially when it came to their harassment toward Anna King, who he really liked. True, he had heard other disturbing rumors about them, but it was complete heresay. What mattered was he had used his power of persuasion to plant the seed in Paul Westcott's mind, and apparently that had been all that was required. He didn't know what the result had been, but he was sure Jackie and Shane had been questioned pretty extensively. They might have taken it as such a grievous offense that they were never going to vacation at Bent Creek ever again. That had been Rick's goal all along. He was very confident his plan had worked. He didn't want to have to deal with that godawful couple again.

With his computer booted up, Rick accessed the administrative area of the company timesheet system. Paul's group was now down to four, which was to be expected. As he scrolled down through the list of those employees who were tapped to work this week's event, he was pleased to see that Anna had logged in for work during this morning's breakfast duty. *Good*, he thought. He'd talked to Anna briefly yesterday morning, shortly after her own altercation with Paul's security team and he frowned at the memory of it. Why hadn't they been as thorough in their communications as they were last year when it came to tapping the help for the private event? Somebody had dropped the ball on that one. Anna hadn't been aware of it, and her reaction was very realistic and genuine. He'd pulled Anna aside shortly after everything was cleared up and had a quick word with her. "I know how you feel," he'd said. "I don't really want to work the next five days either. I got a sick mother at home, and I'll be lucky if I can get a day off between now and tomorrow night so I can make a quick day trip back to Boulder to see her."

"Yeah, well, I don't believe the people that run this place *have* mothers, so they can't empathize," Anna had said. The anger at her treatment was still evident in her face and tone of voice. "But hey, I guess we've just gotta roll with the changes, right?"

"Yep," Rick had said. He had been hoping to continue the conversation, to maybe ask her if they could get together again after one of her shifts. He still couldn't get over the night he'd spent with her; she'd proven to be a very aggressive and sensual lover. She'd also proven to be a woman who knew what she wanted, and what she'd wanted was simple, animalistic and primal sex. None of that sappy cuddling shit afterward, none of that talking about possibly meeting up after the season was over for another date or two, maybe see if things could go to another level, and not even *any* mention of possibly doing this again. Anna had treated the midnight bump and grind they'd engaged in the way a guy would, wham bam, thank you, sir. She'd hardly looked at him in the few days after, as if he were dismissed. *You've served your purpose*, that treatment suggested. Instead, Anna had tossed him a simple, "See you tomorrow," and headed out.

It would be nice to have another encounter with her again, Rick thought, scrolling through the system to see what was in place. He logged out and was trying to decide on what to do next when the door to the coat closet in his office opened a crack and a terrified, shaking voice said, "Rick? That you?"

Rick jumped in his seat, almost biting his tongue. The back of his chair hit the wall with a loud bang and he stood up suddenly as the closet door opened all the way. "Who is that?" he asked, his voice sounding loud and panicky to his ears.

He couldn't make the figure out completely, but he recognized the voice. "Rick, you gotta help me!" And as the man emerged from the closet he saw that it was Brian Gaiman.

"What are you—" Rick began. His heart was pounding and he suddenly felt very frightened. His left hand reached for his desk, hoping to grab something he could use as a weapon.

"Rick you gotta help me, *please*!" Brian babbled. He nearly fell to his knees as he staggered out of the closet and leaned on the corner of his desk, his breath coming in ragged gasps. "The people running this place are *insane*! I need to *find* Carmen!"

"What are you talking about? What's going on?" Rick had instinctively stepped back away from Brian, afraid the missing janitor was going to attack him.

"They had me tied up. They've..." Brian's voice cracked. "They've *killed* people. They—"

The sudden sound of the outer door opening to the administration area, then the sound of approaching footsteps heading down the hall. Toward Rick's office.

Brian glanced toward the sound, his features registering fright. "Oh shit!" he whispered. He looked back at Rick as he retreated away from the desk, backing toward the open coat closet. He put an index finger to his lips—*please, not a word to anybody*! Brian's eyes were black pits of extreme fear. He stepped in the closet and pulled the door closed just as the door to Rick's office opened, revealing Paul Westcott and two members of his security team—Pete Lee and Glenn Rutsey.

Rick, who was still standing behind his desk after his brief, frightful encounter with Brian, looked over at them with a nod and a smile. "Hey guys, what's up? I was just about to step away from here and head to my—"

"Not another word," Paul said.

The tone of Paul's voice cut through Rick's soul, making his balls creep up into his body. For the first time he noticed the grave expressions on their faces. They didn't look too happy with him. Pete was clutching a tan briefcase in his right hand. It looked like his.

"I must say that I am *extremely* disappointed in you, Mr. Nicholson," Paul said. "You can't *imagine* the level of disappointment and disgust I feel right now."

All the spit seemed to run out of Rick's mouth. *They're looking at me as if I've done something*, he thought. *What the hell is going on*? Rick licked his lips and tried to speak, but before he could, Hank beat him to it.

Hank flipped the briefcase around so it laid on the underside of his left arm, its lid facing Rick. A sense of dread bubbled in his gut. That briefcase was his, all right; he'd recognize it anywhere, especially with that large scuff mark on the front. It was a holdover of his tenure with the lawfirm, and he still used it to store important business documents. He'd taken it to Bent Creek because there were several legal briefs he was consulting with some of the guys on, and he normally kept it under his bed, in his suite when he wasn't working, or he brought it down to the office with him and went over things during his lunch break.

Pete began fumbling with the latch as Paul continued talking. "We started searching the senior management and executive staff members' rooms this morning. Look what we found stashed under your bed."

The latches up, Pete opened the lid. The three men stood in front of Rick silently as he looked at the contents of the briefcase.

It was filled to the brim with hundred dollar bills that appeared to be bundled together in neatly arranged stacks.

Looking at it was like being sucker-punched in the stomach. He felt all the wind get knocked out of him.

When he spoke it was hard to summon the words, much less speak them. "I don't...I don't understand—"

"Didn't think we'd catch you?" Paul's eyes were riveted to Rick's. "I can see it in your face."

"Are you trying to frame me?" Rick managed to get out. His heart was walloping madly in his chest and every instinct was telling him that he was in a bad situation, they had him backed into his office with no way out except through the window, and they were accusing him of theft, of stealing money from Bent Creek's wealthy guests. "This has got to be a joke, right?"

"No joke," Paul said. His gaze never left Rick's face. Beside him, Pete closed the Halliburton, snapped it shut, and set the briefcase down on the floor. "Mind telling us how that money got in your briefcase?"

"Your guess is as good as mine!" Rick exclaimed. His voice sounded high-pitched to his ears. Panicked. "I have no idea where the—"

"I saw you leave with a duffel bag yesterday morning," Paul continued. The tone of Paul's voice during this whole exchange was calm and non-assuming, but beneath that there was a level of danger. "Was that the rest of it?"

"What do you mean, 'was that the rest of it?'"

"Parker Goode had two hundred and fifty k in cash stolen from his room from his suitcase. That money was bound together in denominations of thousand dollar bills. That would be easy enough to carry out in the duffel bag I saw you with yesterday, when you had to leave so suddenly to tend to your sick mother." The way Paul said *sick mother* indicated he felt Rick's mother wasn't sick, that he had come up with that story to sneak off of Bent Creek grounds with a portion of the stolen money. It was suddenly evident to Rick that all the talk of Mom being sick, of his eagerness to leave for a day to get back to Boulder to see her, his nervousness about her condition, could have been construed as nervousness over his alleged theft. "Another three hundred and fifty grand was stolen from another couple." Paul regarded Rick with a leveled gaze.

"No," Rick said. His hands were shaking and he was finding

it hard to control the quiver of fear in his voice. "No, you've got it wrong. I didn't steal any money. I don't know how it got there, but I swear to Christ, I had *nothing* to do with any of this!"

Paul nodded at Pete and Glenn. "Grab him."

Pete and Glenn stepped toward Rick and grabbed him by each arm. Rick struggled and started to shout. "I didn't steal that money! I didn't take it, you can't do this!" He tried to swing his fists but he was so quickly overpowered he could only grunt with exertion as the bigger men closed in on him, and then Paul was suddenly looming over him as Pete and Glenn forced him to the ground. He tried to kick them with his feet but they sidestepped his flailing legs easily. Rick felt a spasm of pain in his left shoulder blade as a nerve was pinched, forcing him to the ground.

"This won't hurt," Paul said. Using the side of his hand, Paul swung a blow down on his neck, just below and behind Rick's right ear.

Paul was right. It didn't hurt at all.

It simply knocked him completely out.

Brian Gaiman listened to the exchange in the closet with bated breath, biting down on the back of his hand to keep from screaming.

He couldn't see what was going on, but judging by the brief struggle that became quickly frenzied, then died as suddenly as it started, something bad had just happened to Rick Nicholson.

OhGodohfuckohjesuschristohpleasedontletthemfindme!

The closet felt hot and cramped. His legs were still stiff due to spending most of the past day hiding in Charlie Thompson's closet. After sneaking in to Charlie's room yesterday and finding it empty, he'd washed his hands and face in the bathroom, checking the abrasions on his wrists and ankles. The first thing he'd done was head for the phone at Charlie's bedside. He'd hit

0 to get an outside extension, but then realized that the phone was dead.

Brian had frowned, wondering why Charlie's phone was dead. He'd never bothered to use the extension in his own room—that's what cell phones were for. Somebody had taken his cell phone during his incarceration, so using the extension in Charlie's room was the next best option. But with no dial tone that option was out of reach.

Brian had debated briefly on letting himself out of Charlie's room and trying somebody else's, then decided against it. The wrong person might see him. It was best to wait for Charlie to come back.

He'd sat on Charlie's unmade bed and was about to settle down and get comfortable when another thought occurred to him: suppose Charlie was partially responsible for his abduction? After all, Charlie was the only person who'd known where he was the day he was abducted from behind the storage shed. If somebody had wanted him badly enough, they would have asked Charlie where to find him when he was most vulnerable and alone. Charlie would have been the person to get that information from. Brian couldn't believe Charlie was the person behind the abduction—in fact, he was confident that if somebody had asked Charlie where he was at that given time, Charlie would have merely given him the location in an effort to be helpful. But then surely Charlie would have heard about his disappearance later that day, right? And in the days that followed, he would have been questioned by security, maybe even the local sheriff, right? If so, wouldn't it be safe to say that Charlie would be surprised to see Brian in his room?

Well, sure. But then again, *if* Charlie was partially responsible for his abduction, for whatever reason, he might not react the way Brian wanted him to. He might prove to be dangerous.

How do I determine that? Brian thought.

That's when Brian got off Charlie's bed and crossed the room to the coat closet. He opened it. It was empty. Charlie's two suitcases were completely packed with the exception of a bundle of blue work clothes that were lying on a chair near the luggage rack in the corner of the room. One of Charlie's suitcases was open, revealing his underwear and sock container. His work boots were sitting on the floor beneath the luggage rack. From the way it looked, Charlie had cleared out his closet early in anticipation of getting the hell out of dodge when the private event was finished, which meant he wouldn't be needing his closet.

Brian had slipped into the closet and closed the door. Then he'd settled into a comfortable position and waited.

Eventually Charlie returned to his room. For the next several hours, Brian listened as Charlie watched TV, talked on his cell phone to somebody named Trevor, and eventually turned in for the night. It was his phone conversation with Trevor that confirmed things with Brian, and just like he thought, Charlie had nothing to do with his abduction.

"Oh, but get this," Charlie had said to Trevor. "Remember my partner, Brian Gaiman? That's right, he's the guy that went missing. Just kinda disappeared. Uh huh, that's him. Anyway, our chief of security here, Paul, he told me this morning that they found evidence on the grounds that Brian had gone on a meth binge for the last four days. Yeah, they found his stash, found evidence he'd been hiding out in some empty warehouse on the north end of the property. So anyway, he tells me that if I see Brian that he might be, you know, kinda wigged out. Paranoid and shit." There'd been a pause as Trevor talked. Brian had to strain to hear, his mind racing and his heart pounding at the obvious ruse Paul Westcott had come up with to explain his sudden disappearance. "Yeah, they're not sure where he is. He might have already scaled the fence and taken off. If so, he's in the woods somewhere. Paul contacted the local sheriff's department and gave them Brian's description. Guess they'll bring him back if he's picked up." Another pause. "Yeah, no shit. Fucking tweakers!"

Brian didn't dare fall asleep, lest he snore or something and wake Charlie up. He didn't dare try to sneak out of the closet, either. Instead, he'd stayed in the closet all night.

At some point, he must have dozed off lightly because it was the sound of Charlie rummaging around in his dressers that woke him up. Brian listened, trying to stay calm as he waited for Charlie to get dressed. When Charlie left his room thirty minutes later, Brian had let out a sigh, trying to contain his emotions. He'd never done meth in his life. In fact, it wasn't drugs that had landed him in prison in the first place—it was breaking and entering. Brian didn't like drugs, and he rarely drank. He believed in living clean and healthy. So to hear that he'd been on a meth binge told him that Paul Westcott, and possibly upper management, was behind his abduction. For some reason, they didn't want the local authorities to get a hold of him, but just in case they did, they had a bullshit story already cooked up for them. And of course nobody would believe Brian. After all, he was a convicted felon.

Brian had waited a full five minutes, then let himself out of the closet. He'd waited for his vision to adjust (the lights were off in Charlie's room but the closet had been pitch dark, much like it had been inside that freezer). The time on the digital clock on the nightstand read seven-thirty. Perfect. Before all this had happened, Brian and Charlie used to meet at the employee bar and grill every morning at this time for breakfast. If he was going to escape, he had to do it now.

Before he left the room, though, he'd taken a quick look around for Charlie's master key card, which opened up the employee-only areas of the building. It was on the dresser, near a pile of change and a set of keys on a large key ring; the keys fit various doors and locks on the Bent Creek grounds. Brian had taken Charlie's master key card and slipped it into his pocket. Charlie wouldn't realize it was missing until tomorrow morning. By then, Brian would be long gone.

He'd let himself out of the room quietly. Then, using his

knowledge of the property layout and the way the buildings were arranged, Brian had quietly made his way over to the administration wing. His path led him back outside and around the grounds again. Twice he thought he'd been spotted by the surveillance cameras, but he'd kept moving forward, expecting a spotlight to hit him at any moment, followed by the words, "Stop right there!" just like in the movies. That never happened. Instead, he got to the administrative wing without being seen and let himself in with Charlie's keycard.

He wasn't sure why he picked Rick Nicholson's office as a safe spot. Probably because he liked Rick and felt comfortable around him. Guy was white-collar all the way, the kind of yuppie Brian used to make fun of, but once he'd gotten to know him, he'd liked him.

Once inside Rick's office he'd closed the door and headed straight for his desk. Picked up the phone. Got an open line. Hit the star button, then the nine button to get an outside line.

And that's when he heard the outside door to the administration wing, the door he'd just entered, click open and then close.

His adrenaline racing, Brian had put the phone down and looked around the room for any avenue of escape. His eyes darted to a door set catty-corner to the entrance to Rick's office. He darted toward it, opened the door, saw it was a coat closet, and he closed the door and fought to contain his rising fear as somebody entered the room.

Once he was positive it was Rick sitting at his desk, Brian was at a crossroads. He trusted Rick. He had a good feeling about him, and he knew he wasn't like the rest of the upper management types here. He stuck up for his people. And he was very reasonable. Surely he could—

He couldn't help it. That's when he'd cracked the door open and called out to Rick.

And now he was back in the closet, listening to the aftermath of Rick's confrontation with Paul Westcott and his two goons.

"How long will he be out?" Pete asked.

"Couple minutes," Paul Westcott replied. "The area I hit him in...there's a nerve there in the back of your neck, right behind your ear. Hit somebody hard enough there, it disrupts the electrical signal and the brain interprets trouble and shuts your body down. That's your anatomy lesson for the day, gentleman. Remember it. Just don't hit somebody too hard there, or it'll kill them. Now, let's get Rick out of here and get him to the kitchen."

There was the sound of the three of them maneuvering around to pick Rick up off the floor. Amid the grunting and heaving, Glen said, "You think we should search his office?"

Brian felt his heart lodge in his throat. His breath held, he could only think, *no, please don't search the office, just get out of here, please, just* leave!

"Yeah, we probably should," Paul responded. "In fact, we should probably search every cubical and office in the admin area. Let's get him to the kitchen first."

Shit! Brian waited as the three security guys carried Rick out of his office, their footfalls fading as they headed down the hall toward the end of the wing.

CHAPTER 28

Eight Months Ago

He was at an exclusive private party in a very large house nestled in the foothills of the Saddleback Mountain Region in Aliso Viejo, California. The home was owned by Earl Sanders and it was impressive. Ten thousand square feet, with crown moldings, a high ceilinged great room, and a large deck off the back that overlooked a sparkling swimming pool—it would set Joe back about seventeen million if he were to buy it. Earl had already mentioned to Joe that he was thinking of selling. Joe had feigned interest. Seventeen million was easily within his price range, but he wasn't too wild about the location. It was too close to the foothills. Brush fire territory. If he was going to have another home in Orange County, he'd prefer a place at the beach, preferably perched on a cliff overlooking the ocean. He'd seen such a place yesterday while flipping through a real estate paper and the asking price was thirty-five million. If he was going to pay that kind of money for a California house, it better goddamn well have a spectacular ocean view. The only thing Earl Sanders's home had going for it was a pretty spectacular view of the entire South Orange County area and Saddleback valley.

There were two dozen people at the house, most of them Earl's colleagues. Joe got a chance to talk a bit more with Earl this time, and found him to be a gregarious family man. His wife had taken their kids away for the weekend to Magic Mountain and weren't due back until the following day. Joe learned that Earl Saunders was involved in the overseas investing market. He was also involved in several shell corporations that served as holding companies for other interests, most of them in the construction industry. "I do a lot of business with the Tyler Corporation," Earl had told Joe as they stood at the bar. "I know all their top brass—Steve Bloch, Harry Goldstein, Wayne Sanders. I also sit on the board of a few companies John and George are involved in."

Joe had nodded, sipping his drink. He didn't react, but when Earl mentioned Wayne Sanders's name, his antennae had gone up.

Finally! A lead on the elusive Bill Richards!

Chef Munchel, the chef he'd met last month in Newport Beach, was catering the dinner. John Lansdale and George Spector had wandered over and John had raised his glass at them and smiled. "Come join the party!"

The four of them had talked business for a little bit, then Earl had begged off. "I need to tend to some things for the party," he'd said. "You guys make yourself at home. Enjoy!"

Chef Jim Munchel was ensconced in the huge kitchen preparing the main courses and directing the activities of his garnish and sous chef. Talk about the impending merger from their meeting at the restaurant last month had concluded with an agreement—come tomorrow, the lawyers were going to get together via Skype and agree to the basics per their clients' wishes; then, the paperwork would get drawn up. Things could be legal within another month or so. Wiggling into Earl's radar hadn't come easy, but it was a step closer to Wayne Sanders, whose name was on the articles of incorporation papers Dean had uncovered at the Casper County Deeds office for Apex, Limited, the company that had placed the advertisement for the job Carla had applied for. Apex, Limited had pulled out of the small office space they had rented during the time Carla had supposedly visited them, and a search through industry sources didn't turn up anything on them. If Bill Richards worked for Apex, Mr. Sanders could lead John and Dean to him. That was the theory, and that was the loose plan Joe and Dean had come up with; start digging, worm your way into the lives of these people and make your way to Mr. Sanders and, from there, the elusive Mr. Richards. The last person to apparently see Carla alive.

Joe thought about this as he drained the rest of his martini. He glanced toward the kitchen. "I'll be right back," he said.

George nodded. "You getting another drink?"

"That and some munchies," Joe said.

"I'll go with you." George joined him and together they entered the house and made their way to the huge center island that bordered the kitchen and the living room.

A very large array of Hors D'oeuvres had been placed on various serving trays that rested on one half of the island—various finger sandwiches (capicola, salami, muenster cheese), caviar and crackers, ladyfingers, peeled carrots with various dips, and the requisite potato chips with sour cream and onion dip. Even the wealthy loved chips and dip. Joe picked up a carrot and popped it in his mouth as a young woman dressed in a backless white outfit floated by and asked if he wanted a refill on his drink. She took their glasses and departed to refill them at the bar (which was positioned in the corner near the kitchen).

"Earl knows Chef Munchel pretty well, I see," Joe said.

"Oh yeah," George said. "We all do. Jim caters to some pretty important, influential people."

"Well, I can see why. The food at the restaurant was spectacular."

Chef Munchel noticed them and called out. "Gentlemen! Mr. Spector and Mr. Garrison! Come to the kitchen for a moment!"

Joe and George walked around the center island to the kitchen, trying to stay out of the way of the other kitchen staff. Chef Munchel was standing over the eight burner stove. He held a spoon up in a *here, try this*, gesture to Joe. "What is it?" Joe asked, curious.

"Don't ask, just taste," Jim said. He held his left hand below the spoon to catch any dripping sauce.

The aroma was intoxicating, and the look and texture of the food was wonderful. Joe detected a hint of oregano and spice in the tomato-based sauce. The meat was finely cut, but Joe couldn't tell what it was. Curious, he nodded and let Chef Munchel spoon a bite into his mouth. An explosion of flavor rocked his senses. He chewed, savoring the myriad of tastes. The meat was so tender that it melted in his mouth. "What is this?" he marveled. "It's wonderful!"

"One moment," Chef Munchel said. He spooned a sample for George, who stood beside Joe. George nodded, smacking his lips. "Oh yeah, this is great! Wonderful!"

Jim smiled. He glanced at Joe, a twinkle in his eye as he turned back to the dish that was simmering in a very large skillet on the stove. He moved the skillet away to a nearby counter for final preparation. Beside him, another chef was preparing another batch of the same dish. Must be the main course, Joe thought.

"So what is it?" Joe asked.

"Take a guess," Jim invited.

The taste and sensation of the dish was still fresh on his mind. "The meat has the consistency and texture of a fine cut of chicken, but the taste was vaguely pork-like to me."

"Mr. Garrison wins the Rolls Royce!" Jim cried. He turned his attention back to the stove. "That was pork loin simmered in a garlic tomato-based sauce that is a secret recipe of mine. The pork loin itself is marinated in a lime-based marinade. This dish is being served with rice pilaf and spinach salad with raisins."

Joe's mouth watered at the mention of what was on the menu. "Once again, I have come to the right place."

George laughed beside him. "Jim has a way with food, all right. I don't think there's a dish Chef Munchel *hasn't* tried making."

"You name it, I've cooked it," Jim said, standing nonchalantly at the kitchen as he worked his magic. "I've prepared everything from peanut-butter and jelly sandwiches for kids' birthday parties to five course meals with exotic and rare ingredients for kings and princes in far away lands. I've cooked things most people wouldn't eat if you told them what the ingredients were. I've—"

"You mean like monkey brains and birds nest soup?" Joe piped in, his tone joking. The cocktail waitress had delivered their drinks and Joe took a sip of his.

"Yes, I've prepared both before. Monkey brains are considered a delicacy in some Asian cultures."

George raised his eyebrows. "You've prepared *that*, Jim? I didn't know that."

"Aren't the monkeys still alive when you...you know...eat their brains?" Joe tried not to look repulsed by the idea.

Jim sighed. "I'm afraid that is an urban legend, Mr. Garrison. The dish is usually prepared as part of an ingredient in a variety of Asian meals, and is served with coconut palms and banana leaves. It can be fried, boiled, or cooked in a wok with a variety of herbs and spices. But it is *never* consumed raw while the monkey is alive. You've watched too many movies."

Joe nodded. "I remember in one of the *Indiana Jones* films, the main character was served chilled monkey brains as part of the meal."

"There are dozens of rare and exotic dishes," Chef Munchel said. He was working on preparing another batch of the wonderful pork loin he'd just given Joe and George a taste of. One of the sous chefs had removed the skillet and was dishing portions out over a bed of steamed vegetables and rice. "There is a dish I've prepared that uses the thorax and the legs of the South American Goliath bird-eating spider. That's quite good. I've also prepared dishes with tiger meat, giraffe, and sea turtles."

"I've had sea turtle before," Joe said, recounting a trip he'd taken to New Orleans on business where he'd tried sea turtle and alligator. "I really liked it."

"Would you try some of the other dishes Chef Munchel mentioned?" George asked. He was grinning.

Joe shrugged. "You know, if it was any other chef, I'd say no. But I've seen this man work, and I've tasted his food twice, and I would have to say yes. I'll try anything he prepares."

"*Anything*? Those are some bold words, Mr. Garrison." Watching Chef Munchel work effortlessly at the stove, his fingers deftly pinching the right amount of seasoning into the simmering dish was like watching a skilled magician. "I've prepared dishes utilizing animal parts that are usually disposed of in Western cooking. Lungs, livers, hearts, intestines, and the brains of chickens and cows—you'd be surprised at what you can create out of what most people would find unappetizing."

"I've had *menudo*," Joe said. "And when I was in Pennsylvania on business, I had pig stomach and scrapple once. I liked it."

"So you aren't immune to the leftovers?"

"Not at all."

"That's good to know." Chef Munchel gave Joe a grin. "Dinner will be served shortly. Why don't the two of you find yourselves a place at the table?"

Joe and George left the kitchen and threaded their way through the living room to the large and expansive dining room. "Chef Munchel is an interesting guy," Joe said. "I bet he'll pretty much prepare whatever you want when you hire him for something like this, won't he?"

"Absolutely," George said. The two of them found a place at the end of the table and sat down. "Jim will track down any ingredient within the budget he is allowed, and he is not adverse to cooking dishes that are considered taboo in Western culture."

"Really?"

"Oh yeah." George took a sip of his drink. "I attended one event where the menu consisted of bull penis and the beating heart of a cobra."

Joe raised his eyebrows. "Beating heart of a cobra?"

"Yeah." George chuckled and shook his head. "I wouldn't touch *that*. The bull penis, on the other hand, was pretty tasty."

"What did it taste like?"

"A good filet mignon!" George laughed. Joe laughed too.

As other guests arrived and Earl appeared at the head of the table, Joe unrolled the heavy cloth napkin that was part of his place-setting and set it on his lap. George was halfway finished with his drink. "I think I might have to get Chef Munchel's number," Joe said. "The guys I work with frequently host private parties like this. Munchel would be a big hit."

"I bet he would," George said.

"I might have to talk him into catering an event for me," Joe said, continuing with his train of thought. "Think Chef Munchel would cook for me if I hire him?"

George smiled and looked at Joe. "Mr. Garrison, for the right money, Chef Munchel will prepare anything you want."

CHAPTER 29

Five more days. That's all she had to put up with. Five more days.

Anna King was the only waitress who'd been tapped for dinner service for the private event. Under normal circumstances, it would be a piece of cake. There were only a dozen high rollers at Bent Creek for the private event, most of them consisting of the Board of Directors, which Anna thought was strange. Equally strange was the fact that she'd heard all of them had arrived within the past day or so, with the exception of Wayne, the head-honcho. Unlike Wayne, who Anna had never met, much less caught a glimpse of, they'd all made brief appearances around the grounds in the final days of the season. Currently, all of them except for Drake Johnson and Ben Eastman were still in their suites. Drake and Ben were seated at Table Four having their morning coffee and breakfast, which Anna had just served them.

Anna thought about this as she prepared drink orders—coffee and various juices—and delivered them to the few tables seating patrons. The way she'd heard it, the grounds were being rented by a private party for the next five days. No problem there, but why were all Board members present? The way Anna saw it, there were perhaps half a dozen other people who had remained after the facility closed for the season. Carl White was one of them. Theresa and Mitch Johnson, the couple she'd become friendly with a few nights ago, was another. All three of them were seated at two different tables. The Johnson couple were talking quietly over their morning coffee. Mr. White was reading the *Wall Street Journal*, a bagel with cream cheese and a carafe of coffee at his table. Five guests made for a slow breakfast service.

Chef Munchel was currently performing kitchen duties and it was a piece of cake for him, too. Anna wondered why Chef Munchel had dismissed all of the kitchen staff—including the bartenders—and had only kept her. The way it was explained to her, she was only required to work breakfast and dinner service for the next five days. She wouldn't be required to do clean-up. After her service, she was free to lounge around in her room all day, use the spa and pool, and do whatever she felt like so long as she didn't venture into the private banquet areas (which she wouldn't have access to anyway, being a secured area). She had talked with Barry Young, one of Chef Munchel's assistant chefs, one morning a week or two back, about the private event. Barry had been on staff at Bent Creek for five years, and he thought Chef Munchel was strange. "But hey, they're rich pricks and they pay good." They'd been sitting with a group of fellow employees at the employee bar-and-grill. He was a big guy, his forearms heavily tattooed. He reminded Anna of an English bulldog. "If these rich fucks wanna pay me ten G's for twenty hours of work for the next five days, I'd be down with that."

Chef Munchel broke her train of thought, pushing two plates out at her from the pass. "Johnson's order is up," he said. He nodded at her, giving her a smile. Comrades in arms. Anna smiled back and transferred the orders to a serving tray. Scrambled eggs and bacon on one plate with a slice of orange, and a breakfast crepe with linked sausage framed with fresh cut strawberries on another. Both dishes looked and smelled wonderful. Anna balanced the tray on her left hand and headed toward the Johnson's table.

She had to walk past Carl White's table and the table where

the two Bent Creek board members were seated to reach the Johnson's. She'd had the feeling throughout the morning that she was being observed. It was subtle, and most people wouldn't have noticed, but Anna wasn't most people. She picked up on things like this, and it was especially strong this morning; Carl White sneaking quick glances at her as she took orders from other tables; brief lapses in conversation from the two board members as she passed them on her way to take the Johnson's initial order; and most revealing of all, the Johnsons and their continued appraising glances at her that were becoming more blatant as the morning progressed. And to think they'd been so subtle about what had went down between the three of them earlier. Considering how things had played out last night and this morning, she was surprised to see the Johnson's.

That look on Theresa and Mitch Johnson was clear-cut as she approached their table with their breakfast. Ignoring them, she set their plates in front of them and said, "Enjoy your meal."

"Oh, we will," Theresa said.

Mitch chuckled. "We'll especially enjoy it, Ms. King. I can't wait." Mitch smiled at her. For the first time since meeting him, and spending such quality time with him, that smile sent a shiver up her spine.

She wasn't aware that somebody had approached her from behind until his hand was over her face, covering her mouth and nose. Anna went into immediate fight mode, thrashing wildly. The serving tray dropped to the floor with a loud clang. She drove her right elbow into somebody's abdomen. The man behind her grunted in pain. "You ain't doin' that shit to me, bitch," he said in her ear. She felt his fingers press against her carotid artery.

And in the final seconds before she lost consciousness, Anna saw that the other patrons—the two board members and Carl White—were watching this exchange with amusement, not with rising alarm or horror.

And then she blacked out.

CHAPTER 30

Eight Months Ago, A Few Days After The Event In Aliso Viejo, California

Joe Taylor had tried every search phrase in every available search engine: Google, Bing, Yahoo. He'd clicked on every link the results spit back at him.

And through all that, he'd found nothing he didn't already know.

Information on Chef Jim Munchel, full name James Michael Munchel, was well known to culinary artists and food lovers all over the world. Born March 7, 1961 in Harrisburg, Pennsylvania, Jim was the youngest of three children. He'd put himself through culinary school by managing a B. Dalton bookstore in a mall in Camp Hill, a suburb of Harrisburg. In September of 1988 he was fired for hosting a booksigning by local horror authors John Skipp & Craig Spector after being forbidden to by the corporate office. His firing had no effect on him: Jim Munchel was already on his way to becoming the world renowned chef he would become famous for. He bounced back by getting a job at a restaurant in Lititz, Pennsylvania called Scooters. His cooking became a local favorite and by the early nineties he had moved to Philadelphia and was working at a variety of five-star restaurants. In 2000 he opened his own restaurant, The Pinnacle, in Center City. He opened the Newport Beach location in 2005 and a New York City location in 2008. Despite his success, he refused most media interviews and guest appearances on various cooking shows, most notably *Iron Chef*. "I didn't get into cooking to be a celebrity," Jim Munchel was quoted as saying in a 2009 *Philadelphia* magazine article. "I got into it because I love it and it is pure artistic expression of the highest honor. I enjoy food, and I enjoy preparing meals for my guests. Cooking a meal for somebody is the most pure form of love and kindness one can bestow on another, and it pleases me when people enjoy my food."

The dozen or so biographies on Munchel that Joe Taylor managed to dig up—from his restaurant's websites to his Wikipedia entry, were nearly identical. Only the *Philadelphia* magazine article gave more detailed background information on the chef, and even that seemed too typical, too bland. Joe Taylor had printed the article out and set it to one side on his cherrywood desk for future reference.

Searches on George Spector, John Lansdale, and Earl Saunders were equally unsuccessful. Dean Campbell had been running various background checks on George Spector ever since Joe returned from St. Louis. Between their combined efforts, they hadn't learned much on any of them. They hadn't even learned anything about Bill Richards, the man Carla had last seen for her alleged job interview. The only thing Dean Campbell was one hundred percent sure of was that the company Bill claimed to represent, Apex, Limited, didn't exist.

As for Bill Richards himself, his name was listed in the articles of incorporation and that was where the trail ran cold. Bill Richards was not listed in any state government database—he had no driver's license, no Social Security number. To Joe Taylor, it was as if Bill Richards didn't even exist.

The research Joe had conducted at the Casper, Wyoming Deeds Office had yielded several important finds. One, the building it was believed Carla had gone to for her interview was owned by a very large holding company, Randolph Unlimited, who owned similar property throughout Wyoming, Montana, and Colorado. They did not have a tenant at their Casper location called Apex, Limited or any variation thereof. However, they *did* have a tenant in that location called Ace Corporation, which was a sole proprietorship. It was also a shell corporation for an outfit called Mountain Funds.

Mountain Funds was a commodity trading firm headed by a man named Wayne Sanders.

Joe Taylor pushed his chair back from the computer and rubbed his eyes. The threads were faint, but he couldn't ignore them. Once you followed one, a pandora's box opened, leading you to someplace else. Mountain Funds was one of the companies on George Spector's list of prospectuses. Joe had given that information to Dean Campbell. This morning, Dean called him with some startling news.

"Get this," Dean had said. "Mountain Funds is a pretty legit company. They deal directly with Goldman Sachs and a bunch of other Wall Street players. Their CEO, Wayne Sanders, is also involved in international investing and here's where it gets interesting. One of his clients is a member of the Saudi royal family."

Joe hadn't found that information so tantalizing. "Big deal. The Saudi's have a lot of money in our banks and mutual funds. Everybody knows that."

"Yeah, I know. But ten years ago, a woman filed suit against Mr. Sanders in a New York lower circuit court claiming she'd been drugged while on a business trip to Saudi Arabia with him. She claimed Mr. Sanders attempted to force her into servitude—forced slavery."

That got Joe's attention. "Forced slavery?"

"Yeah," Dean said. "Unfortunately, that's as far as it got. Sanders settled the case out of court on the condition the plaintiff never speak of the matter again. I located her and tried to get her to talk. She ain't talkin'."

"Offer her money," Joe suggested.

"Are you serious? She can't talk, Joe. She's bound by the terms of the agreement."

"Fly out to see her," Joe suggested. "Follow her, make sure she's alone and nobody has tailed you. Then approach her, offer her two hundred grand in cash if she'll tell you everything she knows about Mr. Sanders."

"I'm sure Wayne Sanders settled with her for a lot more than two hundred grand."

"Then find out what it was and double it."

"Joe—"

"I'm serious, Dean. This is a good lead. If Wayne Sanders is running some kind of white slavery ring...if Carla got dragged into it on US soil..." The thought repulsed him. And to think he was more worried about Carla being sold into slavery if she'd gone to a Muslim country like Saudi Arabia. "Money gets people to talk," he said, closing his eyes. "I'll pay anything to get Carla back, Dean. *Anything*. I *have* the money. I will hand over my entire fortune if it brings Carla back."

There'd been a pause on the other end of the line. Dean knew how much Joe Taylor was worth. "I'll see what I can do," Dean had said.

That had been yesterday. Dean was in New York now. He'd located the woman and was tailing her. Joe had received an update an hour ago. He'd told Dean he was working on connecting the dots on his end. And it was all starting to come together.

Wayne Sanders's company had employed Bill Richards. Wayne was connected to George Spector, who was connected to John Lansdale and Earl Sanders by virtue of belonging to the same country club in Wyoming, a big sprawling place called Bent Creek. He'd heard the name in passing at Earl's house a few days ago, shortly after Chef Munchel served dinner. In normal circumstances he might not have paid attention to it. Joe had heard George Spector make an aside to another guest at the party that Chef Munchel often catered and prepared extremely exotic cuisine for a private party he was involved with at Bent Creek. The comment was made casually, but it later gained Joe's attention when the guest began to bug George about it and he mentioned the elusive Bill Richards by name. *How do I get invited to attend something like this? I keep telling Bill Richard's that I'd love to try more of Chef Munchel's more esoteric and exotic food. I actually flew down here hoping I could meet Mr. Richards, but his schedule is terrible. Said he wouldn't be able to introduce me to Chef Munchel. I told Bill that I can pay for it! Why won't you tell me*? And each time, George would brush it aside and try to change the conversation. Joe could tell George regretted bringing it up to the guest, that if he hadn't been so tipsy he might not have said anything. Joe used this opportunity to spring to the rescue. "I'm having an event in New York and I still haven't hired a chef," he'd said. "If Munchel is available to work the event for me, I'll make sure you're invited, sir."

The man had smirked at George. "See, that's how colleagues are *supposed* to treat each other!"

The man had then introduced himself to Joe and given him his business card. His name was Ralph Ferrano, and he was involved with hedge fund portfolios. Joe later learned that Ferrano had never formally met Bill Richards; they'd only spoken by phone. "He was supposed to be here," Ralph later told Joe. By this time, George had excused himself and Joe was trying to learn more about Bill Richards without trying to seem overly interested. "He's apparently very tight with our host, Mr. Sanders. But Earl said Bill couldn't make it."

Joe sat back in his comfortable office chair, remembering that event and others, making the connections.

There was nothing on paper. Nothing official in cyberspace. But the connections existed via word of mouth and recommendation: Joe was now connected to George Spector, John Lansdale, and Earl Sanders. Earl Sanders knew a guy named Bill Richards—presumably the same Bill Richards he and Dean

Campbell were looking for—who also shared a professional relationship with Chef Jim Munchel. George Spector and Bill Richards had apparently attended an event Chef Jim Munchel catered at a place called Bent Creek Country Club.

George Spector and Bill Richards were apparently connected to Mountain Funds, which was headed by Wayne Sanders.

The pieces were coming together, but there were still parts missing.

What to do...?

Joe navigated over to the main website of Chef Jim Munchel's restaurant. He clicked on the *Contact Us* box. The page came up and displayed the address and locations of all three restaurants. Figuring Jim's headquarters was still in Philadelphia, he opted to start with that location. He picked up the extension on his desk and proceeded to make the first of several calls to arrange for a private banquet catered by Chef Jim Munchel.

CHAPTER 31

When Rick Nicholson swam up from the murky depths of unconsciousness, he knew he was facing trouble once he breached the surface.

He opened his eyes. He didn't immediately recognize the room he was in. It looked like a store room. The wall he was facing was concrete and metal shelving had been erected against it. Boxes sat on the shelves. Rick tried to control his breathing and gather his wits, letting his senses report his current state to him: he was lying on a bare concrete floor, his hands were tied behind his back, ankles lashed together. He'd been set down on his left side, facing a bare concrete wall. The air was cool, and as he lay there collecting his wits, he felt another presence in the room.

"He's waking up," somebody said.

Rick felt his breath hitch in. His heart began to trip-hammer. He felt no pain. He remembered being knocked out. His last thought had been of Paul smacking him with a karate chop to the back of the neck, then nothingness.

Footsteps behind him approached. The sound of somebody crouching to the floor. Rough hands grasped his shoulder and turned him over onto his back.

A face leered down at him. Paul Westcott. Standing behind him were Pete and Glenn from Security. They didn't look too happy, either. Paul snapped his fingers over Rick's face. "You hear me?"

Rick nodded. His throat was dry.

"Scared?"

Rick nodded again and gulped. "Yeah," he managed.

"You know why you're in trouble?"

"No." It was the truth. He didn't know why they'd done this to him. It was one thing to be accused of theft by your employer. It was another thing for your employer's security team to assault you and hold you hostage. Did Paul contact the Wyoming State Police? He hoped so. He wanted off Bent Creek grounds immediately, and if being hauled away by the State Police to sit in a holding cell for a day or two until he made bail was the only way out, he was taking it. He would deal with the theft accusation later, through the courts. And he would bust their ass for illegally assaulting and detaining him.

"I'll explain it to you then," Paul said. "You *are* aware of the thefts over the last few weeks on Bent Creek grounds, yes?"

Rick nodded. "Yes."

"And you are aware that two of those thefts were of cash money, stolen from two different guests."

"I didn't take any money," Rick said.

Paul held up his right hand to stop him and continued. "Two hundred and fifty thousand dollars in cash was stolen from one of our guests two days ago from a locked briefcase. The briefcase was in the guest's room. In addition, three hundred thousand was stolen from another guest this past Monday. It was originally thought the thefts were conducted by one of the cleaning staff. *You* were present at most of the questionings of the cleaning staff, and you helped supervise the search of their rooms. I must say that was very clever on your part, Mr. Nicholson."

"I didn't take any money!" Rick stated again, more forceful.

Paul ignored him. "We looked at everybody. We even followed up several leads involving Bent Creek guests that looked promising. None of these leads panned out. Then we decided to search the rooms of our senior staff members. That's when we found part of the money in your briefcase stashed under your bed."

"I didn't take it!"

"How did that money get there?"

"I don't know!"

"It just magically appeared in your briefcase under your bed?"

"I said, I don't know!"

"Do you know which briefcase I'm talking about?"

Rick paused for a moment. When Paul and his security team had walked into his office carrying his tan briefcase, he'd wondered what was going on. He'd recognized it immediately from the scratch along the lid. He took a deep breath. "I have a tan briefcase. I keep important business papers in it."

"You kept a goodly portion of almost three hundred thousand dollars in that briefcase," Paul countered. "The rest you must have smuggled off the grounds in your duffel bag yesterday, when you left to tend to your so-called sick mother."

"I didn't put that money in the briefcase!"

"Then how did it get there?"

Rick wanted to say, *you guys did it,* but he didn't want to provoke a violent reaction. Instead, he thoughtfully phrased his response carefully. "I don't know. Somebody must have it in for me."

"So you were framed?"

"Maybe."

"Who would want to frame you, Mr. Nicholson? Your employees? I find that hard to believe. Your direct reports liked you."

Rick realized that this looked really bad. The looks Paul, Glenn, and Pete were giving him conveyed one thing: they didn't believe him. This made him nervous, and he began to stammer. "I-I didn't have ah-ah-anything to do with this. I sw-swear to God!"

"You *do* realize that all the evidence points to you?" Paul said. "You have key card access to all the rooms. I'm sure with the right amount of investigating, we can connect the dots even further. All it will take will be a search warrant or two, and we can get that easy."

"Go ahead," Rick said, releasing his breath and feeling a slight wave of relief come over him as the implications became obvious. "Get a search warrant. I'll consent to that."

There was a buzzing noise. Paul calmly reached into his breast pocket and pulled out his Blackberry. He put it to his ear. "Yes?" He listened for a moment, then stood up, turned away from Paul. Glenn and Pete looked at him, their features concerned as Paul's expression changed. "Yes, I understand. I'll be right over." He pressed the disconnect button and nodded at his team. "That was Emily. She wants to see us in the main conference room."

The three men stepped away as a single unit. Rick craned his neck to watch their retreat and saw that his first impression was right—he *was* in a storage room. He immediately identified it as the large spare storage room right off the main pantry. Two large walk in freezers sat directly across from him. Glenn and Pete exited the storage room. Paul turned back to Rick. "Don't go anywhere. We'll continue our discussion later."

Then Paul exited the room and shut the door behind him. Rick heard the lock engage.

The moment they were gone, Rick closed his eyes and fought to control his emotions. He had to be calm, had to think this through. He had to get out of this mess and he had to do it carefully. He had no idea how that money wound up in his briefcase. It was obvious *somebody* had to be blamed for the thefts; somebody had to be the scapegoat, and for reasons beyond his comprehension, that turned out to be Rick. Fine. Let them blame him. Let them press charges. Let the State Police take him to jail. Getting off Bent Creek property was the first step. The next step was getting in touch with his former partners at the law firm to seek their help. He was confident they would not only rally to his cause, but would vigorously defend him in the process. When it was over, they might even welcome him back into the fold. He never should have left the law firm in the first place. That had been a mistake.

The more Rick thought this over, the better he began to feel. He would be vindicated. If this wound up in court, he would be vindicated the moment any mention was made of illegal detainment and imprisonment. And with the proper investigation on Rick's part, who knew what kind of dirt he could dig up on Paul Westcott and the rest of the Bent Creek upper echelon? All Rick had to do was wait this out and get out of here.

Rick took a deep breath and let it out. He felt better. He felt confident. When this was over, Paul Westcott and every Board of Director of Bent Creek was going to wish they'd never hired him.

CHAPTER 32

Seven Months Ago

The party was turning out to be a smashing success.

Joe held it at the upper West Side apartment of a close friend, Angus Scott, one of three other people in his inner circle who knew about his efforts to find Carla. Angus was an investment banker. Short, balding, and approaching sixty, Angus had been married and divorced four times. He was currently in a long-term relationship with potential wife #5. "But we'll never get married," he'd told Joe once a few years ago. "No need to give her any incentive to chip away at my estate the way the others did." Angus had laughed about it, but Joe never understood why his friend had never displayed more anger about the divorces. His first marriage was the only one that produced children, and Angus was a great father. Despite his busy schedule, he'd always found the time to attend their sporting and school events, to be a part of their lives. He was even on very good terms with ex-wife #1. Connie was her name. Joe had liked Connie. Still liked her. It was a shame wives #2-4 had been gold diggers. They'd hung around long enough for things to be legal, then they'd filed for divorce and demanded high alimonies. Angus was one of those guys who had the uncanny ability to be attracted to women who wanted nothing more than to transfer a portion of his money to them.

So when Angus offered to host the party at his Upper Westside penthouse apartment, Joe had taken him up on the offer. Angus knew what he'd gone through with Carla's disappearance, and he'd provided a reliable background to the Bob Garrison pseudonym for the reference checks with George Spector and his group. Joe's other close friends—Tom Spellman and Charles Glowacz—had provided air-tight references as well. He counted himself lucky to have such friends.

Booking Chef Munchel had been as simple as making the arrangement with the Chef's business manager. Normally, Munchel had to be booked months in advance. Joe had been prepared for that. Luck was on his side, though. An opening had come up for the weekend of the 10th. Joe had reserved the spot immediately on his American Express card. Then he'd called Angus with the news, hoping his friend could pull strings at the last minute. "I'll make the arrangements on my end," Angus had said. "Don't worry about it."

And now the party had been under full swing since eight o'clock.

Angus and Joe had billed the event as a social mixer for their respective firms. Chuck Glowacz had flown in from Los Angeles. Angus had invited a couple of lower-rung stock brokers from his firm—guys who had never met Joe Taylor and were introduced to him as Bob Garrison to lend verisimilitude. In turn, Joe had invited Dean Campbell, Earl Sanders, George Spector and John Lansdale. In total, there were two dozen guests.

Joe had spent most of the time at the bar in the kitchen, talking to Jim Munchel and his kitchen staff. He drank countless manhattans. He got tipsy. Despite this, he was very aware of Angus and Dean keeping an eye on things. That's what they were here for. Joe's goal was to get into Munchel's inner circle. He was already part of Lansdale's and Spector's. He was on the verge of knowing about their private deals, and despite Earl Sanders being somewhat distant, he was getting to know him better, too. He wanted to get closer to Munchel to learn more about Bent Creek and Wayne Sanders, which would lead him to Bill Richards.

Jim Munchel had prepared balsamic vinaigrette scallops wrapped in bacon as appetizers. Joe had devoured them, finding them very good. He'd also been partial to the escargots in lime-butter sauce and the buffalo frog-legs. When he'd booked the event he'd spent an hour with Munchel over the phone discussing the menu. Joe had picked the chef's brain on exotic cuisine. They'd finally settled on something exotic and tantalizing: the aforementioned appetizers along with braised butterflied leg of lamb, Ostrich steaks, or Reticulated Python flanks for the meat; these dishes were served over either beds of wild rice, sautéed mushrooms and gravy made from pig stock, or broiled banana leaves. The desserts were more traditional, everything from truffles to flan, to various ice creams.

"Are you sure you want the python flanks?" Munchel had asked him. "Your guests might balk at a dish that's so foreign to them."

"Maybe they will," Joe had responded. "But *I* certainly want to try it. And my partner Angus has been chomping at the bit to sample it the moment he saw it on your menu."

"Ah! I see." The menu Joe had referred to was the special menu, accessible only by username/password on Munchel's website after the deposit had been made. It wasn't available to the general public. Sautéed monkey brains had been on the menu, along with live Octopus (in which Octopus tentacles were prepared and served while the Octopus was still alive, braised in a sauce partially made with Octopus ink) and a similar dish utilizing live lobster. The monkey brain dish had been the first thing Joe had asked for, but Munchel reported that he wouldn't have a good source for the ingredient until fall. He'd wanted to go with the live Octopus but was unsure if some of his guests, particularly Dean, Chuck, Tom, and Angus, would be able to stomach it. The python had been the more logical choice.

Once again, Joe dined with Spector, Sanders, and Lansdale,

and maintained a chummy rapport with Munchel after dinner service. He was feeling the effects of the alcohol, too. It made him more outgoing, more agreeable to conversation. His caution and cunning remained, though; he held back just enough to retain that semblance of control so he could remember things later. Besides, he also had Dean Campbell and Angus Scott to cover his back.

When dinner and dessert was over and the mixer resumed in various portions of the spacious apartment, Joe found himself at the large center island talking food with Chef Munchel and George Spector. "That was wonderful," Joe told Chef Munchel. "Too bad you didn't have access to the monkey brains. I would have liked to have had that again."

"Chef has prepared sautéed lamb's brains and duck embryos as well," George said. He took a sip of his drink—a martini. "Ever had those?"

"Sautéed lamb's brains, yes," Joe said, the lie coming across perfectly. "Duck embryos, no. Speaking of which," he turned to George, letting his train of thought take over from his research into such exotic cuisine. "One time on a business trip here I went with some colleagues to a Korean restaurant where we had freshly vivisected lobster and live octopus. *That* was good!"

"I've had that too," George exclaimed. "That's Kim's Place in Lower Manhattan, right?"

"Yes, that's it," Joe said.

Chef Munchel listened as he cleaned the kitchen. "You like seafood, Mr. Garrison?"

"Love it."

"And we know you like lamb and beef from our previous dinners," Chef Munchel continued. "What about pork?"

"That too, and that reminds me." He turned to George Spector. "Here's one...pig fetuses broiled in orange butter sauce. Had that in Minneapolis once."

"That, I've never tried," George admitted.

Chef Munchel was listening to all this with great interest. "I'm pleasantly surprised, Mr. Garrison. I didn't take you for a connoisseur."

"I never thought I would be until my work started taking me to far flung locations." Joe took a sip of his drink. "I had business once in Kenya, in Nairobi. A few days after we concluded our business, several of us hired a travel guide who took us to this fabulous place off in Kisumu in Nyanza Province and the chef there prepared gorilla breasts grilled in mango salsa."

"*Whoa*!" George looked impressed. "Now *that* is a dish. I've only had once myself. Chef Munchel prepared it."

"Was that Silverback breasts, Mr. Garrison?" Chef Munchel asked.

"Yes, they were."

"And where was this?"

"The Kisumu on Dunga Road. The Chef's name was Matubi. Odd man. Nice enough, but odd." Joe had rehearsed this the day before while on a marathon research session. He'd plucked Matubi's name from a cached website on the internet about black market exotic foods.

"Silverback Gorilla meat is black market," Chef Munchel said, his voice lowered as he began to wipe down the marble countertop. "It's easy to prepare, but challenging due to its black market status. I've only prepared it twice. I hope you don't ask me to procure it for you, because I'm afraid my floor price will be *extremely* high."

Joe chuckled. "Don't worry about it. I wouldn't want you to take the risk. Besides, if I want the dish that badly, I'd compensate you generously."

"I appreciate that, Mr. Garrison." Munchel continued wiping down the counter.

"Well, if you decide to employ Chef Munchel's services in preparing Silverback breasts, give me a call!" George Spector elbowed him good-naturedly and downed the rest of his drink. He got to his feet. "I think I need another drink."

Joe raised his glass. "I'll be here."

As George ambled off to the bar for a refill, Chef Munchel finished with the counter. Joe nodded to him. "I know Silverback is taboo. Probably because it's like eating Long Pig. And that's something I've only heard about through an acquaintance who claimed he tried it in South America during some native ritual."

"It was served as part of a religious ceremony?"

"So says my friend Richard." Joe grinned. "But then he was probably stoned out of his mind during the ceremony, so I'm relying on the memory of a guy whose perceptions were pretty impaired."

"So he doesn't remember how it tasted?"

"Not at all," Joe replied. "And I only use the term 'Long Pig' because well...that's the nickname I've heard for it. That it's supposed to taste like pork."

"Is it a dish you would try if given the opportunity, Mr. Garrison?"

Joe thought about it, putting the visual effort in giving him the impression he was seriously considering it. "Yes, I would," he said, nodding at Chef Munchel, not breaking eye contact. "If the opportunity presented itself, I would have no problem trying it."

Chef Munchel smiled back. "Like I said, it's nice to meet a true connoiseur, Mr. Garrison."

CHAPTER 33

Joe Taylor sat at the edge of the king-sized bed in his suite, looking at his reflection in the large mirror that sat perched over the oak dresser. The man that stared back at him was determined, resolute. Inside, Joe felt a slight touch of unease and nervousness begin to flutter in his belly.

Don't think about it, he thought. *Concentrate on the task at hand.*

He hadn't gone down to the dining room for breakfast this morning. Instead, he'd ordered room service—freshly cut fruit, crepes, and coffee. He'd eaten breakfast calmly with the TV news on, not really paying attention to it. Chef Munchel had delivered his breakfast and they'd exchanged pleasantries. He'd killed the next few hours watching TV—cable news, the History Channel, VH1 Classics, not really paying attention to them, just thinking about what lay ahead: a luncheon meeting with the group at noon, in the main dining hall, where Joe would finally get to meet some of the players. Chef Munchel was to make a brief presentation on the menu items for the next few days, then the next few hours were devoted to free-form networking. The main event, the main kick-off dinner, was to commence at five p.m.

When it was closing in on eleven o'clock, Joe had turned off the TV and retreated to the bathroom. He'd taken a long, hot shower. When he was finished grooming, he'd gotten dressed slowly—underwear, socks, a short-sleeved dress shirt, a pair of slacks, tan slip-on dress shoes. Then he'd sat on the edge of his bed and contemplated his next move.

He and Dean had made a loose plan—Wayne Sanders and Bill Richards were present at Chef Munchel's private event this week at Bent Creek. Dean had verified this last week after cracking Bent Creek's computer network. He'd also provided Joe with photos and vital stats on both men. When Dean presented this information to him, his face had held a degree of shock, as if he'd been taken by surprise about something. "I'm going to show photos of both men to you so you'll recognize them. I would strongly advise against approaching either of them, for fear they'll know that you aren't who you say you are." Dean had hesitated a moment before showing him the first photo—Wayne Sanders.

The photo of Wayne that Dean provided showed a thin man with a face that appeared to be chiseled from granite—his chin and nose had sharply defined angles. He was bald, wore glasses, and had piercing eyes that made you want to immediately hunker down and hide, hoping his gaze passed you by. "I'm sure if he tilts his head the right way, he looks like a mad scientist," Dean had commented last week at Joe's home. "Look at those eyes. Guy looks like a fucking lunatic."

And he did, too. Something about the way Wayne Sanders's eyes seemed to glare at you gave Joe a bad feeling for reasons he couldn't adequately explain. He had an intimidating look that probably served him well in the boardroom.

When Dean showed Joe the photo of Bill Richards, he gasped. He could see why Dean had hesitated.

The photo Dean presented was that of Earl Sanders.

Joe had looked at the photo for a full minute before he was able to meet Dean's gaze. "I was able to find a file on Bent Creek's network that contained information on Bill Richards. It's a pseudonym, Joe. It was only used once, during the summer Carla disappeared, and it was used by Earl Sanders as a contact name for the lease of that office space in Casper. In fact, the name was used in the articles of incorporation papers that were filed with the county."

"I don't understand," Joe had said. Looking at the face of a man he'd been cozying up to for the past few months, who he'd shared meals with, had been into his home, had invited to his friend Angus's apartment in New York for that impromptu mixer, set off a worm of unease in him. He looked up at Dean. "Are you saying that...Earl Sanders...that he..."

"No," Dean had stated firmly. He'd leaned over the table in the dining room, where they were sitting. "It doesn't mean he had anything to do with her disappearance. We don't know *what* happened to Carla, Joe. *That's* what we're trying to find out."

"But the idea that Earl Sanders used an alias when he interviewed Carla tells me that this is leading to something very bad, and very *wrong*." Joe could feel the dread intensifying. His heart was hammering madly in his chest.

"And that's why you are going to avoid him when you see him at this event," Dean had said. He'd fixed Joe pensively. "And to tell you the truth, I'm having severe reservations about you attending this thing."

The plan they'd come up with was simple: meet Earl Sanders and Wayne Sanders at this evening's banquet. Get George Spector to make the introduction to Wayne. Engage Earl in conversation about finance. Dean had provided Joe with a dossier on him and Wayne, as well as most of the other Bent Creek board members. He was to try to lure Earl to his suite under the guise of presenting some paperwork to him. Then—

"Your room will be bugged," Dean had said. He'd provided Joe with monitoring devices before he'd left, which Joe had already placed in strategic, hidden places around the suite. "Get him talking. We want him to admit two things. One, that he participates in executive recruitment interviews for Mountain Funds in Casper, Wyoming. Second, we want a confirmation he interviewed Carla for a position. I've given you a script that will help you to guide him toward that goal. Once Carla gets into the picture you need to step in and reveal that you saw her recently, within the past two months, and were trying to get in touch with her. Watch his reaction. The way he responds is going to be what we need to make our next move."

Joe took a deep breath. A part of him was consigned to the fact that in all likelihood it was very possible that Carla was dead. He had taken that fact and tucked it away in the back of his mind to be dealt with later. For now he had to concentrate on going through the motions. He had to get some kind of verification of what happened to Carla. It was still very possible she had been abducted and sold into slavery somewhere. The more Joe thought about it and connected the dots, the more that outcome seemed likely. Earl's connections with Wayne Sanders, billionaire hedge fund tycoon who already had a complaint lodged against him for kidnapping, made this a very likely scenario. Recent investigative work Dean uncovered seemed to suggest that case was the only one that had ended with a good outcome. Dean had uncovered over two dozen missing persons cases that bore several uncanny ties. All of those ties had several things in common. And quite a few of them involved the victims last being seen heading to job interviews for companies that were found to be false.

Two of those companies were from the Casper, Wyoming area.

And in all those cases, the missing person was never found.

The missing shared common traits—they were all young, healthy, physically fit, with no drug or alcohol problems, and they were all between the ages of eighteen and thirty. They were of all races and of both sexes. And they'd all vanished without a trace.

Joe stood up, thinking about everything Dean had found. There'd been the case of Toni Hawthorne, a twenty-four year old law student who turned up missing after telling family and friends she was going to a job interview in an industrial park in Tempe, Arizona. Neither her family nor her friends could recall the name of the company, and phone records pulled from her cellular carrier revealed calls from a number that, according to the initial police report, were from a company that claimed to have no knowledge of her. Dean's later research indicated that shortly after the missing persons report was filed, the company in question dissolved and the phone number became inactive.

Toni Hawthorne's was one of only several cases that bore striking similarities to Carla's.

Dean had quietly looked into the backgrounds of several of the other victims. He'd even contacted Toni Hawthorne's parents. What he learned was heartbreaking—Toni came from solid, middle-class stock. Her parents had never given up hope in finding her and she'd been missing for six years.

One thing that intrigued Joe about the victims was their profiles. Joe had seen a documentary on *20/20* about a middle-class twenty-something woman who had answered an employment ad for a modeling agency that was a front for a sex trafficking ring. The woman had gone through the vetting process thinking it was a legitimate job. It wasn't until she was at the agency's office one day that she was drugged and whisked to another location—a safe house for the operator of the ring. Once there, she learned her fate: she was a forced prostitute for wealthy clients. For the next two years she was ferreted around the world on luxury jets to service wealthy businessmen and government officials, all under the threat of beatings, torture, and worse—the torture and murder of her family if she ever tried to escape or alerted the police.

Joe had seen the *20/20* program and alerted Dean to it. While Dean told Joe that it was extremely unlikely Carla was abducted by a sex trafficking ring—modern day sex traffickers usually traded in runaway minors and adult immigrant workers—he said he would look into it. Months later, when the victim pattern began to emerge from Dean's investigation, it seemed even less likely. "We have male and female victims," he told Joe during one of their meetings. "Unfortunately, women make up the vast majority of victims in these cases. If men are the victims, again, they're usually youths, runaways—"

"Let's just keep that option open," Joe had advised.

And now they were about to put everything into play.

Joe approached the desk and opened the red duffel bag on the dresser. He took out a Kimber 1911 .45 and two loaded clips. He placed the gun and a clip in his front right pocket and the other clips in the left pocket. Then he reached inside the duffel bag and took out a Sig Sauer 9mm handgun. He held the gun for a moment, liking the weight of it in his hands, then placed it in the inner left-hand pocket of his jacket. A pair of clips for the Sig Sauer went into the right inner-coat pocket. He put the jacket on and looked at himself in the mirror. He looked presentable for tonight's dinner. Two handguns and seventy or so rounds of ammunition should be plenty. Hopefully, he wouldn't have to use them.

But if he did...

Joe Taylor contemplated what it would take to get his daughter back. To learn the truth of what happened to her. And he wondered, if the truth was not to his liking, and Earl Sanders, Wayne Sanders, and others among Bent Creek's Board was responsible, if he would be able to restrain himself from committing mass slaughter in revenge.

CHAPTER 34

Four Days Ago

Joe was packing when Dean Campbell called. Joe put the call on speaker and ignored the intensity in Dean's tone as he rummaged in his closet, looking for one of his suit coats. "You really aren't going, are you?" Dean asked.

"I'm going," Joe confirmed.

"Goddammit, Joe, we talked about this! Whatever it is Wayne Sanders is involved in is big and—"

"And I've gone through all of this—the separate identity, meeting Spector and Lansdale and the other guys associated with Bent Creek—for the purpose of learning who Bill Richards is so I can find out what happened to Carla. You found out that Bill Richards was an alias used by Earl Sanders. I *still* don't know what happened to her. Earl is going to be at this fancy shindig being catered by Chef Munchel, and I intend to be there."

"I don't feel good about this," Dean said. "If there was only some way you could have arranged to bring me—"

"You know I made inquiries," Joe said. "And you know how it turned out. Every time I arranged for one of them to even *hint* at the possibility of outside guests, either Munchel or Spector would clam up and get evasive."

Dean was silent. In the past six months as Joe worked his

new business deal with Spector and his company, he'd taken in many private dinners prepared by Chef Munchel. He'd become rather tight with both men. As time went by and he became more friendly with them, he learned that Spector and Munchel seemed even tighter than the usual client-vendor relationship. And as those months passed, and Joe worked his way into their inner circle through his financial wizardry on the market, and through lavish private trips at various *soirees*, Joe began to hear about Bent Creek Country Club and Resorts more. Furthermore, he learned that George Spector and Earl Sanders were members, and that Chef Munchel was the head chef. He'd researched the country club on the internet and, like The Pinnacle, Chef Munchel's restaurants, Bent Creek's website and all the information he found about them was very bland, very corporate-speak. Joe had read through the website anyway, wondering how the resort fit in with all this. By all accounts, Bent Creek was a very typical high-end resort for high rollers. Joe had stayed at such a place exactly once—Woodview Ridge, in the Hamptons—at the urging of a friend and business acquaintance at his old mutual fund firm. All of Joe's expenses were paid by the firm, but he remembered thinking at the time that if he had to be stuck in another establishment full of stuffy, pretentious blowhards again—

"Getting Munchel to invite me was a big deal," Joe said. "I earned his trust. I had to keep it. Even *mentioning* that I was *thinking* of bringing a friend would have been too risky."

Dean sighed. "I guess you're right."

Of course Joe was right. Over the past month, as Joe learned about Bent Creek and its expansive grounds, its riding stables, its squash court, its spacious suites and how the wait staff was selected from the best of the best, it was apparent to him that Munchel was feeling him out. Joe had been intrigued about attending Bent Creek ever since he learned of it by way of the mention of Bill Richards name at Earl Saunder's home in Aliso Viejo, where it was revealed Munchel catered some sort of private event every year. Knowing that was just one way to get a chance to meet Bill Richards and perhaps learn more about Carla, Joe had started cozying up more to Chef Munchel. He'd braved his palate and partaken in many strange and exotic dishes Munchel prepared over the next few months—broiled and pickled pigs feet, veal made from calf embryos, scrambled eggs and sausage made from Platypus eggs and meat, among other dishes Joe didn't have the stomach to *think* about anymore. He'd summoned up his inner courage and partaken in these strange dishes to not only impress Chef Munchel, but perhaps make him a good candidate for an invitation. After all, Munchel *did* mention during one of their many conversations that he had invited select clients to the Bent Creek affair from time to time. "But they have to be true *connoisseurs*," Munchel had said. They'd been at a mansion in Connecticut, at the home of a wealthy banker who was having a party. The banker was an acquaintance of Joe's who was hip to the Bob Garrison alias, and when he heard Munchel was catering the event, he'd made himself available. Neither Spector, Lansdale, or Earl Saunders were in the banker's circle of friends or colleagues, so they weren't present. "You *are* a rarity, Mr. Garrison," Munchel continued. "It's not every day I run across somebody who isn't afraid to sample the exotic or seeks it out. It's even rarer to meet somebody who has admitted to partaking in black market dishes. I must say I enjoy our conversations over dinner."

"As do I," Joe had said. He'd raised a glass of wine to Jim. "To you and your fine culinary skills. May I continue to know them and be enriched by them!"

"Once Munchel extended the invitation to me, I accepted and I knew there was no turning back," Joe continued. "I'd overheard enough anecdotes from George that the private event Munchel catered was really Wayne Sanders's thing. Well, Wayne's and the board of directors that run the place. And over the next several months it was through very carefully orchestrated questions about the event that told me that once you were invited, you were *in*. You weren't allowed to bring a significant other or a relative or friend unless *they* were in, too. As in, already in the circle."

"And they all had to be approved by Chef Munchel," Dean said.

"Yeah."

There was a pause. Joe continued packing. "Do this for me then," Dean said. "Stay put. I'm heading to your place now. I have some things that'll help you."

"Make it quick."

Dean had been at the house forty minutes later. He carried a thick briefcase with him, which he opened in the kitchen. Once Joe saw what was inside the briefcase, his admiration for Dean grew even more.

Dean instructed him on the placement and operation of the surveillance equipment. He also handed over the Sig Sauer and the Kimber, along with the ammunition and clips. Dean knew Joe was familiar with firearms from past conversations and a few trips to a local firing range. "The weapons aren't registered and there's no serial numbers on them. That's why you're using these. As for communication, we're going to use these." Dean handed Joe a cell phone and held up a second one that was identical. "The one I just handed you has one number programmed into speed dial that links with this one, and vice-versa. Both phones have apps that are designed to block wireless monitoring and intrusion, but just in case, we're going to be really vague about what we talk about when you have to call me. I'm going to run a few catch phrases to you that are code. We'll use these phrases to relay key information to each other. Okay?"

Joe nodded. For the next thirty minutes, Dean made Joe memorize the phrases. They ranged from the nonsensical ("The day is hot, but it's going to rain") to the downright ridiculous ("The rat is running away with the cheese"). "Christ, Dean, these sound like something out of some cheesy spy movie!"

"Hey, they work, okay? You hired me for this shit. You listen to what the fuck I have to tell you."

Once Joe had the phrases and their meanings memorized and his bags were packed—including the surveillance equipment and weapons—he and Dean exited the house. Joe locked up and Dean walked him over to his car. "Are you *sure* you don't want to reconsider this?"

"I'm sure." He stood at the driver's side of his black Mercedes. He'd stashed his bags in the back seat and put his sunglasses on. "I have to do this, Dean. Not just for Carla, but for Nina. And myself. I have to *know*."

Dean regarded him for a moment, saying nothing. Then he nodded. "Okay," he said.

CHAPTER 35

When Anna King came to consciousness, the first thing she was aware of was the smell.

It was heavy, coppery, and wet.

The second thing that hit her was her vision. It was blurry, then began to slowly gain focus. It felt like she was lying trussed up on a metal table of some sort, her wrists tied behind her back, her ankles lashed together. She was still wearing her waitress uniform from this morning. The last thing she remembered was somebody grabbing her from behind, pressure around her throat, then darkness. Her assailant must have utilized a pressure point to render her unconscious.

The next thing she was aware of was sound. It was steady and unmistakable. It sounded like a heavy knife chopping through chunks of meat, like one would hear at a butcher shop.

Thuck! *Whap*! Then the tearing sound as tendons snapped and cartilage parted from bone. The sound of a slab of meat being set down on the butcher's block.

She sensed she wasn't alone in the room.

Anna couldn't see everything through her half-slitted eyes, but she could tell she was somewhere in the bowels of the kitchen. The prep room, maybe. She recognized the metal shelving that lined the wall and she identified several large mixers on the high shelf, placed there for storage by one of the cooks before the season ended. Chef Munchel's voice shattered her thoughts. "I know you're awake, Miss King. No sense playing possum."

Whack! Thuck!

Anna slowly turned her head toward Chef Munchel's voice. Her vision swam into focus and her heart almost stopped at what she saw.

Chef Jim Munchel was standing at a large table dressed in his cook's whites. His outfit was stained with fresh blood. He looked at her from across the table, that sly smile playing across his lips. He was holding a very large, very heavy, butcher knife. He looked down at the carcass on the table, sized up his next surgical slice, and brought the blade down again. *Whack!* Anna watched with dumbfounded shock and horror as Chef Munchel ground the blade down between upper thigh and pelvis, cutting expertly through cartilage. He gripped the upper thigh with bloodstained fingers and pulled. It was like watching somebody pull the thigh bone off a turkey. There was a loud crack and the limb was wrenched out of its socket. Chef Munchel grunted and moved the limb aside.

What the fuck? Is that a human body?

"Don't panic," Jim said casually. "I didn't think you'd come around so quickly. Just sit tight. You might not want to watch the rest of this, either."

Anna could feel her heart racing; her limbs felt tingly as her blood was infused with adrenaline. Her eyes roamed down the table Chef Munchel was working at, taking in the carcass he was dissecting. She made out two human thighs, lower legs (minus the feet), dismembered arms and hands, and the torso. A head sat at the far end, but she couldn't make out who it was. Then her eyes focused on another table directly behind Jim and her heart stopped. There was a second chopped-up body lying on that table and this time the head was facing her. She recognized the second victim easily.

Jackie Daniels.

Heart beating rapidly, Anna felt herself begin to panic. She tried to move her arms. No go. They were bound tightly behind her. She tried to move her legs. They were tightly bound, too. She wasn't going anywhere.

Anna looked at Jim, who wasn't paying attention to her. He seemed too pre-absorbed in dismembering what she assumed was Shane Daniels. The decapitated head sitting at the end of the table bore a slight resemblance to Shane—it had short graying hair cut in the style Shane usually favored, but the head was lying on its side, its back facing her, so she couldn't see the face.

The door to the room opened and Anna swung her gaze toward the sound.

Mitch Johnson walked in, smiling greedily at her. He was still dressed in the outfit he was wearing this morning at breakfast. He didn't pay any attention to Jim as he slowly approached the table Anna was tied up on.

"What's up, Mitch?" Jim asked casually. He pulled another large knife from what appeared to be a collection of them from a metal tray. He moved Shane's torso, inspecting it quizzically, as if debating on where to cut next.

"Just want to talk to her, Jim," Mitch said. He didn't even look at the chef. His eyes were focused directly on her.

I was right, Anna thought. *Well, at least partially right. Mitch wanted me again, but not the way I thought. He wants to torture me, cut me up, and Chef Munchel's going to let him do it. Hell, Munchel's probably a part of it, the sick—*

"Why you feel the need to talk to your meals before they're prepared escapes me," Jim remarked casually. He placed the tip of the butcher knife below Shane's sternum and shoved it in with a grunt.

Anna felt her breath hitch. *Meals? They're going to* eat *me*? She cast a wide-eyed look at Mitch, who started laughing.

"I think you scared her, Jim," Mitch said.

Chef Munchel sliced Shane Daniel's abdomen open. "Good! That'll get those endorphins pumping through her blood. Make her taste that much better."

Anna somehow found her voice. "What the fuck are you talking about?"

Mitch grinned down at her. "Not a bruise on her too." He addressed Anna. "I wasn't kidding when I said I wanted to have you for dinner. Remember that?"

Anna didn't reply. She remembered. Recalling that night now brought a sense of revulsion through her.

Mitch was grinning. "You seem shocked."

"Wouldn't you be?"

Mitch appeared to consider this. He shrugged. "Maybe. Maybe not." His smile cracked wider. Anna felt another wave of revulsion at the memory of going to bed with Mitch and his wife, Theresa; they'd been so eager to extend the invitation, had been so willing to be intimate with her, that they'd seemed to let down their guard completely. That was the sole reason Anna had followed up on their invitation. Only now she wasn't looking into the face of a handsome, rich man, one who she thought had been too eager to let his guard down completely. She was looking into the face of a complete psychopath. "Theresa's really going to love you."

Anna's mind was racing. She had to get out of this, and now was not the time to panic. "You're in this with your wife, then?"

"Of course, my darling," Mitch said. "We *paid* for you."

A sickening smell began to waft toward them. Anna grimaced as she realized where the smell was coming from—Shane Daniels's gastrointestinal tract was being scooped out of his abdominal cavity by Chef Munchel. He was inspecting it the way a butcher inspects prime cuts...which is what it was to these people.

"I don't understand," Anna said, turning to Mitch and trying to ignore the stench. "You paid to have me killed and eaten? Who did you pay?"

Mitch turned to Jim. "Should I tell her?"

Jim looked at Mitch and shrugged. "What can it hurt? It's not like she's in the position to go running to the police."

Mitch let out a loud, cackling laugh. "You're right!" He turned to Anna, leering at her. "Let's just say that we have a little fine dining club here. We're all connoisseurs of fine dining and we enjoy the strange and exotic. About once a year we gather here at Bent Creek for a private banquet exclusively catered by Chef Munchel. It's more a cooperative, really."

"A cooperative?"

"Yes. We buy in to rent these facilities from Wayne Sanders and his board. In return, Wayne diverts those funds to employ his resources in obtaining the finest ingredients for our little *soiree*." Mitch chuckled. "Chef Munchel is really working for *us* this week, but I must say that part of our little club really started with *him*."

Anna was breathing hard and fast. "So you pay Wayne Sanders? Is he a cannibal freak too?"

Mitch tilted his head back and laughed heartily. Jim Munchel smiled a little, then stepped back from his work at the table.

"Actually, my dear, we *all* are." Chef Munchel set the butcher knife down and hunted around for another. "Wayne and I actually started this club many years ago. It's a long story, but here's the short version: we knew each other on the food circuit and on the underground hardcore scene in Philadelphia and New York. Wayne was one of my restaurant clients and when we kept running into each other at various dungeons, he asked me if I would be interested in a private job—to prepare long pig for some people he was involved with who had a cannibalism fetish."

"Cannibalism fetish? You mean like sex?"

"Yes." Chef Munchel found the knife he was looking for. He casually flipped Shane Daniels's torso over and began hunting for another section to cut. "The money was good, and I'm always open to new recipes, so I gave it a try. My first dish was a success!"

Despite the shocking allegations, Anna couldn't help but

want to learn more. "How did...how did Wayne...I mean... how..."

Smiling, Jim Munchel paused in his work. "Wayne heard I belonged to a snuff film ring. We had an event once where we screened a film in which the victim was partially cannibalized while he was still alive. Wayne was interested in viewing that film, so I arranged a showing. And because of my willingness to bring him into my circle, he felt he could trust *me* with what he was envisioning. By then, it wasn't about sex at all. It was about..." Jim's face seemed to become reflective. "...it was about experiencing new things. Finding new ways to taste food, to prepare dishes, to make the dining experience more enriching and rewarding."

What Jim was telling her was horrifying, but she couldn't let its sheer awfulness affect her. "So Wayne's behind all this..."

"He's certainly the figurehead," Jim agreed. "He acquired the taste overseas. I'd been intrigued by it ever since a dear friend of mine, Mabel Schneider, *raved* about it. I'd always wanted to try it, and Mabel told me that human flesh can be prepared like pork so..." He shrugged. "When Wayne made his offer I decided to take him up on it. Mabel gave me one of her recipes and I made it my own. It was quite challenging."

"I...I still don't..." Anna was having a hard time trying to wrap her mind around it. She knew what she wanted to say. *How do you get your victims*? But that sounded like a stupid question. She was tied up. That was her answer.

"I noticed you months ago," Mitch said. He was smiling at Anna, watching her calmly. Was that sense of yearning in his eyes really a look of hunger? Looking into Mitch Johnson's handsome features was like looking into the face of a hungry tiger. "I saw you in downtown Denver at a restaurant. You were there with a group of your co-workers, I believe. This was back in April. Do you remember?"

Anna searched her memory and came up with the incident easily. Actually, she *had* been at the restaurant—a popular sports bar across the street from the Denver convention center and attached to the Hyatt Regency hotel—with her former co-workers. She'd been laid off from her job over a year before and still took in lunch with the girls every few weeks. She didn't remember seeing Mitch that day, but she supposed he could have been there, silently watching her, admiring her. "I remember," she said.

"The moment I saw you, I realized you were perfect," Mitch said. "I knew right then that I had to eat you. After your party left, I made a couple of casual inquiries about the group you were with and found out they were from a consulting firm called Tek-systems. One of the waitresses knew your name. That was all I needed."

The implications were obvious. "What did you find out?"

"*Everything*."

Anna thought carefully before proceeding with her next question. "So you found out I was out of work? That I'd been a consultant with Tek-systems and I had been lunching with my former co-workers?"

"But of course."

"And you knew I was working a waitress job in Aurora?"

"Yes, I did."

"You found out where I lived?"

"Where you lived, your phone number, all that pertinent information."

"Did you follow me around when I went out?" Anna asked, her mind racing. She felt a worm of nervousness at the implications, but kept a straight face. "When I went out with my friends on Saturday nights, or when I went to visit my mother on Sundays?"

Mitch chuckled slightly. "We didn't have to go *that* far, dear. Just enough to learn most of your habits so we could lure you away easily. That's always the key, making sure the abductions themselves aren't typical. Instead, people just disappear like that!" He snapped his fingers.

So they didn't learn everything about me, Anna thought. That was painfully obvious by his answer to her last question. She continued, her mind racing ahead of her. "You pulled strings to have me hired for this job."

"*Bingo*!" Mitch grinned again. "Your college transcripts indicated you maintained a 4.0 grade average. Pity those smarts didn't keep you from losing that cushy job you had at Teksystems."

Anna almost said, *yes, it is a pity*, but didn't. She was just about to deal a card in this mind game when a voice called out from the storeroom just off the main pantry. "Chef Munchel? Can you and Mr. Johnson come out here for a moment? We have something to show you."

Mitch Johnson turned to Chef Munchel, who shrugged. Mitch frowned. "They enter the storeroom through the back way?"

"They did," Jim said. He set the butcher knife down on the table. "And I think I know what this is about. Step this way, Mr. Johnson." To Anna. "Hang tight, Miss King. We'll be back."

Mitch and Jim stepped through a rear door and closed it behind them, leaving Anna with a few precious moments to plan her next move.

CHAPTER 36

Everybody was assembled in the main storeroom when Jim Munchel and Mitch Johnson stepped inside. Jim nodded at them, making sure all board members were present, as well as those in the circle who had paid for this season. Wayne Sanders stood in the middle of his loose throng of Bent Creek board members. He was wearing a tan business suit and wire-frame glasses, his bald pate shining from the bright fluorescent lighting. Standing at his left was Emily Wharton and two other board members, Gail Scott and Don Vachss. To his right was Earl Sanders, George Spector, Steve Whittaker, and Amory Patterson. Carl White, Theresa Johnson, and another half dozen or so members of the club were also present. Only Bob Garrison and another couple were missing—James and Beth Tyler, from Connecticut. They'd only arrived at Bent Creek late last night. He would pass the word on to the Tylers and Mr. Garrison himself when his prep duties for this evening's dinner service were over.

Lying on the table was Rick Nicholson, the former Director of Operations at Bent Creek. Jim noticed that Paul Westcott and his security team were conspicuously absent. It figured. Paul, Scott, Pete, and Glenn knew about the club, did not want to be a part of it, and were paid handsomely for their silence, but they also had very weak stomachs. Paul had once told Jim that he didn't want to hear about what was done to the people he sometimes helped subdue and keep within the country club grounds. "I know what goes on," Paul had said, "but I don't want to know the gory details."

That arrangement had worked out splendidly. When Emily told Jim that Paul and his team had identified the perpetrator of the rash of thefts as Rick Nicholson and that she wanted him added to the menu this week, Jim suggested they take offers from other interested parties in the event who wanted to try him. Emily was all for it. Of course, Rick had denied being the thief, even when confronted with the evidence. They had to get rid of him somehow. According to his Human Resources profile, he was completely healthy, too.

Rick was tied up and gagged. His eyes were wide with terror. His face was drenched with sweat. He looked at the assembled board members, at Carl White and the Johnson's, recognition flitting through his features but not comprehending what was happening. The fear was evident in his eyes though. And that was perfect. Just where they wanted him. Fear produced endorphins that made the blood rich with oxygen. Killing somebody at the height of their fear bathed their flesh with those endorphins and gave their flesh a rich, sweet taste. The more afraid Rick was, the better.

"Very good," Jim began. "As you see, this one has just been added to the menu at the last minute. In conferring with Mr. Westcott, we decided not to add the Daniels to the menu due to Jackie's opiate addiction and the uncertainty of Shane's own system. I understand he was a heavy drinker. Alcohol destroys the liver, as you all know, and the liver is such an important vital organ. I'm afraid Shane would taste rather shitty. Anyway, long story short, Rick is a much better addition. I realize this will leave us with a *lot* of leftovers. I can have whatever is left-over from him freeze-dried and over-nighted to your residences with the correct measurement of ingredients and a recipe should you wish to buy in." He looked at the assembled throng. "So, do we have any interest?"

Gail Scott took a step forward. She was in her early fifties and looked like she might be a lawyer in the outside world. She wore a burgundy business suit and her shoulder-length brown hair was pulled up into a pony tail. She gazed appreciatively at Rick's lean, muscular body. She reached out and caressed his thigh, giving it a slight pinch. "Mmmm, nice legs. I bet he has a nice ass, too."

"His ass is mine, bitch," Emily Wharton said. Her tone was joking and she grinned. Everybody in the room laughed.

Jim grinned at Gail. "To be truthful, I am dying to roast his ass cheeks in the oven with my special mushroom gravy. I'll split him with you."

"Deal," Gail said. Her eyes were dancing with anticipation.

"Anybody else?" Chef Munchel said, surveying the room. "He's lean and muscular. He should yield some nice loin steaks and some tasty ribs. And his biceps are nice." Chef Munchel fingered Rick's right bicep. Rick tried to scream through his gag and shuffle away, but was restrained by the awkward position he was laying in. "Just look at those. If health nuts only knew that all the talk about proper diet and good exercise, especially good weight training, only made them more appealing to us as culinary dishes, they'd stop exercising and eat at fast food chains more."

"So true," Earl Sanders said. He was watching all of this with interest. "And I must say it's sad it's had to come to this for Mr. Nicholson. I understand he was a great asset to the management team."

"He was," Emily Wharton agreed. She nodded at Jim. "If you and Gail are going to divide him up, let's adjourn. I need to get back to my suite and finish writing an email to my secretary."

"Very good," Jim said. His gaze swept across the room. "So he goes to Gail and I? Last chance for any other takers."

There were scattered "No thank you's" and shaking heads. Then they started to drift away, retreating from the table and heading toward the outer door that led to the back; Jim usually made it very clear that he didn't want anybody in his kitchen. Mitch raised his hand to get Jim's attention. His wife, Theresa, was standing next to him. "Mind if I take Theresa back to the kitchen?"

Jim sighed. "No, go ahead. I'll be there in a moment."

Mitch and Theresa exited the storeroom and headed to the kitchen. Jim Munchel stood by the table where Rick Nicholson lay trussed up and gagged, his eyes wide with horror and shock, sweat streaming down his face. As the other members of the club left, Jim turned to Rick. "Pity it had to come to this, Mr. Nicholson. I rather liked working with you. No hard feelings, hmm?"

Whatever it was Rick Nicholson shouted, it came out as a series of muffled gibberish. He shouted and strained at his bonds, his face stricken with panic. Jim smiled and shook his head. "I know, Mr. Nicholson. I'm a bastard, and a degenerate, and I'm going to pay for this. Trust me, I will. Mr. Sanders will require that I contribute something if I am to acquire you, and I feel it's only fair. After all, we're taking great risk in presenting you as part of the menu this week. Plus, there *will* be leftovers." He paused for a moment, silently counting down the main menu items this week. There was Dale Lantis, the overweight man from Accounting, who was to serve as a sort of rump roast recipe he had that called for a cut of meat with a high fat content; there was the two bodies cut up and packaged in the freezer that Paul Westcott and his team had procured; there was Brian Gaiman, who Emily Wharton had bought and who, like Anna King, had been lured to Bent Creek at the request of their purchasers because they wanted their meat as fresh as possible. Unfortunately for Emily, Brian had managed to escape. And now they had an extra.

Jim Munchel frowned. He wondered if this was starting to get a bit out of hand. Brian Gaiman escaping was bad enough. Jim was still nervous about that and had wanted to call off the event, but Wayne had insisted, assuring Jim that they were safe. Killing Shane and Jackie was done out of necessity—the disposal of their bodies would be easy enough, but explaining away their disappearance would have to be dealt with. For that matter, so would Rick's disappearance.

While Jim could appreciate Wayne's reasons for wanting to add Rick to the menu, he had to question if it was the right thing. Rick would be missed. After all, the guy used to be a lawyer. He probably had friends that cared about him. Eventually, any investigative trail would come to Bent Creek for Jackie, Shane, and Rick. Paul Westcott would know how to deal with that if the time came, right?

Voices from the kitchen interrupted his thoughts. Laughter, coming from the Johnson's. It was time. "Tell you what..." Jim Munchel said, pulling out the butcher knife from the sheath he wore around his waist. "Nothing personal, but I have to deal with a matter in the kitchen. The Johnson's have paid for one of your former waitresses, Anna King. I plan to prepare five meals from Anna, with the first to commence tonight—grilled steaks, from the flesh carved from her calf muscles. Gail's meal is actually already in the freezer awaiting preparation, so I can put you aside until later. *Bon Apetit*!" And with one swift motion, Jim Munchel drew the sharp edge of the blade across Rick Nicholson's throat. Rick's eyes bulged suddenly and he began to struggle. Jim stepped calmly away from the spray of blood, then headed toward the kitchen, leaving Rick to bleed out.

CHAPTER 37

The hallways of Bent Creek were deserted.

Joe Taylor made his way calmly and carefully down the hall to the elevators. He rode down to the lobby and stepped out, looking both ways, listening. All was quiet.

Joe turned left and headed toward the front lobby. He could see through the large plate glass doors that led to the large marbled walkway that spilled out to the circular driveway and it was deserted. It was still daylight outside, but the sun was going down. It would be dark in another two hours or so. He was fairly certain the front door to the resort was locked. He was also fairly certain that whatever remained of the crew at least two, possibly three members of the security team were still on the grounds. One of them was probably watching him now. Joe noticed the security camera as he walked past the elevator banks and into the lobby. If he was spotted, and if anybody in security felt it was wrong for him to be wandering around here, they would come down and intercept him. He would deal with that if it came. For now, he was going according to plan.

Joe headed for the door to the Administrative area. He paused for a moment, then turned the doorknob. It was unlocked. He let himself in.

He shut the door quietly and stood there for a moment, taking everything in. The Administrative area was dark and silent. It had the sense of emptiness. Joe walked slowly down the hall past cubicles and offices. He had no idea which office to hit first, but his best bet was one in the rear of the Administrative wing that would provide the most privacy. He was to find an office and turn on a computer. In his pocket were two thumbdrives. Dean had given him explicit instructions on how to bypass start-up and go directly to a DOS prompt to change the computer's BIOS. "We're going to change the BIOS so the computer will boot directly from a thumbdrive," Dean had said. "The program on the thumbdrive will hack the password and get us full access to the network at an Administrator level. Once you're in, here's what I want you to look for and download to the other thumbdrive I've provided." Dean had given him a list of files and their possible directories and explained that he hadn't been able to get complete Administrative access when he'd hacked their network earlier. "The program on this first thumbdrive will do the trick. It should take you no more than fifteen minutes to get what we need and get out of there," Dean had said.

The files Dean was after was anything containing personal information on Earl Sanders and Wayne Sanders. "In case we need it for a trial," was Dean's catch-phrase. In reality, there would be no trial. Either Joe would learn what had happened to Carla or he wouldn't. There was the very possibility he would spend the next five days at Bent Creek dining on exotic dishes prepared from human flesh and get chummy with Earl Sanders yet learn nothing about his daughter. And if that was the case, the files he obtained from Bent Creek's computer network might provide them with the information they needed to strike at a later time.

And so help me God, Joe Taylor thought as he reached the end of the hall, his nerves tingling as he sensed that he wasn't alone, *if I find out Carla's disappearance resulted in her being cannibalized by these people, they will be sorry they ever set eyes on her.*

Joe stood there for a minute, his heart pounding. He reached into the pocket of his slacks and pulled out the Sig Sauer. Somebody was close by. He could sense them. He couldn't tell what office they were in, but he had that spidey-sense feeling that somebody was poking around. In fact, they were—

A drawer in the office on his right opened and closed. Another drawer opened. There was the sound of somebody pawing through the contents. Joe listened carefully. The way the search sounded, whoever was pawing through those drawers wasn't familiar with whatever was in the desk. To Joe's trained ear, it sounded like a prowler. Somebody from Security?

From the office, a muffled, "Shit, I'm so fucked!"

There was a good chance that if Joe retreated back down the hall he wouldn't make it. The intruder would either exit the office at the right time and see him and then the chase would be on, or he'd step out of the office at any moment and there'd be a confrontation. Joe couldn't have that. He knew he had the element of surprise and he decided to take it.

Joe stepped toward the open doorway that led into the office and pointed the Sig's barrel inside. The blinds were drawn and all Joe could make out was a wiry man wearing a pair of battered and dirty dungarees and a blue workshirt rummaging through the desk. He reached for the phone on the desk, picked it up, and hit a series of buttons. He wasn't even aware of Joe standing in the hallway, that's how wrapped up he was in his search. Joe took a step forward and got a brief glimpse of the man's face—he looked terrified.

Then those terrified eyes turned to Joe and he gasped. "Oh God!" He dropped the receiver and raised his hands. "Please don't shoot me!"

"Who are you?" Joe said, taking another step into the room and keeping the gun trained on the man.

"I...I'm Brian," the man stammered. He was backing up against the wall. The wave of fear emanating from him was enormous. "Brian Gaiman. Listen, man, it's not what you think—"

"You work here?"

Brian nodded. "Y-yeah."

"What do you do?"

"Uh, I-I'm a maintenance guy."

"Maintenance?"

"Yeah." Brian Gaiman was breathing short, heavy, fast breaths. Joe knew by instinct that whoever this Brian Gaiman guy was, he wasn't part of whatever was going down at Bent Creek. "I just work here man. That's all. Please..."

Joe stepped all the way inside the office and closed the door. The room became darker, but Joe's vision had adjusted enough to where he could make out Brian's figure perfectly. "Don't move," he said. "The minute you move, I plug one in your chest. Got me?"

Brian stammered again, nodding furiously. "Uh-uh-uh ye-yeah-o-o-ok-okay."

"What are you doing in here?"

"N-nu-nothing!"

"Don't lie to me! I heard you pawing through the desk and say that you were fucked. Then you tried the phone. I could tell you weren't calling anybody 'cause you were just randomly jabbing the keypad."

"Something must be wrong with the lines," Brian said. His voice was wavering with nerves. "I can't get an outside line!"

"You can't get an outside line?"

"Uh uh."

"Whose office is this?"

"Rick Nicholson's."

"Who's he?"

"Director of Operations."

"Is he here?"

Brian Gaiman nodded. "He's in big trouble. Paul from Security...and a couple of Paul's security guys...they came in and got him. Knocked him out, dragged him off somewhere."

"What?" Joe's grip tightened on the handgun. "You better explain what the hell is going on right now. You understand me?"

"Uh...yeah." Brian licked his lips and seemed to calm himself down. "You're not...you're not one of *them*. Right?"

He means I'm not part of this, Joe thought, as the realization of what was happening flitted through his senses. Somehow, Brian Gaiman had stumbled onto Bent Creek's dark underbelly. "Just tell me everything you know as quickly as possible. And talk to me in a low voice."

"Okay," Brian said. He still looked scared, but he was more calmed down now than when Joe first entered the office. In a lowered voice he told Joe what had happened to him; how he was working outside on the north side of the property when all of a sudden he was knocked unconscious; how he woke up in what he later learned was a metal freezer; his imprisonment; how he managed to escape and what he found in the freezer next to his that was running.

When Brian got to that part Joe interrupted him. "There were cut up human body parts in the freezer next to you?"

Brian nodded vigorously. "Oh God, yes."

"How many?"

"I don't know."

"Could you tell if they were male or female?"

"No." Brian shook his head. He still had his hands raised over his head, his back against the wall. "I'm sorry, I was too scared!"

"That's okay," Joe said. "Keep going."

Brian finished his story, telling Joe about his escape, how he snuck over to the Administrative area to try to get to a nice quiet place to call the police. He concluded with Rick Nicholson arriving and how he hid in the coat closet, still scared of being discovered. "I didn't know if Rick was one of them," he explained. "I had to...I had to make sure! But..." His voice broke. "I waited too long. Paul and two of his guys came and I stayed where I was and listened to the whole thing. They accused Rick of stealing some money and Rick, he didn't know what they were talking about. I could tell by the tone of his voice. Then they...I don't know how they did it, but they got him, knocked him out. Then they got him out of there."

"And you listened to all this in the coat closet?"

Brian nodded. Joe could tell the younger man was shaking. Scared. "Y-yes."

"How long ago did this happen?"

Brian shrugged, hands still raised in the air. "Maybe thirty, forty minutes ago."

"You were hiding in the closet the whole time?"

"Yeah." Brian licked his lips and swallowed. "As they were leaving they talked about coming back to search the offices. I stayed hidden. I didn't know what else to do. I was scared. I wasn't sure if...you know, if they were still out there. Or when they'd be back."

Joe considered this. Brian was telling him the truth. He felt it in his gut. It was in his face, in his eyes, in the way he spoke, his voice crackling with fear. That decided it for him. "Don't move," he said. "I'm just going to reach into my pocket for my cell phone."

Brian seemed to visibly relax a little. He nodded.

Keeping the gun trained on Brian, Joe reached into his left breast pocket for his cell phone. He quickly called up the speed dial for Dean and put the phone to his ear. He kept his sight trained on Brian as Dean picked up. "Yeah?" Dean said.

"The chair is against the wall," Joe said.

"Now? Are you sure?"

"John has a long mustache," Joe confirmed.

"Fuck!" Joe heard Dean scrambling in the background. "I'll be on the ground with a full deck in thirty."

"We're going to need to do a complete shave," Joe said, then disconnected. Not breaking his gaze from Brian Gaiman, Joe lowered his weapon. "I need you to listen to me very carefully," he said.

CHAPTER 38

When Jim Munchel returned to the prep area of the kitchen, Anna glanced his way, heart racing, her senses fully alert and ready. Mitch had returned a few minutes ago with his wife Theresa. Anna had immediately sensed that she could ignore them as they stood over her and taunted her. She was more interested in what Jim Munchel was doing in the storeroom. She'd heard the muffled voices of conversation, had caught a few muffled screams, then everybody had left through another door except for the Johnson's. They'd left the door open when they re-entered the kitchen area, and Anna was able to hear everything Jim was saying now. She listened carefully and was quickly brought up to speed.

They had Rick Nicholson in there and it sounded like he was in the same situation as she.

Theresa was caressing Anna's left calf, talking to her husband. "Just feel her legs," Theresa said. "She is going to be so mouthwatering."

Mitch's hands had trailed to her left breast. She let it linger there, barely aware of it as he kneaded it gently, feeling its fullness. There was really nothing she could do about it anyway. Besides, her main threat right now was Jim Munchel. She listened to Jim talking to Rick in the storeroom, ignoring Mitch as he said, "I want this breast entirely to myself."

From the storeroom there was the sound of a wet gurgle and

a strangled hiss, then the spatter of liquid as it hit the ground. Anna held her breath. Did Jim kill Rick? Her question was answered a moment later as Jim entered the kitchen, a bloody butcher knife clenched in his right fist.

"Now that we have *that* out of the way," Jim said, approaching the table. He nodded at Mitch and Theresa. "Where were we?"

"Just savoring what we're going to be tasting this week," Theresa said. She grinned at Jim Munchel. She was running her hand up to Anna's left thigh now.

"Yes, of course," Jim said. He placed the bloody butcher knife on the table and began rummaging among the cutlery for another. "I take it we still want to go with your original menu choice for this evening?"

"Of course," Theresa said.

"I wish I could have the breast tonight," Mitch said. He was twirling his thumb around Anna's left nipple. Anna felt a wave of disgust with herself as it grew hard.

"The breasts have to marinate overnight," Jim said. He looked across the table at them, then his eyes focused on Anna's and he smiled. "Don't be so afraid, Miss King. We're going to use every edible portion of your body this week, starting with the flesh from those luscious legs of yours."

"I'm not afraid," Anna said. Her breathing was slowing down. She was directing all her mental energy, all of her willpower on keeping her fear at bay and formulating a plan of action for escape.

"Brave girl," Jim said, still smiling. "But I still sense a little fear in you. Correct?"

"Maybe."

"Don't be. I'll make it as painless as possible. Rest assured that you will be providing nourishment and sustenance for weeks to come for two highly regarded and influential members of society. That should come as great comfort to you, that you will be a part of something big, something important, something powerful. Your contribution may appear small and insignificant to you now, but rest assured that it is *very* important, that you are contributing to something great." Jim paused. He was fingering a clean, heavy-bladed knife. "Would you like to hear how you will be prepared tonight?"

Anna said nothing. Her eyes were locked with Jim's as he stepped around the table, gripping the knife.

"Tonight, Mitch and Theresa will dine on your calves. I will slice two inch thick strips of meat from your calves and rub them with garlic salt, parsley flakes, and pepper. I will take a cold frying pan and fry some bacon, then brown the meat from your calves in the bacon fat. Once they're browned, I'll set them in the bottom of a baking dish for a moment. While the frying pan is hot, but not smoking, I'll add water, sour cream, cider vinegar, sugar, soy sauce and a bay leaf. When this comes to a bubble, I will pour this over the calves. I will cover the baking dish with aluminum foil and bake it at 325 Fahrenheit for about one hour and forty minutes, or until the meat is well done. Then, I will add a garnish of garlic mashed potatoes and steamed vegetables and personally serve it to the Johnson's table." Jim paused, the grin never leaving his face. "They will enjoy it immensely."

Now Mitch was caressing her lower right leg. He leered down at her like a hungry wolf. "Boy, when you break it down like that, Chef, you really make me want to just dive in to her now."

Theresa gave out a little laugh.

Anna felt her heart race again. Her eyes flicked from the Johnson's to Chef Munchel, who began approaching her slowly. He raised the knife slightly, fingering the blade with his right hand.

Anna directed her gaze at Mitch. "Well, I hope I'm worth it then. Too bad all your money was stolen."

Mitch laughed. "Nice play at distraction, dear."

"It's not a distraction, it's the truth. You've heard about the thefts taking place here among the guests for the past week, right?"

"Of course," Mitch said. Jim hung back a little, and she could tell he was waiting for Mitch to end this exchange. "We've *all* heard about it. And I'm not dumb enough to take your bait, my dear. Nobody stole any money from us."

"Think again," Anna said, her gaze locked with Mitch's. "That big check you wrote to Jim and Wayne for this feast is going to bounce, because all the money in that checking account is gone."

This seemed to stop Mitch in his tracks. He glanced quickly at Jim, who shrugged. Jim didn't appear phased.

"He paid you with a check, right?" Anna asked Jim Munchel.

"What makes you think he paid me?"

"Because you probably process the payments and funnel Wayne's portion to him later," Anna said, winging it now, hoping this was the case, for her sake. She knew she was taking a big gamble with assuming this, but she really had no choice—she was in a life-or-death situation here. "You're the one with the restaurant, you have the business accounts set up for private catering events like this. Of course the checks would be made out to you. Mitch wrote you a check. Did you deposit it yet?"

Mitch Johnson glanced at Jim Munchel, who seemed amused by this.

"Well? Did you?"

"Why would it matter to you?"

"Answer the question!" Anna's heart felt like it was going to burst out of her chest, it was racing so fast.

"In a word, no." Jim Munchel's thumb flicked the blade of the knife. The metallic sound his thumbnail made against the steel blade was like Chinese water torture on Anna's brain. "But the Johnson's are good customers. I know their check is good, and besides—"

"The check isn't good anymore," Anna persisted. "The money in that account is *gone*. Trust me." Anna's gaze locked with

Jim Munchel's and for the first time since her predicament, she felt the balance of power begin to shift.

"This is bullshit," Theresa Johnson said. She reached into her Gucci handbag and pulled out an iPhone. She began tapping at the display. "I'll end this discussion right now, little Miss King."

Anna ignored Mitch and Jim as she watched Theresa Johnson access her bank account. She tried to suppress the grin as Theresa put in the account number and waited. Theresa's features turned from one of smug annoyance to stunned shock in seconds. She looked at her husband in disbelief, then at Jim, then tapped the screen again. "This is impossible!"

The grin Anna was trying to suppress made a brief appearance on her face, then settled into a look of defiant triumph. She kept her gaze trained on Theresa as she tapped at the screen again, her face looking increasingly shocked at what she was seeing. "This is *impossible*!"

"What's impossible?" Mitch asked. He didn't sound so smug himself anymore.

"What the—?" Theresa's eyes were wide, her mouth an O of shock. She looked at Anna. "You little *bitch*!"

"What the fuck are you talking about?" Mitch shouted at his wife. Jim Munchel took a step back; to Anna, the chef seemed to look out of place in the midst of what appeared to be a marital spat over money.

Theresa turned to her husband. "The Citibank account has been cleared out! Savings, checking, all of it, it's all *gone*!"

Now it was Mitch's turn to drop his jaw. "*What*?"

"*Look*!" Theresa thrust the iPhone at him, holding it up to show him. Mitch looked at the display and that sense of power grew stronger as Anna watched the look on his face change.

Mitch turned to Anna. "You...?"

"What did I tell you?" Anna said. "Think I lied?"

"Where's our money?"

Theresa was scrolling through the device, her features

stunned. "Ten thousand out of checking, two million out of savings...it's all *gone*!"

"It's not *all* gone," Anna said. "I left you a couple bucks in each account."

"Where's my money, you bitch!" Mitch leaned forward, eyes fiery with anger.

Anna didn't let Mitch's newfound anger get her. She locked her gaze with him, not breaking it. "You thought you had me, didn't you? Well, guess what? Now *I* have *you*! And if you kill me, the money that was sitting in your Citibank, your Wells Fargo, *and* your Morgan Stanley accounts will sit in *my* accounts *forever*. And you'll *never* get it back!"

At the mention of the other accounts, Mitch and Theresa froze. Jim Munchel was beginning to look uneasy. Theresa moaned. "Oh God, you can't be serious..." She began to frantically scroll and tap at the iPhone. Anna watched her, feeling that she had the upper hand completely now. Mitch waited in silence while his wife called up another account. A moment later, confirmation. "*No*!"

Anna grinned.

CHAPTER 39

Paul Westcott entered the dining room and began weaving his way between the tables toward the kitchen, when Chef Munchel and Mitch Johnson emerged from the pass, ready to meet him.

"I came as quickly as I could," Paul said. That was the truth, too. He'd spent most of the day asleep, trying to rest up from the long night before.

"We have a situation," Jim Munchel said. He looked nervous.

"What gives?" Paul tried to appear that he was in control, but inside he felt everything was coming apart. First Brian Gaiman disappeared—and they still hadn't found him—and now this....whatever *this* was. The moment Jim roused him from sleep fifteen minutes ago and told him there was a problem, Paul wished he'd never taken on this job.

As Jim brought Paul up to speed, he glanced toward the entrance to the kitchen from the galley. Theresa Johnson stood there, hanging back. She looked like she'd just learned a close blood relative had died unexpectedly. Mitch was harder to read—he was definitely shocked by something, but there was also a touch of anger about him. Paul listened to Jim, not showing any emotion as he learned what Anna King had revealed to them. "You were able to verify this?" he asked Jim Munchel, his mind still trying to comprehend that Anna had been responsible for the thefts the whole time. *Anna? Anna King? That good-for-nothing, shit-for-brains waitress Alex wanted to fire because she was so bad at her job?* That *Anna?*

"Yes sir, I did," Jim replied.

Paul turned to Mitch. "Did you check the other accounts she mentioned?"

"Theresa checked two of them," Mitch answered. "They were cleaned out. She's...she became too upset when checking the other one and the system locked her out. She kept typing her username and password in wrong."

Paul began to think about how to get themselves out of this. It was clear to him now that Rick Nicholson hadn't been their thief after all—it had been Anna the whole time. How? Surely she would have had some kind of help in this. Paul clenched his fists in frustration, at a loss for what to do. "How much money total are we talking about?"

"Almost ten million dollars," Mitch said, his voice low, deadpan. He looked like he'd just been told his entire family had been wiped out in a holocaust.

"Okay..." Paul nodded. "Take me back there. Let's talk to her."

Jim and Mitch led Paul through the kitchen and to the rear prep area. Theresa joined them, hanging back a bit. She clung to her husband's left arm, visibly shaken and shocked.

Anna King was waiting for them, still trussed up but not looking a bit uncomfortable. To Paul she looked like a completely different person now than the one he'd originally met three months ago when the season first started. That Anna had been somewhat clueless—she'd reminded Paul of one of those dopey reality TV stars with a shoe-size IQ that always got into fights with people; a Snookie or a Real Housewife or a Bridezilla, and then became either enraged when they were forced to face the consequences of their actions or became shocked. This Anna was a completely different person. She was cunning, manipulative, and completely without moral compass. Paul now saw that the previous impression he'd gotten from Anna had been an act. She'd been playing them the entire time.

How much money has she been stealing? Paul Westcott thought.

"So, Chef Munchel just told me you're responsible for some pretty brazen thefts," Paul began. "You've copped to the theft of much of the Johnson's money. Is that true?"

"Guilty as charged," Anna said.

"What about the other thefts we've experienced at Bent Creek over the past three months? Was that you as well?"

Anna smiled. "I throw myself at the mercy of the court, your honor."

"Do you realize that your boss, Rick Nicholson, was our main suspect in these thefts?"

"I did not know that."

"Did you know that Rick is dead now because of your thefts?"

"This is the first time I've heard of it."

"And how does that make you feel?"

Anna looked at Paul, her gaze not wavering. "Are you asking me if I care that Rick's dead?"

"Are you?"

"No. It's not my problem he was blamed."

Paul took a breath and switched tactics. Anna's complete disregard for Rick's death threw him for a loop. "We found half a million dollars in cash under his bed. It was in his briefcase. He claims he didn't know how it got there. We have that money now."

"Good for you," Anna said. Her hazel eyes didn't break their gaze from Paul.

The pieces fell together for Paul instantly. Anna had planted that money in Rick Nicholson's briefcase. How she did it...how she managed to get in his suite, much less sneak the money inside and transfer it to the briefcase, was a logistical problem Paul couldn't fathom right now, but it was obvious to him that Anna had planted this money in the event Rick's suite and belongings were searched in order to throw suspicion off herself. She'd succeeded admirably. If she hadn't confessed to the thefts prior to Jim murdering her for this weekend's feast, they never would have learned who the thief was, and the Johnson's money would have been unrecoverable.

"So you stole the cash from the Westlake's and Mr. Goode," Paul reiterated. "Another one of our members, Carl White, also had money stolen, although this theft was done electronically, out of his bank account. He didn't file a report with me, but he did mention it to me in passing. He was concerned. At the time, I thought that was an isolated incident. Some type of bank fraud or outside hacker activity. That happens. It seems that, in light of this recent confession regarding the Johnson's funds, you're responsible for the theft of Carl White's money as well."

"Haven't we already gone over this?"

"You did this all by yourself?"

"I'm a smart girl." Anna turned to Mitch Johnson. "Told you I was an Alpha in disguise."

Mitch Johnson could only glower in anger.

Paul's mind was racing. With this brazen a theft, it was imperative that the stolen money be recovered as quickly as possible before account managers were notified. "Are there any other victims?" he asked. "Any other guests whose financial accounts you may have looted?"

Anna grinned. "There is. Pity that Mr. Sanders isn't here now. I'm sure he'd love you all to hear what kind of shenanigans *he's* been up to."

At the mention of Wayne Sanders, Paul's blood went cold. Good God, did she get into Wayne's accounts too? And if she did...if she got into any of the Bent Creek corporate accounts and somebody finds out...

Jim Munchel must have noticed the look of shock on Paul's face. "I hope you can understand the delicacy of this situation," he said to Paul.

"Yes," Paul said, his voice low, not breaking his gaze with Anna, who glared at him. "Yes, I do."

"What the hell are you *talking* about?" Mitch seethed.

"Mr. Johnson, shut up," Paul told Mitch. He kept his gaze on Anna. "So," he said, "we have the quarter of a million in cash that you stole from Parker Goode. You have the Johnson's money. And I presume all the other funds from our other guests. Correct?"

"That is correct," Anna said.

"I think it is also safe to assume that you will not return it."

"You must have been a straight A student in college."

Paul ignored the quip. "And you won't tell us how to get it back."

"Nope."

"I can have my security team analyze your laptop computer," Paul said. "I'm sure they'll have passwords and log in information and will be able to reverse whatever computer hacking you may have—"

Anna started to laugh, which produced a finger of fear down Paul's spine. "That's funny," Anna said, trying to control her laughter. "Me, a computer hacker? That's good, but...um... no. You can try to look for passwords to people's accounts on that laptop, but you're not going to find them, even if you do get through my encryption."

"Encryption?"

"Yes. Encryption." Anna cocked her head. "It's the highest available, too. Good luck trying to crack it."

Paul sighed. He could tell that he wasn't going to get very far with Anna tonight. He might have success with her later if given the opportunity, but for now he had to deal with the current situation: Mitch and Theresa Johnson and their arrangement with Chef Munchel and Bent Creek. Closely tied to that was protecting the members of this little event. Killing Anna King now would silence her, but if she was working with somebody else, they would find out something happened to her. And Paul was convinced that Anna had a partner despite her denial. If Anna disappeared, that partner could be trouble for them, especially considering the funds pilfered from the accounts and the players involved. If financial regulators and the government stepped in, started snooping around, it could lead the investigation right to Bent Creek, to the board members, to Wayne—

—to me!

Paul turned to the Johnsons and Chef Munchel. "It seems we have quite the dilemma here," he said. "It's a good thing Chef Munchel didn't cash your check yet." He turned to Chef Munchel. "I take it you are still in possession of the Johnson's personal check?"

"It's at my office," Jim said quietly.

"Very good," Paul said. He turned to the Johnson's, who had been watching the exchange with bated breath. "I'm afraid I have no choice but to instruct Chef Munchel to return your check with our regrets and apologies."

Mitch Johnson's face crumbled. "Wh-what?"

"And then I'm going to have to escort you to your suite, wait while you collect your belongings, and escort you off the property," Paul finished.

"You can't be *serious*!" Mitch screeched. He traded a shocked look with Theresa, then turned to Paul. "You can't do this!"

"It's in the contract, Mr. Johnson," Paul said.

Chef Munchel sighed. "He's right, Mitch. I'm sorry."

"But I *paid* for her!" Mitch howled.

"Your intentions were good and noble," Paul said. "But I have a situation to deal with. Miss King is an asset to Bent Creek at this moment. She's no longer yours." He traded a glance with Chef Munchel, silently conveying to the Chef that this incident with Anna King and the thefts were only the tip of a very large iceberg. Chef Munchel picked up on it and became solemn. Paul turned to the Johnson's, letting his professional side take over. He held his hand toward the door that led to the main kitchen, ushering them out. "Come, if you'll just step this way—"

"Can't you just torture the little bitch?" Mitch said, glaring at Anna. "I'm sure she'll spill all her dirty little secrets if you turn the heat up on her."

"Torture me all you want," Anna said. "You won't learn a goddamn thing about your money."

Paul Westcott gently took Theresa Johnson by the elbow and started to escort the couple out of the kitchen's back entrance. A heavy feeling of dread was settling over him and it turned into a solid weight as he ushered the Johnsons through. He turned to Chef Munchel and Anna King, intending to tell them he would be right back.

And then he heard a noise coming from the pantry where Rick Nicholson's mutilated corpse lay.

CHAPTER 40

Dinner service during opening night of the private event always started early.

Emily Wharton arrived at the dining room ten minutes before the official start time, as always. After the quick meeting with the other guests thirty minutes ago, Chef would be getting Rick Nicholson ready for overnight storage, continuing his prep work for tonight, and would shortly begin preparing tonight's meal. Emily would probably assist Chef by serving the wine. But for the most part, opening night was Chef's show.

Chris and Barbara Shear arrived, dressed in evening wear, looking like they were ready for a night on the town. They smiled and nodded at Emily as they entered the dining room. "Hello, Mr. and Mrs. Shear," Emily said. "Nice to see you."

"You too, Ms. Wharton," Chris said.

One by one, the other guests and board members trickled in. Gail Scott, Harry Rowe, Alan Vath, George Spector, Carl White. All were dressed to the nines in sport coats, clean-pressed dress shirts and ties, dark slacks and shoes, the women dressed in evening-wear that would set their husbands back in the low five figure range; chicken-feed, really. Emily nodded at each one as they passed. The Johnsons would still be in the kitchen, probably savoring Anna's demise by now. They were the only club members that liked to personally witness the slaughter, something Emily wasn't into, the way most people didn't like to watch beef cattle get that hole punched between their eyes while being led down the chute to their demise. She glanced around the dining room; the dozen or so tables that had been set for the event were centered in the middle of the area, each one laid out with the finest silverware and white linen napkins. One of Paul Westcott's security guys—Pete Atkins—showed up for his evening duty at the door to the dining area and Emily acknowledged him with a nod. "About time you showed up," she said. "Where's your boss?"

"He didn't tell you?" Pete asked.

"Tell me what?"

"He called me ten minutes ago," Pete said. "Said Chef Munchel called him to the kitchen. Said they had a situation."

"Well, yes, I do know about *that*," Emily said. "That would be Rick Nicholson. I was there late last night. Remember?"

"This is something else."

Emily felt a flush of dread bordering on relief. "Did they get Brian?"

"No, it's not that either." Pete looked frustrated.

Wayne Sanders appeared suddenly, as if materializing like a ghost. He was wearing a tan suit. His bald head gleamed like a pool cue. For a small, thin man, Emily knew he was incredibly strong and he had a commanding sense about him that belied his physical stature. He nodded at Emily and Pete. "Good evening, Ms. Wharton."

Emily smiled. "Wayne!" She greeted him with a kiss on the cheek. "So good to see you as always!"

"Ah, it's always good to see all of you!" Wayne Sanders stood at the threshold to the dining room, surveying the guests already assembled. A few other board members squeezed past them—Leon Jenkins, Neal Hartley, Earl Sanders. They murmured greetings and weaved their way to their tables. "We're going to have a fine dining season, yes?"

"As always," Emily said.

"I understand you are responsible for arranging an additional menu item this week?" Wayne asked, raising his eyebrows.

"You heard correctly."

"Rick Nicholson? The man I hired as Director of Operations?"

Emily nodded. "Yes."

"Very good. It's a pity that went so wrong. I'm glad we were able to recover from that so quickly, though. I understand Gail bought a piece of him. I might have a sample as well. I was observing him a few weeks ago. Man had a nice body."

"Yes, he did."

Wayne looked at Pete. "And how are you this evening, Mr. Atkins?"

"I'm fine, sir."

"Very good. Someday maybe you'll join us, yes?"

Pete shrugged. "Why not? You people pay me good money to cover your back. You're good people. I respect that. I'd be honored, sir."

Wayne Sanders beamed. "Good! Perhaps tomorrow, then?"

"If it's okay with Paul, sir."

"I'll speak to Paul. It's about time he joined our little club as well."

"Thank you, sir."

"Where is Paul, by the way?"

"Pete says he's with Chef Munchel, sir, back in the kitchen," Emily said.

"Ah, I see." Wayne Sanders surveyed the assembled guests in the dining room. "It appears everybody's here. Shall we get started?"

"Absolutely," Emily said. "I'm *famished*."

"As am I!"

Wayne held his arm out and Emily took it. As they stepped into the dining room, Pete called out to her. "Um, Ms. Wharton?"

Emily and Wayne stopped. Emily turned to Pete. "Yes?"

"There's still one more guest on the way. A Mr. Bob Garrison."

"I'm sure he'll show up soon, Pete."

"Yes, Ms. Wharton." Pete looked hesitant, as if he were worried about something.

"Pete, don't look so worried. You're doing fine. Paul's meeting with Chef, Glenn is manning the security room until midnight, and then Scott takes over until noon tomorrow, and you're here. What could possibly go wrong?"

Pete smiled, as if her little pep talk had put him at ease. "Yes, Ms. Wharton, you're right. You and Mr. Sanders have a great time tonight."

"We will, Master Atkins," Wayne Sanders said. He grinned, like a wolf anticipating a meal of freshly slaughtered sheep.

Wayne Sanders and Emily Wharton stepped into the dining room to begin this year's festivities.

They entered the storeroom through the rear outside entrance. Had they been there thirty minutes earlier, they would have been in danger of crossing paths with almost the entire board of directors and their guests. The board and the guests had retreated to their suites immediately upon making the decision on how to divide Rick Nicholson's body among the diners and were now making their way to the dining room via the main dining room hall.

Brian Gaiman eased the door to the storeroom open as Joe Taylor covered them, keeping a watchful eye out over the rear of the building.

Brian stepped inside and motioned for Joe to follow him.

When Joe stepped inside he let the door shut softly behind him. There was a large fluorescent light on, bathing the room in yellow light. He saw the corpse on the floor the same time Brian gasped in shock.

"Oh my God, it's Rick," Brian said.

Joe held the weapon out in front of him, doing a sweep of the room. He wasn't a trained law enforcement officer by any means, but he knew how to handle a firearm. He cast aside all feelings of self-doubt as he quickly checked the room and found it empty of the living.

"Holy fuck," Brian said, his voice quavering.

Joe took a quick look at the body. Rick Nicholson's arms were tied behind his back, his ankles lashed together. He was lying on his left side, his head tilted slightly back, gagged mouth opened in a silent scream, eyes wide and bulging with fright. His throat had been opened up with a deep, gaping wound. There was a large puddle of blood beneath him. Rick's murder had happened just a moment ago, maybe within the past thirty minutes.

Joe noticed a door opposite the one they'd entered through. "Where's that door lead?" he asked Brian, speaking softly.

"Main pantry," Brian said. He stepped back gingerly from the pool of blood. His face was growing pale. His eyes were wide with shock.

Joe turned toward the two walk-in steel freezers that sat flush against the far wall. There was a noticeable purr of an engine; one of the freezers was operating. He motioned toward the freezers. "Those the freezers you were talking about?"

Brian nodded. "Yeah."

"Which one were you kept in?"

"That one." Brian pointed to the one on the left.

Joe approached the freezers and reached out with his left hand. He gripped the handle of the freezer and opened it.

A waft of cold freezing air billowed out. Brian stepped back and Joe stepped forward, trying to see through the fog of condensation at what lay inside.

The freezer was huge—the size of a small walk-in closet. Meat hooks dangled from the ceiling. Metal shelves lined the walls. Stacked on the shelves on both sides were slabs of meat that were distinctly recognizable as human. Joe made out a forearm, a lower leg, a foot. Several large slabs of meat that were virtually unidentifiable lay wrapped in what appeared to be Saran wrap. To the uninitiated they could be large cuts of beef or maybe pork. But Joe knew better. They were human. Cuts from the hips, the lower torso, the chest perhaps.

Joe stepped back and closed the door to the freezer. He'd seen enough.

"Now what are we going to do?" Brian asked.

Joe was about to answer him when a woman yelled out from the pantry. "Watch out!"

And that's when the other door burst open and a man stepped through. Joe recognized him as Paul Westcott, head of Security. Directly behind him was Chef Munchel. Joe locked eyes with Chef Munchel, who was momentarily taken aback in shock. "Bob," Chef Munchel said.

Paul Westcott spoke into the Blackberry he clutched in his right hand. "Pete, I need you here *now*!" His left hand drifted to the firearm holstered at his hip.

Joe reacted. He raised his weapon, aimed.

Paul Westcott raised his weapon.

Gunfire followed.

CHAPTER 41

The moment shots were fired, the guests in the dining room got up from their places and began to file out of the dining room.

Wayne Sanders and Emily Wharton reacted instantly. They were up and along the far wall of the dining room, making sure everybody exited in an orderly fashion and that coats and purses were in the possession of their rightful owners. Emily knew this *wasn't* a drill—they weren't scheduled to perform one until tomorrow night, per the unofficial by-laws established by the core members of the group. Thankfully, everybody was treating this seriously and were heading out quickly. Pete Atkins was shouting orders into his cell phone, probably alerting Glenn and Scott—he'd already retrieved his weapon, a Beretta 9mm. Theresa Johnson ran out of the kitchen, her pretty bimbo features a mask of horror and shock. "Oh my God, oh my God!" she screamed.

"Shut the fuck up and get out!" Emily ordered.

Theresa stopped at the pass and turned toward the kitchen. "*Mitch*!"

There were sounds of a struggle coming from the kitchen and the pantry beyond. Emily couldn't tell who it was, but she could hear Anna King screaming for help.

Theresa looked torn between wanting to follow Emily's orders and heading back into the kitchen for her husband. A male voice yelled—it sounded like Mitch—and that decided it for her. Theresa sprang back toward the kitchen, yelling his name again. "*Mitch*!"

Orders given, Pete Atkins sprang forward, firearm in hand.

"We need to leave, Ms. Wharton," Wayne Sanders said. For the first time since Emily had known him, Wayne looked nervous, but he was doing his best to hide it.

Emily knew they had to leave. They'd established an emergency plan years ago upon formation of the club. At the first sign of trouble, all members were to vacate the premises immediately and turn over all security decisions to Paul Westcott and his hand-picked team. Paul and his team were to dispose of any human remains left in the incinerator that was set just off the storage room and pantry. Paul and his team had exactly thirty minutes to dispose of any human remains and evidence in the event somebody called the police.

There was another gunshot, followed by a scream. "Mitch! Oh my God, *Mitch*!" Theresa turned, and still screaming, ran back towards the dining room.

Shortly after, another gunshot, and Theresa fell face first on the floor, sprawled near the pass.

Pete Atkins crouched below the countertop that led to the pass. He was talking into his cell phone again and Emily could pick out the frantic tone of his voice.

Wayne Sanders gripped Emily's elbow. When she turned to him she read the stark fear in his watery blue eyes. "We really need to leave. *Now*!"

Emily nodded and let Wayne lead her out of the dining room.

Scott Baker arrived just as Emily and Wayne were halfway down the hallway heading toward the elevators. His weapon drawn, he rushed past as Emily and Wayne walked purposefully toward the elevators. "You and I can take my car," he said. "Glenn should have activated the gates that lead out to Route 7." Route 7 was a rural road that bordered the rear end of the property about two miles from Bent Creek proper. The access road that led to it was seldom used and wasn't known to the general clientele of Bent Creek, nor most of the staff and security agents Paul employed; it was a private road, used only for the board and their guests during the private event. Upon notification of any sign of trouble, the security agent manning the system would have deactivated the gate, allowing for board members and their guests to exit the property swiftly.

"Okay," Emily said. Her heart was racing.

"Everything will be fine," Wayne said. They stood at the bank of elevators, waiting.

Behind them, in the dining room, the battle raged on.

Joe Taylor had taken Paul Westcott down with two shots that hit the Chief of Security square in the chest. He went down with a bloody gurgle and Chef Munchel scattered back to the doorway, missing it by a foot, eyes wide, face flush with fear. Joe pointed his weapon at him. "You stay right there!"

Chef Munchel raised his hands. Surrender.

From the pantry, excited, panicked voices. The woman who'd shouted out the warning kept it up. "Get me out of here! Help!"

Joe motioned toward the Beretta Paul Westcott had dropped. "Brian, pick that up, please."

Brian swooped down and picked up the weapon.

"Chef Munchel, I want you to move over to the corner on your left," Joe said. He had a bead on Chef Munchel and he felt a strange sense of calm now that his worst fears had been confirmed. Somehow, having his worst fears about Carla's disappearance coming to light and bearing evidence was driving his actions, and he was calm and methodical about what he planned to do next.

Chef Munchel did as Joe asked, shuffling over to the corner. In the pantry, a man and a woman were arguing, their voices rising and falling in their panic. "We paid for her, goddammit!" the man shouted.

"Turn around, face the wall," Joe said to Chef Munchel.

"You don't want to do this," Chef Munchel said.

"Turn the fuck around!" Brian Gaiman snapped. Whatever fear Brian had was now gone. He gripped the Beretta by the barrel.

Chef Munchel turned around slowly, hands still raised in the air.

Brian swooped forward and brought the butt of the Beretta down on the back of Chef Munchel's head. There was a sound like a watermelon falling to the floor and Chef Munchel dropped like a sack of meat. His right leg twitched for a few seconds and then stopped.

"Get him tied up if you can," Joe told Brian. Without waiting for an answer, he stepped into the pantry, weapon raised.

The first thing he saw when he stepped into the pantry was a man dressed in a black suit and a white shirt standing over a woman in a mussed-up waitress uniform who was lying on what appeared to be a rolling serving tray. The woman was tied up. The man was holding a large butcher knife, a look of indecision on his face. From beyond the pantry, in the kitchen, a woman was screaming at somebody named Mitch. The man looked up as Joe entered and he raised the butcher knife over the woman on the table. Joe shot him once in the face just as the screaming woman from the kitchen emerged in the doorway to the pantry.

The man went down, dropping the knife. The woman screamed. "Mitch! Oh my God, *Mitch*!" She turned and ran out of the pantry, screaming.

The woman on the table was struggling to free herself. She cast a pleading look to Joe. "Please get me out of here!"

"In a minute," Joe said, walking past her, gun still raised. He crept up to the doorway that led to the kitchen, then stepped through, raised his weapon and fired at the woman running away. He shot her in the back and she went down in a spray of blood.

Return gunfire from somewhere out in the dining room beyond whizzed by him and Joe dropped, taking cover behind the large rectangular grill and stove that lay center in the kitchen. From the dining room Joe heard another male voice, probably speaking into a cell phone or Blackberry. "Get the fuck down here, goddammit, we're in a load of shit!"

You're right about that, asshole, Joe thought. He had eight rounds left in this clip and another three clips in his right slack's pocket. The man who had returned fire was probably one of the three security guards working for Paul Westcott. The other two would probably be on the scene any minute now. Which meant that...

Joe felt the presence behind him before he heard the voice. "Freeze, motherfucker!"

Oh shit! Joe froze, heart in his throat as somebody stepped close to him. "Make one move and I'll blow your brains all over the floor. Now drop the gun!"

Joe took a deep breath, trying to center himself again. He slowly lowered his handgun to the floor.

"Good. Now push it toward the front of the kitchen."

Joe shoved the gun away from him, feeling his defeat grow as the weapon slid down the smooth tiled floor of the kitchen.

The voice behind him called out to the man who'd returned fire from the dining room. "I got him, Pete!"

"Where's Scott?"

Another voice, fainter, from further back in the dining room. "Right here, boss. What do we got?"

"We got somebody who thinks he's the fucking Lone Ranger, that's what we got," Pete said. To the man who had put the drop on him, Pete said, "Glenn! There anybody else with this scumbag?"

"Don't know. I came through Chef's office."

"Where is Chef?"

"Don't know that, either, Pete."

There was silence from all around. Even the woman on the table had stopped yelling for help. Joe only hoped that Brian Gaiman would be his element of surprise. Surely these guys knew that Brian had escaped, right? This was confirmed a moment later. "Who is it?" Pete asked. Judging by the sound of his voice, Pete was drawing closer, but cautiously. "It's not Gaiman, is it?"

"No, it's not Gaiman," Glenn said.

"Where's Paul?"

"Don't know."

Another pause. Then, "I'm coming in. Scott, stay here."

"You got it, bro."

And then, with a sickening mount of dread rising with each footstep Joe heard, Pete Atkins headed toward the kitchen.

Scott Baker stood at sentry duty at the entrance to the dining room, his heart racing.

He'd been awakened from a sound sleep by the blaring of his Blackberry. When he picked it up, Pete Atkins's frantic voice had wiped every trace of tiredness from his system. "Get down here now! We have a situation! We have a situation!"

"Leaving now," Scott had said, and he did. He'd pulled on slacks, shoes, grabbed his gunbelt and keys, and was out of his suite in thirty seconds.

His route to the dining room was taken with speed and agility. Weapon drawn, he'd made his way quickly to the entry hall of the banquet area and quickly went on alert when he drew closer. Pete was shouting at somebody in the kitchen and he heard Glenn's voice as well. He'd heard a single gunshot on his way downstairs and his pulse had quickened. Whatever had gone down had happened quickly. Even the guests had filed out and were gone—they hadn't taken any chances. Scott hoped that they could wrap this mess up quickly and efficiently. He knew that in the event something unexpected like this was to happen, and should they successfully eliminate the threat, the board had promised bonuses for them. Scott accepted that as part of the conditions of taking on this job. Of course he didn't want this kind of trouble—what kind of private security guard wants to put up with trouble that could result in being killed or being convicted of a major felony?—but now that it was here, he was going to do his best to eliminate it, work with his team to solve the problem. That's what he did and who he was. He was a problem solver, a guarder of secrets, a man who protected those who employed him and provided for him.

He watched as Pete made his way to the kitchen. Just beyond the pass, he saw a spill of blonde hair and the top half of a dead woman lying sprawled face down on the floor. From here, it looked like Theresa Johnson. *Holy shit, she's dead*, he thought.

Scott's mind was racing. Glenn would have been manning the security booth when the shit hit the fan. He'd probably come down the back stairs and entered the kitchen through the entrance in Chef's office, which was just catty-corner. Glenn probably dropped the guy there. Scott frowned. Glenn said the shooter wasn't Brian Gaiman. So who was it? Somebody Gaiman had managed to call during the past twenty-four hours? Highly unlikely. Paul ran a tight ship here security-wise. The security control room had wireless monitoring equipment that could intercept cellular transmissions and eavesdrop on conversations. Had they been able to pick up on any kind of cellular call Brian had made, they would have caught it.

From the kitchen, Pete and Glenn were talking. "Who the fuck is this?" Pete asked Glenn.

"Fuck if I know," Glenn said. "I came out of Chef's office, saw Theresa run screaming, then this guy steps out of the pantry and shoots her in the fucking back."

"What's your name?" Pete asked the still-unknown suspect.

"Bob Garrison."

Scott's frown deepened. Bob Garrison was the last minute addition to the event for this week. Chef Munchel had added him. He remembered Paul Westcott being pissed off because he'd been unable to completely vet him, but Chef had insisted this Garrison guy be his guest. Chef was probably hot for the guy. Probably wanted to blow him or fuck him while the two of them rolled around in grilled human loin meat dipped in hot buffalo wing sauce. Figures.

"You're the guy Chef Munchel invited," Glenn said.

Silence.

From Glenn again. "I didn't hear you."

"Yes," Bob Garrison said.

"Where's Chef Munchel?"

"Back there. Storage room."

"Did you kill Chef too?"

"No, I did not."

"What the hell's wrong with you, Mr. Garrison?" Pete asked. "Chef invites you out of the kindness of his heart to this shindig and you go all goddamn crazy. Like goddamn fucking Clint Eastwood."

There was a beat of silence, then Pete barked a command at Garrison. "Rise to your feet slowly. Hands up so we can see them."

Another beat of silence. Scott cast a glance in the hallway, noted it was getting dark outside, then turned his attention back to what was going on in the kitchen.

"Were you in on this with Brian Gaiman?"

"No," Bob Garrison said. "I don't know who Brian Gaiman is."

"So you acted alone?"

"Yes."

"Why?"

Silence.

Pete to Glenn. "I've got him covered. Go check the storage room."

Another beat of silence, then Glenn called out: "Paul's dead. Chef's knocked out. Nobody else is here."

"Shit," Pete muttered. At the mention that Paul was dead,

Scott felt a sense of coldness settle into his belly. Paul was dead? What the hell were they going to do now? From the kitchen, Scott heard Pete Atkins tell Bob Garrison, "You killed Paul!"

"He was going to shoot me."

"I oughta fuckin' shoot *you*! Goddammit!"

Glenn said something to somebody else in the kitchen. "You know this guy?"

Scott strained to listen. It sounded like somebody was crying. A woman. Anna King? It had to be. They obviously hadn't taken her out yet for tonight's dinner. *Jesus...*

"We're not gonna get anything out of her," Pete said to Glenn.

"Yeah, you're right."

Pete called out to Scott. "Everything okay out there, Scott?"

"Affirmative."

"So what do we do with this guy?" Glenn asked Pete.

"I say we pop him."

"But what if Wayne—"

"Wayne isn't here, and we're in charge of maintaining the security and well-being of our clients now that Paul is dead!" Pete barked. "And *I* say *this* guy got killed when we came in to try to save Bent Creek's guests."

Scott felt his heart stop. His attention was wholly riveted to what was going on in the kitchen. He never thought his security duties at Bent Creek would escalate to *this*—he'd taken the job knowing there was the possibility, however slight, especially since he was required to carry a firearm. But now that it was happening, Scott didn't know if he was willing to sign on for another season despite the hefty salary. Carrying a gun while on the job was one thing; using it was a completely different ball game.

"Turn around, motherfucker," Pete said to Bob Garrison.

Anna King started to scream out in a sobbing cry. "No! Please, don't shoot him! Don't!

There was a muffled coughing sound that exploded from

Scott's left and something whizzed past his face. Pete's head rocked to the side in an explosion of blood and he dropped like a sack of meat.

What the hell? Scott thought.

Glenn looked at where Pete had just been standing a moment ago, then turned toward the dining room. For a moment, his eyes locked with Scott's. There was another muffled cough from behind and slightly to the left of Scott, and Glenn was hurled back, as if taking a sharp punch to the chest. He fell against the countertop, his chest suddenly bloody, and slid to the floor, bringing down pots and pans in a clatter.

"Ohmygod!" Scott said. He turned around.

A man Scott had never seen before stepped toward him. He turned the silencer-equipped pistol on him and pulled the trigger and Scott didn't have to worry anymore about staying on for another season at Bent Creek.

CHAPTER 42

Calm down, calm down, calm down. Joe kept repeating this litany silently to himself, ignoring the woman tied up behind him who was mumbling incoherently. Joe opened his eyes, not even seeing the two corpses at his feet. All he could think of was how lucky he was that Dean Campbell and Clark Arroyo had arrived in time.

"Joe?" It was Dean. He was flattened against the wall near the pass. Joe couldn't see him, but he could make out his shadowed form.

"I'm okay," Joe managed. He took a deep breath. His heart was racing like mad in his chest. He felt like he was going to faint. His knees felt rubbery. He put out his left hand to steady himself, gripping the edge of a countertop. He looked at Pete's body splayed out on the floor. The last thing he remembered was Pete telling him to turn around, the gun pointed directly at his face. Joe was on the verge of leaping forward and launching himself at the guy when the shot had taken Pete in the head, dropping him. Until that moment, Joe thought he was a dead man. His call to Dean Campbell had occurred thirty minutes ago. He knew it would take them at least that long to make their way up the winding driveway to the grounds of the country club, then they had to find their way inside. The code Joe had given Dean indicated that Dean and his partner, Clark, were to head straight to the kitchen. It's a good thing those instructions were so concise. Otherwise, he'd be dead now.

"Where's Westcott?" Dean asked.

"Dead," Joe managed. "In the storeroom. We're clear."

Dean emerged from where he had covered himself and a moment later Clark Arroyo, the man Dean had told him about two weeks ago when they'd made plans to undertake this mission, stepped out of the shadows, and Joe Taylor was finally able to breathe a little easier.

They got the woman on the table untied first. As Joe worked on freeing her, Clark made a quick sweep of the rest of the kitchen and the storeroom. Dean stood by Joe, relief and worry etched in his features. "I can't fucking believe this," he said. "This is just...it's just..."

"Believe it," Joe said, working on unloosening the knots around the woman's wrists. The woman had been sobbing in relief, but now she was calmed down and looked at them with relief and gratitude. "It's everything I was afraid of."

Dean shook his head. He still gripped his handgun loosely, barrel pointing to the floor. He surveyed the kitchen, the bodies of Pete and Glenn, the Johnsons sprawled on the floor. "Who are they?"

"They were going to *eat* me!" the woman said. Now free, she massaged her legs, trying to restore circulation. "Chef Munchel...he was going to kill me, prepare me for these... these..." The woman couldn't seem to speak about the incident anymore. Joe reached out to her and held her while she tried to get control of herself. She was older than Carla but in a way she reminded him so much of her.

From the storeroom: "Holy crap, dude, don't shoot me!"

Joe called out. "Brian?"

Brian's quavering voice answered. "Yeah?"

Dean stepped into the pantry. He spoke to Clark, who Joe couldn't see, but he could hear the conversation perfectly. "He's okay," Dean said to the marksman. "He's a victim." Beat. "This one, on the other hand..."

"Don't shoot him, either," Joe said, still holding Anna in his embrace. "I want him alive."

They used the coils of rope that were used to tie Anna King to the table and got Chef Munchel trussed up. Clark Arroyo made quick work of the ropes and had the award-winning Chef tied and gagged quickly. As Clark worked at securing Chef Munchel, Brian Gaiman came into the kitchen, wide-eyed, his face pale. Joe learned that he'd hidden himself back in the freezer when the shit went down. "It was the quickest hiding place I could get to," he said.

"And the smartest," Joe said.

Once Chef Munchel was tied up, Clark propped him up against the wall. Joe stood next to Brian, looking down at the unconscious man. "How hard did you hit him?"

"Hard as I could," Brian said. He shrugged. "I hope I didn't kill him."

Clark knelt beside him, felt for a pulse in the man's neck. "He's alive. Pulse is weak." He pulled back Chef Munchel's left eyelid, watched the pupil retract. "He should come out of it soon."

Joe turned to Dean Campbell. "We need to look for the others."

Dean nodded, turned to Clark. "Phase Two," he said.

Clark got up and Joe turned to Brian and Anna, who were standing near the table where Anna had been tied up. They'd dragged Chef Munchel into the kitchen rather than leave him in the pantry with Rick Nicholson's mangled remains. "I need the two of you to stay here. Can you do that?"

"Where are you going?" Anna asked. While she looked frightened, there was a sense of strength that was coming to the surface that Joe liked.

"We need to try to catch some of them."

"But what if they—" Brian began.

"They're not going to come back," Joe said. He gestured at the bodies of the security guards. "We took down their security team. Everybody else scattered. They're probably in their vehicles heading off the property now, but if we can catch up to a straggler—"

Clark Arroyo slapped in a fresh clip in his handgun. "Let's do it."

Joe handed Brian the Sig Sauer and two extra clips. "Just in case."

Brian took the handgun and clips and nodded. No longer the frantic victim, he seemed empowered now that he'd been rescued.

Joe Taylor, Dean Campbell, and Clark Arroyo exited the kitchen and set off to track down the rest of the board members and their guests.

An hour later they all gathered back in the dining room.

Anna King and Brian Gaiman had carried Chef Munchel into the dining room and braced him against the far wall while he was still unconscious. Brian wanted him moved because he didn't like hanging out in the kitchen where the dead bodies lay. Anna didn't care either way. Anything to abide by what Brian wanted, since he was on her side.

Once they had Chef Munchel out, they brought some chairs over and set them in a rough semi-circle around him. Then they waited.

When Joe Taylor, Dean Campbell, and Clark Arroyo arrived back, Joe looked disappointed. "They cleared out," he said.

"Has anybody been monitoring any of the mobile devices the security guards were carrying?" Dean asked.

"Uh...no," Brian said. He cast a look back at the kitchen and grimaced. "The thought of touching one of those guys just...makes me squeegee."

Clark headed toward the kitchen. "Which one is Paul Westcott?"

"The one in the pantry," Joe said. "Blue slacks and white shirt."

Clark headed through the kitchen to the pantry.

"Some of them left their belongings behind," Dean Campbell said to Joe. "One of the suites' doors was chocked open. It looked like whoever occupied it left in a pretty damn good hurry. They left suitcases."

"There's probably records in the computer system," Brian said. "And if the security booth was being manned, there's probably some kind of list somewhere with their names and addresses."

Dean nodded. "We already have all that information."

"There's one other staff member probably still on the grounds," Brian said. "Charlie Thompson. He's probably in his suite, way on the other side of the property."

"Do we need to worry about him?" Dean asked.

"No," Brian said. "He was tapped by Wayne to be on hand for any maintenance issues that might arise during this thing." He told Dean an abbreviated version of how he hid in Charlie's closet and overheard his former co-worker talking on the phone to his friend about Brian's disappearance. "They were telling the staff that I was on a meth binge."

Clark Arroyo returned with Paul Westcott's Blackberry. "No messages yet. And there's an app here that connects directly to the county Sheriff. Nobody sent out a distress call to them. Lucky for us." He sat down in one of the chairs, facing Chef Munchel.

"So what now?" Brian asked.

"Now we wait for him to wake up," Joe said.

A moment later, Chef Munchel woke up.

* * *

They waited until he was fully conscious.

During that time, brief introductions were made. In the heat of the moment, she hadn't recognized the man she'd waited on over the last few days. She hadn't recognized him as the man who had been so nice to her, who had introduced himself to her as Bob Garrison.

Twenty minutes later Chef Munchel looked at Anna King and she couldn't tell if her former employer was scared, nervous, or angry. His eyes darted from her to Joe, back and forth. He seemed most confused by Joe. She remembered back in the pantry when she was still tied up. Chef Munchel had looked at Joe in surprise, obviously recognizing him.

"Your name isn't Bob Garrison," Chef Munchel said. His voice was slightly slurred.

"No, it isn't," Joe said.

"What is it, may I ask?"

"You can ask, but I'm not telling you."

A hint of a smile on Chef Munchel's lips. "I'm disappointed, Bob. I was so looking forward to our meal tonight."

"So was I." Joe leaned forward, looking down at the Chef. "I've been waiting for this moment for a long time."

The two men stared at each other. Anna had the instinctual feeling that there was something more at play here, something that went back in Joe's history with Chef Munchel when he had fooled him into believing he was Bob Garrison. She had no idea who Dean Campbell and Clark Arroyo were—she assumed they were private investigators of some kind. They surely weren't real police or detectives or federal agents. If they were, more cops and detectives would have been on the scene by now. They were playing this privately, much like the next five days at Bent Creek had been for Wayne Sanders and Chef Munchel's private, exclusive guests who paid lots of money to dine on exotic dishes prepared from human flesh.

"I'm going to show you a photo," Joe Taylor said. "And I want you to tell me if you've ever seen the person in that photo. Furthermore, if you recognize this person, I want to know what happened to them. Every detail."

"Mmm, I see what we have here," Chef Munchel said. There was something about the lilt and tone of his voice that creeped Anna out. "You're a vengeful father, husband, boyfriend, or significant other. Once I tell you what you know about your loved one, you're going to kill me, right?"

"No," Joe said. "I'm not. I just want to know what happened. And why."

Chef Munchel raised his eyebrows. "That's unheard of."

"Not really. Lots of murder victim families get to confront the murderer of their loved ones with these questions every day."

"I see," Chef Munchel said. "You want closure."

"Look at the photo," Joe Taylor said. He reached into his pocket and extracted a leather billfold. "Nod if you recognize her. And be truthful. If you lie, we'll know."

Joe Taylor unfolded the billfold and held it up to Chef Munchel. The chef looked at the photo for a long moment, then nodded. "I remember her."

"What happened to her?" Joe Taylor asked.

Jim's eyes flicked up to Joe's. "You know."

Anna was watching the exchange with bated breath. She could sense the underlying emotion simmering in Joe. Rage. Anger. But most of all a tremendous sense of finality. Of loss. Of confirmation that whoever was in that photograph had been very dear to him and he was finally facing the truth of her demise.

"Who brought her here?"

Jim Munchel said nothing. His eyes remained locked with Joe Taylor's.

Joe knelt down in front of the chef. "I know she came in contact with a man named Bill Richards. She had a job interview with him, for a company that we later found to be false. She disappeared after that meeting. Last week, we learned that

Bill Richards was an alias used by Earl Sanders. We tied Earl to Wayne by the holding company that was used to form Apex, the company we found to be false. The holding company was incorporated by Wayne Sanders." Joe paused for a moment, letting this information sink in. "Tell me how she was chosen."

"Earl chose her," Jim murmured.

"What do you mean, he chose her?"

"I don't know the details. But he probably saw her somewhere. And...she probably looked good to him. So...he learned about her. That's what we do. We learn about them to make sure they'll fit, to make sure they're healthy, that they'll be easily trapped, and their family and friends won't have the resources to find them."

Joe frowned. "Earl misjudged that with her."

Jim said nothing for a moment. His eyes locked with Joe's. "I suppose he did."

"He set up the fake job ad?"

"Yes. Everybody in the club, the heavy-players, they're the ones who pick out their choice menu items. They're the ones who set things up to...how shall I say it? Ensnare them."

Joe said nothing. The tension in the air grew thick. Anna could feel her disgust rise. She thought about Mitch and Theresa Johnson, how they'd picked her out in Denver, Colorado at Hoops, that sports bar she'd been at with her former co-workers. They'd scoped her out at the same time she was sizing *them* up.

Clark Arroyo spoke. "Earl Sanders, a.k.a., Bill Richards, had her abducted and taken here."

Jim Munchel looked up at Clark and nodded. "Yes."

"And I was recruited for this job because the Johnson's picked *me* out," Anna said. Her gaze bore into Jim, smoldering. "Only *I* got the drop on them, too."

Brian looked at Anna, curious. The statement didn't get a rise out of Dean, Joe or Clark. Their attention was still directed at Jim Munchel.

"If you think you're going to take this network down, you are sadly mistaken," Jim Munchel said.

"Am I?" Joe Taylor asked. "Explain."

Jim Munchel let out a little laugh. "Be reasonable. You think you can take down Wayne's circle? You might have me, you might have evidence of murder, but you have *no* evidence of what *really* went down here."

"We have a survivor," Dean said.

He means me, Anna thought.

Jim cast a glance at Anna. "You have a thief. Last time I checked, the crimes Anna King has been admitting to and committing are serious felonies punishable by life in prison."

"I'm not concerned with what Miss King is accused of," Joe said, keeping his gaze locked on the chef's.

"Well, you should be. She's been stealing from some of the richest, most powerful people in the country."

"Don't forget the most depraved, too," Joe said. "This isn't *about* her. This is about you and your network of sadistic low-life freaks who feel they are so above everybody that they feel they have to *eat* people, especially those they feel a sense of superiority over."

"It's nothing *like* that," Jim replied. He was shaking his head. "No, no, no, you've got it all *wrong*! You're making it out as if this is all a symbolic act, like some twisted S&M game. Or a way to feel superior to the commoners."

"Then what is it?"

Jim smiled. "It's because we like the way..." His eyes seemed to grow dreamy. "It's because we like the way people *taste*. There's nothing *more* to it than that. No symbolic act of superiority." He looked at Joe. "We simply like the way human flesh tastes when it's properly prepared."

Anna felt her stomach churn. The tension in the room seemed to grow heavier, a dead, weighted thing. Anna felt her heart race at the thought of what had almost happened to her.

"Think about it, Mr. Garrison. I can still call you Mr. Garrison, can't I? Since you won't reveal your real name?"

"Of course," Joe said.

"What's your favorite dish, Mr. Garrison?" Jim Munchel looked up at Dean Campbell, at Clark Arroyo. "You gentlemen? What dish do you find so mouth-watering that you'll drive clear across town to a restaurant that prepares it *exactly* the way you like it when that same dish is prepared at restaurants closer to your place of residence?"

"I fail to see the analogy," Dean said.

"The analogy is this," Jim said. "The people I serve, the Bent Creek elite who have formed this little secret dining club, will employ extreme measures to partake in a dish they find mouth-watering and irresistible much in the same way when you have a hankering for some kind of beef or poultry dish and you drive across town to dine on it when restaurants closer to you serve similar dishes. The *reason* you travel across town is because the chef at that far-flung location has a certain flair, a certain... *zest* for preparing these dishes. The meat is more tender, more tangy, and the way it melts in your mouth...pure magic! You pay extra in mileage, in time, and in menu price. The people who are part of this club pay extra in mileage for their travel here, in time for the inconvenience in traveling here, and in price due to the risk. To them, the rewards are worth it." Chef Munchel looked at Joe. "We had countless conversations about this, Mr. Garrison. You recall, yes?"

"I do," Joe said.

"I suppose all that talk about how you dined on Silverback breasts was all a ruse, wasn't it?"

"You could say that."

The more Anna listened to Chef Munchel, the more disturbed she got. Listening to him, and remembering what he told her earlier about how he got into this was painting a very ugly, disturbing picture. She could tell that the man Chef Munchel was referring to as Bob Garrison was fighting to restrain himself from physically attacking the chef. Dean and Clark appeared more stoic. The more she observed, the more she had the impression that Dean and Clark were hired guns and that Joe Taylor wasn't simply your average man out to learn the truth and seek revenge. He was that, but he was a lot more too. If he'd infiltrated Chef Munchel and his inner circle, he was cut from the same social strata. He was a man of power and wealth, of a certain prestige. The fact that he had probably been rubbing shoulders with Chef and some of the other members of this cannibal club told Anna that he was very wealthy himself.

But he was not cut of the same cloth as they.

"This was *never* about broadening your culinary taste," Chef Munchel continued. "It was all about one of the oldest motivations in human existence: *revenge*."

"No," Joe said. "It *wasn't* about revenge."

Chef Munchel cocked his head questioningly. "Oh, but it *must* be, Mr. Garrison. You're a lousy liar when it comes to what you hold true to your heart. I saw the resemblance in that photograph. She's your daughter, isn't she?"

Anna noticed Bob Garrison's jaw twitch. Confirmation.

Chef Munchel smiled again. "See? I was *right*! Daddy was coming to find out what happened to his little girl!"

"And now that he's found out, you are going to be sorry you ever met me, motherfucker," Anna said. She stepped forward, emboldened and angry now. Chef Munchel turned to her and before Dean or Clark could stop her, she continued. "The Johnson's may have chosen me for you to prepare as exotic meals for them, but they picked the wrong bitch and you know it. I'm guessing some of your friends know that now too. Emily Wharton, some of those other fuckbags on the board."

"I'm sure they do," Chef Munchel said. His features still bore that beaming devil-may-care look, but was there also a slight tinge of fear there now? "And I can assure you that they will work at uncovering your crimes and finding you."

"They'll have a hard time," Anna said.

"I seriously doubt that."

"First, they'll have to learn my true identity."

Chef Munchel looked as if he'd been hit over the head with a brick. Anna grinned at the chef's expression of shock. "I've got all kinds of tricks up my sleeve, Chef Munchel. If you'd been successful in killing me and feeding me to the Johnson's, a woman named Anna King would be legally dead. She might have even been reported as missing. But that's not my *real* name. And that's why, when you hired me at this place, you let in a real Trojan horse, you stupid piece of shit."

"That's not true," Chef said, speaking rapidly. "Paul ran a background check on you. You were vetted."

"An *illusion* was vetted," Anna countered. "A *conjuration*. A person who only exists on paper!"

The color ran out of Chef Munchel's face. She could tell he believed her. It was in his eyes, which never wavered from her.

"You told me that you started this little cannibal club after meeting Wayne at some weird sex thing," she continued. "Correction: some sick *criminal* underground thing. Torture clubs? Snuff films? That's more twisted and more wrong than anything you can pin on *me*."

"Snuff films?" Joe looked like he'd been slapped in the face with his own bladder. The tension in the air definitely changed when Anna brought up Jim's earlier confessions to her. Jim appeared to shrink visibly at the accusations and Anna took advantage of it.

"I'm not gonna repeat everything you told me earlier," she said, "but that's the gist of it, right? You met Wayne at one of these things. I think you told me you watched some guy eat a human being in one of those sick films, right?"

Jim Munchel said nothing. He looked nervous.

"Wayne later asked if you could prepare somebody for him to eat. He wanted to try human flesh. You named your price and you indulged him."

"It was never about the money," Jim Munchel said.

"*Shut up*!" Anna snapped. She was on a roll now, her gaze directed entirely at Jim Munchel. "Long story short, you and

Wayne formed this separate club. One that consists of rich bastards like you who like to dine on human flesh prepared in a manner that most five-star chefs prepare, oh, I don't know... normal meat items like chicken and fish? Maybe lamb?"

Anna waited for a response. Jim didn't provide one.

"So we've got you guys, then we have the other sick fucks you alluded to before. The guy that ate somebody in a snuff film. The people that paid for it. They're still out there, and your other friends are still out there. Wayne Sanders and Emily Wharton and all those other freaks. I'm going to find them."

"You'll never find them," Jim Munchel said.

"We can find them," Dean Campbell said. He was standing by Anna. She sensed the rage coursing through him. "I have all I need to track them down."

"And I have *all* their bank records," Anna confirmed. "Everybody who was here this season...I have everybody's bank records and log-in data. I may have stolen money electronically from only two of your friends, but I have all their data. Including Wayne's." Anna leaned toward Jim and smiled. "And I have *yours* too!"

Jim Munchel's face turned into a mask of horror. "No..."

"Yes. I do."

"You'll never get away with this," Jim stammered. "We're too well-connected. Wayne's probably working at a contingency plan now—"

"There *is* no contingency plan," Anna said, seizing on this window of opportunity. "People like you and Wayne don't *have* backup plans. I've worked at enough corporate jobs to know that even the so-called biggest firms don't do *shit* when it comes to a complete disaster recovery plan. They may have one on paper for Sarbanes-Oxley purposes, but they don't put the necessary money or training in implementing them. They don't want to because that will take up too much precious money for their senior executives and their bonuses." Anna cocked her head at him. "Am I right, Chef Munchel?"

Jim Munchel said nothing.

"I am going to take them down," Anna said, speaking directly to Chef Munchel.

"And I said you'll never get away with it. They're too powerful."

"I don't care."

"I don't care, either," Joe said. "They can try putting up a defense, but they don't know who they're fucking with. I'm taking your entire network down."

For the first time, Jim Munchel looked nervous. He licked his lips, his eyes darting from Anna to Joe, then to Dean and Clark, who had largely kept silent during this exchange. "You can do whatever you want," Jim said. "But you aren't getting anything from me."

"I don't need to," Anna said. She stood up, patted the pockets of her waitress uniform and remembered that her cell phone was still in her room. She turned to Dean and Clark. "Do either of you have a cell phone? I have to call somebody."

Clark frowned. "No police."

"No police," Anna said. "But I need to talk to my partner."

Dawning realization spread across Jim Munchel's features. "You...you were working with somebody *else*?"

"Maybe I was, maybe I wasn't," Anna said.

Dean and Clark glanced at Joe Taylor, who had risen to his feet. He nodded at them. Clark reached into the front pocket of his slacks and handed Anna an iPhone.

"Thanks." Anna took the phone. "I'll be right back."

Then she turned and headed out of the dining room into the entry hall to make her call.

CHAPTER 43

Mark Copper answered the phone on the first ring. "Yes?" He sounded worried. Panicked.

"It's me," Anna said.

"Hey! I've been trying to call you!"

"I can't talk for very long. I need a big favor right now."

"Are you okay?"

"I'm fine." Anna took a deep breath, her ordeal flashing quickly through her mind. She took another breath. "I'll tell you all about it later. Right now I need your help."

"What is it?"

"Jim Munchel's corporate network. Do you still have access?"

"Of course."

"I need you to get some information for me."

"Sure. Hold on." She waited a moment, glad to hear Mark's voice on the phone. She could hear him typing away at the computer keyboard eight hundred miles away in California. "Okay, launching VPN access now...just a minute..."

A moment later, Mark gained access. "I'm in. What do you need?"

"Grab everything."

"*Everything?*"

"There's not much on that file share. There's a Payroll folder, a folder for Marketing, a folder for Jim and we've seen much of that. Just grab everything and then disconnect."

"Okay. Give me a minute."

Anna sighed. This was going to work. It *had* to work.

"Transferring everything now. You want the Outlook contact folder?"

"Yes. Everything."

"Okay. That might take a few minutes longer to download." Beat. "Uh...you okay? You sound...kind of frazzled."

"I was, but it's wearing off."

"Nothing bad happened, did it?"

"Nothing we can't fix," she said.

"Oh." Mark was silent. She could tell she'd alarmed him. When they'd set this job up, part of the protocol was they weren't supposed to give each other away nor allude to any potential danger on either end. She had to stick to that script even though it appeared she was home free.

"Everything's okay," Anna said. "In fact, we'll probably need to reschedule our meeting."

"Again?"

"Yeah. How's tomorrow night sound?"

"Tomorrow night?" Another beat. "Jesus Christ, I'm just dying with anticipation here, baby. You know that, don't you?"

"Of course I do."

"Files are downloaded," Mark confirmed. "I've got everything. Disconnecting VPN as we speak."

"Great. Encrypt that data and then wait for my call."

"When will you call?"

"I don't know." It was the truth. She wasn't sure what was going to happen next. It was her hope that she could call Mark later tonight and tell him she'd be seeing him tomorrow.

"Okay." Once again, Mark sounded worried. "Be safe."

"I will." She broke the connection and headed back to the dining room.

All eyes were on her as Anna approached; Clark Arroyo; Dean Campbell, the man she only knew as Bob Garrison; and Jim Munchel, who remained seated on the floor, back against the wall, legs splayed out in front of him, hands tied behind his back. Munchel regarded her with a dead gaze. "Well?" he said. "Are we going to end this charade now and get on with whatever it is you're going to do?"

Dean nodded at her. "Who'd you call?"

"My partner," she said. She glared at Jim Munchel. "We have everything we need on this twisted motherfucker."

"Like what?" Dean asked.

"I had my partner hack into Chef Munchel's corporate network. I got all his financial information, marketing info, personal documents, *and* his email files."

Chef Munchel laughed. "Silly girl. There's nothing about the group on that network."

"Sure there is. When Mark and I accessed it a few weeks ago, we found an encrypted file called WLTP. Mark was able to determine it came from another system, like it had been synched from another computer. A personal laptop maybe?"

Chef Munchel's face fell. Watching the color drain from his face did wonders to Anna's confidence.

"Yeah, I thought so. You used your personal laptop in the office. Used your network to save files, back shit up. Lots of small business owners do that. It makes sense to sync the personal laptop's files with the network share, because the network stuff gets backed up, probably to an outfit like Moby or a larger firm like Iron Mountain." She turned to Dean Campbell. "That file probably contains everything on the group, including personal contact information. Once Mark cracks the encryption, we'll have that information."

"How sure are you that he can crack it?"

"Chef Munchel alluded to my being a thief," Anna said. "He's correct. I *am* a thief. But I didn't act alone. Mark helped me. He created an algorithm to crack the encryption of various financial institutions. Long story short, we stole a bunch of money from Munchel's clients. That's part of the reason he's so pissed off at me."

"No kidding?"

"No kidding."

Bob Garrison asked, "How much money are we talking about?"

"Four hundred million dollars."

Jim Munchel was seething with anger. "You fucking *bitch*!"

"Well, that convinces me," Dean said. He regarded Jim Munchel on the floor for a moment, then turned to Bob Garrison. "I think we've taken this as far as we're going to get. You paid me to help you get to the bottom of Carla's disappearance. We learned the truth. I'm sorry it wasn't what we'd hoped for but, considering our present circumstances, I don't recommend we alert the proper authorities."

"I agree," Bob Garrison said.

"I believe we've learned everything we're going to learn from Mr. Munchel," Dean continued. "I don't have the resources to have him transferred elsewhere." He glanced at Anna. "You say he told you things? About this group?"

"He told me enough. Being as he was so pissed off when he learned we had access to that encrypted file that contains his personal data, I think it's safe to say we have quite a bit on this other group."

"You will share this information with us?"

"I'll tell you everything he told me and I'll share whatever files from his network and his personal laptop you need."

Jim Munchel muttered. "Fucking whore. Should've gutted you like a sow."

"Very well, then." Dean Campbell turned to Clark Arroyo. "I think we're done here."

Clark turned to Bob Garrison. He gestured to Jim Munchel with a casual inflection. "Do we need him anymore, sir?"

Bob Garrison shook his head. "No."

Clark pulled a silencer-equipped handgun from a shoulder holster beneath his jacket, pointed it at Chef Munchel, and pulled the trigger three times. Munchel's body shuddered and jived as each bullet struck home, pulverizing brain matter, splattering blood, breaking skull like pieces of pottery. When he went down, rolling over onto his left side, Anna was amazed to see that the human skull was like a fine piece of pottery. When bullets hit it at the right trajectory it tended to pulverize into pieces and not even the network of skin and muscle and sinew that held everything together could hold it together. What was left of Chef Munchel's head after three point-blank shots into his noggin had left him virtually unrecognizable.

Clark Arroyo replaced his handgun. "Anything else?"

Dean nodded. "Yeah. And we have to act quickly about this, but we need to make a plan.

When it was over, they reconvened in the security room.

Anna had never been in the security room. It was accessible from the front desk by way of a keycard. They used Paul Westcott's keycard to gain access. Prior to that, they each set about on their own tasks, as coordinated by Clark Arroyo and Dean Campbell; retrieving their empty shell casings, wiping areas down to erase fingerprints. Dean told Anna and Bob to retrieve all of their personal belongings from their rooms and make a hasty retreat back to security. "There's probably going to be some DNA evidence but—"

"I was careful," Anna said. "I wore latex gloves most of the time I was in my room. And housekeeping was very good about vacuuming and dusting. I'll do a quick clean anyway."

Dean turned to Brian. "Was your room anywhere near Charlie Thompson's?"

Brian nodded.

"I'm assuming after you were kidnapped, they cleaned out your room. We don't have time to look for your belongings. Do you understand?"

Brian nodded again. "I can get new clothes some other time, man."

"Good." Dean clamped a hand on his shoulder and offered him a pensive smile. He turned to Anna and Bob and gave them thirty minutes to retrieve their belongings and meet him, Brian, and Clark back in security.

Anna went back to her room, grabbed her things quickly, making double-sure her laptop and other paraphernalia was securely in her backpack, and all her things were in her suitcase, then she did a quick wipe-down of her room and headed back to Security.

When Anna arrived back, she saw that Bob Garrison had beat her. Clark, Brian, and Dean were waiting for them. Clark was holding a cell phone in one hand—Chef Munchel's, obviously—and Paul Westcott's key card. He swiped the card and there was a clicking sound. Clark opened the door.

The security room was quite impressive. Four computer monitors displayed screens displaying various areas of the grounds. The indoor and outdoor surveillance systems were still working and would continue working long after they left.

Dean turned to Clark Arroyo. "Can this system tell you if the local Sheriffs have been called?"

"Yes," Clark said. He sat down at the desk in front of a computer screen that was displaying some kind of system information. Clark grabbed the mouse and began scrolling through text. "And no, they haven't been contacted yet. At least within the facility." He turned to Dean. "There's always the possibility one of them made a call while they were on their way out."

"Can you find out what suites Jim Munchel and Wayne Sanders were staying in?"

Clark shrugged and turned to the computer. "I can try."

"Get their room numbers," Dean said. "And do a quick sweep of their rooms. Grab anything you can that looks important. I doubt Wayne left anything behind, but if Chef Munchel brought his laptop or another device—"

"I have his phone and I'll check his room," Clark said.

And with that, Clark left the security booth.

Bob nodded at the video monitors. "Do we even want to bother trying to find the backup tapes?"

"Yeah, we need them," Anna said. She'd set her suitcase and

backpack on the floor near the entrance. She and Dean started looking around the security booth. Beyond the command center was a server room that held two racks of servers. The server room was fairly sophisticated—surely not the most high-end state-of-the-art server room Anna had been in with raised floors and good ventilation, but it served its purpose. She saw a door on the other side of the server room. "What's back there?"

Dean headed toward the door and paused for a moment. He drew his firearm and carefully opened the door. It led to a short hallway. Anna followed Dean carefully and just beyond the door and to the left was a large metal door with a large combination lock and a big steel lever. The door was only open halfway. Anna reached out, grasped the lever, and pulled the door all the way open.

If this was a security vault, it was small. The back of it was lined with metal filing cabinets. Resting on top of the filing cabinets were dozens of backup tapes encased in plastic cases. "These must be their backup tapes," Anna said. She pulled them down and began rummaging through them. They were labeled by day of the week and server name. It looked like only one day's worth of backup was missing—the tape from the previous Thursday. Those tapes were probably stored off-site somewhere. "What a bunch of dumb shits. They were too cheap to store all these tapes off site. They must've only been willing to pay for an off-site courier to come once a week."

"Let's grab them," Dean said.

They headed back to the server room and showed Bob the backup tapes. As Anna opened her backpack and stored the tapes inside next to her laptop, she heard Bob and Dean go into the server room. "What about what's recording now?" Bob asked.

Anna joined them in the server room. Dean was surveying the server rack. One of them contained a computer monitor and a keyboard on a pullout tray. He turned to Anna. "It sounds like you've been in computer rooms like this before."

"I have," Anna said. She stepped up to the server rack and pulled the keyboard tray toward her. Using the mouse and several keystrokes, she quickly gained access to the system. "There's tapes in the other servers, but the backup jobs aren't scheduled to kick off until tonight."

"We need to bring down their security system first," Dean said. "Do we do that from here?"

"Yes, I think so," Anna said. She was scrolling through each server. "Give me a minute to see what is what."

"So what are we going to do with Charlie?" Brian asked. He had followed them into the server room and he looked worried.

Dean looked at Bob Garrison, then back at Brian. Clark looked indifferent. "Where's his room?"

"You aren't going to shoot him in the head like you did Chef Munchel, are you?" Brian asked.

"Only if you think I should."

"Fuck!" Brian turned away from the group and began to pace the room.

"What are Charlie's work hours?" Dean asked.

"Four a.m. to Nine a.m.," Brian said. His mouth was a grimace of distaste. "I like Charlie. I don't see him as being involved in this."

"He isn't," Anna said. "They tapped me for duty this week too, remember? Only that was just a ruse. I remember hearing Paul tell somebody that all Charlie was supposed to do was clean the ashtrays and the public toilets and change lightbulbs in the dining room when they went out. He wasn't supposed to set foot anywhere in the kitchen or pantry at all this week. He was basically supposed to be on call if something major went wrong—you know, something electrical, or with the plumbing."

"They would have restricted his access from the kitchen and the dining room," Dean said. He shook his head. "And we don't have time to go look for him now. Where's his room?"

"On the other side of the grounds," Brian said. "Everybody on staff here, including the office people, they had access to their living quarters through the rear of the building. We weren't supposed to be seen anywhere the guests mingled during our off hours. That included the dining area and kitchen."

"So your quarters are tucked away from the employee parking lot?"

"Yeah."

"Then we're good." Dean turned to Anna. "Can you crash their system?"

Anna grinned. "I'd be happy to."

It took them thirty minutes to completely bring down their network.

Anna handed Dean a USB memory stick she'd pilfered from one of the workstations in the data center. "I'm going to give you a quick lesson in erasing a hard drive so the data is not recoverable," she'd said. "The tool you'll use is on this memory stick." She'd downloaded the application a moment before and jotted down a quick set of instructions on wiping the Windows servers. "If they want to pay for it, Wayne and his cronies can hire a good forensic computer specialist to retrieve the data on these hard drive, but if we're lucky they won't be able to retrieve anything."

"This won't do the trick completely?" Dean asked.

"To make it completely unrecoverable we have to set the number of times to wipe the hard disk at 10," Anna explained. "That will require ten reboots and we can't be here to manage that. We're going to have to set these all in motion and hope we can at least cripple them."

Bent Creek had seven Windows and Unix servers and one SAN server. Anna wiped the SAN first, then she and Dean went through each server from two different terminals and keyboards. It took them five minutes each to access each server and begin the process of doing a complete wipe of the hard drive. Once they set the wipe in motion, they moved on to the next. While Anna and Dean brought down their system, Clark, Brian, and Bob made their way to the Administrative area and rifled through various desks. They returned bearing armfuls of file folders.

The phone in the data center began to ring when they were almost finished. Dean and Bob Garrison looked at it nervously, but Anna ignored it.

"We about ready?" Clark asked, setting the files down.

"Just about," Anna said. She was on the last server, the data warehouse server that tracked and recorded all the financial data.

"You sure we have all the backups?" Bob asked.

"We have them all except for last Thursday's. Looks like an outside service picked up the tapes on a weekly basis."

"So they could technically recover," Robert said.

"Yeah, but it would take them weeks," Anna said. The screen of the computer she was sitting at went blank and she pushed her chair away from it. "I didn't see any signs that they had a fallback system in place, like backing up remotely to an outside data storage center. And I don't think Wayne will have the resources or the *cojones* to even *try* bringing this system back up."

"Wouldn't it have been faster to just trash the place?" Clark asked. He was gathering everything together for their trip outside.

"We could've trashed it, but that wouldn't have guaranteed the drives would have been destroyed."

Now with the drives in the process of being wiped and the DVDs and tapes in place, they divided various media and file folders between the three of them. Clark took over, speaking with authority. "I'll lead. We head out in single file formation to the van. We'll leave the vehicle Bob drove up in, since it's a rental. If Bent Creek gets their hands on it, they won't be able to trace it." Clark turned to Anna. "Do you have a vehicle in the front employee lot?"

Anna shook her head. "No. Mark dropped me off."

"Okay. Then we all get in the van. I drive. We'll circle the grounds and exit by the rear."

"The same exit they used to sneak out?" Dean asked.

Clark nodded. "Yes." He grinned and held up another key-card. "I lifted this from Mitch Johnson. I've got the Johnson's cell phone too."

"The security system—" Bob said.

"Is controlled by an outside company," Anna said. "All we did was kill the servers and swiped the DVDs with recorded data. The company that mans the front gates is still running things here, it's just not recording data. In fact..." She glanced at the phone. "That might have been them calling. I bet one of the servers we just killed was theirs."

"What does that mean?" Dean asked.

"It means they're trying to contact somebody here to see what's wrong with their server," Anna said. She pushed the key-board tray back in the server rack. "If this place is closed for the season, I bet most of this stuff is shut off except for the server that manned the security system. I'm sure this system is monitored by somebody, whether it's an outside company or one of Bent Creek's own IT people. They'll probably try remoting in to see what's going on very soon."

Bob looked visibly relieved. "All this technical stuff...I never thought it would be so complex."

Clark held an armful of file folders in a cardboard box. "We ready to go?"

"I am," Bob said. He picked up a box of files, too.

"We're just going to leave the bodies here?" Brian asked.

"Yes," Clark said. "With one minor detail." He reached into his pocket and brought out a knife. "Give me five minutes and we'll be ready to go."

Anna understood immediately what Clark was going to do. "Don't forget the freezer in the pantry," she said.

"I won't," Clark said. He reached for a roll of baggies and twist ties that were on a nearby shelf and left the server room.

Brian looked confused. "What's he doing?"

"You'll see," Anna said.

Ten minutes later they were in a white paneled van that Clark piloted, heading toward the rear entrance.

Once outside the rear entrance, they hit the secondary road that would take them to Route 7.

Once they were on Route 7 heading toward the nearest town, Dean pulled out his cell phone and placed a call to the Willow Grove Sheriff's department.

Thirty minutes after that, they pulled over at a convenience store and bought two bags of ice to keep the meat from spoiling.

CHAPTER 44

Officer Chris Barnes got the call on his four to two a.m. patrol. The message from dispatch was clear—there was an armed conflict at the Bent Creek Country Club and Resort with multiple shots fired. Suspects were to be considered armed and extremely dangerous. Chris responded that he was on his way, switched on his lights and sirens, and made a U-turn on Highway 80 to head south.

As he drove, he listened to the police radio as other officers responded. *This sounds like a big one*, he thought, feeling his pulse surge. *Although why armed gunmen would want to storm a country club for rich snobs is beyond me.* Chris knew that Bent Creek contributed vast amounts of money to the city coffers; they sponsored the Rotary Club in town, they hosted fundraisers and blood drives, they donated to various charities. Rumor had it they donated heavily to the police and fire department. Green River's Police Chief, Andrew Walker, was very chummy with several of the big-wigs that ran the place. Every year around this time, shortly after their summer season ended, Chief Walker always made sure that patrol units pulled double duty around Bent Creek grounds and along the highways that bordered it. "I especially want you to pick up any hitchhikers you may see in that area and deliver them to our lock up," he said. This was an edict that usually went against the grain for Chief Walker. Unless it was found that hitchhikers had a criminal record, Walker preferred they be taken out of town and told to leave, that if they were caught hitching in their jurisdiction a second time, they'd be formally arrested and transported to county. Chris surmised that the reason Chief Walker wanted them taken into custody during this particular week was that Bent Creek didn't want to run the risk of vagrants converging on the area. There were probably clean-up crews and maintenance workers on the grounds the week after the resort closed, getting the place ready for the approaching winter. As far as Chris knew, there was no winter caretaker. Two weeks before the season started in late spring, work crews arrived to prep the place for business. Then the rich and the pampered descended on Willow Grove.

Chris Walker was only a quarter of a mile away from the main entrance of Bent Creek when the call came in and he reached the country club grounds in no time. As he pulled up to make a left-hand turn into the entrance, another County Sheriff vehicle arrived from the opposite direction. The blare of headlights made it hard for Chris to see who it was, and he let the vehicle make its turn into the driveway and followed suit. He identified his fellow officer by the call numbers painted on the hood of the car—Officer Dan McCartney.

Chris followed Dan down the long, winding two lane driveway, feeling his pulse quicken. They passed the employee parking area and a minute later they reached the guest parking and the large turn-around at the front entrance. Dan and Chris pulled up in front of it, dome lights swirling. Chris immediately reached for the shotgun mounted on the dashboard and exited the vehicle.

Dan had his weapon out, a Glock 9mm handgun. He glanced at Chris. "Unit ten and twelve should be here any minute."

No sooner had he said that then they were. Both vehicles parked behind Dan and Chris and Officer Jane Hamilton and John Fish got out. Jane radioed in to dispatch that they were at the location and Dan nodded at them. "Let's go!"

They moved forward in a loose formation. Chris held back a little as Dan reached for the gold door handle and tugged. Locked. He nodded at Chris, who conveyed this to dispatch. A moment later the call came through: *break it down*.

Dan and John went to Dan's vehicle and opened the trunk. A moment later Dan approached the door with a large, black battering ram that they used to bust down doors during drug stings. On the count of three, Dan slammed the butt end of the battering ram into the double-glass doors. They fell apart in thick shards, providing ample entrance. Dan slipped through, followed by John and Jane and Chris.

The early evening shade cast long shadows in the lobby, their footfalls hardly making a sound on the smooth marble floor. They all had a vague idea of the general floor plan, having been made to memorize it when they earned their positions with the Sheriff's department. Chris still didn't understand that one. Bent Creek supposedly had its own private security staff; they didn't subcontract with a professional agency, they employed their own guys. Chris wondered if Chief Walker was in Bent Creek's pocket just a little bit. It wouldn't surprise him. Maybe they used Sheriff resources to provide some additional muscle when needed. That would explain the hitchhiker edict for that week in late September, when the season ended.

The dispatcher had reported that the gunfire had come from the dining room. As they made their way toward the dining room, Chris's pulse spiked. The lights had been extinguished in the lobby, but they were on in the elevator banks and in the rear hallway that led to the dining hall. They weaved their way in secure formation toward the dining hall and eased forward carefully, weapons ready. The entrance to the dining hall was wide open. The dining hall lights were off, but the lights were on in the gourmet kitchen beyond. Chris couldn't see much—the edge of a few tables and chairs. Dan was in the lead, splayed back against the door. He nodded at the others, then weapon held out and ready, he entered the room. The other officers quickly followed.

Chris brought up the rear and he stopped as suddenly as the others had, his mind taking in the scene with numb shock and horror.

The body of a young man lay face down, a handgun lying a few feet away from him. Headshot, to the back of the head from the look of the spray pattern. In the middle of the dining room another body, male, multiple gunshot wounds. The body of a woman lay half in the kitchen, her blonde hair spilled out and matted with blood. Chris tightened the grip on the shotgun. His palms were sweaty.

"There's another victim against the wall," Jane called out.

Chris glanced to his left. Against the wall a middle-aged man, heavy-set, leaned over on his side, his head resembling a crushed watermelon. He was wearing white slacks and a red shirt. No, it wasn't a red shirt, it was white. He'd bled out so much it had completely soaked his shirt.

"Jesus," Chris said.

John and Dan had advanced toward the kitchen and they called back. "Two more victims in the kitchen."

Chris advanced forward, covering Jane as she finished her sweep of the dining room and the area just shy of the kitchen. He got a better glimpse of the woman now—definitely blonde, dressed to the nines, good-looking.

From the kitchen, Dan called out. "Two more victims in the pantry."

John: "Oh my God, will you look at that!"

Convinced that nobody else was on the premises, Chris moved the barrel of the shotgun toward the ceiling. He and Jane entered the kitchen, being careful to step around the bodies on the floor. "What do we have?" Jane called out.

"Gunshot wound to the head for this guy," Dan said. Chris quickly took in the scene in the kitchen—three bodies, blood everywhere, pots and pans lying all over the place, no shell casings as far as he could see. Jane entered the pantry and Chris followed suit. The first thing he saw was the body sprawled on the floor amid a pool of blood. Adult male, mid-thirties, dressed in business casual. His head was tilted back, revealing a gaping wound in his throat. Blood had poured out of the wound in a great cascade, staining his clothes and the floor in a wide pool. The man's hands were tied behind his back and his ankles were lashed together.

"What the hell do we have here?" John asked.

"I have no fucking idea," Dan said. He picked up his shoulder mike and called for immediate backup.

CHAPTER 45

Three Months Later, Manheim Township, PA

When the raid on Carl White's east coast residence was conducted, it was carried out with stealth and cunning surprise.

Carl had been under surveillance since October. Between his five thousand square foot mansion in the ritzy, gated community of Parkwind Estates in Manheim Township, a small rural community in Beverly Hills, his apartments in New York and Chicago, and his mansion in Palos Verdes, California and condominium in Hawaii, federal agents had been able to cover all residences quite easily. All they had to do was gather evidence and wait for something stupid to happen. It only took three months, but it came with a phone call to his Pennsylvania estate LAN line.

The phone call was immediately traced to Jake Chambers, who the FBI had been watching for several months on suspicion of securities fraud. The agent in charge of the investigation had been itching to tie White and Chambers together for two years and he finally had his wish. He hadn't been able to do squat until just recently, when his superiors had finally green-lighted that investigation into Chambers and White warranted closer scrutiny. A court order had been secured with both of their cellular and their LAN phone carriers a few days ago, to try to tie the two together with phone calls. Once Jake Chambers made that phone call to Carl White, the connection between the two was firmly established and arrest warrants were issued, with Carl's taking place in Pennsylvania, Jake's taking place in the Hamptons. Both raids occurred simultaneously. The feds hit so hard, neither man knew what hit them.

Carl had been in his downstairs office when the security system was tripped. He looked up from his desktop, heart racing, and froze momentarily. The house was empty, of course. Jennifer had left him five months ago and had filed an alimony suit against him, which was currently tied up in the court system. Between Jennifer leaving, the theft of his remaining funds from the account he and Chambers had set up, and what happened at Bent Creek, his nerves were shot. He'd been burning money leasing a private jet to ferry him back and forth between coasts, trying to appear that business was normal. But in the back of his mind, business *wasn't* normal. Even Jake had been on edge and Jake wasn't even a member of Chef Munchel's club. "I'm just going to close that account," Jake had told Carl after Carl returned home from Bent Creek and the two of them had a long talk on the phone about the theft. "I'll close it and pretend none of this ever happened."

"That's a good idea," Carl had agreed.

"If those transactions were traced, we're in deep shit."

"I know."

"And if they connect us through phone records or email, our story is simple," Jake said. "We met at the American Bankers Association conference in 2008. That's partly true."

"It is," Carl agreed. It *was* true. Two months after the ABA conference, they were planning on the White/Chambers Hedge fund that had netted both of them close to a quarter of a billion dollars in just one year's time, a fund that had also tanked in the marketplace and had played a big part in the financial meltdown of the last recession. "And I suggest you make good use of that paper shredder."

Unfortunately, Carl didn't follow his own advice. He'd

stewed over the theft. Two hundred and fifty k wasn't much, but it was all that was left in the fund that had, during its height of performance, outperformed others on the market. To see it reduced to such a paltry figure and then to have *that* sucked out of the account...well, it was insulting, to say the least. The fact that the money came out of the account electronically told Carl that somebody at the financial institution had a hand in it. Upon arriving back to his apartment in New York after the fiasco at Bent Creek, he'd made a few phone calls to the principals of the private banking institution where the account was opened. Nobody had a clue as to what happened. The CEO and IT Director had pored over every transaction, every network log, in an effort to trace when and how the money had come out of the account. Despite their exhaustive efforts, the money had seemingly vanished without a trace.

At one point, Carl had to stop worrying about the theft. In the grand scheme of things, it was a paltry sum. On the other hand, he had a bad feeling that the disappearance of the funds meant something bigger was at play. Was this the result of some kind of government committee? The IRS? As far as Carl knew, the IRS didn't snag money out of private banking accounts. They sent nasty letters, paid personal visits to places of business or residence. They hounded you, annoyed the living shit out of you. If you didn't pay up, they froze accounts. They didn't just swoop in and take the money without some kind of warning. And it took them a long time to eventually freeze an account. No way was this the work of the IRS.

Who was it, then? He'd been under the impression it was Rick Nicholson. But a week after the Bent Creek fiasco, Emily Wharton had called with a bombshell. The money had been stolen by a waitress, Anna King. It was unsubstantiated, of course, but she'd confessed, and in the turmoil that followed, Anna had escaped. Her whereabouts were currently unknown. "But I've hired a private investigator to find her," Emily had told him. "Don't worry. We'll find her."

Carl remembered Anna. She'd been quiet, polite, a good

waitress. She hadn't really stuck out from Jim's wait staff at the restaurant. Carl could barely remember what she looked like. He remembered her being reasonably attractive, and the more he thought about her, the more he began to get the sense that she had played down her physical appearance. Her makeup was sparse, her hair wasn't very stylish, and the way she carried herself seemed to suggest that she'd spent her adult working years in the service industry and had been beaten down from it. He wondered now if that was all part of her act, to make her appear invisible.

In the weeks that followed, Carl had thought a lot about her and the methods she might have employed to steal his money, which had come by piecemeal from Emily during weekly phone calls. As a result, he had been lax in destroying his records on the hedge fund account. Instead, he'd tucked them away in a locked file cabinet and continued on as if nothing happened. He got updates from Wayne Sanders and Emily Wharton regarding the Bent Creek fiasco, and despite a scary few weeks of uncertainty, things were beginning to ease up there. Wayne reported that the Willow Grove Sheriff's Department had done what they were paid to do and they performed the task beautifully—they'd covered everything up (Wayne also admitted that Anna or somebody else had phoned the sheriff's department, obviously not knowing that the sheriff's department was in Bent Creek's pocket). The bodies were disposed of in the incinerator on Bent Creek grounds (Wayne's voice had changed pitch slightly when he said this, as if he were uncomfortable talking about it, or something about it bothered him). Wayne made sure Chef Munchel's business affairs were taken care of—his lawyers had done a splendid job of forging the correct documents that stated Jim had decided to move to Thailand and was turning his company over to his trusted manager, a woman named Alice Henderson, who was stunned and surprised at the news. Likewise, Paul Westcott was made to appear as if he'd skipped town as well. Rick Nicholson's demise had been the toughest—apparently, he'd been quite talkative to family and friends in the Denver area about his new gig, and Wayne had been ferrying calls from them demanding to know where Nicholson was. They wouldn't accept the Sheriff's verdict that Nicholson had returned to his apartment in Boulder, packed up his meager belongings, and left for parts unknown. The sneak thief Wayne paid to rifle through Nicholson's apartment and remove certain items, making it appear as if he'd packed hastily and left town seemed to satisfy even the state police. But Nicholson's family and friends weren't buying it. They'd hired a private investigator.

Luckily, there had been no inquiries regarding the disappearance of the Johnson's, nor Shane and Jackie Daniels. Their respective colleagues didn't know about Bent Creek (it was in the bylaws and was similar to the first rule of *Fight Club*—don't talk about Bent Creek...to anyone).

The last phone call Carl got from Wayne was two days ago. "It looks like things are going to be okay," Wayne had said. He'd sounded better to Carl, less tense, the worry out of his voice. He was beginning to sound like his old self. "I've been in constant discussion with other members of the board and we're leaning very strongly toward not holding our annual meeting next season. We thought we'd wait until the following year."

Carl had agreed that would be a good thing. Actually, he had doubts the club could continue. They would need a chef. A chef like Jim Munchel couldn't be found lurking in every restaurant.

What had been more disturbing to everybody on the board was the absence of data on the computers at Bent Creek.

Emily Wharton had reported this to Wayne Sanders shortly after the events that had ended so bloody. Their IT Director, Mark Robinson, had reported to Emily that the daily reports he received via email ended suddenly on September 22, the day after things went to shit. Even more troubling, Mark was not able to remote into any of the servers, much less ping them.

With no way to troubleshoot what was wrong with the network, Emily told Mark that he was to remain at home until he received a call from her that he was to go to the grounds and investigate the matter. A few days after the county sheriff's department performed their cleanup, Wayne and several other board members drove to the grounds to do further cleanup—mop up the blood, get rid of personal belongings of those who died, and deliver a handsome payout to Sheriff Andrew Walker for his cooperation (strangely enough, Sheriff Walker reported that the bodies of Dale Lantis, Rick Nicholson, and the two other menu items that had been secured and stored in one of the walk-in freezers were not present during their cleanup. Carl himself had flown in a week or two later and assisted with a walk-through of the property with Wayne, where he found evidence that the incinerator had been put to use. Sheriff Walker hadn't noticed that, but Carl did; at times, he assisted Chef Munchel with disposal of those portions the group could not consume by cremating them in the incinerator. A glazier was hired to repair the damaged heavy plate glass door in the lobby. Once the interior was cosmetically sound, Emily placed the call to Mark Robinson, who drove up to Bent Creek from his cozy suburban home in Aurora, Colorado.

Mark had been stunned by the damage in the data center—the secure door to the server room had been shattered, the server rack compromised. All drives had been completely wiped of data, the backup tapes stolen. Mark had worked tirelessly for a week to restore data from a week's worth of backup tapes that had been stored offsite by their offsite data storage vendor. He'd made several phone calls to Emily, telling her in a snotty voice that if they'd only listened to him and had all their data saved to a cloud, they wouldn't have to worry about any missing data. Emily had told him to shut his pie hole and fix what he could. And because Mark was very good at shutting up and doing what he was ordered to do, no matter how stupid or against the grain, he did what he was told and performed admirably. Despite his efforts, there were gaps in the missing data. At the end of that week, Mark had submitted his report to the board of directors on what remained missing and what was salvageable. The board was still poring over this information, focusing on the personnel records of Anna King and the scant customer information on Bob Garrison.

Carl cocked his head, frowning. The security panel at his office door that monitored the estate's security system was blinking several red lights, indicating an intruder. He was debating on whether to put a call in to the police—surely they were already on the way now—when he heard the faint murmur of voices coming from outside.

A moment later, several loud booming sounds at the front door. A male voice barked out. "FBI! Open the door *now*!"

Oh shit! Carl dived for the key to the file cabinet where the hedge fund records were kept. As he fumbled the key in the lock, he thought, *I shouldn't have been so goddamn lazy, should have shredded these papers weeks ago*! And as he flipped on the shredder and pulled the first file out, papers spilling to the floor, a series of heavy booms came from the front door and then a resounding crash as the front door banged open and heavy footsteps pounded down the entry hall and Carl knew he was really, truly, fucked now.

They took him quickly, swarming over him, pinning his arms behind his back roughly and pointing ugly semi-automatic weapons in his face as they shouted at him to "get on the ground, motherfucker!" They pushed him to the ground, got his wrists cuffed behind his back with a pair of zip lock cuffs, then hauled him up. It was FBI all right. Black clad, with bullet proof vests and crash helmets. There were no less than a dozen of them running around like ants all over his house. "What are you charging me with?" Carl demanded.

"Securities fraud and a host of other things," one of the

agents said. He was young with a crew cut and appeared to take his job seriously. "You have the right to remain silent. Anything you say can and will be used against you in a court of law..."

And as Carl White was led out of his home, leaving half a dozen FBI agents to paw through his office, the foremost thought on his mind was this all had to do with the theft of his money from that hedge fund, and if it was truly Anna King who had set him up, she were going to be sorry she'd ever been born.

Earl Sanders was scared.

He was standing in his plush living room at his home in Aliso Viejo, California, trying to scrutinize the fine print of the search warrant he'd just been served with. A team of CSI techs were searching the house for various items, and Virginia and the kids were freaking out. They were seated on the sofa in the den, being questioned by several detectives. Earl was trying not to let his nervous demeanor show. "I'm telling you, you have the wrong guy," Earl said, shoving the document back at the detective, who hadn't taken his stony gaze off him since Earl answered the door. "In fact, if you'll excuse me, I'm going to call my lawyer now."

"Detective Giraldo?" one of the CSI technicians called out.

Earl and Detective Giraldo turned toward the CSI agent, who had just emerged from the stairway that led to the lower level of the home. The agent held up something that looked like a test tube strip. "We've got a match, sir."

A match? Earl thought. *A match to what*?

"Mr. Sanders, you're under the arrest for the abduction and murder of Carla Taylor," Detective Giraldo said. He nodded at two other detectives who were standing close by. "Cuff him."

"Wait...*what*?" Earl protested, his heart slamming in his chest at the mention of the name. His arms were jerked behind his back by the other two detectives but Earl paid them no heed. His head was reeling at this news. How could they tie him to Carla Taylor's murder? "I don't know what you're talking about. Who's Carla Taylor?"

"You're also being arrested for the murders of Dale Lantis, Alan Smith, and Rick Nicholson," Detective Giraldo said.

The world went black. Earl felt his knees buckle, but somehow he held on. "What? I don't understand?"

Detective Giraldo raised his eyebrows in surprise. "You don't understand? How is it that you fail to understand, Mr. Sanders?"

"I…I…" Earl's mouth suddenly felt very dry. "…I don't understand how this is happening."

"It's quite simple, Mr. Sanders. Our CSI technicians have matched DNA on the bloodstains and human remains found in the freezer and your work area downstairs. Does that help you understand the charges against you?"

Hearing this did more than help Earl Sanders understand the charges against him. It made him faint from the sudden shock of the news.

All told, a dozen arrests were made across the continental United States that day. All of those arrested were members of the Bent Creek Board of Directors. Media journalists did not seem to notice that Mr. Sanders's arrest bore any links to the arrests of the Bent Creek board members, which was being tagged as one of the largest investigations of criminal financial fraud in recent memory. Instead, Mr. Sanders's arrest was trumped as yet another deranged psycho leading a double life; respected banker by day, sadistic serial killer by night. His wife, Virginia, and their kids were devastated.

Jake Chambers was arrested that day too, on fraud and embezzlement charges, same as his partner in the hedge fund, Carl White. Likewise, Carl White and Jake Chambers were not implicated in the Bent Creek fiasco. A journalist who wrote for the *Wall Street Journal* made a thin connection but ultimately wrote that the White/Chambers arrest was due to a completely separate matter, one that bore no relation to the level of dishonesty and corruption that had brought the Bent Creek empire down.

Emily Wharton and Wayne Sanders were the last board members to be arrested. Emily was taken into custody in her office at Max Brothers, the firm she headed. She immediately pled her Fifth Amendment right to avoid self-incrimination and called her lawyer, who immediately began leaking highly spun stories to the press. Wayne Sanders was arrested at Dulles Airport just as he was about to board his private jet that was scheduled to depart to Italy. Unlike Emily, Wayne's arrest was loud and dramatic and it made front page headline news: billionaire financial tycoon throws temper tantrum on Dulles runway as he's being arrested for committing multiple counts of securities fraud. Those stories did not help his image with the general public, who had grown tired of hearing stories of spoiled rich people anyway. Privately, Wayne conferred with his lawyers and wondered how this could happen. Exactly how had he cheated investors? When his lawyers revealed the evidence the government had against him, Wayne was shell-shocked. Unauthorized accounts opened, funds shuffled around that he never knew about, even cases of funds bought before the prospectus on them was fully known, which constituted securities fraud. In short, all instances were clear setups—the question was, who set him up? He could only think of one person capable of pulling this off: Anna King.

Emily Wharton thought of Anna too while she sat in jail awaiting trial. She went over it constantly in her mind. How the little bitch had pulled one over on all of them. If there was one thing the Bent Creek board of directors had in their corner, it was that they conducted all their business affairs legitimately. When the US government stepped in to bail out the banks, those board members who were affected by the financial crisis played by the rules. They attended hearings on behalf of their various industries; they kept their books opened to federal oversight committees. The only illegal activity undertaken by anybody on the Bent Creek board was the sole reason the club had been formed in the first place—for the procurement of their main ingredient, human meat, for consumption in their secret, extremely exclusive, exotic dining club. That constituted abduction and murder.

But illegal financial and business shenanigans? Never! Drugs, sexual assault and battery, and other felonies? No way. None of the club members had as much as a speeding ticket on their record.

Emily fumed silently in her cell. If they had only gotten to Anna in the weeks after the shit went down at Bent Creek! But they couldn't. Anna had disappeared off the face of the earth. Not even the private investigators she'd hired discreetly could find her. It was as if Anna had never existed.

Emily and Wayne realized they could not bring Anna's name up to their lawyers, much less anybody else, without revealing what *really* went on at Bent Creek. They could only remain in custody on pins and needles as the resort was thoroughly searched by investigators. Despite searching the place from top to bottom and questioning past and former employees and customers, no evidence of foul play turned up. Earl Sanders didn't even say a word despite the charges being levied against him; he was being charged with four murders, based on anatomical and DNA evidence found in his home. Carla's father, Joe Taylor, identified the scrap of clothing found in a sealed-off basement room in Earl's home. The scrap of clothing contained Carla's DNA. Despite their diligence, no mention was ever made to Earl or his defense attorney that Carla had once applied for a job at Apex, Limited, and Earl did not volunteer that information. To do so would only open the door to things he did not want to talk about, especially if he wanted to keep his family safe. He had heard about Wayne Sanders's arrest, and while the billionaire might be behind bars, his reach beyond them was long and dangerous. So Earl kept quiet and let the government paint a very ugly picture about him, one that would compare him to other monsters like Dennis Radar and Gary Ridgeway, the Green River Killer.

Some things were best left unsaid.

CHAPTER 46

One Year Later, Federal Court Building, Harrisburg, PA

Court was in recess and security was tight.

Carl White was escorted to the cafeteria by his lawyer and court-appointed security guard. They were in a section of the building commonly marked off by spectators and jury members, where high-profile defendants were often escorted to private conference rooms, the lavatory, or the cafeteria during lunch and recess. Despite that, the long, wide hallway that led from the courtrooms to the cafeteria was still busy. Lawyers dressed in suits and carrying briefcases walked past, hurrying to their next court appearance. Criminal defendants from all walks of life huddled with family members and friends or legal representation, most dressed up for court. It was a familiar scene to Carl, who was being tried separately from his ex-partner, Jake Chambers.

"I need a pit stop," Carl's lawyer, Ben Ferguson said. Ben was in his early sixties, with grizzled-looking white hair and a mustache. He was wearing a gray suit. They stopped just outside the men's lavatory. "Just give me a minute. You need to go?"

"I'm fine," Carl said.

"Okay." Ben stepped into the bathroom.

Carl's security guard was a man in his mid-thirties named Chris Hodges. Chris was African-American, of average height, but with a weight-lifter's physique. His uniform was always sharply pressed. His threatening demeanor was belied by his personality, which was mellow and easy-going. Carl liked talking to Chris when they were alone together. Chris seemed to like asking Carl for advice on money, ironically enough.

"So what do you think about what I told you last week?" Chris asked, once Ben stepped into the bathroom. "You think what I want to do is feasible?"

"The annuity for your grandfather? Absolutely. It's the only sound thing you *can* do."

"Gramps is pretty adamant he doesn't want it, though. He doesn't want to pay taxes on it."

Carl sighed. "The taxes are minimal. The money the fund will earn through interest alone will be more than enough to take care of the taxes. In fact, he'll *save* more money on it than where he has it now. You said it was a low yielding savings account, right?"

"Yeah." Chris nodded. "He probably earns about two hundred dollars a year on the interest."

"He can easily earn forty grand a year in interest from the accounts we talked about setting up for him. The taxes on *that* interest would be around the same as what he's paying now for taxes on the house, the utilities, the gardener, the home owner's association, all this on a house he isn't even *living* in anymore. His money is just being pissed away. You know that, right?"

"I know that, and you know that, but he refuses to accept it. He says he wants his money where it is."

"Even if his tax bill winds up being the same as all those other expenses put together?"

"Uh huh."

"And he doesn't pay income taxes now, right?"

"Nope."

Carl frowned. Chris had told him that his grandfather's income came from social security and a small pension, which wasn't enough for him to pay federal or state income taxes on. The old man simply didn't want to pay anything in to the government, even if he wound up making more money in interest than what he was collecting from his retirement accounts. He had five hundred thousand dollars sitting in a low-yielding savings account and another two hundred thousand in cash stashed in a bank safe deposit box. "Did you look into that will?"

"Nah, I still gotta do that," Chris said. He was standing casually with his back to the crowd of passersby. Carl was standing close to the marble wall, not even paying attention to who was coming and going past them—to him, they were all lawyers and other defendants, most probably guilty of what they were accused of.

"So what's keeping you from doing it?"

"The time." Chris mustered a smile at Carl. "Nine hour days here, then an hour drive to and from work, dealing with the kids, the wife, the house, that all takes a toll, man."

Carl smiled back and was just about to respond when a female voice floated from behind him. "Spill the beans on Wayne Sanders and you'll get off light, Carl."

Carl started, heart leaping in his chest and whirled toward the sound of the voice. Chris saw the look on his face and instantly went on guard. "What's the matter?"

"Who said that?" Carl was looking around at the crowd of passersby, all those dark colored suits merging into a sea of people that all looked the same, all dressed the same, with no discernable features except...

A flash of burgundy retreating toward the stairs that led downstairs. She was carrying a tan attaché case, dressed in a hip-hugging business suit, shoulder-length hair artfully done. He couldn't see her face, but he recognized her by some kind of instinctual feeling. It was her. Anna King.

"Over there!" Carl said. He started toward the stairs and Chris held him back.

"What?" Chris was tense, on alert.

"That woman! Going down the stairs! She's the one that stole the money!"

People around them began to look in his direction but Carl didn't care. He tried to dart forward again and was restrained by Chris Hodges. Another security guard stepped forward to assist. And as Carl watched Anna retreat down the stairs, perfectly in place with the sea of people on their way downstairs and out the building, he began to panic and shout that they were letting her get away, they needed to catch her! And by the time Ben returned from the bathroom, charging out as he heard his client's panicked voice, the woman Carl was certain was Anna King had already left the building and was walking down Walnut Street to the train station with a satisfied smile on her face.

EPILOGUE

They watched the news coverage together, in Joe Taylor's spacious living room.

Over a year after the incident at Bent Creek that had brought them together, she still hadn't told Joe her real name yet and he was okay with that. There was a lot about Joe Taylor she liked. She was warming up to him faster than she would have imagined. Mark Copper was warier than her, and even *he* was gradually warming up to Mr. Taylor's genuine nature, his heart-felt and honest demeanor. His unfailing support.

Today it was just the two of them, relaxing on a lazy Friday afternoon. Joe had worked from his home office this morning while she had worked out in his home gym, then touched base with Mark via Skype in her bedroom at the other end of the house. She could tell Mark was excited. They had worked hard to bring the Bent Creek board and most of the club members down. And it wouldn't have been done without Joe's support, and the help of Dean Campbell and Clark Arroyo, too.

"You want something to snack on while we wait?" Joe asked. He was dressed in tan khaki shorts and a white sleeveless T-shirt. He was barefoot. He looked more like a middle-age beach bum than a rich entrepreneur.

"Sure. Any of that cut fruit left?"

"Yep. I'll go get it." Joe left the living room and headed to the kitchen.

On CNN, Wolf Blitzer was talking to a member of the

United States Senate about the upcoming criminal verdict expected to be handed down today in what had become known as the Bent Creek Investment scandal, so named due to the fact that all the defendants were board of directors of the Bent Creek Country club in Willow Grove, Wyoming. All eight board members had been tried together. The Bent Creek case was merely one of several cases the United States Justice Department had brought up against various players on Wall Street as a result of the near financial meltdown in the US and global economy over the past few years.

She watched the news, noting that the Senate member was merely doing talking points, same old same old. Joe returned a moment later with the fruit bowl and a veggie tray, leftovers from a social mixer he'd hosted yesterday for Clark, Dean, and Brian Gaiman, who they still kept in touch with and had settled in nearby Glendale after taking a job at one of Joe's companies. Clark had left this morning for preliminary work on another job, something Joe was keeping to himself for now, but she had a strong idea of what it might be.

She plucked a strawberry from the fruit tray and bit into it, savoring the taste. Joe headed back to the kitchen to prepare drinks.

Her mind went back.

Despite her refusal to tell anybody her real name, they'd been drawn together in an instinctual sense of comraderie. Upon leaving Bent Creek, they'd immediately flown back to California on a chartered private jet Joe had leased. Once in the privacy of his home, everybody's guard went down. Brian was still on edge from his close shave; Joe had retreated upstairs to his room, she assumed to grieve over the confirmation of his daughter's murder—Dean had told her in quiet tones on the plane ride the cliff notes version of why he'd been checked in to Bent Creek under an assumed name. She'd understood perfectly. She'd been hired by Bent Creek under her own assumed name, for completely different reasons.

In the weeks that followed, Joe would retreat to his room to grieve privately, usually well after eleven o'clock when he turned in for the night. She could hear him sometimes while she sat downstairs in the spacious living room, watching TV with the sound turned low. Joe Taylor's house was huge—over eight thousand square feet of living space—but in the dead of night it was hard *not* to hear him. He would lose control of his emotions and weep heart-rending sobs that touched her, bringing her own emotions to the surface. But she never let her own emotions spill out of her the way Joe did. She couldn't allow them to. To do so would make her vulnerable, and she couldn't afford that. Not now. Maybe later, but not now. She would know when the time was right. Only then would she grieve for her own loss, which Joe's sobs reminded her of every time she heard him.

She'd almost learned Bob's true identity almost immediately after arriving at the house, even though he never formally introduced himself to her, nor did Dean or Clark ever formally make the introductions. She just learned that his real name wasn't Bob Garrison, that his real name was Joe. She learned this while listening to him talk to Dean and Clark and heard them refer to him by this name a few times. In the days that followed he just became known to her as Joe, and she began referring to him by that name. In days and weeks after the Bent Creek event, she learned that Joe had reported to his estranged wife that he couldn't learn what happened to their daughter, Carla, and that it was best she be declared legally dead. From what Dean told her later, his ex-wife hadn't taken that news well at all. "Their marriage didn't end well to begin with," Dean said. "It's been made worse with Carla's disappearance. It's best that she never learn what happened to Carla."

She agreed.

She was aware of the loose plan to frame Earl Sanders with the murders of Alan Smith, Dale Lantis, and Rick Nicholson. She'd known about it when she surmised Clark had cut a few pieces off their bodies and taken them with him on their flight back to California. In the weeks that followed, she didn't monitor the situation that close, but she knew enough that this physical evidence was planted at Earl's home by Clark a few months later. She'd also learned that Dean had apparently talked Joe into planting Carla's DNA at the Sanders home, to tie her disappearance to him. "He won't dare look at you in court, nor will he call you out, either," Dean had exclaimed. "Because to do so would be opening him up...would be opening the rest of *them* up, to what *really* happened at Bent Creek. If he were to open that Pandora's Box, he might as well be signing his own death warrant." Dean had then shown Joe copies of the contract everybody had signed; they had been stored on the Bent Creek servers, in a secure folder that Mark Copper had gained access to. It was pretty clear from the dense language in the contract that revealing any of the culinary secrets of the Bent Creek elite would be granting the squealer an instant death sentence. Reference was made to an unsolved murder from 1998 in which a wealthy family was slaughtered in their rural Iowa home. The case remained unsolved, the perpetrator never caught.

Wayne's point was well made in this legalese.

Dean had tried to pry her own name out of her but she'd refused, calmly telling him they could call her Anna for now. "I have my reasons," she'd said. Dean had tried a few more times, then suddenly stopped. She wondered if Joe had asked him to stop, but wasn't entirely sure.

Regardless, Joe had unofficially let her stay in one of his guest bedrooms. That first night she'd been shown a room near a cluster of bedrooms at the south end of the house. Dean and Clark had taken two of them, while Brian had been given a bedroom on the north end of the property. Joe's own suite was on the other side of the estate. Private. A few nights later, after their plans were made and back stories were committed to memory, Dean departed to resume his life. Due to the rules of his probation, Brian Gaiman had to return to Wyoming. Joe sent Clark with him for protection. She didn't find out until later that one of Dean's first jobs upon arriving home was to work some magic in getting Brian Gaiman off of probation. Once that goal was accomplished, Brian was whisked back to Pasadena and a room was ready for him in Joe's home. She and Brian became surrogate brother and sister in the months that followed. Brian passed the time by taking several college courses online, under Joe Taylor's name, with Joe's blessing. Computer network security and maintenance. As expected, Joe moved him into a job in this field with a company he owned, Vertex, an internet company in Burbank. Brian slid into the role easily. He'd been given the job shortly after the screws had been tightened on the Bent Creek cannibals, as Joe had taken to calling them.

"Bent Creek Cannibals," she said as Joe entered the living room bearing drinks.

"Very apt name for them, don't you think?" He handed her a glass of lemonade.

"It is." She took a sip of the lemonade. Perfect.

"Isn't it about time for the verdict to be read yet?"

"You know how these things go. Especially since no cameras are being allowed in the courtroom. They'll probably make an announcement from outside as the verdicts are being read."

Joe nodded. They'd been following all the court cases closely. Earl Sanders had pled not guilty to four counts of murder and was convicted three weeks ago in an Orange County, California court. The sentencing trial was currently underway, with the prosecution aiming for a death penalty. Carl White and Jake Chambers had been found guilty in separate trials on multiple counts of fraud in their hedge fund case and sentenced to two hundred years, and one hundred and eight years respectively in federal prison. She had observed Carl's trial close up *and* from afar. Her parting shot to him at the courthouse—having gained access to the federal building under another *nom de plume* thanks to Mark Copper's expertise—had been orchestrated by Dean and Joe. If Carl dropped dime on Wayne and the rest of the board, who were currently not cooperating in any of their trials, the secrets of the Bent Creek Cannibals would break wide open and the ball would not only roll, it would roll downhill faster, picking up other perpetrators and other members as it went along. Joe had his reasons for wanting all of them to pay—from the core members to the occasional high roller who was let into the exclusive club. Subsequent research from the data procured from Bent Creek's servers and Jim Munchel's computer records indicated that there were over two dozen people that had paid to be members at any given time over the last decade; these members had not been present when Joe infiltrated the club under the Bob Garrison pseudonym, and surveillance undertaken by Dean and Clark in the year since indicated that they were not only laying low, they were doing everything they could to distance themselves from the core members in custody. It had been Joe's plan to have Carl sing to the prosecutors, but that hadn't happened. Instead, Carl's blowup at court had caused a delay in his trial. When it resumed, Carl had been even more tight-lipped. He'd been quickly found guilty on all counts against him and sentenced.

"You know they're going to be found guilty, right?" Anna said.

"No, I *don't* know that," Joe responded. He took a sip of his lemonade. "But I hope they are."

"If they are, what then?"

"We move to phase two."

"What's phase two?"

Joe nodded at the TV. "Looks like the first verdict is in."

She turned to the TV. Wolf Blitzer had interrupted his talk with the Senator to a live feed outside the New York City courthouse. A middle-aged woman in a burgundy power suit was standing before a podium, addressing the cameras and throngs of reporters. "...I am very happy to report that the cases of the People versus Emily Wharton and the People versus Wayne Sanders on multiple counts of fraud, embezzlement, and other matters relating to the Bent Creek case have resulted in the verdicts we were hoping for. For Emily Wharton, she has been found guilty on all charges. Wayne Sanders has been found guilty on all charges. There is a Mr. Robert Barker, also named as a defendant, who was also found guilty..."

The woman continued speaking but Anna wasn't listening. She could only grin, reach across the sofa and hug Joe Taylor. "We *did it*!"

"Yeah, we did it, kiddo," Joe Taylor said. He hugged her back, looking at the TV with a sense of vindication. "We did it."

And as the afternoon wore on, more convictions rolled in for the other parties involved. Their outcomes were the same. "Now will you tell me what phase two is?" she asked Joe at the end of the day as the talking heads were debating the results of the massive convictions of the Bent Creek board members.

The sun was going down outside. In the living room, the drawn shades made the interior of the home seem like a cave. The only light came from the large flat-screen TV against the far wall. Joe didn't look at her. He kept his gaze on the TV in his silence. For a moment, she wasn't sure if he was going to answer. Then he turned the volume down with the remote. "Dean and Clark have used every available method of learning your name and haven't been able to." He turned to her. "Why won't you tell me?"

She felt her stomach tighten. "Why now?"

"Isn't it obvious? After everything we've been through together? After an entire *year*?"

"I suppose..." Part of her was still hesitant, a holdover from her past. She hadn't even told him what she and Mark had done with the nearly four hundred million dollars they'd stolen. A few times, she'd sensed that Joe wanted to ask, but he never did. He was giving her time, which was what she needed. She was growing accustomed to him, had grown to trust him. She felt she had even come to love him a little.

"So?"

"If I tell you, will you tell me what phase two is?"

"Yes."

"Before I tell you my name, can I tell you what I want to do?"

"Of course."

"Okay." She took a sip of lemonade, then took the plunge. "Remember what I told you about Jim Munchel? What he told me when I was tied up back in that kitchen, when I learned the Johnson's had bought me? About the snuff film ring?"

"Uh huh."

"He gave me a name. Mabel Schneider. He told me she'd introduced him to cannibalism. That's how he met Wayne Sanders. That's how he got into it."

Joe nodded, encouraging her to continue. "Yes, I remember. Go on."

"Mabel Schneider's dead. She died of natural causes over a decade ago. Her death made national news due to what was found in her home. Do you remember?"

"Yes, I do. Pickled body parts were found in a freezer. Evidence of murder going back over forty years."

"Even her own children didn't know their mother was a monster," Anna said. She could feel the adrenaline flowing through her veins. "I had Mark do some checking on them. They're still traumatized by what happened."

"You know, I still haven't met Mark. When do I get to meet him?"

"Don't interrupt me!" Anna said. She closed her eyes for a moment to regain her composure, took a deep breath. "Mark did some more poking around and managed to piece together past acquaintances of Mabel's. He's still trying to establish solid evidence of whether or not they were involved in this underground world of torture porn, but—"

"Are you trying to tell me that you want to go after the same people I'm after?"

Stunned silence.

"You want them, too?"

"Absolutely."

"Why?"

"I could ask you the same question."

"I asked first."

"Fair enough." Joe Taylor paused for a moment. "I still don't consider my job here—and by what I mean by *here*, I mean the Bent Creek Cannibals—done. We've taken out most of them. The main players, if you will. But there's two dozen others who paid for the privilege to dine on human meat. Dean has identified every person who ever dined on human flesh prepared by Chef Jim Munchel. We're learning some of them either currently have, or at one time *had*, connections with this other elite group that are into torture and snuff films and other horrible things. Things too awful to mention."

She felt the flesh of her arms break out in gooseflesh as Joe regarded her from across the sofa. "Dean and I have done our research on Mabel Schneider as well," Joe revealed. "We started looking into her after you told me about her."

"So you want to go after them to finish the job?"

"It's more than that. It's like when you know there's a pest problem in your house and you've hired an exterminator to get rid of them. They come in, they do a pretty good job, but they don't completely eradicate the problem because some of them have scattered elsewhere, so you can't get them. The remaining maggots regroup. They multiply. And before you know it, they've infested your home again, only you don't know it."

"Maggots..."

"They need to be stopped," Joe said.

She said nothing. Her heart was thumping and she felt completely on edge, a natural high. To think that Joe Taylor wanted to continue with this was just too much for her to consider. It was exciting and exhilarating and scary all at the same time.

"Can we do it?" she asked.

"I think we can," Joe said.

Something about the tone of his voice made her look over at him. He smiled at her. "This is what I want to do. For me, there's no turning back now. The Bent Creek Cannibals may be locked up, but there are others out there just like them. And they *will* commit monstrous acts again if they're not stopped."

"My name's Jamie," she said, the words coming out in a rush. "Jamie Strong. Middle name Marie. I'm..." For the first time in years, she felt tongue-tied. She tried to get around that, but Joe Taylor beat her to it.

He grasped both her hands affectionately, warmly. "Hello, Jamie Marie Strong. I'm Joseph Michael Taylor. And I am so pleased to finally meet you."

Jamie smiled, then laughed. Joe Taylor laughed too. And as the night began, they talked some more, they shared their lives with each other, and they made future plans.

May 7, 2009 - April 15, 2013

Lititz, PA
Fountain Valley, CA
Altoona, PA

ABOUT THE AUTHOR

J. F. Gonzalez (1964 – 2014) was the author of over twenty novels of horror and dark suspense, including *Survivor*, *Primitive*, *They*, *Retreat*, *Back From the Dead*, *Bully*, *Shapeshifter*, *Fetish*, and *The Beloved*. He is the co-author of the popular Clickers series (with Mark Williams and Brian Keene respectively), and with Wrath James White, the novels *Hero* and *The Killings*. He also authored numerous short story collections, non-fiction, screenplays and more, as well as serving as a renowned horror genre historian and the editor of two magazines.

Made in the USA
San Bernardino, CA
19 March 2017